AMANITA

NATHANIEL SEWELL

For ~ Alan Lucas
A creative wandering spirit

"It is during our darkest moments that we must focus to see the light."

— Aristotle

Chapter 1

When Artemis Lamb was a young girl, she never battled with her parents before her nine o'clock bedtime. Never. She bathed herself as instructed by her mother with just enough coconut butter soap and foamy lavender shampoo. As the bathroom water vapor dissipated into the heavens, she dried off with a thick white cotton towel. She folded the towel in half with the seams side-down, smoothed out any lumps, and hung it at the center point over a polished nickel rod. She buttoned up her pink, sea island cotton pajamas that her mother had taught her how to press out the wrinkles with a hot electric steam iron. With the aid from her digital wristwatch she brushed her teeth for two minutes. She then washed away any tub residue, wiped the vanity and mirror, and checked her bathroom for the unclean.

Artemis pranced downstairs into her father's expansive den paneled with quarter-sawn cherry panels and a coffered ceiling that had a aged, comforting aroma. She stood like a soldier on an antique maroon and dark-blue patterned hand-knotted wool rug as she faced her parents for inspection. They smiled as they reached for her, as she climbed up between them and onto the soft vintage tufted, dark-brown leather couch as a mindless prime time television show spewed bias light.

"I love you, Daddy," Artemis said. She hugged him around his neck. "Good night."

"Love you, punkin," her father said. He kissed her forehead. He smiled at her with blue eyes that shared a father's wish for his daughter to experience happiness and joy.

Artemis giggled as she twisted over to her mother.

"I love you, Mommy," Artemis said. She kissed her mother.

"Love you, my darling," her mother said with a velvety Irish accent. She hugged Artemis. "You completed all your tasks?"

"Yes, mother," Artemis said.

"Now off you go, snuggle in tight," her mother said. She checked her daughter's cotton hair scrunchy, colored in green, orange, and white, and rubbed her diminutive shoulders. "Dream you earned a gold medal. We earn our things."

"Listen to your mother," her father said. His distinct snicker reassured Artemis that he would always protect her. "Be our future Olympian. I'll come tuck you in and tell you a mythological story about gods and goddesses. And then you'll dream about great adventures and mysteries."

Artemis hopped off the couch mimicking her father's snickering laugh as she scampered off toward her bedroom. Mr. & Mrs. Lamb swiveled back to follow their only child with a floppy red hair ponytail and a sly grin on her cherubic face, as she crawled back up the wooden stairs centered by a cushioned maroon carpet runner with brass rods.

Her parents certain her behavior *odd*.

At parties and gatherings, they scrutinized their friends and neighbors' wrestling matches with their offspring before bedtime. The tears, the sobbing, the begging, or the demonic screeching for more playtime. So they shared Artemis' kittenish nighttime rituals with their close friends, and they all agreed, she was *different*.

The Lamb's trusted in science and facts. To best care for their precious child, they engaged physicians and therapists. But the healthcare professionals never diagnosed Artemis with anything pathological. The therapists dismissed her claims to have encountered wandering spirits as childhood fantasies. Hallucinations that would cease as she aged. Otherwise, she presented them no clinical symptoms for profound mental illness; She had not checked off any new diagnostic boxes. The experts determined she was peculiar, but otherwise an engaging, happy redheaded child in good health. They speculated with Mr. and Mrs. Lamb that being an only child allowed Artemis to play inside a powerful imaginative inner world. She was a clever, calculating girl, and their observations matched up with her upper ninety-nine percentile intelligence quotient score. And they had deduced she was ambidextrous, but nothing else to worry them.

Every other night back inside her bedroom, Artemis had had a practiced routine. After her father tucked her in and told her a magical story, she set an alarm with her black rubber digital wristwatch, stuffed it under her soft pillow, and slept for several hours. It vibrated and awakened her. Sneaking into her parent's bedroom. She sat American Indian style and waited for her parents to snore. Once she was confident they had drifted off into their deep dreamland, to reduce sound she scooted her socked-feet back toward her bedroom along the home's hallway carpets and tongue and groove wide-planked hickory flooring.

Artemis sat on her oversized beanbag chair within the silence sensing the home's HVAC system cycle on. It blew warm air through a Victorian themed cast iron grille work above her. It clicked off until the room cooled. It clicked back on. She sat back spellbound. Beyond her thin double-paned window she saw along her tranquil midwestern town's blacktopped streets, lined with pruned mature oaks and maples, were a bustling host of wandering spirits. All hallowed over by a golden meridian. They emerged from pitch darkness as illuminated golden particles. They were fast blips down her street as if shooting stars toward undisclosed destinations. Others floated above the manicured lawns like summer fire flies appearing curious and hopeful even during the depths of a frosty winter.

If the Lamb's traveled late in the night, Artemis realized her parents never noticed the nearby wandering spirits. When she asked about them or pointed out a spirit zipping by their four-door sedan, they never believed her.

"Stop with the make believe," they said to her. Her father watched her from the car's center rear-view mirror.

Her mother looked back at her from their car's front seat.

"You're imagining them," Mrs. Lamb said. She winked at Artemis. "Nothings out there, my darling. Someday, when you're older, they'll not be there. I promise."

Artemis gave her mother a tight-lipped smile from the backseat, and she decided never to tell her parents, or anybody, anything else she saw. She concluded no one believed her.

At high school during an ancient world history class, she understood that there are unique events in this world's evolution, or mysterious happenings that occurred that were difficult to explain away. But at college, Artemis' instincts nudged at her that someone was following her. She sensed something nearby her during the foggy morning walks toward class or at Saturday night inside a loud dive bar hanging out with her friends. It was always beyond her visual reach; She knew it. In time, she dismissed the feeling as mild paranoia from school stress; It was not God, or any other hokum she had learned about in her liberal arts college's mandatory religious studies class. Her family had never walked into a church, synagogue or other; She, like her parents, were not Bible thumpers. The only statement Mr. and Mrs. Lamb ever told Artemis before their tragic accident was that there might be a higher power protecting her. She thought it implausible. She suspected it was just random wandering spirits she had grown accustomed too that from time-to-time tried to interact with her. But they were always peaceful spirits searching for answers and seeking a bright diamond shaped crease in the visual spectrum for them to emigrate.

One day, Artemis was in a work meeting; A new file was being assigned to her. She was unaware that soon she would meet her praetorian minder. And her understanding about the supernatural world was about to transform.

"Girl," Wylie said. He was older, wrinkled and bald. He sounded like he was straight out of eastern North Carolina.

"I'm not a girl," Artemis said. She was now a tall, athletic and a striking redhead that lacked freckles.

"True. I'll not tangle with you, you'd hurt me," Wylie said. He tapped atop his yellow oak desk for a pack of cigarettes, even though he stopped smoking years earlier. "You're my best investigator, warning, this file's not pleasant. To be blunt, it's a mess."

"When you use, not pleasant, and the word, mess," Artemis said. "I get knots in my stomach."

The medical malpractice insurance business was not a kind world. The files Artemis investigated were all about after-the-facts, as in, after a physician amputated the wrong limb, or the wrong baby died during childbirth, or the wrong anesthesia protocol gorked an innocent patient's brain.

"We've got millions exposed," Wylie said. He squirmed on his highback leather chair as he fumbled with his thumb and forefinger along the edge of a common Manila envelope. "The captive tower's funded. Actuaries completed the funding study late last year, then some nitwit in Fort Wayne got greedy, and decided we should reinsure the entire deal, the entire tower, but now?"

Wylie hesitated for several moments staring down his long, rectangular office at a furniture grouping centered with a cherry veneered coffee table and cushioned red leather chairs.

"Dude," Artemis said. "What?"

"I'm not sure," Wylie said. He glossed his hand over his bald head. He had enough gray hair left to cover the circumference from ear-to-ear. "I've got this bad feeling with this one. I'm not sure what to say, go manage this mess. Too old these days, I'd put other people in danger."

"Got it," Artemis said. "Anything else?"

"I like you," Wylie said. He hesitated. "I mean in a mentoring way, you understand?"

"What?" Artemis said. She slouched onto a side desk chair. She screwed her brown leather loafers into the side of Wylie's desk. "Cough it up."

Wylie wobbled over toward her. He waved her shoes off the side of his desk. Artemis shifted back and moved her shoes onto the office's light-gray colored loop-pile carpet.

"This is evil, alleged unauthorized cremations, bodies disappearing," Wylie said. He bent forward, his elbows on his knees, and he handed her the encryption passwords for the file within the envelope. He preferred not to use his business email.

"What are you thinking?" Artemis said. "You've got that look."

"Something else," Wylie said. "A lust for money over human dignity? I can't quite figure out from the files. It all reads nice and clean, like they did the family a favor, preventing a toxic outbreak or similar non-sense. I think they make up their excuses as they go."

Artemis thought a hairy spider climbed along her neckline. She acknowledged Wylie. She was not afraid of spiders, but she understood what the sensation meant. If Wylie's thirty-plus years of experience were knocking his instincts into submission; it was bad.

"Why are you of all people afraid?" Artemis said. "You taught me the business. I'm well-trained to take care of myself, thanks to the military, and, a few others."

Wylie stared over at Artemis. He gave her a blank expression, and he sat back and interlocked his fingers over his paunch.

"It's not about money, this time, I feel it. I always listen to my instinct," Wylie said. He sighed as if he expected the worst. "It's the medical records; they are clean, like a clinical risk manager went through them with an exacto knife. But that perfection makes them flawed. It's not drugs, maybe opioids? They are hiding something, messing with the captive's money? I don't know, some tax dodge to keep the doors open?"

Artemis enjoyed the hunt; Wylie's cryptic observations triggered her memories from previous files and dangerous investigations.

"What's my budget?" Artemis said. She stuffed away the envelope and squeezed with her fingertips on the only ring she wore on her left hand.

"Are you kidding?" Wylie said. He shook his head as he shrugged his shoulders. "Nothing."

"I don't understand," Artemis said.

"Unlimited, the word from up the chain," Wylie said. He glanced back over at Artemis. "Your best work is with death cases. There are a bunch of bodies in this claim. We've got batch language in the policy form. Even so, I suspect they'll try to negotiate a big global deal. Be warned, this is bigger than us." He paused, he examined a framed family photo from a time when Wylie had a complete head of hair. "You'll be all alone, they want this kept quiet."

"I enjoy being alone," Artemis said. "I hunt best when I'm out there all alone."

Wylie scooted his chair forward and opened his desk drawer to reveal personal work papers, paper clips, convention nicknacks, and a heavy-looking Glock 34 resting on top. "Have one of these, right?"

"Yeah, straight forward weapon," Artemis said. She examined the German-made weapon. "You know I do. I'll pack my tools. I'm not a gun person, untidy, leaves too much evidence behind."

"Good, pack it, and those other, ah, tools, you use. Drive up there, take a real truck, with big wheels," Wylie said. He piano tapped his wrinkled fingers on the desktop. "When you get into Kentucky, use back roads. Use cash. I'll get you a draft for the bank. Don't report it back to any expense reports. Spend it, then lose the receipts. Understand?"

"Wylie," Artemis said. "With my hair and skin I can't hide."

"I am aware, I have eyeballs," Wylie said. "Get up there, get a hotel room and go introduce yourself to the head of risk management, and their general counsel. The contact names are in the file. I suspect they are all locals, never worked anyplace else, so this is their home. They'll be real protective."

Artemis considered Wylie's counsel.

"They know someone's coming, how long to respond?" Artemis said. She crossed her legs. "If I miss my guess, they've already hidden the bodies, and whatever else."

"We have twenty days to deny the claim. And unless my thinking is off," Wylie said. He shoved his desk drawer shut and locked it. He doubled checked the lock by rattling it with the key. "Both sides are in league with each other, local plaintiff firm. If you just showed up, they might slip up. I need you up there. Be careful, this file will get nasty. I just know it."

"You always told me, none of us has clean hands."

Wylie grinned. He sucked in a deep breath, held it, and released it through his pug nose. He looked through his offices' smoked glass windows out toward a high-end country club. The course filled with snowbirds, and locals racing golf carts down wide fairways playing chaotic left, right Army golf.

"We were greedy, shortsighted, that's on us," Wylie said. He shifted his office chair backward and forwards. "We got into bed with snakes. I don't want you to get bit, but we have to clean up this mess. Artemis, you understand, this could sink us? I'm too old to redo my resume."

"I got it," Artemis said. "I'll find the problem."

"I do not doubt you," Wylie said. "The Company conceals from me your other work, mostly, but they're pleased. I keep getting files they demand I assign to only you. Do an old man a favor, be careful."

"I'll have my tools," Artemis said. "I'm cautious by nature."

Artemis got up and marched toward Wylie's closed office door. Wylie sprang up, he stopped her. He hugged her tight, like a father hugs his daughter.

"You get back here," Wylie said. He looked downward as he backed away from her as she opened the door. "Hear me?"

Artemis punched Wylie on his shoulder.

"Don't go all squishy," Artemis said. "I got this."

Artemis drove from downtown Tampa, Florida across the Gandy Bridge over blue waters being disturbed by powerful fishing boats knifing across leaving behind them turbulent wakes. Brown pelicans glided nearby the bridge with their wings out, floating, just before they dove for an unsuspecting pescatarian meal.

Back home inside her modest apartment in downtown St. Petersburg, she shut the window blinds. For the next three days, she reviewed the underwriting files, the claim files, and loss data. Artemis thought Wylie prophetic. The electronic medical records were perfect, almost textbook like. For a medical malpractice insurance claim investigator, it meant something sinister. She searched the Kentucky town's map, and she found a hotel chain near the hospital where she would set up operations.

Artemis sat back, considered her options, and thought her first trip into Selene, Kentucky required a late-night visit to the local cemetery. The wandering spirit world was always the best local source for her because they had already experienced their eternal truth.

Chapter 2

Artemis stared out her hotel room's tempered glass windows within downtown Selene, Kentucky. She searched from the third floor for any wandering spirits. But the township's streets and avenues were dark, still and calm. It appeared like any normal American hamlet washed in minimal pale light from a line of faux antiqued street lamps set in front of a fancy town square centered by a granite and marble courthouse built from a make-work project from the mid-1930s. She got up and put on her down parka that covered her below her pants pockets and headed downstairs to walk outside into the frigid air.

"Git ya truck?" The valet said. He stood inside the hotel chains ordinary lobby, as he chatted up the uninterested female late-shift desk clerk who did not glance up at Artemis. The lobby had an over-used smoker scent eliminator system, as she stood near a mid-century ash tray stand set in a corner near the front doors.

"No," Artemis said. She stopped. "What's the best route over to Most High Cemetery? I don't live here."

"Not sure I'd be out there, ma'am, this time a night," the valet said. He rubbed at the intersection of his ample belly and well-worn belt. "It ain't criminals, it's stray wolves, bears. The druggies - they be up in the forest, it gets thick up in there, an easy place to hide."

"I imagine," Artemis said. She pushed open the front doors to step outside as the valet followed her. She looked back at him.

"Be careful," the valet said. "Never know."

"I made a promise to an old friend, for his mother, maybe light a candle," Artemis said. She unzipped her parka and opened it. "No worries, I'm packing. What's that odd smell?"

The valet lurched back and scratched behind his ear. Artemis suspected from the flabby ear piercing it was a former host for a larger earring. He shifted half his plump body outside, and the other squished behind the glass door.

"Coal ash, how some still heat things up here. Well, I reckon I'd head down three blocks, good you be carrying, I tell ya that," the valet said. He pointed forward, as he studied Artemis as the fog vapor rolled from her warm body as she zipped up her parka. "Turn right at Central Avenue, up there's a CVS. It'll be 'bout half-mile on down the right. I'll go with ya, need be?"

"No, I need to be alone with her," Artemis said. She slipped the valet ten dollars. "But thank you. I'll be back soon enough."

Artemis ignored the valet's partial smirk as he snapped the currency between his smoker's fingers as he let the door shut behind him with a thud. She bundled with a maroon and brown Irish Shepherds scarf that was her mother's, as she walked the route beneath a crescent moon; she could see above Orion's Belt blazing a milky white in the clear night sky. The shoveled snow banks looked like piled lengths of lumpy soiled white linen. She stepped with purpose along the pitted and cracked cement side-walks, under stripped bare oak trees and modest brick buildings that had been active and vibrant from a time before the internet and strip centers. A red-light blinked above the intersection where she turned at the corner, across from her the CVS and she stepped by the neighborhood's murky front porches with two still having post-Christmas lights flickering greens and reds. As the valet directed, she saw the thorny iron gated cemetery, dotted with moon lit bleached headstones, and shadowed by ancient tenta-cled oaks. It was strange to her she had not seen golden particle wandering spirits, or any sign that they were active. She stopped. She sensed someone or something watching her, not following. A powerful energy she had never encountered.

The cemetery appeared old as Artemis pushed open the wrought- iron gate with a scalloped-picket profile that ached at its rusty joints. A spent cigarette and black flecked paint collection was at the bottom of the square post. As best she could see the grass park-like setting appeared manicured. She stepped beyond the first column of headstones. She stopped and stared across the cemetery in all directions. Nothing. It was as if the wandering spirits had escaped from her vision. But her instincts whispered that something was nearby, lurking within close range.

Artemis spotted a little girl. She hovered at the back of the cemetery. In life she was petite, fragile and wore a common department store dress. But then the little girl evaporated into the cold air.

At Artemis' right side, there was a black demonic presence that floated near a child statuary set above a grave. And then another dark presence appeared to her left, but it was farther away and near one of the cemetery's back wrought-iron gates. She turned around and counted all the cemetery's gates, there were seven. They designed the cemetery into a significant circle with nine circular family plot sections. Artemis well-aware what she saw were demonic spirits. But they remained sentinel like and had not drifted toward her or menaced her. For the first time in her life, Artemis wanted to back away and run toward the hotel. Her training kicked in; she screwed the toe of her boot into the grass.

"You're here, I can sense you," Artemis said. She stammered. She puffed out foggy breaths as she moved farther across the cemetery toward the center where she stood before a Greek-pillared white granite mausoleum. A voice emanated from behind the impressive structure fronted within the angular pediment by a haunting female winged faux Greek statue holding a bow and arrow protecting a singular fawn.

"You know me, Artemis."

Artemis glanced back and forth at the demonic spirits; they had not drifted toward her.

"Show yourself," Artemis said. She wiped her face glossed with moisture from the dense nighttime mist. "Who are you?"

"How should I appear? We've never met - formally."

"As you are, I'm confused," Artemis said. She thought it was an odd question from a creepy sounding voice. "Stop hiding."

"Always remember, Artemis, I am an idea, a spirit–I am not human."

"You are dead, I get it," Artemis said. She pressed her left hand against the frozen white granite. It felt real. She was not lost inside a vivid dream. "I think. How do you know my name?"

"Oh, I'm so much more, as you might say in your English language. Perhaps your father would have spoken of me using Greek or in Latin words, or found me in Egyptian symbols?"

Silence rained for a few moments, but for the interlocked tree limbs fighting with each other as the invisible breeze antagonized them. Above Artemis a dark particle cloud slithered over her and it caressed the monument like a frothing black wave across a dark sand beach shrouding the Greek statuary and ornate columns. It flooded downward in a black-ant like mass and formed into a giant black King Cobra head. Its muscled body with giant feathered black wings; its hooded face appeared prepared to strike at Artemis as it levitated from its coil, its skins scales tightening as it was steps across from her.

"What - tha?" Artemis said. She resisted the temptation to step backward. Her eyesight transfixed on the massive snake.

"I have many names…" the serpent growl-hissed, it revealed its sharp white fangs. "In many languages, but for you, what should you call me?"

"I–," Artemis said in a whisper. She gawked at the hulking snake that kept wiggling its long forked tongue over near her. Mucus dripping from the pinkish-black tip ends. Its breath putrid like a rotting dead animal decomposing in the forest.

Artemis sensed her skin tingle. She lost the ability to breathe. She realized why the wandering spirits hid, lest they end up in Hell. She was certain she could not escape from it; a powerless sensation from being trapped.

"Fine, I'll pick, I am Satan."

"What?" Artemis said. She reverted to her military training; she focused on calm thoughts, on facts. "I don't understand this, what are you."

"Still not afraid, Artemis?" Satan said. It growl-hissed. "Still a nonbeliever? I am The One."

And then snake form disappeared into black particles, meshing together into a dense gooey orb.

"If I am to die," Artemis said. She clenched her hands, and stood still, and solider like. "I'm not afraid. I accept my fate. I know God will accept me. I never understood, until, now. I think?"

"That's too easy. I enjoy torture," Satan said. The gooey orb sounded like it was digesting a rat. "It's fun to hate. I want to teach you to hate, too."

"What do you want?" Artemis said. She wiped her eyes, she blinked rapidly. "I have nothing. I have nothing on me. I don't want to die."

"I want you, I want your earthly soul, Artemis Lamb," Satan said. "I have watched you from afar. I watched this magic little girl grow up, and you have come to me, join me? I'll show you true power. I want you. Don't you desire me?"

"No, never," Artemis said. The air dried out her mouth; her lungs burned. "Where's God, if God exist." Artemis' mind scrambled for last second ideas. "God exists?"

The orb floated upwards it caressed the statuary. It purred as it hovered back down near as Artemis thought it inspected her down to her genetic code.

"Not how things work," Satan said. "I could bring back that young soldier you loved, the one you think of when you touch that ring on your finger, join me?"

"Why are you so obvious? No," Artemis said. She thought it best to engage Satan, or her own imminent death meaningless. She realized Satan could kill her at any moment, so there was something else it wanted. She waited. She shivered. "What have you done with them, I can't see them?"

The orb floated closer toward Artemis. She thought it was considering its next move. It gave off a stench.

"I take the ones I want, the rest remain searching. I enjoy watching them suffer," Satan said. The orb big cat like growled. "You're correct. I am the reason you cannot see them. I blocked you. Artemis, protector of little girls, who cannot have her own girls. Named by her dead parents after the goddess of the hunt and the moon. I know this to be true. I was there that starry night."

Artemis resisted her tears. It was poking, prodding, and jabbing at her - easily locating her weak spots.

"Leave them," Artemis said. She stammered. "Leave me alone."

The orb glided backwards and floated around her at head level taking a panoramic view of Artemis shaking, and shimmering.

"What was his name?" Satan said. "Your dead lover-"

Tears sprinkled from Artemis' eyes. They glided down her face. She sniffled.

"Benjamin," Artemis said. She breathed in a deep breath through her long nose. She wobbled at her knees. "Benjamin, you know that-"

"Ah yes, Benjamin. Let's see, money will not tempt you. I've tried that. You've accepted being childless, all alone, being without Benjamin," Satan said. "I can make you a bargain. I can bring Benjamin back for you. Join me? And he'll be waiting for you. You can worship me together."

Artemis lacked the ability to stop her tears. Her mother had always taught her to be honest, and honest tears flushed toxic fear. She stared down at the brown grass, her shoulders ached. All she had left was a whisper as snapshots of her Benjamin popped open in her mind.

"No…"

And in an instant the black orb transformed into a tall, handsome, young man wearing a tailored suit with a fashionable bow tie and colorful pocket square.

"Now, you see me in a human form. I am The One, from now on, you deal with me," Satan said. It pointed at Artemis, its fingernails sharp and dagger-like. "I gave you three chances, you denied me three times. I've done this before; it didn't end well on Earth for that fellow. But he's a story for another day."

"Why are you picking on me?" Artemis said. Her knees were bending, her thoughts clouded as if she were caught in a cold sandstorm. Her mind being pelted with conflict. "I'm not afraid."

"It's what I do, for hell's sake," Satan said. Its smile was wide-toothed perfection. "Get it, a little play on words from your English language. I hate my work; It's not work after all if you hate what you do. But to be clear, yes, you are afraid." Satan pointed at Artemis' forehead. "You keep lying to yourself inside that gifted brain. It blocks out the truth. I hate the truth."

"Then kill me," Artemis said. She dropped to her knees. "I'll die like a soldier before I fail Benjamin."

Satan, in a false human form, strolled toward her. It observed her. Its hands stuffed inside the pants pockets.

"Like I said, too easy," Satan said. It sighed with a guttural tone. "Perhaps I'll come visit you back in old St. Pete, I have fun down there, too. I have fun everywhere, all at the same time. I'm God's gift to humanity. God sent me and my minions down here after our coup attempt. But you invaded my hate filled fun, here in the Appalachian forest."

"Leave these people alone," Artemis said. She thought it was a pointless statement; she lacked any power over Satan. She looked up into the stars wondering if God existed and why had it left her life to Satan's whims.

"You're not stupid," Satan said. "You can see those demons, they are not that bright, get it? Yes, God left you for me. You've been a project of mine. I told God I would turn you into my image."

"No," Artemis said. She whimpered. "No, I guess I believe God exists, now, why now?"

"Fine, I'll explain. Demons are dark, not bright, get a sense of humor," Satan said. It winked at her. "I've been having great fun, mass killing of humans I manage. I've got the synthetic fentanyl project moving along. Besides, I've allowed you to investigate your little cases. Silly human beings, but this one, whoa, you might be over your head. I think your boss, Wylie warned you, bodies disappear, remember, in his office?"

Artemis was curious why she was not dead.

"What do you want?" Artemis said. She squinted her eyes. "You want something, otherwise I'd be dead."

"I want to play with you. I'll make some predictions," Satan said. It steepled its fingers together. "You'll get to see my favorite human flaw, what my favorite deadly sin, guess what it is?"

"I don't understand," Artemis said. She remained fixated on the brown grass and the white granite monument. Her mind swirled with incomplete thoughts, and uncertain reasons lost within a living nightmare. She touched the grass; it seemed prickly real. Her knees sensed the frozen soil. She blinked her eyes, her vision cleared. She pinched her cheek. She touched the granite surface, again.

"Come on, play with me," Satan said. "You're a tough girl. I'm your ultimate test. You've always wondered why you saw the wandering spirits. I'm the answer. Pick me, Artemis. Pick me."

Artemis closed her eyes. She pushed herself up off the hard ground, and she made herself open her eyes, and she stared over at Satan.

"I don't know," Artemis said.

"Guess?" Satan said. It nudged at her, its jackal shaped eyes glowed dark blue iris' and flamed outward reds and oranges across the milky sclera. "Or, my demon's feed on you for a thousand years."

"Greed," Artemis said. She spat out the word as she huffed, she gulped, her mouth as dry as sandpaper. "Or, lust, no wait, it's greed."

Satan nodded in agreement. It pointed at Artemis.

"Ah, smart girl," Satan said. It started to stroll behind Artemis crushing the frozen grass under its shiny shoes. Its high-pitched cackle sounded like a satisfied hyena. "Greed, I hate greed. It's my favorite. Although lust is a close second, humans are such horny creatures. The others are boring, but - sometimes useful," Satan said. It kept strolling and poking at Artemis. "But, greed, oh, how I hate it - so. I love nothing–hate's so satisfying. I think you should nibble on some hate, it'll fill your soul with a dull void."

"I'm not giving you my soul," Artemis said. She waited for the final blow. "Kill me- please leave Benjamin's spirit alone."

"Nope, you denied me three times," Satan said. It leaned in near Artemis. It whispered in a suggestive tone. "Look at me, Artemis. I'm gorgeous. I'm not human, but if I were, good Devil, look at me. Let's go play while I'm in this human body, you want me, wouldn't that feel amazing. I am amazing. Remember Benjamin and being at one with him? Take me back to your hotel. I'll light you on fire."

"Never," Artemis said. She spat at the ground. "Never."

Satan continued to stroll. It poked at her shoulders. It patted her on the head. It growled and hissed.

"Pity," Satan said. "I'm one hell of a human lover."

"I'm not afraid," Artemis said. She grasped her fingers and hands together. "I'm not afraid. Be not afraid. Be not afraid."

"Yes you are, I know the good book reads, be not afraid," Satan said with a sarcastic tone. It shrugged. "I know you've read it. Don't worry, no demons will do my work with you, it's all me. Fair warning, you can always run home like a little girl back to Wylie?"

"No..."

Satan kissed Artemis on her cheek with hard, dead lips.

"Until we meet again, Artemis Lamb. I'll be watching," Satan said. It whispered. "Don't eat the mushrooms."

It evaporated into an expansive fog like an unfurled pirate battle flag cruising upward and away from her as if at sea toward a black clouded summer storm. And it glided over the monument. And on cue the demonic spirits disappeared.

Artemis stood alone within the quiet cemetery. She looked up into a nearby oak tree, along a sturdy limb a black-winged raven watched her. She hugged her body, shivered to her core as she turned to stagger back toward the hotel.

Chapter 3

Artemis hooked the laminated Do Not Disturb sign outside her hotel room's front door knob. With her down parka zipped up, she flopped backwards with her boots still laced up, and she squirmed onto the queen-sized bed. She rolled the surrounding stiff mauve comforter into a warm cocoon. She clutched her mother's scarf as she tried to sleep. But Satan invaded her vivid dreams and her memories of Benjamin. And the moment he died in her arms. His hazel eyes fading as he bled to death while lethal bullets rained over them like a cruel metallic sandstorm. She wrestled with the specters in her mind until almost dawn. And then she got up without switching on the lights. She folded the scarf, shed the parka and boots, and she clicked on her computer. She sat on the hard wooden chair with an overused pad and began to review the claim files and the legal documents.

Later that morning she decided she would march into the hospital to find her contact names. As Wylie recommended no need for her to schedule an appointment. It was a calculated journey to find the truth before legal maneuvers blocked normal conversations.

Artemis sipped black coffee, she sat back on the desk chair. It creaked at the machined joints. Curious, she got up and walked bare-footed over to her bedroom windows. Within the night's last light-gray remnants, she saw the wandering spirits had reappeared as they flashed golden streaks along the sidewalks banked with fresh snow drifts as they radiated through the unsuspecting local souls walking toward their own early morning destinations. A sign from Satan. But Satan would not disappear. She turned toward the bathroom to take a long, hot shower to steam off Satan's stench.

~

"Artemis?" he said. He had a greasy blond comb-over, and his ruddy face advertised that Kentucky Bourbon was his best friend.

"Yes," Artemis said.

"I'm Gene, Gene Haskel, general counsel, ah, she's Loretta Dean, head of clinical risk management. Why that's an unusual name?" Gene said. He unbuttoned his blue sport coat. "We weren't expecting anyone from our reinsurance partner, least today and all, guess it's gotten serious, sending you up here?"

"Good to meet you," Loretta said. An impish, androgynous looking middle-aged woman with black hair from a box. Wearing on over-sized red cardigan. "I guess. I mean good to meet you. You have an unusual name?"

"My father was into antiquities," Artemis said. Stone faced she watched Gene and Loretta for personal ticks that might tell her their true thoughts. She could tell her comment did not answer the question; It was Gene's lazy brown pupil and Loretta kept looking at him for answers. "Greek mythology, Artemis, goddess of the hunt, the moon, so forth."

"Oh," Loretta said. She glanced over at Artemis and then back over at Gene. "You don't look Greek."

Artemis was certain Gene was the decision maker, and Loretta was his stooge.

"My mother was an Olympian, Irish national team, javelin thrower, bronzed in the pentathlon," Artemis said. She shrugged like it was common knowledge. "They met at the 1984 Olympics in Los Angeles, as they say, love at first sight. So, I'm here, with my blazing red hair, and the rest is history."

They sat across from each other inside a long conference room cluttered with fancy high-back chairs, gold leafed framed portraits of the hospital system's long since deceased former CEO's, and a statement making mahogany eagle claw-footed table. A ponderous antique grandfather clock broke up the silence by marking each second with a tick, tick, tick before it chimed at the bottom of the noon hour.

"This lawyer makes some tough allegation," Artemis said. She acted like she was reading her file notes from her computer tablet's screen. "A lot of dead patients, any ideas where they are heading?"

Loretta stared over at Gene, he waved with the back of his left hand for her to talk.

"Drugs," Loretta said. She cupped her plump fingers together on top of the table. "Terrible affliction, we try to save them all, but it's these pain medications, and all, not much work up in the coal mines, easy for them to get hooked."

"To be clear," Gene said. He wiped his sweating forehead with his chubby fingers. He sniffled and swallowed but his nostrils kept draining. "Sorry, the building's blasting heat today, they never get it right. But we don't get them hooked. We have to deal with them, can't turn them away. As the good book says, *Heal the sick, cleanse the lepers, raise the dead, cast out devils: freely ye have received, freely give.*"

"Such a God fearing man," Loretta said. She gazed over at Gene with her hands pressed together. "I am so thankful to work for you."

Artemis resisted the urge to vomit in her mouth.

"I'd like to tour your facility, the clocks ticking," Artemis said. "The files read like a textbook, nothing else I should know? I'm just getting started with my basic investigation. We'll deny the claim. He's gotten his certificate of merit, so forth."

"We can take you for a tour," Loretta said. Her smile looked like false teeth from a stegosaurus. "We take great pride in our risk management, our electronic health records are the best in the region, invested a lot of money to comply with the federal government's mandates."

"I can see that. Do you have any insight how we should respond?" Artemis said. She clicked her pen fashioned with a recording device that she slipped back into her breast pocket.

Gene shifted on his seat. His rumbled blue sport coat begging at the seams for a smaller occupant.

"Oh, this is a fishing expedition," Gene said. He waved his right hand palm and fingers forward. "Sorry they've lost family, I can appreciate their frustration. But we are above reproach; Our records are clean."

"Yes, they are spotless," Artemis said. She stared over at Gene, she glared at him long enough to cause him to look away from her. "Anything I should know ahead of time? Altered the files after the fact?"

"Oh lands," Loretta said. "Never, that would be wrong."

"And, it would be criminal," Gene said. He pulled at his wrinkled white cotton shirt sleeves. "No, ma'am, we would not allow this hospital to deal in a fraudulent sewer."

"I assumed," Artemis said. She smiled with her lips pressed together. "But I had to ask, you understand?"

"Yes I do," Gene said. "It's your job. I'm sure you're experienced, seasoned, the reason you're here to protect us."

"If we have all the facts," Artemis said. She considered Gene's statement and his conniving tone. The simpleton would be easy to manage. "We can at least develop a strategy to protect the hospital's interests, and our own. Caduceus Re hired me for a reason. It's not personal; it's about the facts."

"I hope you can make them go away," Loretta said. "Not nice to question Dr. Demetrius. He's a brilliant leader."

Artemis retrieved two business cards from her dark-green handbag. She glided them across the shiny wood grained table.

"Here, my card, come across anything unusual, call me," Artemis said. "I'd welcome your call, or email, it's those minor details that might make all the difference. I wanted to come up, introduce myself, you know the routine."

Gene rubbed the embossed business card between his thumbs and fore-fingers.

"Lamb," Gene said. He hummed a church song. "As in Lamb of Christ, such a God centered last name, Artemis. Lamb of God."

Artemis thought Gene should work the late-shift at a local religious broadcasting network like the television stations she had noticed channel surfing last night as Satan kept pestering her mind.

"Oh such conviction," Loretta said.

"Let's take a walk," Artemis said. She thought Gene was as honest as a dating site photo. "Always helps me to visualize the campus while I review the files. Have to start from a basic understanding. It's my process."

Gene stuffed the business card inside his sport coat pocket.

"Why not," Gene said. He glanced over at Loretta. "Loretta I have another important meeting, can you escort Artemis?"

"Why yes," Loretta said. She got up and waved Artemis toward the tall conference room door. "We're proud of our hospital campus, it'll be my pleasure."

Artemis strolled with Loretta along the busy hospital hallways and corridors. Loretta sashayed across the marble floors pointing out the labor and delivery section, the catheter labs, surgical suites, and all the human services offered by the facility. Artemis ignored Loretta's attempted conversation as she noticed passing by a large window down seven stories at the hospital's rear loading docks there were many, active eighteen-wheel trucks spewing diesel fumes into the air. Artemis stopped, stared downward and tapped on the window.

"Loretta," Artemis said. She grinned. "You all eat a lot here? You've kept mentioning the new cafeteria."

"What?" Loretta said.

"Down there, I'm kidding," Artemis said. She tapped on the window with her right forefinger knuckle. "All those refrigeration trucks, they are at-it, in and out, in and out. That's not body parts being shipped out?"

"Oh, nothing I know about," Loretta said. She peeked through the window down at the trucks. She shifted away from the window as if she'd gotten got masturbating. "Must be delivery day. I don't know."

A fat man wearing a short-sleeved shirt defied the cold air opened the rear of the truck container; It was empty. Within seconds sturdy forklifts loaded it with stacks of shrink-wrapped boxes on wooden skiffs. Artemis felt Loretta tug at her left forearm.

"Did I show you our cafeteria?" Loretta said. "I know I've talked about it, but you must see it."

"No-"

"Oh then, come with me," Loretta said. Her pace quickened over toward the shiny chrome elevators. "It's all brand new. I'm sure you'll love it."

"Ah," Artemis said. She removed Loretta's tight grip. "Maybe next time, I've a plane to catch back to St. Petersburg, but thank you."

"Pity," Loretta said. "It's chicken fried steak day. Gene loves chicken fried steak."

Chapter 4

"This file has land mines," Artemis said. She paced in front Wylie's wooden desk. The office splashed in diffused morning sunlight. "Wylie, you're right, this might get expensive, and nasty."

"What's it like?" Wylie said. He crinkled his face and scratched the top of his nose. He sipped hot coffee from a steaming office mug. "The people, I've never been in Eastern Kentucky."

"Like I went back in time, town stinks like sulfur. I wonder if they have actual clouds in the sky. Sorry, I'm half-kidding," Artemis said. She held her hands up as she kept pacing back and forth. "The hospital creeps me out. Had to come back home, to work this file through my mind. I picked up a strange sensation up there."

"Good on you," Wylie said. After he read Artemis' file notes, he looked up at her. He tapped his ink pen on the computer's flat screen monitor. "What's this business with commercial trucks?"

Artemis stopped pacing, she leaned her hands on Wylie's desk.

"Just a weird observation," Artemis said. "They were loading stacks of boxes onto these refrigeration trucks; they were not delivering anything. All the effort I'd imagine was like a distribution center after you buy something on-line. I've never seen an operation like that at any hospital I've investigated."

"You sure?" Wylie said.

"Positive. They were empty as they opened the back, I watched a fat guy walk inside," Artemis said. She pointed forward at Wylie's side office windows guarded outside by live oaks with haunting Spanish moss hanging from limb-to-limb. "Risk manager got antsy, pulled me away from the windows, then wanted to show me their cafeteria."

"They're peddling body parts?" Wylie said. He coughed with a raspy chuckle. He sipped coffee. "I love that coffee smell, makes me happy. But geez, I'm full of phlegm this morning."

"That's a lot of body parts, it's odd, seen nothing like it at a hospital," Artemis said. She shrugged. "Loading them with the efficiency of a German automaker. In broad daylight with death cases hanging over their heads."

Wylie pondered Artemis' comment.

"Doubt it, ah, go relax for a few days," Wylie said. He thumbed and fore-fingered his right earlobe. "Schedule a meeting with the plaintiff attorney, see where we sit before we deny the claim."

"That was my instinct," Artemis said. She leaned back, crossed her arms, and started pacing again. "I'll get them setup and get back up there, clocks-ticking, need to respond."

"Yeah," Wylie said. "We've got less than twenty days, and then the dark suits get involved. We need to get them managed."

"I think we better get a firm with local roots," Artemis said. She stopped pacing. "If this gets to a trial, better have a legit lawyer with a twangy accent, not unlike how you sound."

"I'm being authentic," Wylie said. He half-grinned. "The wife digs it. I sound normal back home, you'd stick out like a fire engine."

"I stick out like a fire engine," Artemis said. She walked toward the open office door. "Later…"

Artemis drove back home to St. Petersburg, she flicked her car keys on the kitchen counter, and took a walk in the warm air. As she strolled along Beach Drive within the touristy crowd, she heard an odd voice.

"Art-em-is, Art-em-is…"

Artemis stopped and she searched for a familiar face. But there were none, those that moved by her in both directions along the well-maintained concrete sidewalk in front of colorful clothing and shoe boutiques and busy outdoor restaurants, were all strangers from all walks of life. And they were all with the living. And she realized there were no wandering spirits, either. She held her breath aware only one entity had the power over the dead.

"Artemis, deny me again?"

Artemis looked down; The voice emanated from an older man, with a significant paunch, wearing blue jeans and a fanny pack. She stepped closer toward him.

"Do I know you?"

"Oh please, check me out. This body's about done for," Satan said. It patted and squeezed the flabby belly. "Didn't take care of himself. Heavy smoker. I borrowed him from the nearby hospital, they told the family he's resting comfortably. So I inhabited him. Maybe I strip naked and go streaking before he croaks, an awesome and memorable way for a grandpa to go out?"

"What do you want?" Artemis said. She evaded making any eye contact with the humans exiting a nearby shop then rambling nearby them into the next boutique. "You enjoy creeping me out, you know I can't stop you."

"Well, well, so tense," Satan said. It scratched its groin next to its bulge. "Aren't you my new friend?"

"We are not friends," Artemis said. She stood resolute. "What?"

"Fine," Satan said. It sat on a concrete bench next to a large bronzed feminized crocodile figurine that it caressed like they were passionate lovers. "Look at the boobs on this thing, wish it was real. So, I brought you a present, and it's not Halloween."

Artemis turned away. Warm for the winter season even by central Florida standards, but she felt a chill wash across her skin as her face blushed crimson.

"What gives?"

"Well, my dear, it's not a full moon tonight," Satan said. It kissed the bronzed crocodile, tried to slip it tongue, but the hard bronze denied it entry. "Be that way crocodile girl. But, go your way, have your Guinness at The Moon Under Water. Chat up your favorite bartender, Alan. After, walk out the front doors from The Moon, go stroll like you need some air beneath those banyan trees and tell me what you see. You'll love it darling, I am so, so creative. I hate you so."

"You said you enjoyed torture," Artemis said. She crossed her arms; she stared down at her brown loafers. "Right?"

"I do, all for hate, I'll teach you hate," Satan said. It waved her away with a dismissive hand flick. "Move along, I need to get it on with my crocodile girl. I'll get arrested humping this thing, otherwise read on-line tomorrow about my streaking adventure up Central Avenue. Oh, and Artemis. My gift for you is bespoke, the best gift comes from hate, you'll see."

Artemis turned bit-by-bit and stumbled away from Satan. It blurred her vision to imagine what waited. But she kept shuffling her loafers each step navigating in front of the restaurants and shops. She faltered under a maroon dining tent; but she kept staring down at the concrete, as she evaded tourists, their bored children or hearing the families lost in aimless conversations or them looking down at their smartphone screens for walking directions to museums. Glancing side-to-side, she spotted a safe haven, and stopped inside a fine art gallery. The air conditioning, the quiet shop, and the beautiful creations helped her to better grasp reality. Her breathing calmed. From inside the galleries kaleidoscope of vibrant colors she gazed through the glass windows over at the banyan trees curious what awaited her. Her thoughts blocked as if by the steam from a witches caldron for an unknowable gift from Satan. She gulped. She breathed in deep breaths, held them and breathed out.

"Are you okay?" A lady said. A man Artemis guessed was her husband stood close behind her. She had seen them before.

"Oh?" Artemis said. She stopped shaking. She wiped away the sweat from eyebrows. "I am. I'm just distracted from work. Panicked from the stress, sorry."

"We understand," he said. He patted Artemis on the shoulder. "We've kept this place open, somehow."

"Be well," the lady said. "It'll get worked out."

"Thank you," Artemis said. "I like your gallery."

They smiled and acknowledged Artemis as she left the quaint shop and walked out and then back along Beach Drive. She sat on a wooden stool at the far end of the bar inside, The Moon Under Water. She drank her Guinness, as the bartender Alan ambled back over closer toward her from the other side of the dark wood bar. He wiped the amber marble top with a white dish towel.

"Now lass," Alan said. He was an older man, brown haired who said he hailed from Wales; a professional bartender that engaged his regulars like a kind priest within a confessional. "What's the matter?"

Artemis clutched the cold Guinness glass with both hands. The restaurant was lively, plates and glasses clashed as they were being loaded by a husky busboy into a above the counter commercial grade dishwasher.

"A tough file," Artemis said. "My typical workday."

"Ah, now, tell me more," Alan said. He beamed as if you had heard the lament ten times that day. "You have an unusual job. I'm not made for such things. Too much death and despair for me."

"I think my life might get worse," Artemis said. She sipped the Guinness. "Do you think Karma's for real?"

Alan stopped cleaning the bar area. He leaned his right elbow on the bar and shifted over closer to Artemis.

"We were in India," Alan said. He whispered as another bar guest sat down nearby them. "I was in military intelligence, you know. Hush, hush. They took it serious. I promise you that."

Artemis considered Alan's comment.

"I think I have a good heart," Artemis said. She stared behind Alan and over at the liquor bottle line set in front of a wide decorative mirror centered with an embossed white Welsh Dragon. "I don't hate anyone. I think."

"That's Karma," Alan said. He pointed up toward the British West Indies themed ceiling fans. "Only you know your heart, with your god. It's how Karma works, at least, the best the Hindus told me. A multi-directional thing I think. It's beyond my brain."

"Then someone owes me," Artemis said. "I hope. Cash me out."

"Come back soon, Artemis," Alan said. He smacked the paper order ticket in front of her. "Keep breathing. Keep smiling."

Artemis finished her Guinness. She paid her bill with cash and trekked away from The Moon Under Water's front doors. As Satan had instructed her, she stepped across busy Beach Drive by dodging fancy cars, valets, and she strolled over to underneath the two dominating banyan trees. The trees covered with green, oval-shaped leaves, and a circus tent like effect from the descending areal root system. She stared over at the pleasure boats and the yachts moored within the dark harbor that simmered from reflected evening lamp lights. A wolf moon blazed with a red tinged glow as she watched the golden wandering spirits drift undetected amongst the living. It was the first time she had ever seen them all slow down, and glance over at her as if they were being watched by an overprotective parent. But then she realized Satan had all power over the dead. And then, there her Benjamin waited for Artemis. He levitated just above the grass. Radiating next to a ghost white painted Renaissance themed statuary of a maiden staring out at the gulf waters waiting for her sailor to return from the sea. Artemis walked over toward him across the grass park, and away from the banyan trees where children played, yelled and teased each other.

"Why?" Artemis said. She tried not to cry; she tried to keep her composure. "Why haven't you gone on my love."

Benjamin held his hands out, even though he could not touch Artemis. He appeared like a grainy hologram.

"I'm not lost," Benjamin said. "I love you."

"I love you," Artemis said. "Satan tortures the living and the dead. Go on, I'll be fine. Maybe we'll meet again. I'm not sure how it all works beyond me, in the existence that awaits you."

Benjamin was silent for several minutes. His image fading and returning trapped between realities.

"I need your help," Benjamin said. His voice sounded hollow, undulating. "Satan knows the truth. I'm waiting for my daughter. To see her safe, you can protect her. I know your skills."

Artemis stepped closer to Benjamin's image. To those nearby their naked eyes noticed Artemis talking to a statue. But they ignored her because St. Petersburg was a wacky town with former military personnel roaming the streets with untreated profound mental illnesses.

"I didn't know you had a daughter?" Artemis said.

"I was trying to tell you. I made a mistake," Benjamin said. He looked downward. "But then, I took a bullet before... I'm sorry."

"Where is she? I know we don't have long," Artemis said. She stepped back. "Satan sent you. This is not random, where is she?"

"Kentucky, near a town called, Selene," Benjamin said. "She's trapped, she's a child. Her mother's a drug addict."

Artemis understood every human being held onto secrets because each person had their reasons. But in time the truth emerges like water vapors rising from a warm stream meeting cold mountain air and universal equilibrium will reign even beyond death. Satan devoured secrets for its own purposes to conceal the truth. Artemis' mother had taught her without releasing the truth a person was not living in freedom. And Satan was having great fun at her emotional expense.

"What's her name?" Artemis said, softly. She allowed the tears to slide down her cheeks. "I'll find her, you know I will."

"Laina Lynn," Benjamin said. "She's about seven or eight. She'll be eight soon. I can't protect her, and Satan knows she exists. There's a cult there, they search for little girls like Laina."

"Satan knows we all exist," Artemis said. She wiped her eyes with her fingers. "Satan knows all our names, faces, we cannot hide. I just hope if there is God, it is watching. But I'm not much for believing in the singularity."

"I will not go on, I'd rather burn in Hell than not try to protect her,"

Benjamin said. His image began to flicker. "Without knowing she's safe. Satan blocks me from her. I don't know why."

"I'll find her," Artemis said. "I have to figure out my target. The Company never interferes; they point me at the problem. I have some time to clean up the mess. While up there, I'll help her out."

And thick clouds formed and blocked out the moon's glow, and Benjamin disappeared as he whispered, "I love you."

Artemis stood looking at the decaying statuary. Satan shared Benjamin for a reason and then concealed him from her using random weather patterns. But she understood Satan was not random. It did not work that way.

Now confident she was Satan's target. But why her? Or worse, was she living a bad dream or had she lost her mind?

Chapter 5

"So, I'm some hayseed lawyer?"

"No, you're well-educated. I studied your background," Artemis said. She sat across from the plaintiff lawyer, Jerome Jenkins. His law office within easy walking distance from the hospital's front doors. But it had taken Artemis' assistant several days to set up the meeting. "Friends call you, J-Square? It seems you're a busy man."

"Yeah, it's my nickname, grew up here, high school basketball star which helped get me Ivy League educated," Jerome said. He was tall and redheaded. He had blue eyes that did not accept nonsense. "Don't think you being a red too, going to cause me to go soft on this case. Get me?"

"I get you," Artemis said. She deposited her black tactical backpack between her boots. "I figured we can at least talk about the case before we have to respond and get the defense counsel involved."

"Please send in one them pretty boys out of Lexington," Jerome said. He twiddled his silver fountain pen between his fingers. "I enjoy whipping them in court, trust me, they've met me."

"Not sure, yet," Artemis said. She sat back and opened her arms. "Maybe we can come to an understanding without them? And you don't sound as twangy as everybody else."

Jerome stared at Artemis' face. He smiled with his lips tight, he sat back on the conference room chair. The conference room smelled clean, and they kept it spotless. It had a shaker style table, the room decoration minimalist.

"I work at it. I've been out in the world. What's with the tattoo?" Jerome said. He pointed his pen across the table over at Artemis' right hand. "All nice and hidden, but I noticed, how'd they find you?"

Artemis rubbed her right wrist with her other hand. She thought of Benjamin. She acknowledged Jerome.

"Friend's birthday," Artemis said. "I prefer to remember his birthday, he's no longer with the living."

Jerome covered his thin lips with his long fingers.

"Fair enough, sorry," Jerome said. "Most med-mal folks are pasty-white old farts like me trying to act all tough and sinister. You're rather easygoing, but very aware, you are ex-military?"

Artemis stopped rubbing her wrist. She accepted the fact Jerome made his living creating mental subterfuge, being observant.

"They taught me the basics, and then special forces," Artemis said. She gave Jerome a hard, squinted stare to cause him to squirm. "I'm a well-trained medic, bounced me out. Got recruited into medical malpractice. I guess they figured I had the stomach for it, medical training, at least it's always interesting."

"Well, I'll be, few women in your world," Jerome said. "Guess I'll not tick you off, either way, thank you for your service."

"Sure, I was lucky," Artemis said. She unzipped her backpack and retrieved her tablet. "Hospital files look air-tight, where's your evidence."

"I like you," Jerome said. He slipped on his reading glasses. He opened a legal file folder. "Get with it, good on you. I'm old school, like to have the paper and pen in my fingers."

"To be clear," Artemis said. She gripped the tablet computer. "Sorry for anyone you knew, opioid addictions a horrible problem."

Jerome glanced over at Artemis. He acknowledged her point.

"Yeah, I grew up with the families," Jerome said. He unbuttoned his dress shirt sleeves and rolled them up to about mid-arm to reveal his hairy freckled skin. "I committed us to this cause, it's not just about money."

Artemis focused on keeping calm and resolute. She had heard the - *not just the money* - canard from every plaintiff lawyer that had ever filed a claim, created a television ad, newspaper ad, radio ad or the billboards dotting the highway landscape as she drove her rental truck toward Selene.

"Really?" Artemis said.

"Ms. Lamb, for now, I'm funding these cases, it's expensive, which you all calculate into your strategy," Jerome said. He glanced over at her from above his common drug store reading glasses. "This is my hometown. I know everybody. And your hospital has a lot of explaining to do. All I see from them is making money by getting innocent people hooked and then getting paid again by pushing them into their rehabilitation facilities. And human beings don't go into a hospital and then come out after being cremated. I find those DNR's the hospital waved in my face are suspicious, at best. And don't get me started on the consent forms and every employee is under NDA's, poor people want to keep their jobs. I have an expert panel prepared to corroborate our allegations. Already knocked out the certificate of merit. And I don't think your client cares about the standard of care. Shall I continue?"

"At least call me, Artemis," Artemis said. "Ms. Lamb makes me sound old. But the records show your clients had problems, soft tissue injuries, so forth, our physicians were following the standard of care. We have experts on our side, too. Preventing a potential outbreak from toxic bodies. They have solid reasoning behind them. Unless you have solid evidence, we'll be prepared to fight it out based on the medical records."

Jerome set his readers on the table. He pondered Artemis' statement. He looked over at an antiqued framed photo of what Artemis guessed was a bride and groom's wedding day. It was perhaps one of his children given the expensive frame style and his loving gaze.

"Once that hospital sold, taken over by your client, toxic bodies? Nonsense," Jerome said. He huffed and combed his thinning hair with his left hand fingers. "Figured they'd focus on making money, and not patient care. They have not disappointed me. The people that own that hospital don't show their faces here in Selene."

"Hospitals are businesses," Artemis said. "Nothing illegal turning a profit."

"True," Jerome said. "But not at the expense of human lives. And don't think I don't notice how busy that hospital is. I hear they're into a lot more than direct patient care."

Artemis considered Jerome's comment. She was not confident her earlier observations concerning the refrigeration trucks would have been a useful topic. Certain Jerome knew of the refrigeration traffic, and he was holding his knowledge back for another inconvenient moment. She thought him a smart, seasoned personnel injury lawyer that understood negotiation tactics.

"The reason I'm here," Artemis said. She stuffed the tablet back inside her backpack. "We'll fight this out, might take a long time, a lot of money."

"That's all true," Jerome said. He leaned forward across the conference table. "But stock exchange traded companies don't like bad press. I'm not sure you all want to drag this matter out, either?"

"We'll see, I accept your points," Artemis said. She stood up and reached forward to shake Jerome's hand. "Let's keep talking, in the meantime, I'll be in touch."

Artemis left the office that from a former time was a two-story family residence. She walked down the town's Main Street blanketed with enough sunshine that warmed her above the freezing mark. She thought Jerome knew where he was navigating his case. He had investigated the hospital down to every tongue depressor. And her client was cryptic, secretive and pompous.

As Artemis strolled toward her hotel along the sidewalk, after she walked by an elementary school where the playground was crowded with children playing, she recognized the handsome face. Satan lurked the sidewalk wearing denim bib overalls and a bright red hunting cap with earflaps. It waved at Artemis like it had a spastic tremor and it skipped over to stand next to her.

"Honest plaintiff lawyer," Satan said. It rubbed the bodies hands together like it was warming up in front of a raging fire. "Imagine that, he's honest, but Jerome's been up to no good."

"Don't you ever give it a rest?" Artemis said.

"No, I'm Satan…"

"I have a job," Artemis said. "Why are you bothering me in the daytime? You have me during my sleep. Will you let me sleep?"

Satan put its hands on its human form hips; It stared into the pale blue sky. It patted Artemis on her back.

"Artemis, I know your real job, you are great at it. I'd say being ambidextrous makes you gifted. Are you leading with the left, no wait, you're coming with the right. I have enjoyed your previous performances," Satan said. Its voice tone smart-aleck and whimsical. "I am the great deceiver, remember that you are my human plaything. I could inhabit Jerome. Who else could I play with? Questions, questions, but you're correct. Jerome knows a lot more than he's telling you, for now. I am quite pleased with this hospital; they are doing Satan's work. Get it, that's me."

Artemis stopped and stared over at a weathered red bricked pharmacy. The windows covered from the inside with paper. A for-lease sign taped inside the wide front window, encased with an old metal frame. Next door an empty barber shop. The blue and red striped pole no longer operated.

"You'd do a lot more than body parts, killing people's easy for you,"

Artemis said. She stared over into Satan's dead eyes. "What are you doing?"

Satan smiled. It clapped its hands.

"Now you're using that brain," Satan said. It leaned in closer to Artemis. She winced from sniffing its body odor. "That thing lucky genetics gave you between your ears. Until next time. Oh, go find that little girl. She's off-limits, for now. I get bored torturing children. And tonight, it's a full-moon, just saying. I do my best work during full-moons." Satan stepped back and howled as it disappeared into the air.

Chapter 6

Artemis discovered an address for Laina Lynn's mother, Ruth Lynn, after a basic internet search. She drove her rental truck into the Appalachian forest teeming with trees, rocks, vegetation, and fauna along the narrow, circuitous blacktopped county roads. She dodged several hulking coal trucks that spat coal black dust across her windshield as she drove near them and the unforgiving shaved greenish-grey limestone and shale mountain sides.

Artemis found a two-pump gas station next to a single story grocery store with a metal roof. She parked her truck on a gravel surface in front of the grocery store. An old-fashioned Coca Cola sign made of porcelain was bolted next to the front screened door. She walked inside over dusty wooden planked floorboards and found an older man with a buzz cut. He waved over at Artemis from behind the counter.

"Can you help me?" Artemis said. She pecked with her right hand forefinger on her smartphone. She positioned the screen so the man could read the address. "Any idea where I can find this?"

He put on his ill-fitted black frame glasses, stared at the smartphone screen, and nodded.

"Sure can, just up the road, on the right," the old man said. "But it's empty, nobody home, as Ruth Lynn's over in the hospital."

"Why?"

"Drugs," the old man said. "Poor girl went and got pregnant, again.

I'm not sure what to say. I bet the baby died. Sad. A sad story, if were to ask me."

Artemis stood back and glanced over near a half-full metal rack filled with moon pies, fig newtons, and off brand potato chips.

"What about her daughter, Laina Lynn?" Artemis said. "She's a friend of mine's daughter."

"Ain't seen her a late," the old man said. He squinted his eyes. "Them drugs are powerful, evil stuff, ain't like getting a handle of Kentucky nectar, them drugs they'll put you down. All they need is a tiny amount."

"Sorry," Artemis said. "I don't understand. Handle?"

"Bourbon sweetie, you're standing in Kentucky," the old man said. He tilted his head sideways as he examined Artemis from her boots up to her red hair. "Get the big bottle, got a handle on 'em. Cheaper, it lasts for weeks if you are a real drinker."

"Oh," Artemis said. She smelled stale popcorn. She glanced over at the chromed machine spackled inside and out with stale popcorn mounds, yellow caked butter and salt flecks. "I've never, well, it's not my thing."

"Laina Lynn's like a feral cat," the old man said. He poked his tongue into an irritable spot on his upper teeth. It sounded like a mouse squeak as he pressed his fingers against the spot. "She's got nobody, hadn't seen her, like she disappeared. Maybe over at the hospital."

"Well, thank you, I'll go there," Artemis said. She pointed toward outside to the serpentine road canopied by oaks, pines and maple trees. "This the same way out? I feel like I'm lost in a labyrinth. I've never gotten lost."

"You seem like you got a little angry in ya," the old man said. He chuckled as he scratched his unshaven chin. "If I poked at ya. I ain't poking, to be clear, you'd whip me."

"I'm not angry," Artemis said. "I'm lost… anybody think to place signs for the roads."

"It's a problem, but I reckon that you'd be fine going back that way," the old man said. His forehead revealed long horizontal wrinkle lines and vertical ones between his bushy brown eyebrows. "Best be careful up in here, I know my way, but, there's been some weird happenings. Up higher in the old forest, they say them weirdos up there praying at trees, don't like it. Best to avoid them."

Artemis studied the old man's brown eyes, she thought he was being blunt and honest. She opened her coat to reveal her holstered weapon.

"I can take care of myself," Artemis said. She zipped up her parka. "But, thank you for being honest, up front."

"Nice gun, I know you can handle it," the old man said. He leaned farther across the quarter-inch thick pressed-wood counter. "Be extra careful, it ain't just one, there's a bunch roaming. I've had some come in for whatnot, they don't act right. They ain't from here, like you."

"They're alive?" Artemis said. She held her right hand up. "I mean, they're sort of, pale lookin', unfocused?"

"I guess," the old man said. "Sweetie, they seem drugged up to me. They pay up in cash, even so, I'm prepared. That's why god invented shotguns."

"Sorry, ah, stay safe," Artemis said. She handed the old man her business card. "What's your name?"

The old man again put on his ill-fitting eyeglasses. He stared above them back over at Artemis, and down at the business card.

"Virgil Sammons, ma'am, call me Virgil," Virgil said. He glossed his hefty fingers over the expensive card-stock. "Fancy card, from down in Florida. Caduceus? You work for the hospital?"

"No, we only consult. I don't work for the hospital," Artemis said. She noticed Virgil stepped backwards and stood taller. "Not an employee, I investigate liability cases for our company. Hospital's a client. I'm trying to figure out a legal problem. Happened to be in the neighborhood, figured I'd help my friend."

Virgil crossed his burly arms.

"Not sure what to think 'bout you…"

"I would feel the same," Artemis said. She zipped up her parka all the way under her chin. "I came looking for Laina Lynn for her father, he's gone, but he, how do I say this?"

"Benjamin?" Virgil said. He sighed at the cruelty of life. "I knew him, he was a good boy. Sorry he got mixed up with Ruth Lynn. She's a mess. But last I checked, the boy died. They never told me where, just that he'd been killed fightin' for us."

Artemis stared down at the dirty vinyl flooring that bent upwards at the corners from underneath the heavy soda pop machine. The machine had a constant hum from an oversupply of electricity.

"I was there, can't say where," Artemis said. She wiped her eyes with her thumb and forefinger. "I was a medic, tried to save him. He died with me holding him. After the bad guys stopped shooting; his team stood there crying with me. That's all I can say."

Virgil and Artemis avoided eye contact. Virgil glanced down, murmured to himself and leaned his hairy elbows against the counter.

"That's terrible," Virgil said. He coughed. "I reckon you're all right, and all."

"I have a job, the hospital has some issues, coincidence about Benjamin's girl," Artemis said. She rubbed her forehead. She bumped her boot against the molding strip cracked at the joint. "I was checking up on Laina Lynn. For Benjamin. I have no kids, but if the situation were reversed, he'd have done it for me."

"I believe you," Virgil said. He reached behind and pulled out his wallet, opened it, and stuffed Artemis' business card into the empty paper cash section. "If it were me, I'd go search inside that hospital, she might be there. Where I'd go if I were her, be near her mama."

"Yeah, good idea," Artemis said. She stepped forward and shook Virgil's hand. "Thank you, if I can help, or you remember anything, call me. I'll find her."

"I'll be fine," Virgil said. "Go find Laina, and as for you, get out of here before it gets nightfall. Since they sold the hospital, been now a year or so. Stay in town, you'll be safer there."

Artemis stepped toward the metal front door. She stopped and turned back around.

"Stupid question, sorry," Artemis said. She gripped the door's metal handle. "What's Laina Lynn look like, I've never met her?"

"Oh, I get ya," Virgil said. He studied up at the moldy grey specked ceiling tiles. He pointed back over at Artemis. "Bout your shoulder height, dishwater blonde. She's got Benjamin's hazel colored eyes, she'll look right through ya, like you're a ghost."

"Thanks," Artemis said. "I'll find her."

Artemis exited the grocery, drove the truck over to the gas station side where she refueled. As she finished tightening the fuel cap as the temperature had dropped below freezing. Within the dusk and light cast from a single telephone pole across the two-lanes road between thick oak and sycamore trees appeared a white stag with sturdy antlers. Walking with the muscular stag was a Native American warrior, a wandering spirit. Artemis guessed the warrior had traditional tribal markings; he held a long spear in his right hand.

The warrior acted as a protector for the stag; as they blended at the intersection for the living and the dead. The healthy twelve-pointed stag scratched at the grass, dirt and weeds with its front hooves. It snorted foggy breaths through its snout, and it bit off a brown leaf that winter had not taken. The warrior relaxed and stared over at Artemis. She waved at him. He appeared curious how she had the vision to see him. Then the stag turned and trudged back up within the dark forest's protection. The warrior shouted over at Artemis from his native tongue and he turned to follow the stag back into the woods.

Chapter 7

"Can I help you?"

"Yes, yes please," Artemis said. She strode up to the hospital's information counter next to the security station. An older lady with wispy gray hair sat behind it and she smiled up at Artemis. "I need a visitor pass. I work with the risk management department, they said I should come over here for a pass, can you log me in?"

The lady shook her head in agreement; she reached forward with her right hand palm open, her wrinkled hand with swollen knuckles tremored.

"Honey, I need to see your driver's license."

Artemis handed it forward, and she turned to scan the packed lobby area seeking a child that matched Laina Lynn's description. It was a similar scene for every hospital Artemis investigated. Disease and human malfunction attacked all walks of life. And it left those not afflicted to wait and ponder the uncertain future.

"Here you go, honey," she said. She tapped on a sign-in sheet.

"Please sign in on this form."

"Thanks," Artemis said. She clipped the badge onto her jacket. "Oh, wait. Can you tell me the room for Ruth Lynn?"

And within seconds Artemis had Ruth Lynn's room number. She walked deeper into the hospital. As she foraged along corridors, the typical hospital smells enraptured her and the color-coded lines that directed healthcare staff toward the correct floor. She took the stairs and avoided the elevators. After a brief exploration she located the labor and delivery floor and she began her search for Laina Lynn. But she realized as she glanced into patient rooms there were many woman intubated and surviving off life support. She thought about her claim file and the allegations that the hospital had misused the informed consent form and cremated human remains without the families' knowledge. Her instincts inside her brain were thumping at her at full-tilt.

Artemis acknowledged the busy nurses behind the nursing station. She located Ruth Lynn's patient room. The intubated woman's wilted body hooked up to life-support with IV lines connected to oblong nutrition bags. A ventilation machine cycled and it kept pumping oxygen into a no longer pregnant cadaver. A monitor above blipped her vital signs in hibernation across a square-shaped monitor. And curled up into a corner of the room, hidden underneath the half-rail bed, a tiny child balled herself within a thin daisy yellow and lavender blanket.

Artemis kneeled down, she reached forward to touch the child's canvas tennis shoe. The child shook from being chilled and noticed. She studied back at Artemis with one hazel eye as she spied over at her from underneath the blanket's protection.

"Are you Laina?"

The girl inspected Artemis. She yanked the blanket closer.

"Yeah," Laina said with a whisper. "Who are you?"

"I'm a friend of your father's," Artemis said. "Do you remember your father?"

"No," Laina said. "I don't have a father."

Artemis sat back, she retreated and sat American Indian style.

Her hands and arms open in a non-threatening pose.

"I'll help you," Artemis said. She spoke with a low tone, slow

cadence. "I came to say hi, check on you and your mom. Have you eaten?"

Laina shook her head side-to-side. She scrunched farther away from Artemis. Artemis shifted away and gave Laina distance and time.

"I'll be right back," Artemis said. She stood up, walked out of the room, and over toward the curved nursing station fronted with a dark laminate paneling and white composite countertop.

"Pardon," Artemis said. She pointed backward with her righthand thumb. "The child inside the room, I'm friends with her father."

"I'm listening to you," the nurse said. She wore a navy-blue uniform with a tubular stethoscope draped over her neck. She kept her eyes on a flat-panel computer screen. "But I can't help her."

"Does she have any family?" Artemis said. She kept her parka closed to hide her side-arm. "I'm happy to help, if I can."

"We aren't coldhearted," the nurse said. She blew a puff of air from her bottom lips. "We're at a loss, they have the patient on life-support, hoping to keep the baby alive. Are you family?"

"She looks dead, I'm sorry," Artemis said. She tapped on the countertop and over at the busy work stations and nurses monitoring computer screens or inputting patient data. "Sorry, I'm a former medic, military, her pulse is weak. It's a brutal call. I get it."

The nurse took off her stethoscope and placed it behind the computer screen and an over-active LCD call-light display.

"Yeah, it's brutal," the nurse said. She frowned. She glanced side-to-side at her hollow-eyed colleagues. "Not my call, but-"

"No, I don't understand," Artemis said. "You've got several others up here on life-support."

"Yes, I know," the nurse said. "The hospital expects us to keep them all alive. I'm not sure why they follow this protocol, not my call. I need my job."

Artemis considered if she should tell the nurse her true identity. She did not enjoy being dishonest. It blocked her ability to reason between right and wrong. She pondered the situation, but then the girl Laina emerged from the patient room. She wore a tattered dress, tennis shoes, her long dishwater blonde hair in tangles. Artemis was certain her hazel eyes came from Benjamin. And as Virgil warned her, Laina's gaze examined her soul.

"I thought you left me," Laina said. She clutched the safety blanket. "Who are you?"

Artemis waved Laina over toward her.

"I'll never do that," Artemis said. She looked back over at the nurse. "All right if I take her to the cafeteria?"

"Please," the nurse said. Her telephone rang. The line panel blipped three red dots. She turned to examine a white eraser board with names written in black. Physicians in surgical smocks strode close to them. "I don't think she has anyone, no one but you've come to visit her mother."

"No family?" Artemis said. She backed away. "I'll get her some food, but protective services, shelter?"

"This is not a big city," the nurse said. She glanced back over at Artemis. "We've kept her hidden so far, but our homes for kids can be nightmares up here in the mountains. The nurses have tried to help her, but we've families too. We ain't hard-hearted."

Artemis stared down at Laina who was now holding her hand. She acknowledged the nurse.

"I'll take her," Artemis said. She nodded. "You okay with that, for now?"

"Please, disappear," the nurse said. She leaned forward and she whispered without making eye contact. "Get her out of this hospital. Poor things mama's gone, the baby's gone, hear me?"

"I heard you," Artemis said. She turned, encouraged Laina to walk along with her and away from the busy nurses station. In all her case work over the years she knew the overworked nurses in every hospital kept the facility working and they knew all the hospital's secrets. She stopped, turned and reached into her purse and withdrew a business card; she placed it on the counter.

"I'm up here on a legal matter," Artemis said. "This little girl was my deceased lover's child, it's a coincidence. Random. However, if I need some help, have some questions, help me out?"

The nurse examined the business card set on the shiny white counter. She pushed it back over toward Artemis.

"No," the nurse said. "I need my job. But listen to me, keep the girl out of here, we'll act like we never saw her."

Chapter 8

Artemis sat on a ruby Naugahyde bench seat across from Laina behind a white formica-topped table at an all-night diner. She draped her winter parka over Laina's diminutive shoulders. Laina would not look down at the laminated menu, she sat back, huffed, and scanned the busy restaurant. She watched other nearby restaurant guests eating, drinking, and chatting about non-reality television shows or common obstacles life had thrown at them. The diner had given into a non-smoking restaurant.

"You can have anything on the menu," Artemis said. She glided the menu over closer to Laina. "I've got this, don't worry."

Laina glanced down at the menu written in block letters. She squinted. Her soft eyelashes like two butterflies resting on flower stems. Artemis realized Laina could not read the menu. The silence told her the truth as Laina fidgeted with the laminated menu corners rocking it side-to-side.

"Mama said I was a dead weight," Laina said. Scrunching back inside the warm parka. "We don't go to restaurants."

"Well, I don't think you're dead weight, you need to eat a good meal," Artemis said. She tapped on the menu. "What do you like?"

"I don't know," Laina said. She shivered on the bench seat.

"Okay, if I order for you?" Artemis said. She managed her emotions. "Don't stress, I'll not abandon you. You're Benjamin's girl, you're now part of my tribe, hear me?"

"I guess," Laina said. She pushed the menu forward, pulled her legs up and hugged them. She kept staring over at Artemis. "Thank you. Are you my mother's friend?"

"What do you like?" Artemis said. She gripped the laminated menu. Gliding her right hand thumb top to bottom. "Hamburger, French fries… want a strawberry milkshake?"

"Sure," Laina said. She sniffled. "If that's all right?"

"Cool, I'm your father's friend," Artemis said. She tried to smile. "Let's get some comfort food. I'll burn off the calories."

A plump waitress with tired eyes limped next to their table. Her ink pen speared into her kabuki actor styled black haired bun.

Artemis made the orders choosing foods she thought a little girl might like. She picked deep-fried foods, but it was about Laina; it was about Benjamin's child. The waitress backed away from the table and ambled toward the fry cook station splattered with grease, she handed the paper ticket to the skinny older man wearing a paper hat surrounded with heat and steam.

"Do you go to school?" Artemis said Laina.

Laina shook her head. She crinkled her face.

"No," Laina said. "I ain't been for a while."

"It's all right," Artemis said. "It's okay. I was talking, just curious. I knew your father, Benjamin, ah, well."

Laina gazed out the restaurant's window into the dusty parking lot. At the street corner, a single street lamp offered a minimal pale light across the drab environment.

"He's dead, best I know," Laina said. She touched the cold window, huffed a warm breath curious to examine her fingerprints. "Mama said he was never coming to see me. You know, I held her back and all. I always held her back. Tells me all the time."

Artemis smacked her lefthand on the formica-topped table near Laina, rattling the chrome topped salt and pepper shakers.

"He would have," Artemis said. She reached forward and tapped near Laina. "He was a brave man. I think you would have loved him. I know he loved you. He told me."

"He left me behind," Laina said. She squirmed. "It's all right, I'm bad luck. Ma say I'm bad luck."

Artemis thought Laina was hard inside her frail body. The little girl had seen and experienced countless disappointment, heartbreaks over and over for almost the first decade of her life. Her eyes no longer had happy expectations for a trip to Disney World.

"What if I told you I was there? The moment he died," Artemis said. Glaring at Laina with a certain truth from her blue eyes. "Your father was a brave man. He had courage. He was not afraid."

Laina peeked back over at Artemis. She inspected Artemis' face; she scanned every centimeter of Artemis.

"You knew him?" Laina said.

"He sent me to find you," Artemis said. "No kidding."

"How?" Laina said. She crossed her arms. She sat back. "I don't believe you-"

"I'll prove it," Artemis said. She considered her words and how best to talk with a child. "I'm not sure if it will make sense, but I am telling you the truth. I don't lie. My mother taught me to be truthful. She told me the truth frees the spirit."

"Why did he die?" Laina said.

"He was a solider," Artemis said. "He was fighting bad people, sometimes soldiers die for others, like you, and me."

"He's dead," Laina said. "How did he tell you to find me?"

Laina enraptured herself deeper within Artemis' winter parka. The waitress brought over two strawberry shakes with paper bendy straws. She set one in front of Laina, her eyes told Artemis she was eager to taste the pinkish sugary drink. But she did not make any movement toward it. Artemis thought Laina had been beaten enough that she no longer wanted to experience any more beatings.

"I'm able to talk with spirit people," Artemis said. She nodded her head. She shrugged. "Sort of like ghosts. It's the truth."

"I believe in ghosts, I seen 'em," Laina said. Her forefinger touching the condensation bubbles emerging on the plastic glass. "My dad is a ghost?"

"It's for you, yes, he's a spirit," Artemis said. She gripped her shake and sucked through the paper straw. "Laina, see, try it, it's tasty. I don't have sugar much, I'll get a headache."

Laina shifted her finger higher, slow, measured, and she touched the round tip end of the straw with her righthand forefinger. And then she shifted, she moved forward, and sucked at the straw opening until she tasted a bit of the pink strawberry shake. She half-grinned, glassy-eyed as she released the straw and sat back, hunching down expecting wrath after disobedience.

"There you go," Artemis said. Curious if Laina had seen ghosts or imagined them. "You like it? I like mine."

"I like it," Laina said in a whisper. She backed farther away from the shake, but never taking her gaze off the shake. "Can I have it? I don't want to get into trouble."

"Yes," Artemis said. "It's all for you, but you don't have to drink it all, it's up to you."

Artemis wondered how Laina had endured what she suspected were the years of abuse, both physical and mental. Artemis tried to hide her feelings, she relied on her training to focus on facts, and not emotions. She wiped her eyes. But she felt her skin blush and her ears burned red hot.

The waitress returned with plates covered with cheeseburgers, french fries and onion rings. She set a steaming plate in front of Laina who leaned her fingers against the side of the table and she spied up at the deep-fried delights.

"What are you hiding from, sweetie?" the waitress said. She slid the paper guest check over toward Artemis. She winked at her. "Clear your plate for your mom. You need to eat, get some weight on those skinny bones."

"Thank you," Artemis said. She placed enough cash on the ticket to cover the bill plus a good tip. "Keep it all. I don't need a receipt, but I'm her father's friend. I'm no mother."

The waitress looked down and realized it was a nice tip.

"Well, thank you, dear," the waitress said. She smiled at Artemis just before she walked away from the table and slipped the bill and the cash into the front pocket of her dirty apron.

At first, like the shake, Laina was hesitant, cautious. But with Artemis' encouragement, and her example, Laina's hunger gave in and she gobbled down the hot food, the cold drink.

"I need to do some work later," Artemis said. She sighed. "It's a full moon tonight, but you can stay with me, my hotel room's warm, you'll be safe there. The hospital's not a good place for you."

"What about my mama?" Laina said. She talked with her mouth stuffed with french fries. She chomped down and she chomped and soon the french fries vanished and the strawberry milkshake disappeared as the bendy straw tip end gurgled like a plumber clearing a backed-up kitchen sink.

"She's not going anywhere," Artemis said. She crossed her arms. "I'm sorry, she's in terrible shape."

"Yeah, she's done it," Laina said. She pointed over at Artemis' half-eaten plate of food. "You want your onion rings?"

Artemis slid the plate forward.

"All yours," Artemis said. She grinned. "That's the spirit."

Artemis navigated Laina back to her hotel. She stopped at the front counter, and got Laina a room key, and advised the house staff to keep an eye out for her encouraging them with a cash spray. She got Laina to her room, turned on the television, and surfed with the remote for a show to watch. She snuggled Laina into the double bed and turned down the lights.

Artemis was confident Laina would be safe for an hour because Laina dosed off into a deep sleep. Artemis left the television on for Laina's comfort if she awoke in a strange room. And then she made a trip back to Most High Cemetery.

❧

"Oh, how you have complicated your life," Satan said. It was in the form of a dark particle orb. "Couldn't resist the little girl, her Mom is not quite into my world, yet."

Artemis stood near the second row of the icy cemetery. She was confident Satan wanted to keep something hidden within the circular park-like setting. The air and the breeze spiced with a sulfur scent. The wandering spirits had gone into hiding again, certain if Satan wanted her dead, she would be dead.

"You know what I'm thinking," Artemis said. Her hands stuffed into her coat pockets. "What's going at the hospital?"

"Ah, you're learning," Satan said. "You cannot hide from me, or your God the father, we are beyond you. We watch you humans."

"What are you afraid of?"

"Are you being obtuse?" Satan said. The orb floated beneath a white granite cherub, spinning around it and then farther up into the darkness. "It's the other way around. I'll reveal in my good time. And my time is limitless."

"The dead always tell the truth," Artemis said. "The spirits have nothing left to hide."

"Ah, you're thinking," Satan said. "Yes, I am the great deceiver. The dead don't fear the truth; They fear eternity. So you'll wait for it, one clue at a time."

"Why?"

"My enjoyment, to hate, to watch human greed," Satan said. The orb glided down and over near Artemis. "You should go up into the mountains, find your new friend, Virgil. He'll show you the place. There's a great big tree, where foolish humans worship me. A Prophet Higgs Boson, he is their cult's leader; It might be good for you."

"And what," Artemis said. "Get murdered?"

"No harm will come of you," Satan said. "You're correct, if I wanted you dead, you'd already be dead. Consider that Artemis. You become a wandering spirit, lost, searching for a crease in the light. Oh, the hate I would share with you."

"Why are you so interested in me?" Artemis said. She searched the cemetery for demons or spirits. But the icy surface was deserted, and the grass tip ends sparkled beneath the moonlight. "I'm an insignificant human."

"No, you are not. In due time," Satan said. It started to glide upward and over the monument. "Go up into the forest. I think you'll enjoy the show."

Chapter 9

"My mama's dead…"

"No, Laina, you don't know that," Artemis said. Laina scrunched under the bedsheets, her head pushed into a pillow, her tangled hair shrouded her hazel eyes. "Let's hope for the best."

"You done a bunch pushups," Laina said. "I seen you."

"Good, I'll teach you how, besides I needed to warm up, it was cold outside," Artemis said. She hung up her winter parka. "My job requires physical fitness. They help me relax. I hope your Mom recovers."

Laina shook her head. She squished her nose with her right hand palm.

"The nurses say they're keeping her alive for a few more days," Laina said. She sneezed. "They was talking in the room. I listen."

Artemis shifted the wooden chair over near the hotel room's windows. She sat down and studied Laina's face. Artemis thought Laina did not appear upset that her mother was dead; She was beyond acceptance. Laina's hazel eyes told her that story. Artemis thought Laina's eyes were active, observant and more intelligent than her scruffy appearance. If she were born into another family, she would have been a good student, a popular girl.

"What else have you heard?" Artemis said. She leaned her elbows on her knees. "What have you seen as you've been roaming the hospital? At the diner tonight you told me you can see ghosts."

Laina scanned the two bed hotel room like she was searching for a deep secret. She shifted over closer to the lamp; she clicked it on. Her face covered in bright incandescent light.

"They ain't here?" Laina said. "We're safe here."

"They?"

"Like in the hospital," Laina said. "There're these things inside, they scare me."

"Sweetie," Artemis said. She got up and sat at the end of the bed. "Be specific, where in the hospital, what did these people look like? Tall, fat, so forth…"

Laina scrunched her legs toward her chest. She closed her eyes, covered them with her hands, and then she opened them.

"Dark," Laina said. She looked over at Artemis from above the blanket line. "They growl at me, in the night."

"Tiny dark spots? Or, orbs of light?" Artemis said. She was certain Laina had seen demonic figures. "All moving together, did they notice you?"

"I can't see them," Laina said. She scrutinized the dark hotel room without moving her head. "But I know when they're there, they came for my mama. They took her ghost, I figure."

"Did you tell the nurses?" Artemis said. She covered her mouth with her right hand. "I mean what you heard?"

"No," Laina said. She shook her head. "They don't like me."

"It's not that," Artemis said. She paused. "They have work to do, it's not your fault."

"At nights I walk inside the hospital, it keeps me awake," Laina said. "I go up to the cafeteria, sometimes they give me food."

"They feed you?" Artemis said.

"Most of the time, they have extra," Laina said. "Lots times, they warn me to go hide. There're these people they want me to hide from. They must be important."

Artemis rubbed her chin. She wondered what else Laina had seen or heard. But it was getting Laina to remember in context. Her training taught her to provide visual cues, factual clues that the human mind could grasp onto for visual clarity.

"Where do you hide? Be specific, the exact spot," Artemis said. "What did it smell like? Was it warm? Is the room big or small?"

"They push me under the kitchen counters, in the cafeteria. They told me to be quiet," Laina said. She glanced up at the ceiling. She blinked in repetition as if her long eyelashes were floating in static motion. She stopped blinking and paused for several moments. "My best place, dark room, it's warm. It smells real clean, I ain't seen no one go in during the day after I wake up."

"Who are they?" Artemis said. "The people that help you."

"People in the kitchen," Laina said. She looked behind Artemis. "Some doctors help me, they buy me food. The nurses do, too. They real nice to me. But they tell me to hide, be scarce."

Artemis got up, she started to pace toward the bathroom door, and turned around and paced toward the hotel room's windows.

"Are there others like you? Girls, boys."

"I've seen some," Laina said. Her eyes followed Artemis. "Seen some get caught. I stay by myself. I don't need them."

"You're brave," Artemis said. She stopped pacing. "What's the dark room like, I know it's warm. Are there, ah, a long line of metal drawer like things, with people sleeping inside?"

"No, that's the morgue," Laina said. She nodded. "I seen it, too. I stay away from it; it scares me. They be growls the one time went. The fat man in the morgue explained it to me. He said it's not a place for a child to visit. I don't walk there no more."

"I can imagine," Artemis said. She crossed her arms, walked over near the hotel room's windows. She examined Laina's reflection in the windows. "Do you sleep at night?"

"No, not smart," Laina said. She shook her head with intention. "That's not smart. I go to sleep in the morning, during the day. The nurses don't bother me. I stay out of the way."

"Go back for me, in your mind," Artemis said. She touched the window with her right hand fingertips. She glanced back over at Laina. "The warm room, imagine you're inside, when you go inside, can you describe it? Is it dark? How big is it?"

Laina's eyes scanned the hotel room. She fiddled with her fingertips at the edge of the blanket. She closed her eyes.

"They look like mushrooms," Laina said. She nodded. "I saw mushrooms before, in the forest, Mr. Sammons showed me. He told me not to ever eat them, he told me they might make me go crazy like my mama. I don't want to go crazy."

"Mushrooms?" Artemis said. "Sure?"

"I'm sure," Laina said. "Mr. Sammons never makes things up."

"How big's this room?" Artemis said. She gestured with her hands in the air. "Long, tall, when you hide, where in the room do you go?"

"All over," Laina said. "Some times they turn on rain, it rains on the mushrooms, but stops. I have warmer spots. I can see just enough to hide from anyone that comes inside."

"Is that your favorite spot?" Artemis said. "Inside the hospital, the big room."

"Most part," Laina said. "It's close from my mama's room. They let me sneak in, I know they see me. I think it's a safe place for me to hide. I stay out of the way."

"Think you can sleep?" Artemis said. She flicked on the business desk lamp. She stepped over and turned off the lamp between the beds. "I'll leave on that lamp. I'll be over in the other bed, you're not alone, okay?"

Laina shifted under the bedsheets. She pulled the covers up beneath her chin. She looked up at Artemis.

"Are you all alone, too?" Laina said.

Artemis sat down on Laina's bed. She brushed back Laina's hair from covering her eyes.

"You don't have any family?" Artemis said. "Uncle, Aunt… grandma, grandpa?"

"No, they all gone, I guess," Laina said. "It was mama and me. I never met no one else, mama said my grandma was dead."

"I'll find them," Artemis said. "I promise. I'll protect you."

Laina's eyes misted.

"I don't like being all by myself," Laina said. She sniffled.

Artemis pulled the bed covers up and snuggled in Laina.

"Sleep," Artemis said. "I'll be over here, you're not alone. We'll figure things out in the morning."

Chapter 10

"We are efficient with our payment models," Loretta said. She readjusted her hospital provided tablet on the conference table. "It's all about understanding the government codes. ICD-10 was created to capture data, and we have accepted the mandate."

"We developed a unique platform that combs through the aggregated data to enhance our value-based scoring," Gene said. His eyes appeared as if he'd self-congratulated himself. He sipped what Artemis assumed was coffee from a mug with the hospital's brand across the outside. "It's our company edict, we provide quality patient centric care, at the right place, at the right time. But we have to get paid for our efforts."

"I understand, but what about these requests for records?" Artemis said. "On its surface, the claim has some serious charges, cremation without consent, so forth?"

"HIPAA, we are cautious to protect our neighbors," Gene said. He interlocked his swollen fingers. "We focus first on compliance with government standards, tested our consent forms in court, and they have stood up. We're in the right."

"Artemis," Loretta said. She glanced over at Gene. "We review and release as much patient record as possible, but there are proprietary tests that we cannot share. And ninety-days can be a tough number for us to accept."

"You're certain your position will stand up?" Artemis said over to Gene. "If, and it's a long time away, we take this into court."

Gene leaned forward onto the conference room table. His blue sport coat had lost its gold sleeve buttons leaving behind dangled threads wanting acceptance.

"Notwithstanding," Gene said. He paused. "You are under an NDA, so anything I tell you going forward has a legal privilege."

"Just as long as you are not involved with fraud, or criminal activity," Artemis said. She glanced over at Loretta who was fidgeting with her ink pen. "We'd decline coverage, or at least issue a reservation of rights letter. Where are you headed?"

Loretta got up and left the conference room after Gene gave her a sign. She closed the door behind her.

Artemis waited for Gene to talk. Wylie taught her well, allow the silence to become your friend. It was about making your client or prey squirm and wonder.

"I'll be blunt," Gene said. "The community needs this hospital; it needs it to stay open, to care for the community."

"We agree," Artemis said. She sat back in the high-back chair. "I'll do everything possible to protect the hospital."

"Well, in as such," Gene said. He tugged at this sport coat lapels. "Our masters in Nashville, they guide our decision-making these days, you know this?"

"I do," Artemis said. "I am aware of them."

"Good, good," Gene said. He wiped perspiration beads from along his forehead just beneath his shiny blond comb-over. He glanced over at her with his lazy brown eye. "All the hospitals have a mission to be a closed-loop system, you understand?"

"I do," Artemis said. "You're a profit center."

"But, being a not-for-profit," Gene said. He smirked like a mafia accountant. "Allows us some, flexibility, tax and so forth. But yes, each facility has to meet our goals, or, well. I'm searching for a new job. And being as the coal business has died off, I'd be moving from Selene. I'd end up in Lexington, or Louisville, maybe Cincinnati. I don't want to find out."

"So, if I'm following your words, body language, are you saying some of these claims are in fact, accurate?" Artemis said. She opened her arms. She sat back. "I'd rather not have us end up dealing with a surprise FBI visit."

"No, it depends on your perspective," Gene said. He waved over at Artemis. "It's like the standard of care, to a civilian. They might not appreciate how medicine, genetics if you will, how it all works as a practical matter."

"Get with it," Artemis said.

"For example," Gene said. He stared over at Artemis, his shoulders hunched inward. "The one on life support, the little girl you're helping. Which I embrace, it's what Jesus would want you to do. She is an innocent in an evil world."

"Okay, I guess," Artemis said. She assumed that Gene knew she had been in the hospital. The place had video cameras monitoring every patient room, stairwell and the exterior walkways. "I'm just helping out an old friend. I'll find her family. But she's not involved with these claims. Or is she?"

"The patient is close to death, lost the baby," Gene said. "Sad situation, unfortunate, but we manage these problems every day. These poor folks end up on Medicaid, so for us to get compensated, we extend their lives in the hopes they might come out of the induced coma, but long enough to meet the government codes."

Artemis covered her mouth with the back of her hand. She thought punching Gene in the face was not a good response. She avoided eye contact.

"I don't believe this," Artemis said. "First do no harm…"

"Oh, I agree, yes I do," Gene said. "But, we have to work, as I said, in a somewhat flexible standard. To both care and, well, get paid for that care. I accept it's a tough view. But it's an honest statement I'd express in court."

"I'll say this," Artemis said. "I've had some, ah, interesting cases over the years. I'll give you credit, you're honest about being corrupt. You're mad if you think our expert witnesses will play along."

Gene squinted his eyes and half-grinned over at Artemis.

"You're an arrogant youngster, you don't know what you don't know," Gene said. He leaned forward, his moist palms on the conference table. "But you'll keep your mouth shut. Besides, we can prove our standard of care. It's all in the records; our patient records are clear, timed, date-stamped, and transparent; we don't hide our methods."

"But that woman should be pronounced dead and given over for a proper burial," Artemis said. She huffed. "That child should be in protective services, or better. I'm not sure what to think."

"That's your opinion, not a fact," Gene said. "And, unless you tell me different, you're not a doctor. It's Dr. Demetrius' decision. He'd be the one on the witness stand, not you."

"Fair enough," Artemis said. She stood up. "I don't like you, or your little friend. But I have a job to do; records or not, the dead always reveal the truth."

"I would agree," Gene said. He sat back, his significant paunch stressing this white dress shirt's buttons. "Good luck with the little girl. I think you should do us all a favor, get her out of Selene, it's not a good town for her."

Artemis left the hospital and marched over toward Jerome Jenkins' office. She stepped inside and surprised the young boy at the greeter station.

"I need to see Jerome," Artemis said. "Now."

The boy scrambled from his desk chair where he was playing video games. He disappeared down a side hallway. After a few brief moments, Jerome Jenkins appeared at the open doorway for the hallway. His baby blue cotton shirt sleeves rolled up to his elbows. His readers dangled from a stretchy eyewear cord.

"Well, well," Jerome said. He grinned over at Artemis like a parent catching their teenager coming home after curfew. "Did you get saved? Here to convert me, or what not? You look angry…"

"How much?" Artemis said. "What's the number."

Jerome walked farther into the waiting area. He leaned both arms onto the cherry veneered front reception counter. He contemplated Artemis' statement.

"You being serious?" Jerome said. He pursed his lips.

"Yes," Artemis said. "Off the record?"

"Sure, I'll play along," Jerome said. "I can keep my mouth shut, but I think I know what you're about to tell me."

"Then tell me," Artemis said. She slung her backpack down.

"Those people over at that hospital," Jerome said. He searched Artemis' eyes. "Sanctimonious, and corrupt, about right?"

"Perhaps you're right," Artemis said. She clenched her back molars. "On the record, got a number I can take back?"

"Lady," Jerome said. "You've got blue eyes that could burn a hole through steel."

Chapter 11

"Laina," Artemis said as she dried her red hair with a thin ecru cotton towel. "I need to go back home, report in, do you have other family where I can take you? Anybody?"

Laina smiled as she sat on the edge of the hotel bed watching a funny cartoon cast from the hotel flat screen television. She heard Artemis' questions. She stared forward trying to disappear.

"Can I stay here?" Laina said. She searched Artemis's eyes from within a destitute void. And after a split-second, she stopped and slumped an acceptance. "I can go back. I'm a big girl."

"Let me work on this. I had a weird meeting at the hospital this morning, needed a good workout after that," Artemis said. Laina's hazel-eyed gaze brought memories of Benjamin. His eyes were now Laina's eyes. "Don't want people thinking I kidnapped you. I'm not sure what to do. I don't want to get arrested."

"I'll go back inside," Laina said. She stared forward. She sniffled. "But, my mama's dead. She ain't waken' up."

"Let's go over to see her," Artemis said. She flung the towel into the bathroom. "Tell her, and the nurses you're with me. When's last you were home?"

"I can't remember," Laina said. She fumbled with the television remote. "A few weeks, I'd guess."

"Do you have a change of clothes at the hospital?"

"No," Laina said. She set the remote next to the television. "I just wear this. I'm fine."

"That's not acceptable," Artemis said. She paused for a few moments and pointed at the bathroom. "Get in there, shower up. We'll do our best with what you have for now."

Laina shrugged. After several minutes, Artemis opened the bathroom door as steam escaped. Artemis noticed Laina had bathed and put back on her dirty clothes. Artemis stopped her. She shared one of her long blue sweaters, it covered Laina from the turtleneck top on down her fragile body appearing like a fashionable little girl's long dress.

"Feel better?" Artemis said. She examined Laina and patted her on the shoulders. She folded back the sleeves. "You look spiffy. You do smell better. A little perfume?"

"Thank you," Laina said. She giggled. Her hair still wet. But she smiled up at Artemis. In an instant she hugged Artemis at the waist. "I like you. Can I stay with you? I'm a good worker. I'll clean. I promise."

"No worries," Artemis said. She patted Laina on the head. "Let's get moving. I've got work to do."

Artemis combed through Laina's hair, and she unraveled Laina's dishwater blonde tangles. After Laina's hair dried, they got some hotel breakfast, and Artemis walked with Laina into the busy hospital lobby. They made their way to the floor where Laina's mother existed on mindless life support machines. Artemis strolled up to the nurse' station. It was the same nurse from the night before.

"Yes, I know, it was a long night," the nurse said. She acknowledged Artemis. She wore a dark-blue uniform. "Pulling a double, I need the money. We don't have enough staff."

"How long's the lady got left?" Artemis said. She pointed behind her with a right thumb. "I brought the kid to say goodbye."

"Not long," the nurse mumbled. "I think we've got her beyond the required days. CMS rules they tell me. At least the hospital gets paid. I reckon I get to keep my job."

"I get it. I respect your work," Artemis said. She looked back over at the patient room door across the marble flooring. "I'll look after the little girl. She's my dead lover's child. But I don't want to get arrested?"

"No bodies going to come, I'll not give you up. The girl is on her own. Sad. We get this mess all the time," the nurse said. She didn't look up from staring down at the computer screen. "Find her a home. Or, better, give her up to protective services. Let them deal with the mess."

Another nurse in a dark-blue shifted over next to the other nurse. She stared down at the same computer screen. Neither nurse looked up at Artemis.

"Keep her out of here," the new nurse said in a blunt tone. "She needs to move on, otherwise, they'll use her for their experiments. Here me?"

"Why?" Artemis said. "Experiments?"

The nurses looked at each other, careful not to look back over at Artemis. But after nodding at each other they glanced up at Artemis. And then both examined a hanging file acting as if they were reading the patient chart.

"Sorry," the new nurse said. She blew her stringy blond hair off her face. "This hospital's walls have ears, and we need our jobs. Just disappear with her. Please."

"Yep," the other nurse said. "These walls have eyes and ears, and I don't know what else. Gather her, and leave. It's for her protection."

"They'll cremate the remains?" Artemis said. "I'll not ask you about the experiments. I get where you're coming from."

"That's what I, they tell us," the nurses said in unison. "Please, get her out of here," the nurse said. "We've got to get

along. I hope you understand."

Artemis tapped on the white colored nurse's station, she turned and stepped over behind Laina who was standing motionless with her armies at her sides at the patient room door opening, staring inside.

"Laina," Artemis said. She sucked in a deep, deep breath, and she let it release through her open lips. "Say goodbye to your mother, I think. I think it's best."

Laina stepped over toward her mother. As the life support machines rattled, they pumped oxygen, and the monitors blipped vital signs. She observed the body with a useless baby bump covered with a greenish hospital sheet and white cotton blanket. She touched her mother's right hand; she pulled back as if she had touched death. And then Laina spun and ran out of the room. Artemis let her pass, she looked inside and saw no signs that her mother's spirit remained in the room. She was certain Laina's mother dead, whispering a prayer for the dead even though she was a non-believer. An act her mother had taught her. A moment to express respect for the spirit world. She turned around and saw down the long hospital hallway Laina sitting on a mahogany cushioned bench, being ignored by strangers with their own problems, staring down at the marbled floor. Artemis strolled toward her uncertain what to say, what to do.

"I'm sorry, Laina," Artemis said. She kneeled down on her left knee and gripped Laina's tiny left hand. "We'll figure this out, don't worry. I'll not abandon you, I promise. You're Benjamin's girl. I'll not fail him."

"What does it feel like to be alone?" Laina said. Her eyes searched over at Artemis' for answers. "I'm a big girl now. I need to get a job. I have to make plans."

"Accept the facts, your mom's gone, I'm sorry," Artemis said. The hospital's antiseptic scent was off-putting and the reality that Laina had to accept her mother's death. "Think positive, focus on facts and then you can sort of feel better. That's what I do. I've been alone since I was a teenager. My parents died together. I know how you feel. I promise things will get better, it takes time."

"Where will they take me?"

Artemis thought about her life. She considered the nurses' recommendations. She twisted to look back over at the active nurses' station as they investigated patient rooms.

"Let's take a road trip, hang with me for a while," Artemis said. She gripped Laina's left hand and shook it. "Can you get inside your home? I think we should pack up your things."

"I think so," Laina said. She leaned forward and whispered. "Mr. Sammons has a key."

"Ah, Virgil. Let's start there," Artemis said. She stood up with her right hand out in front of Laina. "I've met him, where's his grocery?"

"Down the highway, we live down the road," Laina said. She grasped Artemis' hand. She slinked forward and walked with Artemis. Laina never looked back toward her mother's room. She just walked stoically out of the hospital. As she got inside Artemis' rental truck. "I'm a big girl now. I'll get a job. Maybe I can work at Mr. Sammons' store."

Artemis drove her truck with Laina away from the hospital's parking lot stuffed with a used car collection and mud splattered trucks. Laina glanced back through the trucks back window. She then looked over at Artemis. Her vision blocked by bright sunlight flashing through the windshield. She sat up straight and clicked in her safety belt.

"Laina, you navigate," Artemis said. "Can you help me?"

"I know the way," Laina said. She pointed to turn right at the traffic light that was flashing a yellow caution. The brown hillsides, and the thick forest crowded the busy two lanes road. The town side fronted it with single story shops, muffler repair and gas stations. Artemis gunned the engine.

～

"Florida?" Virgil said. His blue eyes searched the thin white clouds above Artemis as if Florida was an imagined place for him with endless soft sands, limitless palm trees, and skinny topless girls sipping rum based pina coladas. "My, my, I'd never return."

"Bad idea?" Artemis said.

"No, I think it's great," Virgil said. He jiggled the metal key to open the polyethylene paneled trailer door. "Laina you'll be a good girl?"

"I don't know," Laina said. "I'll try. I guess."

Laina entered through the aluminum framed door dented at the bottom from many frustrated nights and drunken boyfriends. On the inside there was a darkness and a moldy stench. Artemis and Virgil followed in behind her careful to not touch anything.

"Damn," Virgil said. He covered his nose. "Laina, you can't live here no more, this ain't right."

Laina scurried farther inside the single wide trailer as if she could run to an exact spot blind folded inside a coal mine. The trailer stuffed from laminated flooring to black mold blotched ceiling tiles with dusty items unsellable at a low-rent flea market.

"I guess mom was a hoarder," Artemis whispered over at Virgil. She crossed her arms. "This is toxic."

"The state pays the rent," Virgil said. He stared down at the floor, and up and over toward the unkept kitchen. "I had no idea. I don't nose into lives. Not my way."

"No child should live like this," Artemis said. "I don't have any words for this. It's not real, but it is."

"No kiddin'," Virgil said. He kept his hand over his nose. "You just take her, get her away from here. This is no place for a child. If anybody asks questions I'll cover for ya."

"Thanks," Artemis said. "Call me, you have my card."

Artemis nodded over at Virgil. Virgil stood near the filthy kitchen area, he continued to stare down at his dirty boots as Artemis stepped forward between indiscriminate magazine and musty newspaper piles. A well-worn fabric couch was covered with a green bedsheet hidden beneath with more magazines and boxes stuffed with junk collections. She stepped down a narrow hallway. Within a small room on her left, toward the trailers far end she found Laina's bare room. But for the cardboard castle that Laina had fashioned as a hideaway from depravity. Artemis kneeled down and discovered Laina hunched down from within her den with her hopeless gaze searching for sunshine but expecting darkness.

"Laina, I promised your father I'd find you," Artemis said. She resisted her tears. "Leave it all behind, just come with me. You must trust me. I'll get you new things, I promise. It's my duty. It's my honor to help you."

"You promise?" Laina said. "Mama never kept her promises."

"I always keep my promises," Artemis said. "Come with me, I'll protect you. I loved your father. I'll not fail him."

Artemis held forward her open hands and arms. Laina scurried out from her cardboard den, and they left the trailer that Virgil would soon set on fire and reduce to forgotten rubble.

Chapter 12

"He offered how much?"

"Twenty million, not much from the captive tower, but he knows we'll pass on that amount," Artemis said. She sat across from Wylie in his office. "But, I think he might get it, if he gets us into a courtroom up there, locals stick together. Maybe a lot more. And I don't like these people at the hospital. I've got this hunch about them they are a sneaky bunch."

"Not sure I agree, assuming we can get that far, move to the change of venue," Wylie said. He sucked in a deep drag of air from his former smoker's mouth. "If they can prove no intent to harm, it's a reasonable standard of care, we'll get our experts to corroborate it, we'll be all right, I hope. Unless our witnesses blow us up?"

"I don't think juries enjoy seeing innocent human beings on life support," Artemis said.

"I cede your point," Wylie said. "But they didn't execute a DNR before they walked into that hospital, bad on them. And it appears vast majority were drug addicts."

"He's got something else," Artemis said. Her tone flat. "He knows twenty million for a global settlement seems like a steep number, but after it gets hashed out, not much left. He's waiting for a bigger payday."

"That's my thinking, smart, went fishing to see what this hospital's hiding," Wylie said. He gripped his nose with thumb and forefinger. He paused. He tapped his hand on his desk. "He knows we'll deny him the offer, something else out there, a bigger problem."

"Trying to set us up for bad faith?" Artemis said.

"If it's just what you've seen," Wylie said. "He'd take the per occurrence limits, what's it, a million per? Twenty millions just enough to tempt us, he's smart. He's being coy."

"Yeah, he's also hooked into all the locals," Artemis said. She sipped water from a paper cup. "Hospital takes the first million per with a ten million aggregate, we've reinsured with a million buffer, towers a half billion over all the coverages. Wait. They split the liability tower, two hundred fifty millions exposed."

"About ten percent of the overall liability tower?" Wylie said. He crossed his legs, he started to rock his chair back and forth. "He's not interested in settling, he's waiting us out."

"Get back up there?" Artemis said.

"For sure," Wylie said. "Go poke around without asking for permission, find this, what's his name?"

Wylie leaned forward and put on his eyeglasses.

"Demetrius," Artemis said. "A Dr. Demetrius."

"Yes, that's it," Wylie said. "Never heard of a Greek doctor practicing in Appalachia. Strange times in healthcare."

"They act like he invented planet earth," Artemis said. She wiggled her hands beside her face. "Staff whispers his name like he's all powerful. We've dealt with these types before."

"Well, he's our key witness," Wylie said. "Figure out if he's useful, or, if we need to hide him. I don't need that type on the stand, or at a mediation, sinks us even if the facts say otherwise."

"Got him lined up," Artemis said. "I'll meet with him, and the general counsel, who I do not trust."

"Part of the job," Wylie said. He snorted like a packhorse. "They need not like us, and now it's our money that is exposed. Let's figure out this doctor. Let me know if he'll sink us, or worse."

"I got it," Artemis said. She almost stood up, but sat back down. She emptied the water from the paper cup. "Question, got a recommendation for a pediatrician?"

Wylie leaned forward, he squinted over at Artemis with his hands on his desk. He leaned back with a surprised grin and interlocked his fingers atop his belly.

"You need an OB first, got something to tell me?" Wylie said. He stared over at Artemis. "Perhaps you mean a veterinarian?"

"Little girl I came across," Artemis said. She crossed her arms as she looked up at the square ceiling tiles. "I couldn't just leave her to the streets. She's with me until I can find her family."

"Just me, but," Wylie said. He pulled open his middle desk drawer, he picked a leather folder from the paper and trinket mayhem. "Most people do that at animal shelters, reason I don't go inside them. I'd take the entire inventory."

"It's stupid, she's about eight, I think? She's a deceased friend's kid, total coincidence," Artemis said. She avoided eye contact with Wylie. "I need her checked out. I don't have any custody. But, I just want to help her out before she ends up in the system. Make sure she's as healthy as possible; the kid needs a break. And well, tell me, have I lost it?"

Wylie winked at her as he dabbed his forefinger and thumb as he turned the pages for his preserved expert witness catalog. He hummed as he glanced over at Artemis as he searched for the contact information.

"I got it, but keep it quiet," Wylie said. He turned the folder around and pushed it over toward Artemis. "Take her to Dr. Langendorpher, I'll call her. Good physician, knows how to keep things under control, and for the right reasons, understand?"

"I do," Artemis said. She snapped a photo of the contact information with her smartphone. "Thanks Wylie, I appreciate you sharing."

"Thirty years in this business should be worth something," Wylie said. He snapped the folder closed and stuffed it back inside the desk drawer. "Where is she?"

Artemis opened her purse and dropped her smartphone inside.

"With Alan over at The Moon, I don't want to deal with a daycare, they'd turn me in," Artemis said. She shrugged. "He's ex-military, he'll look after her, I thought a safe place for her until I get back home."

"Well, bring her in next time," Wylie said. "I love little kids, they're honest, they lack a filter. Wish I could have kept mine at that age. But your eyes tell me something else, what's up?"

Artemis got up from the chair, and she hesitated at the office door. She did not turn around leaning her forehead against the thick wooden door.

"Wylie, she's my dead lover's child," Artemis said. She glossed her fingers over the doorknob. "I have a responsibility to protect her. I cannot fail her, or Benjamin. I feel I need to step-up, and take responsibility for her. Am I being stupid?"

Wylie got up and sat at the end of his office desk.

"I'll help you, you're not stupid, you're human trying your best in a small world, weird you ran across her up there," Wylie said. "They don't tell me much, but I know your other job. A dangerous job. The girl might cause you to lose focus. Got me?"

"I do. I haven't quite figured out the problem," Artemis said. She gripped the doorknob. "I just don't need any loose ends. I've never taken care of a child. And it's dangerous up there, and they don't like me."

"Be careful," Wylie said. "If need be, I'll look after the girl. Wife and I have an empty house these days."

"I'll keep that in mind," Artemis said. She opened the office door. "You were right."

"Pardon?" Wylie said.

"This file," Artemis said. She stood up straight. "This files going to get nasty. I can sense it."

Chapter 13

His eyes, Artemis thought. His dark eyes penetrated, probed over at her as if being observed by the eyes of a predatory animal.

"Am I younger than you expected?"

Artemis hesitated, she scanned across the conference table over at Gene Haskell. He foamed at the mouth. She then stared back over at Dr. Demetrius.

"Yes," Artemis said. "But I knew that, you're well trained, curious what attracted you to this hospital? Not to be rude, but your credentials can get you into any hospital you choose."

"You are not nice," Gene said. He stared away from Artemis and then nodded over at Dr. Demetrius. "She's not our friend. At least she's honest about her opinions."

"I finished college at sixteen," Dr. Demetrius said. He was a large man, raven haired with an olive-toned complexion. "Medical school was straightforward. After specialty training, I got a PhD in mycology for the fun of it. But, to the root of your question, freedom here. The government's eyes do not waste their time out here. It's beautiful."

Artemis remained quiet, still, and considered the moment. Dr. Demetrius enjoyed being Dr. Demetrius. She was certain that was the flaw she sought. But his demeanor was too easy, too obvious. She sensed evil; she was certain Satan was in control of Dr. Demetrius. It was just a sensation.

"Freedom?" Artemis said. "Why?"

"Yes, freedom," Dr. Demetrius said. He had a sinister, confident wide-toothed smile that every orthodontist hoped to replicate. "To practice heal-ing, to advance our culture. To discover new medicines."

Gene coughed. He leaned toward Dr. Demetrius.

"She's under an NDA," Gene said. He sneered over at Artemis. "But I would advise caution, again, she's not our friend."

"Now, Gene," Dr. Demetrius said. He held his left hand up. He had long fingers and wore a Buddhist bracelet. "She's not been a friend, you mean, yet. Can we be friends, Artemis? Besides, I love your Greek name and your red hair. Greeks don't have red hair."

"This is business," Artemis said. She closed her tablet. She stuffed it into her backpack. "How about you take me for a hospital tour, show the place off?"

"I'm not sure," Gene said.

"Why not," Dr. Demetrius said. He smacked his hands on the confer-ence table. "Wonderful idea, I hate wasting time in pointless meetings. Let's get moving, shall we?"

Dr. Demetrius stood up and encouraged Artemis and Gene to follow behind him. Within the hospital corridors he acknowledged staff, patients and their family and friends like an all-powerful emperor strolling within his domain wearing a flowing pure white lab cloak. He pointed up at certain treatment areas. He waved over toward staff working in common catheter labs or active surgical suites. But then Dr. Demetrius sauntered into the obstetrics ward. He twisted around and faced Artemis with an expectant expression.

"This," Dr. Demetrius said. He opened his arms wide apart. "This is where I do my best work."

"We have adopted precision medicine," Gene said. He slouched forward huffing from being out of breath. "Our, I mean, Dr. Demetrius has developed artificial intelligence algorithms to improve our treatment procedures."

"Quite, true," Dr. Demetrius said. He pointed at Gene. "Someday we'll have quantum learning, the practice of healthcare will advance beyond today's understanding."

Artemis watched Dr. Demetrius, she realized he followed her gaze toward the empty patient room where Laina's dead mother had been kept alive. A nurse strode by them. Within the nurses station the telephone system loud and blinking red dots.

"Not sure I understand?" Artemis said. She made certain to stare at nothing and ignored the nurses behind their station. "AI's over my head, I've read about it."

"We don't need to stay here, do we?" Gene said. He wiped his forehead. "Seems its gotten a bit warm in here."

"In this hospital," Dr. Demetrius said. He ignored Gene. "Life emerges within these simple walls, but I believe we have so much more. I want to show you my mushroom farm, I'm amazing."

"Mushroom farm?" Artemis said. She crinkled her face. "What?"

"This is all confidential," Gene said. He nudged over near Artemis. "We have a thriving campus, under Dr. Demetrius' leadership, we are entering a new era to heal the sick, protect God's innocent ones. We are way ahead in our learning."

"Yes," Dr. Demetrius said, dismissively. He pointed over toward a hulking man who stood behind a thick window. "But we must wear a respirator, the mushrooms have a constant blooming during the day. They calm at night, under my control. I am careful with my darlings not to over stimuli."

"I don't remember any mention within the files," Artemis said.

Artemis followed Dr. Demetrius walk by the security guard room, Gene behind her as they moved down a well-lit, narrow hallway with a marble floor, and over in front of a solid looking metal door that puffed open after Dr. Demetrius' thumb print was scanned in a biometric machine. He waved his hand across a sensor. As they stepped forward, within the room it was quiet and calm. The sounds came from the HVAC system that sounded like a sleeping giant.

"What I'm about to show you," Dr. Demetrius said. He adjusted the respirator over his face. He secured it. And then he inspected the respirator on Artemis' face. "I must protect emerging science at all costs. We don't want to make any mistakes with bacteria, viruses, I am cautious with discovery, it must be exact and replicated, over and over."

"Cloning?" Artemis said.

"Not cloning," Dr. Demetrius said. "I must make certain our drugs and other discoveries are from solid, testable science."

Dr. Demetrius pushed farther pushing back the thick door that exhaled from the inside like a satisfied lover. Artemis thought she was entering an alien world that appeared always at dusk, centered by tall space ship sized containers. "This is a strange surprise, it's huge, like a giant warehouse, right here, this is not in your files. We don't insure this in any way, shape or form."

"It's super secret," Gene said. "Word from Nashville. We've taken our exposure off the radar, for now."

As Artemis entered, she sensed the moderate temperature. It was as if long gray clouds blanketed the containers from the ceiling down like a dense African forest dripping moisture. It sounded like a sedate rain.

"We keep the room at a constant sixty-five degrees Fahrenheit," Dr. Demetrius said. He sounded odd speaking over at Artemis from within his respirator like they were standing on the moon. "That way the mushrooms continue to grow, we need these respirators from the constant spores being released from the mushrooms. That sound comes from humidification, my children need moisture, not too much, not too little. A sort of Goldilocks environment, if you'll excuse the cliché."

"This room is massive," Artemis said. She stepped farther forward over the terrazzo flooring. "Your children?"

"We have a large facility," Gene said. "It's maintained, our work is too important."

"Our?" Dr. Demetrius said.

"Sorry, your work," Gene said. "I know it's your work."

Artemis stared across the dusk at stacks and stacks of tall, square storage units. They used each shelf, covered in spiderweb like mesh sheets. They appeared to have blue inked dates, times and serial numbers written across the bins front.

"I don't understand this?" Artemis said. She stood near a sturdy round steel pole, and she looked up toward the top bin. She guessed it was twenty feet to the top. A sliding rack ladder rested within an easy distance from her.

"A new world, we need new drugs," Dr. Demetrius said. He gripped the pole. "Solid, my children are safe, secure. Have you ever studied mycelia?"

"No," Artemis said. "Not sure I understand this."

"From the mushroom rot we are trying to discover a new form of penicillin, humanity is becoming resistant to antibiotics, anti-fungals," Dr. Demetrius said. He tapped on a container. "This is made from mycelia, it's a perfect green storage solution. I am pleased with my progress, it will save many unborn children. Do you know what kills more humans in epidemic proportions inside hospitals?"

"Sepsis," Artemis said. "It's almost impossible to sanitize a facility, just a fact."

"True, very good," Dr. Demetrius said. "Candida Auris, nasty superbug. I must discover how to kill it before; humanity pays the cost. It has been hiding for thousands of years, until now, now it has spread, and it kills innocent people. I must stop it."

"Dr. Demetrius is so skilled at growing mushrooms," Gene said. "The trucks, those trucks you were curious about, we donate the overflow, we are always giving back."

"What's over there?" Artemis said. She pointed at a solid looking chrome door with a porthole window.

"Nothing much," Gene said. He gazed up at the exposed steel ceiling joists. "Genetics lab, I do not understand what they do all day."

"Emerging science, Artemis," Dr. Demetrius said. "With computer power, we are drilling further into the human genome, foods, drugs, and an unknown discovery, all from fungi. The fungi rule the world. They are not animals or plants. And they are ten times larger than plant and animal life. Consider that?"

Artemis stood up straight. She gulped realizing this was the room Laina had described. She turned to examine the security door. She wondered how a little girl could have snuck into this room and safely hid through the night. And without a respirator, her fragile lungs, her tiny body being attacked at a microscopic level. She felt her stomach muscles tighten like she were doing her morning sit-up routine. And she thought of Benjamin.

"This room is always locked?"

"Mostly," Gene said. He stared at Artemis like a spaceman examining a rock on a distant planet. He glanced over at Dr. Demetrius. "Your call."

"At night, when the mushrooms calm down," Dr. Demetrius said. He shifted closer to Artemis. "We'll let children from lost parents sleep inside here. They feel safe hidden in the bins, it's dark, and the sporing activity has slowed down. It's nothing for concern. Unlike right now during their peak sporing time, that's why we keep it locked down, not to disturb my darlings. But at night, they all rest, I let them relax. I think they like children nearby, sedates them both."

"We let them sneak inside," Gene said. He shrugged cryptically. "We have cameras everywhere, poor things have no place to go."

Artemis was certain they were sharing half-truths with her. She tried to hide her body language.

"Well," Dr. Demetrius said. "Let's keep moving along."

"You're certain?" Artemis said. She pointed over toward a line of empty bins. "They don't need respirators on for their protection."

"Oh, I'll sleep in here," Dr. Demetrius said. "Sleep inside some night, you'll see, it's like a mist now, but at night the room is clear as a starry night sky. It's like camping out in a forest, you'll sleep like a baby, I promise."

Artemis searched for the lower level bins. She wondered which one's Laina had slept in. She needed to take her to a pediatrician as soon as possible upon her return to St. Petersburg. Above her she sensed movement, like a tiny helicopter hovering above her.

"By the way," Gene said. "Thank you for taking that little girl into your home, such a kindness, she has no family, we looked into it, just sad at that age to be an orphan."

"Ah, great news," Dr. Demetrius said. He clapped his hands. "We are overflowing with them, good for you. I'm sure Gene's god would approve, right?"

"God loves them all," Gene said. "All the little children."

"I'm sure you believe that," Dr. Demetrius said. He patted Gene's shoulder like a parent treats a naïve child. "My god lives in science and emerges in the fact crucible. Without data, without drawing facts from data, we are just wishing. An accidental discovery like penicillin is rare."

"What's your goal? What's flying up there, in the bins?" Artemis said. She waved up into the air and looked at the vast space packed with bins. "This is not just a fad; you're up to something much larger."

Dr. Demetrius pressed his hands together like a Buddhist monk at sunset.

"Artemis," Dr. Demetrius said. "As the world evolves, we must evolve, or get left behind. Mycelia is the largest living organism on planet earth; they surround us. It's how they feed; they need water and nutrients to grow."

"I would advise caution," Gene said. He wedged between Dr. Demetrius and Artemis. "She's not our friend, well, yet."

Dr. Demetrius contemplated Gene's comment. He backed away. He turned to walk toward the far doorway where Gene explained a genetic laboratory existed. He stopped and turned back toward Artemis. He pointed upward.

"Those are my drone robots," Dr. Demetrius said. "They monitor and tend to their needs. My darlings are never alone, like the fungi out in the forests."

"That's amazing," Artemis said. She watched a drone hover above a large bin overgrowing with a mushroom variety. It clipped some growth; it cleared away dead plant life. "I don't know what to say." "Antibiotics, drug resistant germs," Gene said. He nodded over at Dr. Demetrius. "We, I mean, Dr. Demetrius has been working on new antibiotics, people are becoming drug resistant, we need new ones."

"Mushrooms all have unique gill patterns, they are mysterious, they hide beneath their true selves," Dr. Demetrius said. He sighed. "Like our fingerprints, they are so unique, so special, they fascinate me, my children need care."

"Have you entered clinical trials? What phase?"

"Not yet," Gene said. He stood farther between Dr. Demetrius and Artemis. "We've made a corporate commitment, it takes time to build out the infrastructure."

"Have a good day," Dr. Demetrius said. He pointed his right hand forefinger upward toward a busy drone humming above a bin. "Just remember, mushrooms are good, and evil, all at the same time. I can harness the fungi, you'll see. Sometimes from death, we create new life."

"You have this controlled?" Artemis said. "This has nothing to do with the claim files?"

"Nothing, I will never breach my oath," Dr. Demetrius said. "We care for our patients as best we can. We work in a diligent, thoughtful pattern to save them all. By the way, what you see in here is just the beginning."

"Let's move along," Gene said. He stumbled toward Artemis.

"Good day, Artemis," Dr. Demetrius said. He turned and opened the lab door. He disappeared behind it.

Chapter 14

"Milady, a word?"

"What are you now, Satan?" Artemis said. She examined the sharp featured middle-aged man. He had active pale blue eyes and thinning caramel brown hair. She started to walk away knowing it would harass her. "What? A Brit this time."

"Not sure we have described the FBI as Satan?"

"Sorry, force of habit," Artemis said. She stopped walking, stood still and turned toward the man in front of an abandoned pharmacy building made from timeworn red bricks, the gray concrete channels flaking away collecting along the sidewalk from being attacked by brutal winters and humid summers. "FBI? You sound like a Brit."

"I'm Welsh, the names Nero Beaky, special agent," he said. He flipped open a wallet to reveal his badge. It appeared official. He opened his jacket to display a holstered weapon strapped to his sturdy frame. "Moved here with my father as a child, can't quite lose the accent. I blame it upon the parents, at home, they only talk in Welsh."

"What do you want?"

"Your client," Agent Beaky said. He buttoned his jacket. "They are rather secretive and appear profitable in an age when hospitals like this close or go into bankruptcy, why?"

"No idea," Artemis said. She gripped her hips. "Guess you know my business and my background?"

"It's what we do," Agent Beaky said. "Ex-medic, you're a tough lass, been shot at by bad guys."

"That's not a secret."

"Might we have a coffee?" Agent Beaky said. He winked at Artemis. "If you have some time."

"My hotels across the next block," Artemis said. She waved him forward. "Walk with me. Let's do the drill."

They started to step down the concrete sidewalk. They dodged an older woman wearing a blue silk scarf over her gray hair curled into a tight bun. She pushed a packed metal grocery store cart. The old lady ignored them, but she also stone-faced watched them march just beyond the front of her cart.

"The hospital owns your hotel," Agent Beaky said. "They got into a franchise deal. Smart to have it down the street."

"I think they own the entire town," Artemis said. Outside the hotel she acknowledged a hotel valet. "Is that a big surprise?"

"No, it was a smart business decision," Agent Beaky said. He held open the hotel's smoked glass front door. They marched by the chubby valet who Artemis also acknowledged. "Ah, this will do us well."

"Why are you bothering me?"

"Not sure I can say," Agent Beaky said as he sat down on a cushioned chair next to a square table set near the breakfast bar that was being cleaned by the hotel staff. "I'm just up here asking questions, listening to locals. It's impossible to be about here without being noticed, like that old lady back there. I'd bet she called the local police."

"I'd imagine you're right," Artemis said. "At least you're not redheaded, and tall for a chick."

"True, but I have this accent. I'm not trusted. I'm an outsider," Agent Beaky said with a mischievous wide-toothed smile. He leaned his elbows on top of the table. "Where's your liability claim headed? Lots of death up here, the local lawyer seems prepared to scrap it out with the hospital."

Artemis shifted forward and took in a deep breath. She studied Agent Beaky's face, his intense, playful eyes as she smelled a fresh pot of coffee being brewed.

"You know I'm under an NDA?"

"I suspected," Agent Beaky said. He again winked at Artemis. "But I also suspect you don't want to get pulled in over your head. Not a client to risk jail time and get, as the saying, a loss of your liberty."

"I'm not over my head," Artemis said. "Cute."

"Ha, I like your spirit," Agent Beaky said. He pointed at Artemis. "You're a spunky lass, almost a proper Irish girl. You'll take it easy on me, now, so, help a boy out, what can you give me?"

Artemis understood the statement.

"Not sure about you," Artemis said. "But let's just say, they might scare me if I were a patient."

"I've gotten that hint," Agent Beaky said. He grunted. "Thank you. Are you aware of a so-called tree of life, out in the woods?"

"Nothing," Artemis said. She looked behind him and then refocused on Agent Beaky. "Old man out at a grocery mentioned weirdness, nothing else."

"Weirdness?"

"Not sure," Artemis said. "It was a comment in passing, he tried to give me some advice to watch out for a group, nothing else."

"Ever heard of Profit Higgs Boson?"

"Never, that's an odd name," Artemis said. Satan was not the type informant Agent Beaky would appreciate. Artemis kept that supernatural wonder to herself. "Not that I remember hearing from any actual human-beings."

"Seems he has quite a following," Agent Beaky said. "Women, men, an entire army, a cult leader. Studied about the type at academy, first time in my career to deal with a real one, rather creepy fellow."

"So what?" Artemis said. She shrugged.

"Yeah, it gets strange, if I must," Agent Beaky said. He hesitated. "It will be important to find them, observe them from a distance. I'm just not sure where, any ideas? I think it connects them back to the hospital, not sure why, but it's in my bones. I never question my Welsh instincts, they have never failed me."

"I'm only half-Irish, I don't see how this has anything to do with the hospital, or my file," Artemis said. "My Mother always told me to tell the truth, and I'm not sure what to think of you, or this tree, and yes, it sounds odd."

"I accept your point," Agent Beaky said. He observed to Artemis' left-side at the hotel lobby being mopped and cleaned by a Hispanic girl with a long black ponytail. He contemplated. "I'll put you at ease. I'm lost up here. This is an alien country for me, not like a normal city or town. I suspect you've learned this."

"Yeah, they are clannish, Scot-Irish. I read an article about the local history, they are known not to like outsiders," Artemis said. "Tribal in a way."

Agent Beaky stared back over at Artemis. He calculated his words. He pursed his lips.

"If you'll help me," Agent Beaky said. With his left hand fingers he gripped his square, shaven chin. "I'll try to return the favor? I'll be blunt, I need to find this group. They're dangerous. They've been rumored to abuse women, girls."

"I'll play along, why dangerous?" Artemis said. She considered it might be a good time to visit Most High Cemetery. "I'll do some work tonight, maybe something will emerge from my file notes."

"Can you help me find this tree of life?" Agent Beaky said. "If just an introduction."

Artemis sat back and crossed her arms. The hotel valet scratched his plump belly as he tried to chat up the Hispanic maid. She was certain he would fail in his efforts, again.

"You have my attention. We should go visit the old man at the grocery," Artemis said. She remembered the lost Native American and the roaming white stag. "I can find it, his name is Virgil. Yeah, Virgil Sammons, he knows a friend of mine. He'll know where to go."

"Ah, many thanks," Agent Beaky said. He tapped on the laminated fake wood table top. "I need to find a local with knowledge. Otherwise, I'll find myself with the troubles about me. My superiors will question my methods."

"Don't get your hopes up," Artemis said. "He's a heavy drinker, likes the hard stuff. But if this group is messing with kids, and you think the hospital is connected. That's all I need to know."

"I'm Welsh," Agent Beaky said. He sucked in a deep breath. "I'd not trust him otherwise if he didn't like a proper pint."

"Give me your contact information," Artemis said. She pulled out her smartphone; she tapped in the password. "Here, put in your number, I'll call you in the morning. I have an idea what to do, just let me do some checking, I have my ways, my peculiar methods."

Agent Beaky tapped in his information, he handed the smartphone back over to Artemis.

"I'll be waiting," Agent Beaky said. "Till tomorrow then?"

"Fine with me," Artemis said. She clicked off the smartphone. "I'm an early riser, sleep very little. So I'll be early."

Agent Beaky stood up, he leaned forward and shook Artemis' hand.

"I welcome working with you," Agent Beaky. "Until then."

"Sure," Artemis said. She leaned her head to the side. "Curious, why Nero?"

"Sorry?" Agent Beaky said.

"Why'd they name you Nero?" Artemis said.

"Ah, not sure," Agent Beaky said. He glanced back over at Artemis. "I'm not Roman, or Greek. It's not even a family name. I think my Mother liked it."

"My old man was an antiquities dealer, biblical scholar," Artemis said. She smirked. "Some say Nero was a code for 666, from the Book of Revelations. I'm half-kidding, not sure why I remember these useless facts. My old man told me these stories, daily, growing up. He was so passionate."

"I don't think I'm the anti-Christ, as best I can tell," Agent Beaky said. He staccato laughed. "At least not today, my beloved Catholic mother would have a good laugh at that one."

"Sorry, I'm kidding with you," Artemis said. "If you were the anti-Christ I know something that would not rat you out, in fact, likely cheer you on, if you were mister end of times."

"I welcome your call," Agent Beaky said. He shook his head as he turned and strolled away.

Chapter 15

Artemis stood outside of Selene's circular shaped cemetery. The forbidding iron gates were rusting into oblivion. She searched beyond the bars for demonic spirits or signs for Satan's presence. But it appeared quiet, still, blanketed within a grayish, frosty sub-layer. High above in a hoary oak tree perched a black-winged raven. It eyeballed Artemis as she walked into the cemetery grounds like a sentinel protecting the dead. It croaked down at her.

Across the cemetery near the back gates, she saw a young girl, a spirit girl fluttering above a granite monument. Other wandering spirits bolting by her like golden lightning streaks or they skidded to a stop, confused, inquiring about her solitary existence. The little girl glistened within a golden corona as she waited for Artemis to approach her.

Artemis closed the gate that creaked at its welded joints, the rust chipping away its usefulness. She stepped within the rings and walked beyond the arranged family plots. She walked with a purpose by the massive white granite monument, and then on toward what appeared to have been a young girl.

"Who are you?" Artemis said. The girl a grainy hologram. She wore the clothes from her life, a frilly dime-store dress.

"I don't know," the girl said. Her voice resonated as if she talked to Artemis from inside a tin can. "I'm told to stand here, to wait for you, and then I can go on."

Artemis backed up. She inspected the cemetery searching for Satan. It controlled the spirit girl. Satan blocked the little girl from cascading through a kind crease within the light spectrum. Satan's last moments to torture her. It was nearby; It was the solution for the girl's odd behavior. And Artemis expected the worst.

"Who?" Artemis said. "What's your name?"

The little girl stared over at Artemis.

"Am I dead?" The little girl said. She pointed down at the monument. A name was chiseled into the granite and beneath the name were beginning and ending dates. Artemis kneeled down; She held her smartphone's flashlight above the rough surface.

"Are you," Artemis said. "Lilly, Lily-Ann Combs?"

The little girl looked down at Artemis.

"That's my name," Lily-Ann whispered. Her pale lips fashioned into a slight frown. "Where am I? I'm afraid. I see dark things."

Artemis stood up, and she stuffed the smartphone back inside her coat pocket. She wanted to hug Lily-Ann, but she knew it was not possible; as if trying to hug a mist.

"You're in what's called, limbo, it's temporary," Artemis said. She breathed through her half opened mouth. "Can you see a light, a place to go? Go there, god or something like that waits for you. I think."

A harsh breeze brushed back Artemis' hair. The ground was hard and frozen under her boots. The moon's glow revealed a white-tail deer trotting toward a 8-point buck. They grazed together on wild mushrooms that had emerged beneath a dead elm tree splayed across a woodland field.

"I saw it," Lily-Ann said. She shook her head up and down. "But then, I woke here. I'm just here. I don't know why."

"You are waiting for me?" Artemis said. She reached forward over at Lily-Ann, her hand glided through Lily-Ann's aura. "Why?"

"Mushrooms," Lily-Ann said. "Don't eat the mushrooms. I'm told to tell you, don't eat mushrooms."

Artemis thought about Laina. She looked down at the brown grass. She nodded back over at Lily-Ann. She thought about Dr. Demetrius and wondered what evil the man had wrought against this community.

"Did you eat them?"

"Yes," Lily-Ann said. "I trusted them. I trusted them."

"Who?" Artemis said.

"My mother, she gave them to me," Lily-Ann said. "She promised me they were good for me."

"Dr. Demetrius?" Artemis said. She made herself keep her arms open and welcoming. She resisted her urge to scream. "Did he give you mushrooms, when?"

Lily-Ann's eyes focused on Artemis, her head gestured back and forth.

"Not a doctor. From the forest, they picked them," Lily-Ann said. "Profit Higgs Boson picked them for me. Before…"

Artemis stood up tall, and solider like. She sensed that a forbidding story was about to arrive. She had no reason, but her truth seeking eyes and subconscious yelled at her.

"I don't want to ask you," Artemis said. She closed her eyes and whispered a prayer for peace, a prayer for Lily-Ann's soul, and that if a god really existed, it would accept her into a serenity.

"Ask me," Lily-Ann said. "You have to…"

Artemis acknowledged Lily-Ann. She crossed her arms. She breathed in a deep breath; she held the breath and then released it.

"How did you, ah, die?" Artemis said. She could not stop the tears from coming; The news from Lily-Ann would be terrible. "I'm sorry. I wish I could have saved you."

"Profit Higgs Boson," Lily-Ann said. "My mother gave me away, she gave me to him."

Lily-Ann's face had accepted her fate, a fate written into her eternal four winds. It was about facts. Artemis squeezed her face with her fingertips. She did not want to probe further, but she had to keep investigating. She realized there were other girls like Lily-Ann and she now feared for Laina's safety.

"What happened?"

"He took me, did stuff to me," Lily-Ann said. Her spirit body dangled within the darkness like a lost doll hung by a cotton rope from a thorny tree limb. "My mother just watched, I kept looking at her begging her to save me. He took my heart from me after I ran."

Artemis gripped her hands into fists. She stepped closer to Lily-Ann. She growled as she leaned forward with her shoulders.

"Your heart?" Artemis said. "What do you mean?"

Lily-Ann nodded at Artemis. She pointed her right hand fingers back at her once fragile chest.

"Don't eat the mushrooms," Lily-Ann said. She began to disappear into golden grains water-falling downward. "Don't eat the mushrooms."

And before Artemis could ask another question, to prod Lily-Ann for clues. Lily-Ann dissipated and her spirit washed downward across the monument. And Artemis sensed she was no longer alone with Lily-Ann's spirit. The wandering spirits in limbo had all gone into hiding. She knew what was behind her.

"I warned you," Satan said. Artemis turned to see the handsome man from before. Dressed as if a new suit from London's Savile Row, with high-polished dress shoes. A red silk handkerchief pocket square dangled as if from a proper ladies man uniform. "This is not a pleasant place for you, you might be over your head."

"Let her go," Artemis said. She corkscrewed her boots into the ground. "Let that little girl go on, please, ah, please."

"She's gone, oh how quaint, you're so nice," Satan said. It waved Artemis' questions away with the flick of its sharp fingernails. "But you've learned about Profit Higgs Boson. Now, to be clear, I hate Profit Higgs Boson. He does such bad things. He thinks himself a god particle. And he worships me. And for that, after his human body dies, he'll get to burn in hell, forever, with me laughing at him. Go figure."

"Why do you hate children?"

"I hate every human. I hate animals. I hate happiness," Satan said. It tapped, it tapped and tapped its right dress shoe on the ground. "It makes my work much easier, but don't get all squeamish on me, you have so much to learn. I trust you like mushrooms?"

"I don't understand," Artemis said. Her hot breath fogged a constant cloud in her face. "I can't possibly understand you, whatever you are."

Satan leaned back against a concrete monument. It stared up at the raven. It waved at the bird, and the bird dropped dead. Its carcass spasmed, it shook as it clawed in space. Then it was still.

"It's so obvious, mushrooms, the fungi," Satan said. It wiggled a fore-finger over at Artemis. "Without death, like the dead bird over there, you have no life on earth. The fungi are everywhere; they create rot. The magic mycelia. Those white-tailed deer out there ate mushrooms. Mycelia birth food for your human body, or digest your remains under the soil. A vast army under your fancy hiking boots."

"Why are you telling me this?" Artemis said. Certain Satan enjoyed toying with her mind, she gave up trying to conceal her thoughts as it was pointless and impossible.

"Clues, learn about the fifth kingdom. Fungi are not plants or animals; they are all on their own," Satan said. It grinned as it winked at her. "I hate you. You should go up into the forest, take your new friend, Agent Beaky. Virgil will guide you. Go find Profit Higgs Boson. Warning, he's a bad man. The reason I hate him so, so much, which is a huge compliment coming from me. If I hate you, god help you. Or will the God help you?"

"It has nothing to do with the hospital," Artemis said. "Other than making me sick to my stomach."

"Oh, yes it does, this will only get nasty, you used a perfect adjective," Satan said. It smiled like a male model at a photo shoot. It pointed over at Artemis as it stepped forward. It sauntered over toward Lily-Ann's grave. "Little girl gave you advice, didn't she?"

"What?" Artemis said. She examined the grave's monument that Satan pointed down at. "I don't understand."

"Don't eat the mushrooms," Satan said. It smacked its hands together. "Remember? Pay attention, Artemis. What did I tell you the first time we met? So, I decided a treat for you tonight, someone you once loved. I don't know what that means, you're all gooey inside."

Artemis closed her eyes, she dropped to her knees, and she whispered a prayer. She prayed for guidance from God, as she thought Satan would soon take her life. As she looked up, Benjamin floated within the night sky like a condemned prisoner.

"Artemis," Benjamin said from beyond. "Be careful…"

"Oh, this is so delicious," Satan said. It howled. "Oh baby, be careful. Wha, wha, wha, don't cry Artemis. Don't cry, boohoo."

Artemis reached forward to grasp at Benjamin. She pushed back on her knees. She leaned back and stared up at Benjamin.

"What am I to do?" Artemis said. She whimpered. "I'm losing it."

"You and Laina are both in danger," Benjamin said. His grainy image wavered. "Go home, leave this place. Take Laina."

"How sweet, but go on, my dead slave," Satan said. It snapped its fingers to reveal a white cloud puff. Within the bulbous puff appeared the image of a large man. Satan concealed the man's face. "Tell Artemis what I showed you."

"He's coming," Benjamin said. "He is evil, please, protect Laina, he's pure evil."

"Good boy," Satan said. It snapped its fingers again, and Benjamin's image evaporated. It clapped. "I cannot resist. I hate twisting you, playing with you. Dr. Demetrius? He's even scared of this one, oh, a hateful, greedy one. I hate him, so. He's a bad man."

"Why?" Artemis said. She gripped her thighs. She spat at the ground, she dry-heaved.

"Ambition, he's fueled with greed," Satan said. "This one's got real ambition. I hate his greed, oh, greed. He's a disgusting human. Has a lustful streak, too. Seems he has issues with females."

Satan dissolved into black specs; It formed into a gooey orb, and it floated away into the night sky toward the three-quarter moon.

"I don't understand," Artemis said. She covered her face with her hands. "Let Benjamin go…"

"You will understand soon. I'll keep Benny nearby for now," Satan said from beyond. Its voice sounded like a whisper inside Artemis' mind. "Don't eat the mushrooms. Go out into the forest, you'll enjoy the show. I promise."

Artemis gulped, she exhaled a heavy breath. She steadied herself. She got up. The raven's dead body gone. She stumbled out of the cemetery. She zipped up her parka as she walked along the concrete sidewalk observing the dark homes, the stoic trees. She was confident Virgil would know where to find Profit Higgs Boson and the tree Agent Beaky had mentioned.

Determined to avenge Lily-Ann's death. She had to get back home to Laina; She needed Wylie's help. She stood still accepting the raw winds and winter's chill. But her mind blazed with tasks.

It was in those moments that Artemis sometimes regretted her gift. But her mother always told her not to fear the truth, and now Satan existed. And if Satan existed, somewhere she hoped there was a peaceful, omnipotent god. A god she could not understand that allowed little girls like Lily-Ann to be abused and murdered.

"Please, God, I want to believe in you," Artemis said in a whisper. She started to stride down the sidewalk. A red CVS sign blazed against the darkness. "Please exist, please help Benjamin. Help me protect Laina."

Chapter 16

"I don't think so, better, no way, not goin' to happen…"

"It's of utmost importance, if you please sir," Agent Beaky said. He pushed his hands across the grocery store counter toward Virgil. He was wearing dark mountain hiking clothes with modern lightweight boots. "Again, if you please? You are vital."

"I ain't goin' up there," Virgil said. He wiped his mouth with the back of his thick, hairy hand. "It's dangerous, take a two-handle just to build up the nerve."

"Pardon?" Agent Beaky said. He turned to look quizzically back over at Artemis. "Two what?"

"Bourbon bottle, I think?" Artemis said. She shrugged at Agent Beaky. Curious how the store with a claustrophobic ceiling height remained open since it lacked any other shoppers. But the gas station seemed steady income from having magnetic insertion credit card readers at the pumps and no nearby competition.

"She's got it, right, that's right," Virgil said. He thrust his forefinger over at Artemis. "I'd need to drink for a week, them people are crazy, lunatics, I tell ya, ya hear me?"

"I do," Artemis said. "But I think they killed a little girl, about Laina's age."

Virgil stood up tall, his shoulders back and closely gazed at Artemis. He poked his tongue down into the gap between his front bottom teeth and his jaw line where back in his youthful days he hunted and fished until the darkness crept and he escaped from the forests clutches. He'd stuffed Red Man chewing tobacco, or dipped Skoal from a tin can for calm courage. Artemis knew it was his instinctive tell, his reliable behavior that his mind shifted, his body engaged to take action.

"I ain't got no child," Virgil said. He coughed to clear his throat. "But I reckon I'd step in front of a bullet to protect a child. It ain't right, you don't pick at kids."

"They murdered a little girl," Artemis said. Her voice soft, certain. "Her name was, Lily-Ann."

Agent Beaky leaned back, he let his left hand dangle at his side. He examined Artemis like any good detective who possessed ears.

"Pardon, milady," Agent Beaky said. He kept his eyes on Artemis. "How might you know this?"

Artemis avoided eye contact with Agent Beaky. She fumbled and rearranged the groceries candy bar display. She used to share a milk choco-late with her father when they evaded her mother's dietary methods while shopping for culinary discoveries at a bespoke market.

"Word on the street," Artemis said. She bit down on her lower lip. "I overheard people talking at the hospital. Picked up the name there, perhaps you can investigate the name?"

"Ah, right, right," Agent Beaky said, suspiciously. He opened a notepad and scribbled on the paper. "I've no cell strength up here. Can't text the name to myself, but I'll do that, straight away, a name, please?"

"Lily-Ann," Artemis said. She stuttered a muffled last name. "I'm not exact with the last name. The nurses, it was the nurses gossiping. A kid that ran off, I think."

"Right, right," Agent Beaky said. He snapped shut the notepad. "I'll not look away. I'll track her down, build my file."

"You're a terrible liar," Virgil said. He stared down at Artemis' water-proofed tactical boots. "Cell strength will get better higher-up, inside this valley it's sketchy. Hike-up, and it'll get better."

"Will you help us?" Artemis said. "Please."

Artemis certain Agent Beaky had not accepted her response. Confident Virgil knew of the girl; It was his grinding jaw, his narrowed eyesight. And Virgil had been hip to Artemis' cryptic response.

"I guess we'll all be packing?" Virgil said as he pulled out from under the countertop a heavy, well-used .38 revolver. "This might slow one down, doubt it'll do any killin', unless it's a gut shot, you know, close range."

"That won't be necessary," Agent Beaky said. He waved his right hand forward. "I'm adept at firearm and defensive procedures."

"You ever been up in these hills, alone?" Virgil said to Agent Beaky. He picked up the worn revolver grip the two-pieces held in place by a single center screw, pointing the four-inch carbon-steel barrel downward. "This will get you a head start."

Agent Beaky opened his jacket to reveal his service weapon.

"Understand, I assume you're permitted?" Agent Beaky said. He examined Virgil's revolver, and nodded back over at Artemis. "If you can take us there, I'll deal with them, if need be."

"Let's go, I'm packing," Artemis said. She stuffed the silver packaged candy bar back into the display. "It'll get dark soon. I don't want to get lost out there."

"Not goin' to happen," Virgil said. He yanked up the grocery store counter, limped into the store, and turned to fold it back down and shifted it in place. "I never get lost up in the hills; Worst case, I have a guide friend that'll find us. This is my home. I could crawl home in the darkness."

～

Artemis, Agent Beaky and Virgil trudged up into the gradual climb into the Appalachian hillsides. A dense thicket poked and slashed at their pants, and boots as they squished bubbly mud puddles, the underbrush blanketed with dormant broad-leaf kudzu that during the coming springtime Artemis was confident it would bloom into an idyllic greenish forest. The cycle repeated over thousands of years from birth, life, death and renewal. A logged tree stump's pale yellow flesh rotting in place swarmed over by ivy crawlers, ferns, and repurposed housing for nervous varmints.

"I can't believe you got me out here," Virgil said. He gripped a high beam patrol man's flashlight that begged for fresh 5-D Cell batteries. "I've gotten old, I ain't spry no more."

"It'll be all right," Artemis said. As she stepped up the brown hillside. "You view everything based on bourbon?"

"It helps me manage my stress," Virgil said. He sucked in deep breaths. He spat at the ground. "You should try it, next thing, it's the next morning."

"No thanks," Artemis said. She sniffed. "Got that?"

"Yeah," Agent Beaky said. He sniffed. "Like smoke from a fire, better, kerosene, oily smell."

"It's glowing yellow up a ways, it gets dark up here, quick, the trees can close in on ya," Virgil said. He clicked off the flashlight. "At the crest of the hill, other side I expect them havin' their meetin'."

"I see it," Artemis said. She crouched down. "Let's get closer."

"Let's just keep it slow, and real quiet like," Virgil said. He kneeled down on one knee onto a limestone rock outcropping. He scanned the area like a hunting dog. "Let my eyes adjust to the dark, I knew them to have big boys roamin', lookin' for interlopers like us. They get all wacky about their meetings from what I hear."

"Sorry?" Agent Beaky said Virgil.

"Security detail," Artemis said. "Let's keep moving."

"Very well," Agent Beaky said. He held up his hand. "Wait. If we get separated, what's the plan?"

Virgil scratched his unshaven chin.

"Run back to the grocery, that's what I'd do when I panic," Virgil said. He pointed down the steep hillside that evolved into a suffused dark-lavender woods under Orion's Belt. Its string of three bright stars being lurked by reddish-orange Betelgeuse. "Run to that road, turn left and you'll find it. It's a half-mile, hopefully less. I'm old, but I'll make it."

"Good, it has gotten quite dark," Agent Beaky said. "Artemis?"

"I got it," Artemis said. "Let's do this."

Virgil turned and continued to saunter up the traversing old, bare brown dirt path carved from a time when the area was explored by woodsman like Daniel Boone, inhabited by Scot Irish coal miners, gold prospectors, and 1930s moonshiners. It weaved between age-old oaks, birch and ash trees, and timeless jagged blue-gray limestone and shale outcroppings. The forest floor eternally moist, and it smelled earthy and dank and bore grass shoot clumps wherever nature allowed. The venerable trees bark and barrel chested rocks were blanketed with damp, spongy moss, hardy mushroom clusters, and ferns.

"Hear that?" Virgil said. He wiped his sweating face with his tan workman's coat sleeve. "A party or something, but it ain't a party. I'll guarantee ya'll."

Agent Beaky crawled facedown like a snake wiggling by Virgil and made it to the crest of the leafy hillside. He hid behind a barnacled oak trunk, pulled from his coat pocket a hands-free binoculars, slipped them over his eyes appearing to inspect the area below.

"They've gathered near a big tree, twenty or more," Agent Beaky said. He waved Virgil and Artemis upward. "They are not much farther, keep down, but they're thirty feet below our spot. A perfect location, thank you Virgil."

"What's that," Virgil said as he pointed downward.

Beneath the massive tree, a partially naked young woman, light-haired with sinewy legs escorted a white furred lamb with a dangling rope. Like the young woman, the lamb seemed oblivious to its predicament as it fixated on the sparking fire; the tiki torches fueled with kerosene. It sniffed at the ground.

"A lamb?" Artemis said. "This is not funny."

"That's one giant tulip poplar," Virgil said. "Bet it's close to hundred feet high. I can never figure how the winter breeze don't tumble it. Nature's amazing if ya sit a spell."

"What do you guess," Agent Beaky said. "Twenty-five, thirty foot diameter? Hundred plus year old specimen."

"I'd say," Virgil said. "It's a big one. If they don't cut-'em down, I've seen taller ones. Like seeing giants talkin'.'"

"It's not the tree," Artemis said. She gripped her hands into the dark, moist soil hunching down on all-fours behind a hefty sandstone boulder. "It's the mushrooms, look near the tree roots, they are everywhere. Into the tree, across the ground."

And from another universe hidden from human existence Artemis heard a playful whisper. "Artemis, Artemis... I can see you Artemis... look for me, I'm near The Profit Higgs Boson. See me, holding a torch? This dude thinks he's a god."

Artemis glanced over at Virgil, he seemed entranced. Agent Beaky appeared to ignore them. But that voice whispered again.

"Artemis, remember what I told you? What did I tell you... or what did Lily-Ann tell you? Artemis... Artemis... say it?"

Artemis squinted her eyes and scanned near the tree. A man wearing a white ritual robe with a pointy hood, poked the torch he held upwards, thrusting upwards again, and again as if to draw her attention. It was the handsome Satan from the cemetery.

"Sacrifice a lamb," Virgil said. "Big dudes got a fancy lookin' sword. That ain't for show, tell ya that."

"No kidding, I'm dreading this," Artemis said. She stared down behind her at the forest floor casting haphazard shadows from the weak yellow light. She wondered if the worms beneath the brown twigs, dark leaves remained hidden through winter, hibernating until they emerged from the black soil during springtime. She wanted to hide with them, but it would have been pointless. Satan could follow her anywhere she traveled in life or death. "They sense I'm nearby."

"Pardon?" Agent Beaky said. He snapped his glare over at her. "How might that be?"

"Don't eat the mushrooms," Artemis said. She shut her eyes, remembering Lily-Ann's wandering spirit. "Don't eat the mushrooms."

And Artemis heard Satan's laugh. "Good girl. Those two cannot hear me; It's just you and me, what a great show I have for you tonight. This humanoid thinks he's a god, Profit Higgs Boson. Higgs particle, god particle, get it? I hate him. For now, let the show begin. They've cast me tonight in a minor role. But I am required to provide a lustful, thrusting truth. I hope you enjoy the performance. I'm amazing. These women just stare at my beauty."

The lamb was lead before the big man wearing a demonic long horned goat mask. Dressed in a similar white robe, but he had a golden sash. He held out a small wooden bowl as dutiful followers picked the forest floor for mushrooms. They placed them inside the bowl and backed away into their pre-determined positions. The lamb sniffed; It glanced up at the dominate man with its innocent black eyes. It ignored him as it bit down at the brown crabgrass and spindly weeds.

"A sword, quite right," Agent Beaky said. He refocused the binocular lens with a round dial next to the right-side lens. He grunted. "That's a Kris, it's decorative, they made the blade wavy on purpose. It's for rituals. I suspect the animal is being sacrificed this evening. If you have never experienced this practice, turn-away, cover your ears. The animal will scream. The slicing sounds are off-putting. I needed counseling to manage the first-time, after I investigated these practices. Brutal."

"They know I'm here," Artemis said. She whispered to herself. "They will put on a show for me."

"How's that?" Agent Beaky said. He did not stop monitoring the scene. He kept texting himself notes to his muted smartphone.

"Oh, it's a hunch," Artemis said. "That's all, maybe my brain is playing tricks on me."

"Might you be a clairvoyant?" Agent Beaky said.

"Ah, now what ya callin' her?" Virgil said. He stared back and forth at Agent Beaky and Artemis. "Never heard about a family up here named that, Clare Fovant?"

"I am, been gifted from birth," Artemis said. Her eyes locked on the doomed lamb. "Instincts, the hospital, it's part of this. It has to be, my stomach is in knots."

Artemis, Agent Beaky and Virgil kept low and close together. They heard the aggressive man shout what they suspected was a satanic chant. The group practicing a demonic worship service. The symbols were all there in front of them. An upside down Christian cross fashioned from tree limbs hung and swayed from a sturdy branch like a hanged captive prisoner by a ruthless dictator as a community warning. They had scratched a pentagram within a wide-circle beneath a lacquered table. And Artemis was the only human aware Satan was in their midst.

"Artemis," Satan said. "This nut job talks in gibberish. I have not an idea what he's saying. But seems it's for me, funny. I hate these humans."

"Show time for the lamb," Agent Beaky said. He stared over at Virgil and back over at Artemis. "Turn your heads, if need be, I'm required to develop evidence, it's my job."

The lamb started baaing high-pitched resistance as if an elementary school child blowing through a hard plastic flute in music class. They tugged the lamb over toward the bowl full of mushrooms. It sniffed the fungi. It's furry body relaxed as it nibbled the mushrooms.

"Don't eat the mushrooms," Artemis said in a whisper. "Oh, god, don't eat them."

"Well," Virgil said. "That's weird. Figured they'd have done something worse. They didn't eat know mushrooms, either, or whatnot."

"Wait for it," Agent Beaky said. "They are all focused at the lamb; they took it off the rope, letting it roam among them, strange. But a forbidding signal for the lamb."

"I get it, jokes on that lamb," Virgil said. "Wouldn't mind getting tugged about by a rope with some of them honey's, for land's sake. I'd be freezin', but they all perked up."

"Focus," Artemis said. "They are all high, addicts, doubt they even know what they're doing down there."

"Yeah, I reckon," Virgil said. "Them drugs, zap ya brain."

And as the lamb seemed to enjoy its freedom, it began to tremble and stagger. It squealed as if questioning the humans for what they had fed it. It stumbled like a drunken Halloween guest until it flopped onto the ground. Its hooves writhing in tremors, trotting in space. It stopped. It stilled.

"Those mushrooms, that only took a few minutes," Agent Beaky said. He squeezed off some photos from his smartphone sans a flash. "This group is up to something bad. I'll need more evidence."

"You all notice something weird," Virgil said. He coughed. "Now that ape's got that fancy sword back out."

Artemis heard the whisper float over from Satan. "Artemis, this is so wicked, but you must wait for it, it's about to get worse, and worse. And these women cannot wait to take me; the dead lamb set them on fire. And I admit it. I genetically gifted this body. You'll see. My performance must be authentic. I'm a professional. I have a reputation to share pure evil."

The muscled man wearing the demonic mask gripped the Kris sword, and he carved the dead lamb into bloody chunks, hacking it into random sized flesh and bone pieces. He served the group members portions into small individual bowls. The members spread the bloody, white furred meat and bones around the base of the soaring tree in a crisscrossed pattern and in an expanding circle over the pentagram symbol until they scattered all the lamb's remains beneath the tree. But for the severed head, which the goat masked man placed next to the tulip poplar's craggy bark, and robust base.

"Why are they stepping away from the tree?" Artemis said. "This is so odd. Why did that woman take off her clothes? Stop that."

"Focus on them," Agent Beaky said. "They all seem to understand their role; this is a practiced ritual, it is not random."

The trio remained hidden behind tree trunks, evergreen bushes, and sandstone boulders but a hush descended over them as if their collective instincts formed into a singular understanding that something unexplainable was about to happen. The sounds from below were the crackling fire, torches spitting kerosene and the soft breeze swaying the bare tree limbs. The demonic group held hands, chanting, in a circle around the tulip poplar.

"I guess they praying," Virgil said.

"A satanic, wait," Agent Beaky whispered. "The soil it's shifting beneath their sandals."

"Ah, what's that they're doin'?" Virgil said. He nudged forward. "That ain't normal like, never seen this."

"Ground is cracking open," Agent Beaky said. He started to video the scene using his smartphone. "Artemis, if you have your smartphone, perhaps you can video as well? Need a backup."

"I'm with you," Artemis said. "I don't believe this."

Artemis pressed her thumb against the red smartphone icon, as she pointed the camera lens down at the scene. Long fishers and crevasse split open the rich dark brown soil to reveal a white skeleton like network that sucked the animal's flesh and bone down into the abyss. It devoured the lamb in seconds. And then the soil magically healed over the openings, the cracks after it had digested the lamb chunks including the severed head. The group stepped closer in as tiny mushroom caps began to appear sprouting near the tree, zigzagging along the ground as if pushed up by a hidden underworld farmer from Hades sharing a bobbly mushroom crop.

"There are things you see in life," Virgil said. He covered his eyes with his hands. "You can't forget, but wish you hadn't seen, geez. It was like they were popping mushroom popcorn. I don't believe what I saw."

"I warned you," Agent Beaky said. He blew a whoosh from his lungs and out his open mouth. "Let's move along before they notice us. I'm troubled by this, I'll need to report back. The bureau will need to get resources out here."

"Great idea," Artemis said. "I don't understand what just happened, that tree, or its roots ate the lamb?"

"Artemis," Satan whispered. "Don't leave now, maybe you should join us, come enjoy our celebration. The new mushrooms will take you on a magical trip, I promise. Dr. Demetrius would be amazed. Hint. Hint. You can eat these for fun. It has no effect on me. So, my performance is about to involve that curvy brunette, and maybe the husky blond teenager with huge boobs. She needs a good spanking. I'll let them decide their fate. It's authentic hate."

"Just give it a second," Artemis said. She stopped crawling. Sat up began to take another video with her smartphone. "I have a hunch. I'm not real eager, but, just thinking."

"Fine with me," Agent Beaky said. He remained resolute and focused on the scene. "I try to trust hunches, the subconscious. The best discovery comes from that inner world we don't understand."

"Ah, them girls all got naked," Virgil said. "Whoa. That one's got some perfect ears, if ya get me. The cold makes her perk up."

"I'll behave with my comments," Agent Beaky said. "Much respect Artemis. I trust we can all be professional."

"Ah, sorry," Virgil said. "I, well, good on you."

The young women gave themselves freely and were being used by the men into performing sex acts and being attacked by multiple men. The muscular man kept the goat mask on and chose his partners first, and the others followed his lead. Artemis shook her head, avoiding any further eye contact as she turned away. The woman had complied like prostitutes. She was confident induced from hallucinogenic mushroom consumption.

"Lust, not greed, those women don't even know where they are," Artemis said. "Let's go, that's disgusting, nothing more to see."

"Typical carnal activity, for this group type," Agent Beaky said. He and Artemis started to crawl away from their vantage point. It was pointless to remain watching human degradation, but they realized Virgil was still observing the show. "Virgil?"

"Aha?" Virgil said. He appeared glassy-eyed. "Sorry, I'll stay here if need be? Help you all investigate things."

"Come, or you'll go blind," Artemis said. She jumped onto the path and started to hike down the hillside. "Besides, you need to get us out of here."

"Oh, yeah," Virgil said. He tottered, pushed back and limped down, and over the leaves and dirt. "Good idea, they'd have hypnotized me."

And from over the hillside, Satan whispered again to Artemis.

"Oh, don't leave now, Virgil wants to stay. My part in the performance is just beginning," Satan said, sarcastically. "Watch me pull this one's hair. I might bite her neck. I'll bend her over this table and teach her discipline. Can you hear me spanking her? She didn't even scream. But you got it right, my second favorite human flaw, lust. Oh, this human lusts for me. And this fat one is begging me, Artemis, don't leave, these wenches are just getting warmed up for me. And I can play along into eternity."

"Please leave me alone," Artemis said. She wiped sweat from her eyebrows. "You're not real."

"Pardon?" Agent Beaky said Artemis as they hiked down the steep hillside. "Were you talking to me?"

"Nothing, I can't unsee that crap," Artemis said. "Just talking to myself, bad thoughts, negative energy."

"Ah, after what we saw," Agent Beaky said. "Much agreed."

"Now Artemis," Satan said. "To think these fools worship me, and someday when they die. I'll remind them I don't care. They'll hate me, oh how rich. Oh this fat one, she'll do anything I want. I hate her. I should teach you to hate. Hate does not satisfy the soul. It has a dull, dead void quality. I'll teach you. I promise."

And Satan cackled and howled, as its laugh resonated through the trees and within the cold forest until Artemis made it back to the blacktopped road. The surface glistened in lavenders and blues within the darkness from a singular street lamp and the clear interstellar night sky.

"I don't want any part of that place again," Virgil said. He unlocked the metal grocery door and opened it.

"Don't worry," Artemis said. "I'll leave you alone. I'll keep you posted about Laina, cool?"

"That'd be appreciated," Virgil said. "I'm too old for this, my heart 'bout popped out up there."

"Ms. Lamb," Agent Beaky said. "Let's drive out of here, perhaps we should get back and have a moment to go over our findings?"

"Y'all go do that," Virgil said. He shook his head and his shoulders. "I need to go find me a handle, and some ice."

Chapter 17

"Ms. Lamb?"

"Yes," Artemis said into her smartphone. She set it on her nightstand while using the speakerphone function. She rubbed away morning haze from her eyes. "I can hear you."

"This is Dr. Langendorpher," she said. "Only reason we are speaking is Wylie, understand?"

"Yes," Artemis said. She pulled up the smartphone after plugging in her earpiece. She searched for the hotel room's coffee maker. "I have you off speakerphone, sorry. I just woke from a nap, hard night, working late out in the field."

"Try pulling an ER shift in your seventies," Dr. Langendorpher said. "Your odd acquaintances, Alan and Mikey brought a minor over to my practice, are you her parent or guardian?"

"No," Artemis said. "She's the kid from my deceased boyfriend. Her mother died, a drug addict. I'm trying to find her next of kin, but, in meantime, I'm just trying to help her out, keep her out of the system. That's all. I doubt she's ever had a health checkup."

"Well, I can lose my license, you understand?" Dr. Langendorpher said. "I trust Wylie. He said I can trust you, we understand each other?"

"Yes, I need an expert evaluation," Artemis said. She held the smartphone as she got up and stepped barefooted on the carpet over to the coffee station. "I'm just looking to help her out, and how should I say this, just looking for your expert opinion. It's what Wylie and I do, investigate medical malpractice cases."

There was silence for a few moments on the other side of the smartphone's cellular connection.

"We understand each other. I'm not accepting her into my practice, but purely for an expert assessment," Dr. Langendorpher said. Artemis heard her sigh. "Now, that's over with. She's a precious baby. I'll never turn my back on a child in need. Let the medical board try to take my license for treating a helpless child."

"Yes," Artemis said. "I felt the same. They left her all alone."

"Ms. Lamb, let me get to the point. They have abused this girl, she's a mess," Dr. Langendorpher said. "Where do I start?"

"I suspected, someone's using her for experiments, call me Artemis," Artemis said. She glided her fingers through her tussled hair. "She was living in a hellhole."

"Very well, Artemis. Your sentiments were correct," Dr. Langendorpher said. "She's had a wearable device taped on her back, between her shoulder blades in a spot she'd never touch. Who ever did it knew the precise spot where to place it?"

Artemis clutched her smartphone, she filled the coffee maker with water, picked a coffee pod, flicked on the machine and strode over toward the hotel room's windows. Diffused sunlight splashed into the twin double bed room. The coffee machine gurgled hot water and gasped out steam.

"I'm not certain I understand," Artemis said. "But I have a sick feeling you do."

"Someone's monitoring her, from there, I am certain," Dr. Langendorpher said. "They track her movements, her vital signs. After I found the wearable, I didn't remove it. But I got curious and scanned her from head-to-toe."

"What else?" Artemis said. Her lungs puffed out condensation Rorschach test blobs against the icy window. She wiped them away. "Wearables are too simple, what else?"

"Her righthand, between the thumb and forefinger," Dr. Langendorpher said. Artemis thought the doctor's voice sounded passionate. "Implanted a microchip, just under the first Dorsal Interosseous Muscle, someone knows where she is at all times. Like she's a little lab rat. I've never seen a real one, read about them, just a disgusting part of misappropriated science."

Artemis stared through the windows and noticed her perplexed reflection gazing back at her. It was as if she were a living image of herself trapped inside the smoked glass panes.

"Her lungs?" Artemis said. She walked toward the coffee machine, grabbed a paper cup and filled it.

"That's interesting," Dr. Langendorpher said. "You're a few steps ahead of me, why did you ask that?"

"I discovered where Laina was sleeping inside the hospital," Artemis said. She slowed down to consider her words.

"Go on," Dr. Langendorpher said. "I need all the background data I can gather."

"Hospital has a dark room where they grow mushrooms, fungus, it's temperature controlled," Artemis said. "Ah, for clinical research, new drugs. Something about penicillin, antibiotics. I don't understand the entire science; It makes logical sense to me long-term; But, they say it's a safe place to sleep."

"I do not agree, at all," Dr. Langendorpher said. "But I'd need not see it, inspect it. Laina's lungs are coated with spores; She's infested with fungi."

"This is terrible," Artemis said. She shifted to turn toward her workstation. "I'll send you cash from the company."

"No," Dr. Langendorpher said. "Send me a file. I'll invoice you all. I want this kept as an expert opinion."

"Better idea, thanks. I'll figure it out with Wylie," Artemis said. "What's the next steps?"

"I need to take tissue samples," Dr. Langendorpher said. "I don't need your consent given our understanding."

"Do what you can," Artemis said. "I owe it to her father. He was a good, an honest man. A solider."

"Good news, and I don't even need to look at the samples under a microscope," Dr. Langendorpher said. She paused. "And I have a soft spot for military children."

"I don't understand," Artemis said.

"Fungi can be lethal, Artemis," Dr. Langendorpher said. "If the spores were from say, I looked it up, Amanita muscari. The girl would have developed liver damage, and given her weakened immune system, she'd have died a horrible death."

"Can she be saved?" Artemis said. She closed her eyes, stood still and breathed out. "Tell me."

"I'll manage this girl," Dr. Langendorpher said. "Take a breath. Don't get stressed, I've got her under my care."

"Thank you," Artemis said. She sat down on the edge of the hotel bed. Her neck muscles relaxed, staring over at the paper cup releasing steam. "I'll be back home soon. I'll come visit you."

"Another item to consider," Dr. Langendorpher said. "GMOs."

Artemis grimaced.

"I tried not to consider this," Artemis said. "I guess it's sometimes better to remain ignorant, but go on."

"Mushrooms, or better what's making the mushrooms, stuff under the ground," Dr. Langendorpher said. "Can you get me some samples?"

"I think so," Artemis said. "What else are you thinking?"

"I did some study," Dr. Langendorpher said. "Sweet girl's results got me wondering. I was afraid I'd end up down a rabbit hole wasting my time, but then that pesky internet."

"I eat mushrooms," Artemis said. "Perhaps I shouldn't."

"You're on to me," Dr. Langendorpher said. "Ever heard of CRISPR? I'm sure it's an issue in your world."

"Not yet," Artemis said. "We've been monitoring the issue, I don't know much about it."

"You will," Dr. Langendorpher said. "Genetic modification of food is one thing, scary if in the hands of a madman. It'll branch out into human testing."

"Ah, if I follow," Artemis said. "That's a big lift, as in. I don't even like to think it."

"As well," Dr. Langendorpher said. "Modify the Genome, make slight genetic alterations through a food source."

"Nobody, even government types," Artemis said.

"Correct," Dr. Langendorpher said. "Would you ever suspect a hospital in nowhere, Kentucky?"

"They send me in to clean up messes," Artemis said. "I think I found my mess."

"You do have a mess," Dr. Langendorpher said. "Interesting side bar from researching Laina's case, appears death cap mushrooms, read an article, Amanita phalloides. There's an infestation happening, right under our feet. It's a monster they woke up."

Artemis wrote the words, death cap, in pencil on a hotel notepad set on her workstation.

"I'll check into this," Artemis said. "Thank you."

"I'll manage this girl, give her fancy milk thistle, she'll be fine," Dr. Langendorpher said. "But I'm not sure what else might go on inside her tiny body."

Artemis ended the smartphone conversation. She sat in front of her computer screen and typed in CRISPR. It provided her with a long string of sponsored ads for self-service gene editing businesses. All she needed to do was swab inside her mouth, share the saliva with a hidden laboratory. And then Artemis realized her DNA would be available for the world to inspect and analyze in government or other databases. She read a science paper abstract, CRISPR, clustered regularly inter-spaced short palindromic repeats, and associated protein 9, CRISPR-Cas9, it was a technology to edit genes in organisms. The human organism.

"Mycelia," Artemis said to the computer screen. "The largest organism in the world."

And from beyond Artemis' hotel room. She heard the whispered words of Satan.

"Now you're thinking," Satan said. "I'm always found in the teeny, tiny genetic details. Keep with it girl."

Artemis got up and stepped over toward the hotel room windows clutching the warm paper cup. She examined below her the wandering spirits searching for answers within a golden meridian. She wondered what had she stumbled into in little Selene, Kentucky. And she understood why The Company had assigned her the file.

Chapter 18

"You've been up in the forest?" Artemis said. She stared down at the Jenkins Law office's pastel colored shaker style carpet created from timeless workmanship. They had stretched it out over a thick padding that also absorbed sound. "Been near that tree, those mushrooms?"

Jerome Jenkins tapped his long left forefinger over his pale lips. His office chair shifting side-to-side.

"Yes," Jerome said. "A brutal group. I try to avoid the area these days. I warn friends to not go hiking up in there."

Artemis studied Attorney Jenkins' blue eyes, the cadence from his voice, and his blank expression.

"You called the FBI?" Artemis said. She set her backpack down.

"You're the only person they'd take serious; It's obvious."

"Insight's spot on," Jerome said. He glared over at Artemis. "If you live in a place long enough, you know everybody, every squirrel, every blade of grass, and, if something is out of sequence, I'll notice."

"They killed a little girl," Artemis said. Her gaze locked onto Jerome. "Don't ask how I learned that. It's a fact."

Jerome grunted in agreement. He slipped his eyeglasses on, read a line from a document he was writing, marked the entry. He took in a deep breath through his open mouth.

"So we are clear," Jerome said. He pointed over at Artemis.

"We're off the record, we're just talking, amongst friends."

"I understand," Artemis said. She shrugged.

"No, the answer is?" Jerome said. He kept pointing at her.

"Please."

"Off the record, yes," Artemis said. "I'll keep quiet."

"Good, good," Jerome said. He got up. Set his readers back down.

"Let's take a stroll. I want to show you something. Leave your backpack; It'll be safe here. Besides, you are not a fancy purse, girl? Not into expensive purses."

"I am not, I have a basic one for business meetings," Artemis said. She stuffed the backpack next to the cherry veneered desk. "You love this place?"

"I do," Jerome said. He waved for her to follow him.

Artemis walked along with Jerome down the downtown streets in Selene, Kentucky. He pointed out the new high school, the diner where he used to eat sliders on Friday nights, and cruised in his junker with teenage friends wondering how he'd escape the town.

"I do, it's home," Jerome said. He stuffed his hands inside his all-weather coat. He grinned looking over at Artemis. "I had to learn the hard way, sometimes you have to leave, kick some flat tires, make some mistakes to realize what you had. I was lucky, I'll die here, happily. I have no regrets."

"How do you get by?" Artemis said. She stopped walking and stuffed her hands inside her coat pockets. "Have enough work, how do you pay the bills? It takes a lot of money to fund a med mal case; We're just getting started with my investigation."

Jerome waved over at a middle-aged couple, they drove along by them from the opposite direction. He gave Artemis a sheepish grin.

"Like them," Jerome said. He pointed his left thumb back toward the four-door sedan that kept rolling along the two-lanes road. The car stopped at a blinking red light. "I've known them before they got married, any legal work, they come to me. It's straightforward work. I've made a few healthy licks over in Lexington. I'm in a good spot. You are aware?"

"I am. You have a solid reputation," Artemis said. A man inside a rusty truck, smoking a half-burned cigarette honked over at Jerome.

"Robert Charles," Jerome said over at the man. "Good on you, partner. Keep that thing going, impressive."

The man inside the truck wearing bribed overalls, smiled over with browning front teeth. He gave Jerome the Queen's back hand wave and drove his squeaking carriage down a bricked side street.

"Why the FBI?" Artemis said. "Local police not good enough."

"They've looked the other way, it's about greed," Jerome said. He nudged Artemis at a street corner to follow him down a cross street. They walked in front of a CVS. "Let me show you. It will help you all understand."

And Artemis realized her hotel was farther down, the CVS was the same one she had marched by toward Most High Cemetery.

"Cemetery?" Artemis said. She continued to stroll with Jerome.

She saw the pointy gates, the oaks, and the headstones. "You really know how to treat a girl."

Jerome acknowledged Artemis' comment. He pulled up the iron handle for the cemetery front gate, and they started to step across the grass. And then a concrete walkway. The funeral home's workers had set a blue tent over a freshly dug grave. The dirt pile covered over with a green tarpaulin.

"I'll end up here, maybe a nice day like today," Jerome said. He pointed over at a section. "Family plots over there, they'll drop my dead carcass in a hole, like that grave over there. If I'm lucky, the pastor will say something nice over me. Throw dirt on my coffin and everybody can go about their day."

"You're a believer?" Artemis said. She saw a black raven staring down at her from the same oak branch from her last visit. It wiggled its beak and studied Artemis with black eyes. "Sorry, don't mean to be personal."

"No worries," Jerome said. "I am. I pray there's a loving god, but it's not for this world. This world is full of evil. The truth to your question, read the book of Job, ever read it?"

Artemis noticed they were strolling toward a grave she had already visited. She stared down at the tombstone for Lily-Ann.

"I've always been interested in religious studies, but, I'm not a believer. My father was an expert in antiquities, drilled Bible, mythological stories into my head," Artemis said. She pointed down at the gravesite. "Why are we here?"

"This the little girl, Lily-Ann?" Jerome said. He kneeled down and whispered a prayer, he made the sign of the Holy Cross with his fingers, and he gently, lovingly touched the headstone.

"I think so," Artemis said. She sighed. "Yes, it's her."

"They found her out in the forest, dead," Jerome said. "The photos taken at the scene, not the way a sweet little girl should die. I'll leave it at that."

Jerome stood up, he glanced away from Artemis. He was oddly
quiet and still. Artemis crossed her arms, thankful it was a bright sunny
day so her skin would absorb natural vitamin D.

"You knew her?" Artemis said. She contemplated Jerome's
emotions, why he had turned his back to her, and the headstone.

"Not really, I remember her as a baby. I remember her birth was
a happy day for her grandmother, the family," Jerome said. He turned
back around, but kept looking downward at the brown grass. "We knew her
grandmother. My wife and I both knew her grandmother from childhood.
It's a strange sensation when you realize you're old enough that your high
school friends are grandparents."

"I guess it's all about perspective," Artemis said. She turned
and examined the modest cemetery. "I hope to live long enough to find
out. But I don't have any guarantees, not with my career."

"You're right. Yes, being older becomes a blessing," Jerome
said. "And in truth, I practice law for the pure joy. Now, it's fun to
tangle with the likes of you and your people."

Artemis inspected the cemetery. Strange to her to observe the
headstones, the plots under the clear skies. She didn't feel an evil presence. It was a simple, peaceful certainty.

"What drives me is the unfairness," Jerome said. He appeared to
contemplate his life. "God blessed me in many ways; It's embarrassing
to me that this girl, an innocent child." He paused. He sniffled. "She was at
the wrong place, with the wrong people. I fail to understand. But I don't
question god. I hope a god's out there."

"What happened?" Artemis said. She closed her eyes and waited
for the truth to emerge. She sucked in a cold breath. "To Lily-Ann."

"Found her little body out there," Jerome said. He waved out
toward the hulking brown hills covered with thorny trees and jagged
rocks. "She'd wondered off, Mother was an addict. Fentanyl, heroin, an
overdose got her, not sure where died. Before, she was a good girl. Auto
accident caused her back to go out. Pain meds got her addicted."

Jerome squinted his eyes. He pulled out a white handkerchief and
wiped his nose.

"That's terrible," Artemis said.

"Yeah," Jerome said. He wiped away tears from his eyes with the
clean handkerchief corner. "Well, Lily-Ann had been half-eaten, wild
animals, so forth. It wasn't the animals fault, they were hungry."

"That's awful," Artemis said. "Makes me sick and angry."

"The medical examiner from over in Lexington said she'd eaten mushrooms they call, death caps?" Jerome said. He looked up into a nearby maple tree appearing to examine the rough bark. "Yeah, that's right. They figured she'd gotten lost, got hungry. The mushrooms must have appeared like something from a grocery store. She ate the wrong thing. She never had a chance out there in the wilderness."

Artemis searched Jerome's eyes. And she was now aware they were being watched. There were several undead spirits floating nearby, staring at her. She hoped Lily-Ann had moved on into another universe. A peaceful place where children's souls exist with happiness and joy. But she was certain those spirits were there because Satan wanted her to see them. They were a reminder.

"Something else? Right?" Artemis said. "The reason you called the FBI."

"Correct," Jerome said. "The local police, they're corrupt. I ignore them. I assume they know who murdered Lily-Ann."

Artemis averted eye contact with Jerome.

"I've been up into the forest," Artemis said. "With an FBI agent, a local grocery owner, Virgil."

Jerome nodded his head. He crossed his arms.

"I'll keep quiet," Jerome said. "And?"

"I'm not sure why, I figure the hospital's involved. The FBI agent is being way too obvious," Artemis said. Out of respect, she kneeled down to gloss her hand across Lily-Ann's grave marker. "But there's a group out there, they're nuts, all into mushrooms and worse."

"Virgil?" Jerome said. He sighed. "He's not a bad guy, drinks too much. But he's got a soft heart. He took you out there?"

"Yeah," Artemis said. She looked back up at Jerome. She shielded her eyes with her right hand to block the bright sunlight.

"It's not an easy spot to hike into," Jerome said. "You'd need a guide, right?"

"Absolutely, it's not home for me," Artemis said. "But you've been up there?"

"Yes, I have seen things I wish I had not seen," Jerome said. He sauntered back and forth on his heels. "Us talking, right?"

"Yes," Artemis said. She stood back up. "I saw a ritual. If that helps jog your memory."

"That group murdered Lily-Ann," Jerome said. He shook his head in disbelief from a reality he knew existed. "They sacrifice animals, sometimes people. But there's never any evidence left behind."

"You saw it happen?" Artemis said. "After…"

"Yes," Jerome said. "They're smart, sick, but quite smart. They

don't leave a lot of loose ends. Very little evidence, you can video them, but without hard evidence, the legal system will kick the case back out. Videos can be faked. Not the type file to start over. Until they found this child. Poor thing, she ran for her life. I cannot imagine one of my own in that situation. It hurts my heart."

Artemis pulled out her smartphone.

"If I show you something," Artemis said. She held the smartphone

screen made from aluminosilicate glass forward. "It's disturbing."

"I can handle it," Jerome said. He sucked in a deep breath

through his nose. "Besides, I'm old. I have a strong faith. They can't chase me away from the truth."

And Artemis pressed the play icon, and the iPhone video of the

tree, the mushrooms, the goat masked man and the lamb sacrifice that had played out before the ground opened up to consume the animal.

"I did not expect this," Artemis said. "This had nothing to do

with your med mal claim, but now it does. Thanks to your friends at the FBI getting me to play along. It's sick. It's troubling. I think I know someone behind this mess."

Jerome stared across the cemetery. He nodded.

"She ran," Jerome said. "I'm certain now. They tried to

sacrifice her to an evil I do not want to tangle with."

"Sorry?" Artemis said. "What else, it's in your eyes."

"Lily-Ann," Jerome said. He scowled at Artemis. "Her mother was

never found, presumed dead. I suspect I know where she's decomposing. Like I said, overdose victim. Lily-Ann's body had bruises and slash marks on her. They had violated her body. They are mentally deranged, sick. I think abusing a child the worst crime."

Artemis was certain what Jerome was about to tell her next. But

Lily-Ann had already told her the truth. It was a truth that Satan enjoyed, but she wondered why a loving god would allow it.

"Worse?" Artemis said.

"Someone, a sub-human had carved her heart out," Jerome said. He

sniffled. "Left her body behind, must have gotten spooked away, wild animal, something, before they got to drag her back to that tree. It had to be something like that."

"Any DNA left behind?" Artemis said. "I don't want to think what they did to her. It makes me angry."

"Nothing they could trace," Jerome said. "Body was in pieces, decomposing. You get the picture."

"They created whatever that thing is," Artemis said. "I'm not sure how it connects direct to the hospital. But for our purposes, between us, I do have a sick feeling. My instinct is not good."

"Mycelium," Jerome said. "I did some research after I saw what you saw up there. It's what lurks under the soil. I expect your Dr. Demetrius has something to do with it."

Artemis turned to face Jerome.

"Genetics?" Artemis said. "You know about Dr. Demetrius and his mushrooms? His experiments?"

"I do," Jerome said. "Small town, my dear, we all know each other's business."

Artemis stepped away from Jerome.

"But you don't have the proof you need, yet?" Artemis said. She stared at Jerome. "I know that you're searching, you've nothing solid. The medical records don't help you. And it's become dangerous to go out there. The hospital's kept in almost total lock down; Administration seems obsessed with squeezing out a profit. And the local police are not your friends. You and your clients are isolated. You all need hard evidence."

Jerome gripped his nose with his right hand fingers, he stepped forward and paused.

"Smart lady, but the hospital's got cameras everywhere. I can't just walk about without them noticing me, they'll escort me off the campus," Jerome said. He started to walk toward the front gates. "The police are not interested in investigating her death. I hoped that the FBI might open a case. But that hospital and those kooks out there, they are connected. And when I find out, I'll get my evidence and I'll get Lily-Ann justice."

"For now, let's keep talking," Artemis said. She started to walk with Jerome. "It's not something I'll share with the company, yet?"

"I do. I honor your willingness to seek the truth. We'll argue, but afterword we'll break bread," Jerome said. He pointed forward. "Thank you, I'll open the gates, allow me to be a gentleman."

"Besides, I might need your help," Artemis said. They walked beyond the iron gates. Jerome closed them and flipped down the iron lever. "It's a personal matter, a little girl, total coincidence."

"There are no secrets in the mountains, about Benjamin's girl?"

Jerome said. He walked just in front of Artemis. His dress shoes crushed loose concrete aggregate. She followed him back toward his office building. "I'll help you, or at least try. I'll keep it separated out. Looking for her next of kin?"

"I guess you've been watching me, too," Artemis said. She shrugged. "I think that's the best option for her. She should be with her family, stay here with people she grew up with."

"I'll ask around," Jerome said. "Bound to someone that'll take her in."

They went back to the office. Artemis retrieved her backpack.

"I'll be back in town in a week, we should talk then," Artemis said. "Determine where we both are."

"I welcome your visit," Jerome said. He waved at Artemis as she left his office.

As Artemis left the Jerome Jenkins Law office behind, ahead she saw Satan sitting on a long wooden bench set at the side of an empty building on a gravel surface. It was wearing a heavy denim coat and a plaid red wool hunting cap. It was whittling a hickory branch.

"Artemis, my dear Artemis," Satan said. It pointed the knife at her. "I've been waiting for you. I like this human body, the new outfit makes me look local. Like the bib overalls, I'm being authentic, immersing into my role. What do you think?"

Artemis stopped walking. She shifted her black backpack and gripped the shoulder sling. She stared down along the concrete sidewalk and the road with a fading reflective white middle stripe.

"What?" Artemis said.

"Look, I'm whittling a whistle," Satan said. "I'll give it to you, just in case, for an emergency."

"Thanks," Artemis said. She was stone faced. Her feet frozen. "What?"

"He's all in," Satan said. It chuckled. "He's into Jesus, god, he has swallowed the whole deal. I cannot quite get into that brain, yet. Almost got him when he was young. I inhabited several hot babes, but he resisted. Sad. He wanted to be in love. How sweet, yuck."

"He's not for sale," Artemis said. "Nor am I."

Satan took the whittling knife and sliced its human left thumb.

"Look, human blood, Artemis. I'm bleeding, can you save me?"
Satan said. It examined the red blood dripping down and splattering on the concrete near its steel-toed boots. "It hurts this body, if I let it keep bleeding, this body dies."

"Keep bleeding," Artemis said.

"That's the spirit," Satan said. It smiled. It sniffed the wound like an animal hunting for prey. "Hate, oh I can feel your hate, thank you. I'm encouraged by you, Artemis. I'm making progress."

"What do you want this time?" Artemis said. She stared down at Satan, it snapped its fingers and stopped its thumb from bleeding. It healed the wound in an instant and dissolved the blood pools.

"See, I clean up my messes, too. But I wanted to ask if you enjoyed the show?" Satan said. It set the knife down. "Sorry, you missed out on the lust part; They all seemed to like my efforts. It was quite the fun, I got into debasing those women."

Satan kissed the air, it pushed the body's hips back and forth.

"I'm glad I left," Artemis said.

"I knocked those girls out, I made them quiver," Satan said. It opened its mouth to reveal a forked tongue. It oggly eyed up at Artemis. "Prophet Higgs Boson, dear me, he beat his girl to death. I enjoy his temper, he rages. He fed her to the mycelia. He's got mumsy issues. Poof. His dead girl's gone into hiding in the spirit world. I'll harvest her at project end. She's all mine. She made a contract."

"What's with the mycelium," Artemis said. "Not normal to eat an animal or a human."

"Ah, get to the point. I hate that about you, efficient with time," Satan said. It inspected its whittling. The cream-colored reddish scrub hickory wood fragrance was strong. "You stumbled onto a good clue while you were talking about Lily-Ann. The genetics. The mycelia and those mushrooms. Now what could be happening?"

"Yeah?" Artemis said.

"I'm proud of you," Satan said. It smiled with a menacing gaze that another show was on Artemis' future play list. "If you were smart enough, and you wanted to do something awful, but appear to be doing something wonderful?"

Artemis shook her head. She gripped the backpack strap, and shifted the weight forward.

"I don't understand," Artemis said. "You're being cryptic."

"It's all part of your journey. I created this journey for you,"

Satan said. It handed Artemis the hickory wood whistle. "Here, take it, give it to Laina. She might use it as an emergency whistle."

Artemis held the soft wood whistle in her fingers, as Satan

dissolved into the late afternoon air. She held the whistle in her hand positive it was a sign from the Evil One.

Chapter 19

"Where has this child been?" Dr. Langendorpher said. She took
off her rainbow styled eye frames and set the retro eyeglasses on her
metal desktop. "She's bright, sweet girl, but her bodies a mess, lungs
inflamed like she was a mushroom farmer."

Artemis sat down on a nearby cushioned side chair.

"Like we agreed," Artemis said. She crossed her legs. "She's
part of a new file, a hospital client? Wylie and I have to manage it,
investigate the claim before it goes to a suit phase, and the media gets
involved."

"Agreed, we understand each other, the games people play," Dr.
Langendorpher said. She glanced up at the ceiling. "Now, who is she? I
think you mentioned a boyfriend, military?"

Artemis uncrossed her legs. She leaned forward.

"My deceased love, she's Benjamin's," Artemis said. She stared
downward at the medical offices spotless cream colored tile floor. She
paused. "He's gone, died fighting bad guys, with me. I found out later,
Laina was his child, by accident, a cruel coincidence."

"Where?" Dr. Langendorpher said. "Where's this hospital?"

"Selene, Kentucky," Artemis said. She glanced over at Dr.
Langendorpher. "Why?"

"I have no idea where that is," Dr. Langendorpher said. She
pursed her lips. "But they are sophisticated. Whoever they are, Laina is

someone's experimental pet. I don't like it; a child should be protected, not abused by science."

Artemis got up and started to pace inside Dr. Langendorpher's office. She glossed her fingers over medical textbooks, several dogeared PDRs, and long since out of print medical journals.

"I suspected," Artemis said. "I have an NDA over me, but since you're helping with the file, I guess we can speak in the open."

"I would need to review all the facts for an expert opinion?" Dr. Langendorpher said. She hissed. "The medical records."

"You feel me," Artemis said. She tapped on the bookshelf. "The hospital is decent sized, multi-disciplinary, OB, across the line patient services."

"Wow, not what I'd expect," Dr. Langendorpher said. She interlocked her fingers across her waist as she scooted back. "How do they keep the place open, wouldn't seem enough population there to feed it?"

"My thoughts, as well, they a strange bunch," Artemis said. She held her right hand under her left elbow to support her arm. Her fingers squished over her lips. "But the place is a modern, well-managed faculty from the outside looking in. But…"

"Let me guess," Dr. Langendorpher said. She held up her hand like the dark haired smart school girl from the back of the class. "Large genetics lab, experiments with mushrooms, for new drugs that will save humanity? Or other nonsense about saving Mother Earth."

Artemis stared back over at Dr. Langendorpher.

"Why saving humanity?" Artemis said. She held her gaze over at Dr. Langendorpher. "You're being quite specific."

"Laina, they infested her lungs with mushroom spores, all different types, like I told you on the phone," Dr. Langendorpher said. "I cleared her up, you know that. But it was not without some serious anti-fungals, with an anti-inflammatory course. She might be an asthmatic for the rest of her life. Otherwise, I got all her human problems checked out."

"Not surprised," Artemis said. "But you filled in a lot of information with no knowledge, never been there, how?"

"Artemis, please," Dr. Langendorpher said. She leaned onto her office desk, supported by her elbows. Her white lab coat stretched at the sleeves. "I follow emerging science, like any physician. But the healthcare community needs to discover new antibiotics, as a species we are becoming drug resistant. It's all true. Penicillin was discovered by accident, fungi killed the bacteria. Fungi have their own kingdom, mold, and yeasts; They are ten times the size of plants and animals. In other words, first place I'd go looking for answers to this tough healthcare riddle. The fungi."

"Ten times?" Artemis said. She stared down at Dr. Langendorpher.

"What else, give it up, you look like you're holding back."

Dr. Langendorpher leaned back and crossed her arms. She winked over at Artemis.

"You know," Dr. Langendorpher said. "To the uneducated and self-important government types, all you need is one of those medical cookbooks near you. Treat the human condition, step-by-step, which is bullshit. They are self-entitled morons. Open the page over there in the cookbook where you treat real time, a screaming, crying baby that only communicates with its eyes and vital signs and a nervous mother peppering you with questions?"

"Wow," Artemis said. "You're not kidding."

"I'm still a country girl at heart. I only cuss when I'm mad," Dr. Langendorpher said. She got up without losing her stare over at Artemis. "Medicine is about art and science, after a while, your instincts lead you in a direction; you should follow your instincts after you've been educated and gotten seasoned with patients. Come here, why don't you follow me down the hallway."

"I guess I should," Artemis said. "You're leaving me behind."

Artemis walked alongside Dr. Langendorpher down toward the clinics nuclear and radiology laboratory signage. Dr. Langendorpher found an empty office within the steps of a hulking PET scan machine.

"Artemis, that monster over there," Dr. Langendorpher said as she pointed at the machine centered with a donut hole like portal with a spongy patient platform, surrounded by a round mass encased inside prefabricated materials. "It's a fancy machine, does PET scans and MRI, a terrific combination. A game changer, but expensive."

"Never seen one," Artemis said. She stared through the office window and out at the resting medical leviathan.

"We got one," Dr. Langendorpher said. "No one knows it, administer, good man. He squirreled away some grant money, or other financial magic, regardless, it's here."

Artemis sat down next to Dr. Langendorpher.

"Put Laina through it?" Artemis said. She appeared blank faced, and her eyes stared at the computer screen. "What showed?"

Dr. Langendorpher glanced over at Artemis.

"Nothing I've ever seen," Dr. Langendorpher said. She toggled
the computer mouse and clicked on icons until she found Laina's electronic health record. "If I had gotten caught, I'd have lost my license. I
didn't have any authorization, but I did it anyway."

"I don't understand," Artemis said.

"I had a PET and MRI performed on Laina," Dr. Langendorpher
said. "Without pre-authorization, plus she's a minor. Get it? But I went
looking for something. I wasn't sure what I was looking for, mind you, but I
felt down to my mortal soul something suspicious was inside that child."

Artemis gulped. She blew slowly through her open mouth. She
pursed her lips together.

"What then?" Artemis said.

"Tech thought I'd lost my mind," Dr. Langendorpher said. She
toggled the mouse icon. "Gave little Laina a drink with F-18 fluo-
rodeoxglucose in it, a radiotracer mind you. She was so sweet, oblivious.
She just laid over there, gave her some earphones and let her pick the
music."

"Was she scared?" Artemis said. "I would be."

Dr. Langendorpher waved Artemis' comment away.

"No, I told her it was just part of a basic physical, she fell
asleep," Dr. Langendorpher said. She studied the screen, and then she
clicked an icon to open a computer file with a 3-D image. She pointed at
the screen. "She's healthy, except for those little critters, look close at where
the radiotracer accumulated."

Artemis at first only saw red shades, pale greens, and deep blue
colors. But then from her medical training she started to notice tiny
spots within the bright red areas.

"The dark spots, as you move from each image," Artemis said.

"They move, they shift just a little."

"You're good for a med mal girl," Dr. Langendorpher said. She
double-clicked the computer mouse to blowup the cranial scan image.
"Those things are the size of human cells, almost undetectable. I think
what you see are microbots, fueled by either a magnetic field, or a laser
system. A sort of solar energy panel on the roof of a house, but in this case,
microscopic."

Artemis leaned in closer next to Dr. Langendorpher. She watched
in horror as the dust like spots move like tiny spiders across Laina's
brain matter.

"Why?" Artemis said. She held her breath and blinked her

eyelids. "What do you expect?"

"I think someone," Dr. Langendorpher said. She picked up on some nearby movement, some random conversations within the laboratory. She quickly closed the Laina's patient file. She turned toward Artemis. "Someone is using those things to monitor Laina, not just her vital signs. I think someone's building a base line from her body."

"The mushrooms," Artemis said. She turned toward the door as the nearby conversation grew louder. "Genetically modified, so are the spores, quite specific?"

"We should take a walk," Dr. Langendorpher said. She turned off the computer screen, she got up acknowledged a lab tech who was prepping a patient. "I hope you enjoyed the tour, Artemis. Let's walk into the hallway."

Dr. Langendorpher had her hands inside her white lab coat's pockets. She acknowledged her colleagues, blew a kiss over at the haggard nurses, and orderlies.

"She's been a lab rat, for sure," Artemis said. "Like you said, I'm lost."

"It's someone skilled in surgery inserted a monitor in Laina's right hand, between the thumb and her forefinger," Dr. Langendorpher said. She squeezed the spot within her own wrinkled hand. "This is the spot, leave it alone. It's their poker tell; It'll lead you back to them."

"They are tracking Laina," Artemis said.

"You need to be careful," Dr. Langendorpher said. She stopped walking and touched Artemis' forearm. "Unless I missed something, they'll want their pet back. Those microbots are dying, slow, but steady. They need energy, do you hear me?"

"I hear you," Artemis said. She smelled the disinfected environment; she stared down the busy, well-lit gray marble hallway. "I won't note the claim files, but I'll tell this to Wylie."

"Yeah, I think you should, just for your own protection," Dr. Langendorpher said. She started to scamper along. "Let's act like I was just practicing some safe clinical experiments, just to see how the machine worked, nothing more, you know, for a healthy patient, got the kid a baseline and all."

"Noted," Artemis said. "You're so kind."

A crowd of focused care givers hustled by them as Dr. Langendorpher stopped and gripped Artemis' left forearm.

"Be careful, hear me?" Dr. Langendorpher said. She glanced up and down the hallway suspicious, uncertain. She gripped Artemis' forearm with a clear intention. "Like I said, this is a sophisticated outfit. I think Laina's in danger. I can feel it. And I suspect she's not the only one, and by the way, you'll be right there with her."

"It's my job," Artemis said. She stepped back and shook Dr. Langendorpher's hand. "Thank you, I'll keep Wylie up to date."

"Don't stress, he'll call me anyway," Dr. Langendorpher said.

She walked away, briefly glancing back at Artemis, and she disappeared down a side hallway.

Artemis left the medical facility. She pondered Satan's comments, the wooden whistle and wondered if she were, in a strange reality Satan's lab rat lost inside an invisible evil labyrinth that Dante could never have imagined.

Chapter 20

"Is this Ms. Lamb? A Ms. Artemis Lamb?" A voice said from Artemis' smartphone speaker. The voice had a heavy southern accent with a slight twangy elongated vibration at the end of the sentence.

"Yes," Artemis said. Her scalp tingled from a dreadful expectation. The phone number on her smartphone screen was from central Kentucky. "Who are you?"

"Glad we found you, oh heavens me," the voice said. "I'm Mrs. Patti Thompson with Child Protective Services, here in Kentucky. We received an anonymous inquiry from our hotline about you and a child named, Laina Lynn."

"Sorry," Artemis said. She started to pace. "I don't understand?"

"You have a child, Laina Lynn?" Mrs. Thompson said.

"Yes," Artemis said. She shifted in front of her apartment windows. "She's safe. I'll protect her."

"I have no doubt," Mrs. Thompson said. "But, we have laws here, you are aware you can't pick up a child off the street, and take the child without working with our system. It's about protecting the child. I'm sure you appreciate my position."

Artemis looked up at her apartments skip trowel ceiling texture.

"I'm not about to break any laws, I do," Artemis said. She sucked in a deep breath. "I've helped her out, her mother died. I suspect you know this."

"Yes, I understand you," Mrs. Thompson said. "That's our understanding, hospital informed us, the mother's cremated, mercifully, you know. I feel for the child."

"I get it, I'm not a kidnapper," Artemis said. "Have you found any next of kin, aunt, uncle, someone close to her father?"

"Not yet," Mrs. Thompson said. "But, we'll need you to bring Laina back, we must have a hearing. We have a process to follow, you understand?"

Artemis searched her apartment for a clear plan; she dreaded what was about to happen down to her bones. Her joints ached.

"I'll comply," Artemis said, dryly. "What am I to do?"

"You've kept the girl?" Wylie said. He sat up straight on his high back office chair. "How's this got to do with the file?"

"Weird coincidence," Artemis said. "You know it."

"I do," Wylie said. He held his wrinkled hands up. "I need more information, or I'll take you off this file. I need your full attention."

"I realize that," Artemis said. "The girl has no one, and being Benjamin's child, cut me some slack."

Wylie sat back and nodded.

"All right, girl, but you can't just keep her, it's illegal," Wylie said. "But you realize that general counsel, Gene something or other, he hates you. I suspect he's your mole. Been complaining up north, he stopped calling me. But to them and me, it means you're doing your job."

"He's a drunk," Artemis said. "He's easy to manage. I have a hearing, for Laina. I'll get this resolved."

"I get it," Wylie said. "Sorry, I have to let them think I grilled you, told you to focus, you realize that?"

"I do," Artemis said. "I'm duly informed."

"So, that's over with," Wylie said. He smirked. He blew her a kiss. "I don't ask about your personal life, tell me about the boy, and his child. I'll help you out if need be, Dr. Langendorpher loved her. Said she's a sweet little jewel."

Artemis sat down. She stared down at the carpeted office floor for several minutes. She wiped away the tears.

"After my parents' accident," Artemis said. She stared behind Wylie at a common office picture within a silver frame. "I fled into a hole. I learned to enjoy being alone. Got out of college, recruited me in, so I went all military. I was a good medic. I was."

"Scary stuff," Wylie said. "I believe you."

"Yeah, once big bullets whizz by your skull, changes how you view things," Artemis said. She gulped. "Anyway, I met him over in Afghanistan. He was a good solider, a born leader."

"I take it was a tragic romance?" Wylie said.

"Correct, but he just understood me," Artemis said. She grinned as her eyes watered. "He loved my red hair, told me to keep my helmet on to avoid snipers. I thought he was funny. Well, I didn't need his help given my other job."

Wylie got up and walked around his desk and sat on the twin side-chair and across from Artemis.

"Go on," Wylie said. "That desk gets in the way. We're just talkin'."

Artemis closed her eyes, she whispered a prayer to a being she never understood, or assumed never existed. She realized if Satan existed, perhaps an all powerful force existed. But her mind swirled with conflict. She needed facts.

"We were in a forward position," Artemis said. "Word came back, we moved in for support, hit them with air power. Tough job."

"You don't need, to," Wylie said before Artemis held up her right hand to cut him off. "None of my business."

"Let me just say it, so you'll understand," Artemis said. She blew oxygen into her lungs and back out from her quivering lips. "I get emotional, I allow it. My mother taught me to allow it and then let it go. Clears my mind. Well, I found him. They had leaned him against an ASV's tire, sniper, got him in the neck."

"Oh damn," Wylie said. He crinkled his face. "I'm sorry dear."

"Blood was everywhere, the firing stopped. After, his team stood there crying, guns pointed down," Artemis said. "He just went limp. I lost him, never loved anyone like him. It's life."

"Says a lot," Wylie said. "Hardened tough guys cry for you."

"All I could do was hold him," Artemis said. "Too late, he died staring up at me. I was powerless, Wylie. I hate that feeling."

Wylie and Artemis sat together in silence. Minutes that seemed longer to Artemis as she remembered Benjamin's handsome face, his kind eyes, and his courageous hazel eyed gaze as he slipped from life into the spirit world.

"I'll come help you," Wylie said. "If need be?"

"No," Artemis said. She stood up. "I'll do my job. I'll get back up there, sort through this mess."

"Come here," Wylie said. He got up, and he hugged Artemis. He clutched her shoulders. "Be careful, my friend. This old man's not dead yet. If I need to, I'll be there."

"I hope so," Artemis said. "Thank you. But I'll handle this, I always have, you taught me well to investigate med-mal. But I have other skills that I need to deploy, so let me go."

Wylie walked back behind his desk.

"Just be careful," Wylie said. He shifted about his family photos set across his credenza. "I don't know why I fiddle with these stinkin' pictures when I get nervous. Go get the job done, and back here."

"Why are you being cryptic?" Artemis said.

"Instinct," Wylie said. "And the fact FBI's been up there poking around, which I take it, you realize things get back to me?"

"I do," Artemis said. "Sorry, I kept quiet, not sure where they're headed."

"Get up there, I'll play stupid," Wylie said. "I talked with Dr. Langendorpher."

"Not surprised," Artemis said.

"Your little girl is part of this," Wylie said. He glanced at Artemis. He nodded. "Follow her, they want that child back. And I bet, if you go say hello to this Dr. Demetrius, we'll get our answers. After, I think you'll find your mess waiting for you."

"You're right," Artemis said. She started to leave the office.

"What was the accident?" Wylie said. He looked back over at Artemis. He sat down on his office chair.

"Pardon?" Artemis said. She held the doorknob turned down without opening the door.

"Your parents, you've never told me," Wylie said. "What was the accident that took them?"

"Oh, gas leak, just bad luck," Artemis said. She shrugged. "I was away, teenager, summer camp. The police said they died in their sleep. They never woke up."

Wylie glossed his hands across the desktop. He flopped files on top of files. He repositioned his flat panel computer screens.

"In a way," Wylie said. "A merciful death, to go to sleep and not awake."

"I guess," Artemis said. She twisted the doorknob. "I've never worried about money; they took care of me. I miss them every day. But I never got to say goodbye. That fact bugs me. A cruel twist."

"Maybe you'll see them again," Wylie said. "In Heaven."

"Stop it," Artemis said. "I'm not a true believer, you know that. I think there's something out there, beyond us, just not a dude winding all the clocks."

"Well, I guess we'll both find out," Wylie said. He waved over at Artemis to encourage her to leave. "Some day. And get back home."

Chapter 21

"What are you really doing?"

Dr. Demetrius stood up from behind the fancy conference room table. He waved over for Gene to remain behind with Loretta.

"Have I ever taken you for a tour of my lab?" Dr. Demetrius said to Artemis. "It's remarkable. Even by my standards."

"No," Artemis said. She glanced over at the despondent Gene and his lackey, Loretta. "But I guess I'm about to."

"You sure?" Gene said. He started to stand up. "I think unwise."

"You stay, Gene. I'm in charge. Follow me Artemis," Dr. Demetrius said. He swung open the conference room door. Artemis followed him out and into the hospital's main hallways. He grinned over at Artemis as he strode down the hospital's internal avenues, and toward the door for his mushroom farm.

"I guess we're back to the farm?" Artemis said. "Do I need a respirator?"

"No," Dr. Demetrius said. He covered his nose and mouth with his hand. "Just walk, hurry, cover your nose, we'll be fine."

They went inside the darkness, the vast room hummed with drone activity, and at the end of the massive room, Dr. Demetrius pressed his thumb into a finger imprint device as simultaneously his left eyeball was scanned by a biometrical laser. The solid-state door disengaged the lock, and it popped open as if to exhale its last breath. But Artemis turned from an instinctual nudge and looked behind her at a little spirit girl. She said,

"Artemis, I see you. I know you'll protect me." And she smiled and giggled and hid within an empty bin. The little spirit girl was alone, mischievous, peeking above the bin for answers. But there were no other wandering spirits in the room to guide her toward a crease in visible light. Artemis frowned aware she was powerless to help her. She waved over at the spirit girl in hopes she didn't feel isolated. But it occurred to Artemis that Satan blocked the child from moving on, a warning it tortured for sport. It tortured children. Artemis turned.

"What is this?" Artemis said. After she stepped inside, uncovered her nose as she stood behind Dr. Demetrius.

"Want to go on a trip?" Dr. Demetrius said. He pointed over toward a laboratory table. A black granite top with a double sink, an arched silver faucet with two gas hookups at the rectangular end. A nearby Bunsen burner waited for gas and a light. "Those mushrooms over there will take you on a trip without ever leaving, and those over there, will kill you, after you go into liver failure."

"Are you obsessed with mushrooms?" Artemis said. She crossed her arms to ensure she touched nothing on the workstations or refrigeration cabinets. Concerned Dr. Demetrius might leave an invisible bacterial trap for her that would penetrate her skin. "What do you plan to do with these?"

"For now," Dr. Demetrius said. He strolled farther into the square laboratory space. "Nothing but testing, my real love is the mycelia, the structure underneath the mushroom. I think that's the answer for humanity, for the world's population."

Artemis watched Dr. Demetrius point at different mushroom varieties. He took out a sharp-edged gardening tool and with great care, surgical, he opened the rich potting soil surface within one of the larger mushroom containers.

"What am I looking at?" Artemis said.

"See there," Dr. Demetrius said. He disturbed a ghost white network of what Artemis thought looked like tree roots and a delicate veinous system. "This allows life, it's almost like humans circulatory systems, examine there, the main artery and all the offshoots?"

"Yes, I get what you're saying," Artemis said. She started to reconsider what she had seen with Virgil and Agent Beaky out deep in the forest. And what Satan had shown her. "What is it?"

"Mycelia," Dr. Demetrius said. He peeled it back with the gardening tool. He held the fibrous network on his fingertips. "Glide your finger over them."

Artemis hesitated, she stepped backward.

"I don't think so," Artemis said. "No."

"They don't bite," Dr. Demetrius said. With his right hand he gripped Artemis' forearm. "Just touch them. Use your fingertip. I want you to sense something about my mycelia. This unique secret, my discovery."

Artemis was cautious, she hesitated, but touched the organism above Dr. Demetrius' finger. It felt like a pile of worms pushing through the dark brown soil after a summer storm.

"That was weird," Artemis said. "Like wiggly worms."

"They are alive," Dr. Demetrius said. He smiled as he slid his fingers back and covered over the soil. Gently patting it down. "Let me repair my invasion, but this one needs time to grow and nurture her offspring."

Artemis scanned the laboratory. It had been cleaned and wiped down in every nearby work station to where the chrome surfaces almost sparkled under the tubular lights. To her left, the laboratory had more work areas hidden in darkness down a long tiled walkway. A line of metal top-heavy isolation machines with thick viewing panels and glove-ports set next to each other waiting for the next experiment.

"Does this have anything to do with the hospital?" Artemis said. "You all have a serious claim, reason I'm here."

Dr. Demetrius appeared to ignore Artemis' question as he lovingly repaired his digging marks within the wet soil. He glided his fingers over the area like a master pastry chef glossing over a cake with dark brown icing.

"Better now, my darling?" Dr. Demetrius said toward the soil and tiny mushroom bulbs. "See Artemis, they can feel my presence, your presence, they can sense your feelings. This one needs to go into the farm and get cared for and monitored. A mushroom's purpose is to reproduce, to share its spore. It's about survival."

"You're truly obsessed with mushrooms," Artemis said.

Dr. Demetrius stood up tall, and he grinned over at Artemis. He nodded at her as he walked over toward a deep sink and washed his hands. He encouraged Artemis to follow his example, and she washed her hands.

"Can never be too careful," Dr. Demetrius said. "You know, that's how they discovered penicillin, by accident, the fungi was left to roam in a hospital, Saint Mary's in London."

"I don't understand?" Artemis said. She wiped her hands dry. "What are you telling me?"

"Antibiotics, it's obvious," Dr. Demetrius said. He grunted. "What are humans becoming immune to?"

"Oh, I don't know," Artemis said. She sensed Dr. Demetrius' dismissive comment was her way inside his mind. "Sorry, I'm not that smart, like you."

"I know," Dr. Demetrius said. He started to strut down the laboratory corridor with Artemis following. "It was a man, Alexander Fleming, 1928. He left his bacteria, streptococcus alone in his lab. And perhaps a simple open window, allowed fungi to find his bacteria samples, and it did what fungi spores do, it needed to survive, so, it ate the bacteria, killing it."

"Let me see if I can catchup," Artemis said. She was certain now something connected the cult in the forest to Dr. Demetrius. But, it was too obvious there was something else. "Your team, you, they are working to discover new antibiotics?"

"To protect human kind," Dr. Demetrius said. "The hospital system lucked out to recruit me here. They allow me freedom to experiment as I wish without interference, my budget, I get zero pushback."

"No accidents here, all these stations, swept clean?" Artemis said. "Eliminate any random bacteria, viral or other."

"Exactly, HEPA filtration," Dr. Demetrius said. "I cannot allow a discovery to just happen like some all powerful god granted me magic power, or other nonsense. I'll unlock the fungi secrets all with my brain and insight."

"Where are we going?" Artemis said. She scanned farther down the corridor at the side-by-side chrome finished doors sealed in thick black rubber.

"You've seen my farm," Dr. Demetrius said. "This is my lab area, but now, I'll show you where I keep all my children. A place to grow before I share them with the farm."

"Children?" Artemis said.

Dr. Demetrius patted Artemis on her shoulder.

"In a way," Dr. Demetrius said. He smirked and shrugged. "I know I'm obsessed. I'm excited to show you my passion. Forgive me."

"Thanks for sharing," Artemis said.

They stopped in front of a tall refrigeration door. Dr. Demetrius pulled open a side panel, he slipped on latex gloves and opened a sealed packet. He gave Artemis a pair of gloves and an identical packet.

"We need to suit up," Dr. Demetrius said. "Cover your shoes and put on this germ proof suit."

"Ah, respirator time again," Artemis said. She peeled back the packet opening.

"Quite," Dr. Demetrius said. He put on the pale green suit, hooded his head, positioned his protective glasses, and respirator while Artemis did the same. He examined Artemis and inspected her respirator and any potential coverage gaps. "Good, you're covered, now we can enter."

"You aren't kidding around," Artemis said.

"No, I am not," Dr. Demetrius said. He pressed in a passcode hidden within a covered side chamber. "This door will open, and then you will be in the presence of my children. Do not touch any surface, anything, do you understand?"

"Yes," Artemis said. She waited for the door.

The door released the locking mechanism with a low clink. He pushed the door inward. A water mist was being sprayed over a round metal plat-form with drainage ports that Dr. Demetrius stepped onto, he held up his arms, and then waved for Artemis to follow his example as he stepped across hidden by the gray mist.

"I try to keep as much contamination out as possible," Dr. Demetrius said. Artemis followed him farther into the room. "But spores, fungi, they are aggressive and microscopic creatures."

"It's quiet in here," Artemis said. "Weird."

"Yes," Dr. Demetrius said. "Inside this low-light, my experiments are in their infant stage, just beginning to grow and to form. It's like a nursery."

"You have them all sealed off?" Artemis said.

"Not quite," Dr. Demetrius said. "We filter the oxygen as best we can, nothing escapes this room, but it's not a perfect closed loop. I think that's impossible for my purposes."

"When do you expose them to bacteria?" Artemis said.

"Smart," Dr. Demetrius said. He pointed farther down toward another laboratory area within the center of the chambered rooms. "Down there, we take bacteria, some are dangerous, there we share mushroom varietals, and then we wait."

Artemis examined the empty laboratory surrounded by sealed mush-room lockers. It appeared like a room for a detective to interrogate a crim-inal down at a police station.

"Place a dish with the bacteria on the table," Artemis said. "And, one of these?"

"Exactly," Dr. Demetrius said. He looked up and down the hallway at his experiments. "If my children kill the bacteria, I know I'm discovering, altering its gnome, the mycelia become stronger, resistant. I make minor alterations to their genetic code."

Artemis remembered the helpless lamb from the forest. She looked at a long line of emerging mushrooms.

"How do you fertilize them?" Artemis said. She closed her eyes as she was certain she would not get a truthful answer, but she was certain she had discovered the truth. "They need more than just moisture."

"Ah, you have as the cliché," Dr. Demetrius said. He glanced back Artemis. "A green thumb?"

"I used to like to grow my food," Artemis said. She crossed her arms as she sensed her heart beating faster. "Not in downtown St. Pete, not an option, but I wish I could."

"Okay, I think I follow," Dr. Demetrius said. He sounded suspicious. "Always know the source for food; it's the source, it's where the magic happens."

"You have an array of mushrooms growing inside," Artemis said. "What's your secret?"

"Now, now Artemis, I'll perhaps let you know that some day," Dr. Demetrius said. "But consider, with the discovery of new antibiotics, or better, someday I'll influence the mycelia to create human organs, we'd alter humanity. Lungs created from your DNA, bespoke to your genetic needs."

"You have a vast mind for these things," Artemis said. And then she sensed Laina's mother was nearby. It was not a spirit. It was a powerful sensation that she understood what was Dr. Demetrius' secret fertilizer. "It's what we eat. Right?"

"It's the mycelia, they are voracious, it's the saprotrophic fungi, they allow the world to grow, by eliminating the dead," Dr. Demetrius said. He shifted and turned around walking toward the exit door. "Let's get out of here, my children need quiet time, they need to feed."

"I have never seen such a thing," Artemis said with a whisper.

"Artemis, it's like a government, or a religion, think about it," Dr. Demetrius said. He started to stroll back toward the platform and the ghostly mist. "It's in front of you, it's obvious, but what it's doing is hidden underground. It eats away your soul. It alters society without a shot."

"You are a mysterious man," Artemis said. Behind her respirator and protective eyeglasses, she was blank faced, puzzled by all the emotions and thoughts crowded into the same space within her mind. "What am I to do about these claims, you have a lot of dead patients."

"Oh, back to your investigation," Dr. Demetrius said. He huffed. "I'm not a lawyer, but they need evidence. I don't think they have any evidence, do they?"

"Not yet," Artemis said. "I think that's a key point. They have theories based on the medical records."

"That's your job," Dr. Demetrius said. "To protect my and the hospital's interests?"

"Yes," Artemis said.

And from a place beyond reason, from beyond space and time, Artemis heard Satan cackling.

Chapter 22

"I'm not sure how to say this?"

"Milady," Agent Beaky said. He glanced over at Jerome Jenkins. He twisted his legs toward Artemis. "Best way, say it out straight."

"I'm curious why I'm even here? Or better, why you two are in my office," Jerome Jenkins said. He sat behind his office desk staring over at Artemis and then over at Agent Beaky. "What am I to make of you two?"

Artemis sucked in a deep, reflective breath. She held the breath for several heartbeats and huffed it down toward the pastel-colored rug. Her vision swirled with a strange peripheral haze.

"She called me," Agent Beaky said. He held his hands up.

"I need your help," Artemis said. "Both of you."

"What?" Jerome said. "Never had a medical malpractice talking head ask me for help. Unless it involves the child?"

"Well then," Agent Beaky said. He wiggled on the office chair. "I'll not be too proud, sing away."

"I have to be careful. I'm under an NDA. And I don't want to get fired. I like my work, and adhering to an ethical standard," Artemis said. She paused. "Cameras are everywhere in this town. I'm always being watched. You both know that."

And Artemis heard Satan whispering in her mind.

"Yes," Satan said. "You are always being watched, go ahead, tell them your little secret. Things will get even funnier. This journey has turned out better than my plan."

"Let's keep this moving along," Jerome said. He crossed his arms. "My desk is covered over with work to do. I don't get paid a salary."

Artemis acknowledged Jerome's comment. She sat forward with her elbows on her knees.

"It's always the addict," Artemis said. "Fentanyl, opioids, right? They die and nobody cares about them."

Agent Beaky and Jerome Jenkins stared at each other for several moments. And they nodded at each other as if they had switched a bright light on to reveal a hidden truth left in plain sight.

"I'm confident where you're headed," Jerome said. He leaned forward on to his desktop. He twirled an ink pen between his fingers. "Let's play a little game. So if asked under oath, you did not reveal propriety evidence. I'll ask you questions, Artemis, and you can say yes, no or maybe, fair?"

"Yeah," Artemis said. Inside her mouth, her tongue glided across her front teeth and remained glued to the spot. "Ask what you want. I'll try to play along. I don't have any hard evidence, but my sensations are raw and sickening."

"Good, I suppose," Jerome said. He tapped his forefinger over his lips. "No one cares about a dead addict?"

"I would say, yes," Artemis said. "That's true. I don't think it's unique to this town."

"It would be a good idea to add," Jerome said. "Several new ICU beds? For those in need, poor addicts. Happen to get paid coming and going, it's a business coincidence?"

"Yeah," Artemis said. She nodded. "It would be important to keep your options open."

"Let me see now," Agent Beaky said. He leaned over onto the sharp corner of Jerome's desk. "Not losing out on any government money, as it were, crying shame not to offer services."

Artemis looked over at Agent Beaky. She nodded.

"Smart criminal," Jerome said. He sighed. "Would figure out a method to cause the evidence to disappear?"

"Easy now," Agent Beaky said. "I'll not look the other way for what I'm getting the hint."

"I appreciate that," Artemis said. "But I'm not sure where I would hide my evidence if I were a criminal."

"They don't ship just mushrooms?" Jerome said. "Other things."

"No," Artemis said. "A growing product menu. I'm amazed how science stumbles into creating body parts from rotting tissue."

"Mushrooms need rich soil," Jerome said. "They need a good place to grow, moisture, fertilizer?"

"Careful," Agent Beaky said. "I don't like your tone."

"Yeah," Artemis said. "I would imagine that's the magic. But I've not earned a PhD in mycology."

Jerome pushed back from his desk. He pondered what Artemis said, and what she had not said. He stared out his office's side windows with his hands over his paunch. The window's square muntins shared no white paint strays with the clear reflective glass that blocked out the gray, cloudy afternoon. The painter had been clean and precise when the home was rehabilitated into a welcoming office setting.

"Medical records," Jerome said. He pinched his right earlobe. "They don't always tell the story, just snippets, points and dates in time?"

"Yes," Artemis said.

"But they provide proof, let's say," Jerome said. "A human being existed and was in fact within a hospital?"

"Yes," Artemis said. "And if the records are perfect. It might be easy to prove they were, at least, treated."

"I guess, it's about Narcissus' weak spot?" Jerome said.

"Pardon?" Agent Beaky said Jerome.

"Wait for it," Jerome said. He waved Agent Beaky back. "Ego, pride's a deadly sin, slithers up and bites."

"Yes," Artemis said. "An Achilles heel."

"What if, just asking, you got inside this narcissist's inner sanctum?" Jerome said. "Happened to spot things Narcissus meant to keep hidden. But that darn ego."

"Yes," Artemis said. "Just a sensation, nothing hard."

"Sloppy," Agent Beaky said. "If I follow, not a good move."

"Difficult to get any useful proof?" Jerome said. "Hard to get inside without a warning shot from a local, cameras, passcodes. It's all clamped down under constant surveillance."

"Yes," Artemis said. She pondered for several moments staring over at Jerome and back over at Agent Beaky. And Satan whispered in her mind.

"Go ahead," Satan said. "Offer them the bait, it will make this so much fun. Your performance is meaningful, moving. I feel your authentic do-gooder spirit. You assassin."

"Artemis," Jerome said. "I'm a man of my word, we are dancing with the devil, and more like, a murder?"

"I don't think, murder," Artemis said. She clutched her backpack's arm straps. "I don't. But more of a composting issue after the fact."

"I'll keep my cool," Agent Beaky said. He grunted as he frowned. "We can't show up on a hunting expedition without a warrant and basic evidence. Judge would laugh us out of the courtroom."

"And our friends across the way, they are proud of their green initiatives, but," Jerome said. He fidgeted with the ink pen. "They would wipe down the facility until it sparkled, and that would be the end of our expedition. My cases would all die."

Artemis surged up off the office chair. She treaded toward the office's six-panel door with a polished brass knob and three hinges. She gripped the cold knob and opened the door and closed it.

"The little girl," Artemis said. "They turned me in. I have to turn her over to child protective services."

"I was waiting for this, keep the door open, it is a bit warm in here," Jerome said. He shifted onto his left elbow. "Gene reminds me of an old west huckster peddling tonic water out the back of a chuck wagon. Corrupt, vindictive and full of greed."

"It had to be him," Artemis said. "He's in this mess."

"Little girl?" Agent Beaky said. He sighed. "Is she well?"

"She's still alive?" Jerome said. He winced. "Right?"

"Yes," Artemis said. She stepped back and gripped the office chair's backrest. "I have her. For now. Nervous about this hearing."

Jerome sat back, swiveled back and forth with his office chair staring up at the plaster ceiling. He stopped and pushed forward.

"You have a confidential claim file?" Jerome said to Agent Beaky. "The cult activities. So forth."

Agent Beaky wiggled his eyebrows and smiled. He crossed his legs and arms into a safe cocoon.

"A connection to our show out in the forest?" Agent Beaky said. He sneered. "I've been reporting in, but it's been getting static back. They are starting to question my sanity. The smartphone video turned out grainy and dark, not much help or evidence."

"Strange, the same thing happened to the video I took," Artemis said. She glanced over at Agent Beaky. "So, I don't have any facts. Not sure it'd be safe to go digging out there in the forest without an army."

"And we have a little lab rat?" Jerome said. "I've heard rumors. Our prideful friend has been playing with the mice's genome."

"Yes, I'm positive," Artemis said. She nodded back over at Jerome.

"The real rat's been experimenting with the little innocent mice. They track the mice's vitals and movements."

"I recognize what to do, this conversation ends," Jerome said. He surged up from behind his desk. His hands on his waist. "Where's the girl?"

"With me, like I said, for now," Artemis said. "But soon, I have a court hearing. I'll need a lawyer, got a referral?"

"I'll help," Jerome said. He gripped his readers dangling on his chest. "You have court documents for my review?"

"That might seem unusual," Agent Beaky said. He leaned against the desk. "Perhaps an outside counsel? Might seem an ethical dilemma if you appeared. And would draw attention to our relationship."

Jerome nodded over at Agent Beaky.

"At this point, we should be cautious," Jerome said. "I don't like this whole setup."

"I'll reach inside our legal panel," Artemis said. "We have a lot of lawyers willing to help me in hopes we give them files."

"Even so," Jerome said. "Keep me informed. I recommend someone local, so forth."

And Artemis heard Satan laughing and chuckling. "Oh, Artemis. Please go on. You kill me, but you can't, I'm Satan my humble assassin sweetheart. I hate you."

Chapter 23

"Tell me about these death cases."

"I'm not sure what you're asking me," Dr. Demetrius said. He shrugged holding his hands up. "It's a hospital, people are born, we heal most, but manage, if you will, death. Cycle of life."

"Yes," Gene said. His puffy hands typed on his tablet without looking over at Artemis. "EHRs all in line, up to date, what's missing in your mind, Ms. Lamb?"

"They appear way too clean," Artemis said. She stared over at Gene. "What would a plaintiff lawyer conclude?"

"We follow national standards," Gene said. He glanced up with his unposed lazy eyes. He shrugged. "They've got nothing but here-say, good luck with that, correct Dr. Demetrius?"

"True, I appreciate the enterprise being in line with the national record keeping push," Artemis said. She leaned back on the conference room chair. She glanced over at Dr. Demetrius. "But I think most had addiction issues, opioids, so forth, I've read it's an epidemic here?"

Dr. Demetrius unbuttoned his lab coat. He pushed his elbows forward across the shiny conference table.

"Blame it on us Greeks?" Dr. Demetrius said. He smirked.

"I don't understand?" Artemis said.

"You learn anything about Greek myth?" Dr. Demetrius said while steadily holding his gaze at Artemis. "I love your short, red hair, you look like you could have been a warrior goddess."

Artemis sensed his unwelcome advance. The truth hidden behind Dr. Demetrius' dark eyes. She looked back over at Gene who had ignored the comment.

"Let's be professional," Artemis said. She stared at Dr. Demetrius. "Right? Go on."

"I meant no offense," Dr. Demetrius said. His hands up. "Besides, I'm stating the obvious, so forgive me for being honest."

"Let's keep moving this," Gene said. He rolled his right hand forward in a circular pattern. "Greek myth?"

Artemis pointed her gaze over toward Gene to encourage Dr. Demetrius to continue with his comments. She pursed her lips and let the creepy comment pass along into history.

"Story of Adonis, he was a beautiful young man," Dr. Demetrius said. He smiled as he opened his arms. "Loved by Aphrodite and Prosperone, but he had a rather unfortunate accident with a wild boar, it killed him. He bled out from a horn impact into his thigh. It was hemorrhagic shock."

"So?" Gene said.

"Exsanguination," Artemis said. "He died in minutes."

"Yes, very good, Artemis. In fact, some scholars think the goddess Artemis took him out as spite against Aphrodite," Dr. Demetrius said. He laughed and hummed. "But, thanks to Zeus, Adonis moved from the living, to the dead in Hades, and back to the living."

"I'm not following you," Artemis said.

"But you understand life and death, my point," Dr. Demetrius said. "Experts offered that Aphrodite's tears after Adonis' death created the poppy plant. The Greeks used the poppy plant for a variety of purposes from antiquity."

"I'm clueless?" Gene said. He searched Artemis for ideas and over at Dr. Demetrius. He loosened his red tie and unbuttoned his baby blue dress shirt collar. "Where are we going?"

"People, catch up, the opioid crisis has been a problem for thousands of years," Dr. Demetrius said. He waved Gene away with the back of his left hand. "People have pain, physicians prescribe, for example, fentanyl. We use it for anesthesia without negative outcomes. But when it is used in the wrong way, we end up with addicts coming to our facility usually inside emergency transport."

"I understand now," Gene said. He tapped his hand on the conference table. He leaned over at Artemis. "We have to help them either way, you understand? They are God's children."

"Thus, all the additional ICU beds?" Artemis said.

"It's the logical move," Dr. Demetrius said. He sat back. "We cannot add beds, for certain services without government approval, it's nonsense to me. Get them any bed you want, either way we do everything in our power to help them, to heal them."

"It's how we manage healthcare, we need a certificate of need," Gene said. He scratched his head. "I don't make up the rules, community standards. The state must approve our services from a needs assessment; it's a formal process. You know the process."

"I get it," Artemis said. She paused for several moments staring down at her tablet. The screen was dark having timed out fifteen minutes earlier.

"What are you thinking about?" Gene said.

Dr. Demetrius leaned his head on his right hand like a bored teenager stuck in a high school civics class.

"I'm not sure how it looks," Artemis said. "The hospital gets paid for care either way. Prescribing, pain meds gets the patient hooked. And then treating them as addicts, when they return, might expose us. An easy avenue for an attorney to make a case. You both follow what I'm saying."

"It's all about the data, we can support our services," Gene said. His lazy eye ogled over at a former CEO's portrait. "We make a healthy profit for our, not for profit."

"Should I work for free?" Dr. Demetrius said. "My research has taken great steps forward. I'd hate to move on, I like it here. But I'll not be a part of this political game."

"This is my job," Artemis said. She closed her tablet. "I consider the medical facts, the outcomes, against what a lawyer might plead in a court of law."

"This is about money," Dr. Demetrius said.

"It is," Artemis said.

"Ms. Lamb," Gene said. He coughed. "If we don't make a profit, we go out of business. Dr. Demetrius cannot advance science, healthcare without those resources. All we do is react to what is happening in society, and yet, we are to blame?"

"I'm not saying, or expressing that," Artemis said. She wondered how Gene had finished college. "You know that, but we have a nasty global claim to defend. I think he's fishing, for now. He keeps bringing up the trucks?"

"I see," Dr. Demetrius said. He drums tapped his hands on the table. "Have you not taken Artemis over to our processing facility?"

"Ah, no we have not," Gene said. "I don't see how that applies to these medical malpractice claims."

"But, it's part of your facility," Artemis said. "That we reinsure above your minuscule self-insured retention."

Gene scowled over at Artemis. He pressed his left earlobe with his thumb and forefinger.

"Let it go," Dr. Demetrius said. He pushed his hands downward. "Breathe my chubby friend. Breathe."

"It's top secret," Gene said. "I don't care if the locals wonder. I just don't want to invite outside interests. They'll get a sniff to our work, a lot of money is at stake."

"The world will eventually find out after they approve my patents," Dr. Demetrius said. "You know that?"

"Tell her," Gene said. "I cannot stop you."

Dr. Demetrius' eyes opened wide as he grinned over at Artemis.

"What is the largest organism in the world?" Dr. Demetrius said as he excitedly looked back over at Artemis. "It's impressive."

"No clue," Gene said. "She'll have not a clue, that's been, until now, our secret."

Artemis remained quiet and allowed them to talk. Get the client or plaintiff talking and shut up, and listen.

"I've told you this," Dr. Demetrius said over at Gene.

"Well, I must have forgotten," Gene said. He shook his head. He glanced over at Artemis. "Why are we going down this worm hole?"

"It's my work, that's why," Dr. Demetrius said. "You all make a lot of money while I'm saving the planet. One plant at a time."

"Someone might misunderstand those plants," Gene said. "I'm saying, I'm not judging. I'll leave that to the master, to god the father."

"Why?" Artemis said.

It was the best question and the simplest question. Dr. Demetrius and Gene instantly locked onto Artemis.

"Tell her," Gene said. He huffed. "She'll keep quiet."

"I know," Dr. Demetrius said. His wide toothed movie star smile was his poker tell. His white teeth shone with ego. "Part of the Amanita genus, my mushrooms. But it's really the mycelia. It's not the mushrooms; they are her fruit, it's the mother ship, underneath that matters."

"You lost me," Artemis said. "You showed me your fungus, they creep me out. But I'm a simple claim handler."

"For example, in Oregon," Dr. Demetrius said. "A mycelia have grown under the ground, better than two thousand miles in diameter, deep within a dense forest. It feeds off the living and dead trees, and the rot, amazing."

Artemis realized that Satan was nearby her. It was as if something, or someone was clapping their hands together in a childlike manner in her mind. "I'm in the details."

"GMOs, legal products," Gene said. He pointed at Dr. Demetrius. "We are selling samples; It's an active online business that the system has kept secret. It's non-public, only invited bio-technology, universities, mind you. We account for the revenue as medically related, for now. But, in time, we must make an announcement."

"It's amazing," Dr. Demetrius said. "I can hardly sleep. I'm discovering a whole universe."

"Genetically modified organisms?" Artemis said. Her eyes started to look down at the table and move back and forth as she processed the information. "Mycelia? The stuff you showed me in your lab."

"Exactly," Dr. Demetrius said. "How do you feed the world, enrich the Earth's soil? The answer is mycelia; the mushrooms are my darlings fruit; it's that simple. It's laughable that we walk over them, it's all under our feet."

"To be clear, these are safe mushrooms, and," Gene said. He sort of focused his lazy eyeball over at Artemis. "This has nothing to do with a malpractice claim?"

Artemis acknowledged Gene's comment.

"The trucks breed questions," Artemis said. "That's all I'm saying, it's obvious."

"We know," Dr. Demetrius said. "But, it's none of their business. The staff keep quiet; otherwise, they'll be unemployed. It's not a good place to be unemployed."

"Jobs are tough to come by, here," Gene said. He squinted.

"I gather that," Artemis said. "What else should I know about your research? Hospital might get state visitors, look at your licenses, if you're not careful."

"Dr. Demetrius," Gene said. "Remember her role?"

"I know, but she's so cute," Dr. Demetrius said. He looked over at Gene, and over at Artemis. He shrugged. "I invented mycelia, planted and used to build safe, mind you, safe mushroom crops. And used in a vast variety of methods."

"Not the magic mushrooms," Gene said. "Or, what do you call them?"

"Oh, death caps is the trade name, and others, again, they are part of the Amanita genus," Dr. Demetrius said. He sat up straight on the conference room chair. "Amanita phalloides, again, from the Amanita genus, poisonous, in fact they resemble edible mushrooms, but they are deadly. Never eat wild mushrooms."

"Got it," Artemis said. She stared over at Dr. Demetrius with an open, accepting face ignoring his suggestive comment. "Go on."

"Penicillin was an accident, as I've pointed out," Dr. Demetrius said. "But if my theories are correct, and I'm certain they are, the mycelia are the root to a god like solution, if you'll excuse my nonsense. But I'm right."

"Of course," Artemis said. "I should advise you, I'm a non-believer."

"Me too," Dr. Demetrius said. He winked at Artemis. "I gave it up years ago."

"We've had some, shall I put it," Gene said. He wiped his sweaty face with a handkerchief. "Break-ins, we have a nearby group that worships magic mushrooms. A weird guy calls himself, Prophet Higgs Boson, has followers, the reason we've kept the lab secret, and in a locked down area."

"Oh, the mycelia amaze me," Dr. Demetrius said. He gazed up at the conference room ceiling like a curious newborn. "They are under everything, they live beneath the soil like a vast network feeding off the dead, the trees."

"As you can see," Gene said. "It's not related to those claims, we'll talk soon, once you have a plan?"

"Correct," Artemis said.

"Time to go," Gene said. He shut off his tablet. And he hurried Dr. Demetrius out of the conference room.

"Another visit to my lab?" Dr. Demetrius said to Artemis as he stood at the doorway. "You'll love what I discovered."

"Time to go," Gene said. He patted Dr. Demetrius on his shoulder. "Let's keep moving. Thank you, Ms. Lamb."

"I'll take you up on that," Artemis said. "Maybe next week, or sooner?"

Artemis sat alone in the conference room. She heard outside the fancy door the normal, everyday hospital activity. There was a shrill sounding ambulance alarm, three floors down at where she was certain was the emergency department. She contemplated the show she and Agent Beaky had seen in the forest. Dr. Demetrius's lab. It was what lurked underneath the ground; It was that fact that she was certain Prophet Higgs Boson and Dr. Demetrius had a connection. But Dr. Demetrius wasn't hulking like the goat masked cult leader. Dr. Demetrius' expression after the name came out of Gene's mouth, Prophet Higgs Boson. He would never have ignored such a comment about his research, protecting his mushrooms and his sacred mycelia. It was the reason The Company had sent her. The Company sanctioned her to kill a societal menace. The question Artemis had to answer was her kill to be only Dr. Demetrius or this Prophet Higgs Boson, or was it both?

Chapter 24

"You should have hired me, like I told you, to," Jerome said angrily. "Or at least another local attorney."

"Agent Beaky made me paranoid about using you, sorry, what can I do now?" Artemis said. She sat outside the Greek themed columned sandstone courthouse with marble floors on a metal park bench. "I hoped one of my company firms could handle a simple custody case in family court."

"Lexington lawyers are not welcome here," Jerome said. "You should realize that, always, always get a local. They know the judges, the staff, and they'll tip off if someone's up to no good."

Jerome Jenkins thumped down next to her. He stuffed his smartphone into his all-weather coat pocket. They had watched a distant relative emerge from nowhere, and the family law judge allowed her to take Laina away in a four-door sedan with a faulty muffler. Laina shoulders slouched as she looked away from Artemis as she got into the car's back seat. She didn't look for Artemis out the back window as the junker gasped away.

"I should have known better," Artemis said. She wiped her cold face; the bench seat was unforgiving and harsh. "I have a bad feeling about this. I think I got set up. It was that toad Gene."

"Am I hired?" Jerome said. He patted Artemis on the right shoulder. "I'll give you the family rate. I'll keep this quiet; but you'll need a local. And besides, I'm the only real game in town, you need me. I'll win."

"Yes," Artemis said. She stared forward. "Help me."

"I'll track her down," Jerome said. "I'll get her back."

Artemis pulled out her smartphone; she handed it over to Jerome. He glanced over at Artemis and then down at the smartphone screen.

"She's wearing a GPS watch," Artemis said. She looked back over at Jerome. She pointed down at the screen blipping coordinates. "I can track her with that smartphone. At least for awhile."

Jerome pressed on the screen.

"I see," Jerome said. "Smart."

"I told her to never take if off," Artemis said. "Never, ever take it off. I hope she listened."

Jerome handed the smartphone back over to Artemis. He crossed his long legs, his dark-gray slacks had a sharp crease. He coughed with his fist in front of his mouth. He stretched his left arm along the bench back.

"They'll take it," Jerome said. He sighed. "It'll get pawned off by sundown, you recognize that?"

"I do," Artemis said. "Thought I'd show them easy candy, bait them away for searching her body."

"What's so special about this kid?" Jerome said. He watched the nearby street traffic coast up and down Main Street. The community alive with normal daily activity. "Benjamin must have been your soul mate for you to take her on. These family matters can become tangled, and messy."

Artemis took back the smartphone. She gripped it like it was a talisman with magical powers that would lead her back to Benjamin and protect Laina.

"I've loved one man, I don't let many into my life," Artemis said. She stared down at the smartphone. "Other than my father, yeah, it was Benjamin. And Laina's his daughter. Somehow, I ended up here, in part, because of you."

"You're joking," Jerome said. "Now it's my fault?"

"No," Artemis said. "It's a random deal, but the girl clouds my brain. I think something did this for a reason."

Jerome sat contemplating life for several moments. He tapped his black dress shoe on the concrete sidewalk and acknowledged several local business people and lawyers that strolled nearby them toward the courthouse's intimidating solid brass doors.

"Life has so many turns," Jerome said. "I wonder sometimes if it's all so random, or not. If there's something beyond us, and I'm playing my part in a cosmic play."

Artemis shrugged her shoulders, crossed her arms.

"It's all to random," Artemis said. "How'd I end up coming here, sorry, but it's in the middle of nowhere."

"No offense taken," Jerome said. He smiled. "It's way to quiet for most, but I love it here. My kids grew up in this Mayberry; it's my little spot in this heaven."

"Do you think a heaven exists?" Artemis said.

"I doubt it," Jerome said. He winked at Artemis. He pointed up at his forehead. "But that's why we have hope. It's that tiny nugget in our minds that an all powerful god's out there, in the cosmos, waiting for us with winged angels."

"I've never been a true believer, but, I want to," Artemis said. She held up her hands over her head. She stretched. She yawned. "I've wondered, my life has gotten strange. And I've lived a wild life."

And Artemis heard Satan's chuckle. Satan whispered to Artemis from beyond her and nearby her all at the same time.

"Strange?" Satan said. It spat out a robust cackled. "That's all you got for dear, sweet, Jerome?"

"This hospital's dirty?" Jerome said. Unaware that Satan was communicating with Artemis. "I'll prove it."

"Dirty might be an under statement," Artemis said. She closed her eyes, hoping that her madness would evaporate from within her mind. "They are a difficult client. I'll say that. I'm not sure if I'll keep my sanity after this file."

"Well, I guess I'm in an ethical dilemma," Jerome said. "Helping you, and I'm about to file my suit in a month or so. You all will deny my claim?"

"Yes, but we'll agree that the staff here does help a lot of these people," Artemis said. She nudged her head over at the modest street traffic. She pointed at a kaleidoscope of people walking and talking like disciplined soldier ants maneuvering in different directions near the courthouse steps and along the bricked side-streets. "And you need some evidence, don't you?"

"We have some fine doctors," Jerome said. "Majority of the staff are good honest, folks, but we have something else going on, now don't we?"

Satan hummed a racist minstrel tune with a banjo twang.

"Oh, you humans are so much fun," Satan said. It was as if Satan had sat between Artemis and Jerome. "Ethics? Tell me an Aesop's fable. What nonsense, you humans worry about what? Begging like sheep for better points with the big guy? Come live with me for eternity, we'll never discuss ethics. And, I will show you a wild existence."

"What if you put the hospital out of business?" Artemis said. "You'd not be so popular here."

"I'll give you that," Jerome said. He pointed at her with his right hand forefinger. "Are you okay, you seem, well, distracted?"

"Sorry, I'm stressed," Artemis said. She leaned back and crossed her legs. "Too many voices going in my head at once."

"I bet," Jerome said.

"Oh, Artemis," Satan said. "Jerome's one of those true believers. He'll go find Laina, protect her, and still go after Dr. Demetrius. He should have angelic wings, like I used to have, but, they took those away from me after my coup attempt. And, I have others that lost wings with me. It was not my best moment in eternity. Now, I exist to create human conflict. As in the mind of my favorite assassin."

Artemis rubbed her eyes, she sucked in the frigid air through her nose. A deep breath into her lungs.

"I'll play this straight," Artemis said. She tried to act like she'd heard nothing from within her mind. "They have the electronic record keeping but we both know it's way to clean."

"I think so, too," Jerome said. "But I have families with questions and loved ones they never got to say goodbye."

"Oh how sweet," Satan said. "He's so nice, yuck!"

"Laina has another tracking device on her," Artemis said. "They'll never find it."

"Well now," Satan said. "Aren't you showing your cards, as the human cliché, my, my, you are such a trusting soul with this one, you don't trust anyone. This is not how you play Texas holdem. Let the river flow where it wants. What gives?"

"Where?" Jerome said.

"It's military grade, an item I obtained from an old friend," Artemis said. "I stuck it on her lower back, she was sleeping. She'll never know it's there, and it's almost invisible."

"What?" Satan said to Artemis. "You're giving up real intel, you must trust this human, I might pass-out. But I never pass-out, I'm not human. I'm not even a spirit."

"You are serious?" Jerome said. He sat back and looked up into the brown, thorny hillsides. "I'm so naïve to these things."

"Yes," Artemis said. "I suspected Gene had this hearing rigged before we walked inside the court room. He's just being himself."

Jerome remained quiet and still for a length of time. He noticed the last snowfall had melted into the soil. And two brown squirrels scratched up a scabrous maple tree arguing and chasing each other.

"You kind of scare me," Jerome said. He covered his eyes with his left hand from sunlight as a wrinkle emerged across his temple. "My instincts are nagging me about you, you've seen real action?"

"I love that child," Artemis said. She stared back over at Jerome. "She's all I have as a connection to what matters to me."

"I understand," Jerome said. "I've an amazing wife of over thirty years. I love her and my children with my life. But you are an intense lady, like you can see everything going on outside the courthouse behind us without turning around."

"He's not getting it," Satan said. "Maybe give him a hint, what you are about."

Artemis acknowledged Jerome. She shifted and gave Jerome the dead eyes of an assassin. Eyes that preyed on its target. Eyes that hunted its target.

"They hired me to deal with these messes," Artemis said. "Protect the house. My boss and I talk in code. We both know this is a nasty case, it'll get worse before I'm finished. The girl has complicated my work. I don't need her complicating things, but she's a reality I have to accept."

"We do have a serious drug problem," Jerome said. He avoided eye contact with Artemis. "We have an epidemic, in part from the hospital, and now out there in the county. It's killing our children."

"I'll find the source," Artemis said. "It's my job."

Jerome shifted away from Artemis. He glanced away from her. He paused, he nodded. He held his breath and looked back over at Artemis.

"They?" Jerome said. "That's not the language of a medical malpractice claim manager. You have a peculiar language. But your blue eyes, to be blunt, you terrify me."

"They - is the correct pronoun," Artemis said. Her lips flat. Her face expressionless. "They are who they are, I don't ask questions. I'm trained to deal with problems. I'll deal with the mess my way and eliminate it. A societal mess."

Satan laughed as its voice almost spasmed with hate.

"Oh, that's so true," Satan said. "I know this. I've tried to scare you; you begged me for the kill shot. Oh, if Jerome understood what you're capable of, oh, but Benny knew. You turned him on fire with your skills. Your inner-self is so truthful. I hate that about you. But, you'll scare ole sweet Jerome. Careful killer. Go easy on the man."

"Can you tell me about," Jerome said. "They?"

Artemis stuffed her hands into her coat pockets.

"No. Let me put it this way," Artemis said. "They are not evil, but they are careful, cautious with their assets and resources. I'm a shared resource."

"Okay, I guess," Jerome said. "You did just hire me. What you tell me goes no further."

"Dr. Demetrius has been a problem, that's not a big secret here," Artemis said. She stared forward. "He's dangerous. I'm here to clean up his mess. But I think there is someone else. I can feel it."

"You're not a claim manager," Jerome said with a certain cadence that emerges from experience. "I'm a small-town lawyer doing his job. But you're not a med-mal investigator. You're different, you are on a razor edge, lady. But you appear calm. I think you're hunting."

Artemis thought about the fact she had discovered from Benjamin what love meant, not just a physical act between two horny bodies, but bonding with a human being into a lovers coil. From the pain she had learned to seal off after her parents accident, learning to navigate life on her own terms. She had her mother's Olympic athletic body, her disciplined nature, and her father's curious mind. Within her heart, their loving fire burned within her soul. But she had come across Benjamin, he rekindled the idea of love, and he had altered her journey. And because of Benjamin, Laina had become her prime one.

"I prefer to work alone," Artemis said. Her face blank. "You're an honest man, Jerome. I like you. You'll help me get Laina back."

"I'll get her back," Jerome said. "I promise."

"Well, well, Artemis," Satan said. "You're opening up today, what should I do next? You're being nice, not calculating. It's not the side I like to see from your soul. I hate you."

"I seek the truth, the facts," Artemis said. "The Company operates from facts, not innuendo, clear, cold hard facts. I track down facts that lead me to a conclusion."

"You are way ahead of me?" Jerome said. He grunted. "You've got this whole situation scoped out."

"I do. It's my job," Artemis said. "The facts are emerging, Dr. Demetrius can't help himself. He's digging his own grave for me, but he's got a connection with this prophet. I need to figure these two out; they're a problem for this community. They are impacting beyond this town. It has to stop."

"I agree. I'll do my part. I have to look after my clients' interests first," Jerome said. "This is my home. You appreciate my position."

"It's scary out there for some people," Artemis said. She shifted forward and got up off the park bench. "I cannot control this little girl's situation, she is not in my world. But Laina's special to me. I'll help you get your claims closed, but you help me with her."

"You weren't a common medic?" Jerome said. He gulped. "I'm curious, no offense intended."

"No, but I was good at it, I liked saving someones life," Artemis said. She nodded as she stared down at Jerome. "I'm clairvoyant. It helps me sort out messes. But I adhere to my code of conduct."

"We thought so," Jerome said. He recrossed his legs. "Before our meeting, Agent Beaky assumed you were a clairvoyant. Said you admitted it. See things we can't see…"

"Yes. Enough about my work," Artemis said. "What's the next steps for Laina? I'm afraid for her. And this Dr. Demetrius, she was inside that hospital all alone with him lurking about without any restrictions or ethics."

"It's straight forward legal process," Jerome said. "But the court will have serious questions."

"I don't want this complication," Artemis said. "But I'll not abandon her."

"One thing I would expect," Jerome said. "They'll work with us, if, and only if, you're prepared to adopt her?"

Artemis expected the question. For the second time in her life she was prepared to let another human being inside her world, a place where her work was her sanctuary.

"Yes," Artemis said, flatly. She wiped the tears from her eyes. "I'll take her in. I don't know any other way to live."

"You fascinate me. You go cold and hot, a snap of a finger," Jerome said. He crinkled his face. "They'll do a serious background study, you sure? Or, I can research her family, see if I can locate a better home for her to live."

"I get it," Artemis said. She cleared her eyes. "That's easy, The Company, they will take care of that part. It's simple. I want her in my life."

"I'll do my best," Jerome said. He held out his right hand. Artemis shook it. "Deal, please help clean up my hometown. Protect my people. I am certain you mean us, or me, no harm."

"I will. If my boss Wylie approves this, he'll help me," Artemis said. She shifted back. "Let me know what I need to do. I need to go find this prophet that goes by this goof name, Prophet Higgs Boson."

Jerome inspected the courtyard area. He leaned toward Artemis.

"He is a dangerous man, weirdo thinks he's in league with Satan," Jerome said. "I have no idea where he lives; he's elusive. But he's become a local menace. Be careful. He has his lieutenants everywhere reporting back to him."

"I'll find him," Artemis said. She walked away, but she stopped and marched back over toward Jerome. "If she's abused, in any manner, you'll tell me?"

"Without question," Jerome said. He waved back at Artemis. "I'll get her out of there, first thing."

"She's personal," Artemis said. She sniffled. She scanned the area. All she saw was a quiet town going about the day. "If they so much as touch a hair on her head, I'll kill them. I'll kill all of them."

"I believe you," Jerome said. He squirmed on the bench. He held his hands up. "I'm on your side."

"Good, sorry," Artemis said. She stomped her left brown loafer into the concrete. She wanted to take back her words, but she was certain Jerome was an honest man living amongst snakes. "Don't mean to scare you. Sorry. We need to understand each other. Again, Sorry. I shouldn't have said that, you must realize Laina's my prime one. I'll do what I have to do to protect her."

"No worries from me," Jerome said. "I'm thankful people like you exist. But I don't want to know what you know. Ever."

Artemis turned and marched down the Main Street the casual traffic coasting by her, a yellow caution light blinked above the street, and a few seniors citizens were comparing grand children photos and then she stepped on toward her hotel. She noticed Jerome did not budge off the bench until she had disappeared from his line of sight. Along her path as she walked past a red brick building Satan sat on a rickety wooden bench again whittling with a pocket knife and this time smoking a joint.

"These humans seem okay with pot, Mary Jane, wacky-weed," Satan said. "Odd smell, but this body seems to like the chill feeling. I'm being groovy, baby."

"Why do you whisper in my ear?" Artemis said. "It's annoying, and you make me question my sanity."

"It's what I do, I cause humans to snap," Satan said. It inspected the pinewood for flaws. "Besides, you scared poor Jerome, you went all assassin at him, quite touching. I sensed your authenticity."

"He'll protect Laina. I'll protect him and this town. I needed to make him an asset," Artemis said. She stood still and stared down at Satan. "You'll leave her alone?"

Satan took in a deep drag. It puffed out the smoke.

"I don't make those promises," Satan said. "You know that, but this cannabis is nothing compared to opioids, fentanyl. Hm, oh, how oh, would Prophet Higgs Boson make his money?"

"It's obvious," Artemis said. "Leave the girl alone, please?"

"Not up to me anymore, remember my favorite sin?" Satan said. "You've invited other parties to our play, you'll see."

"I don't understand," Artemis said. "You're being whatever you are, again."

"You will," Satan said. It carved off a length of pinewood with the sharp pocket knife as the joint dangled from its lips. "Go back out into the forest, at night. Go alone, use your talents. You don't need Virgil or any living or dead spirit to guide you to the site. There you'll find answers. This will be your magic clue. And, you're welcome."

It snapped its dirt cracked yellowish fingernails and dissolved into the afternoon air. It left behind the pocket knife, pinewood, its pungent scent and a smoldering joint.

Chapter 25

Artemis foraged deep into the thick Appalachian old-growth forest smoth-ered with invasive large leaf kudzu, expansive thorny underbrush, and towering tree families. To save time, she scaled up the steep rocky mountain sides, dangling from climbing ropes sliding and pulling her body up through stainless steel carabiners, quickdraws, and rope tighteners. The darkness unmasked by her night vision glasses. Her Glock 9mm holstered to her side. A ballistic knife strapped to her right thigh. Her black nylon boots splattered with brown mud.

After scaling over limestone and sandstone shear cliffs, she found the giant tulip poplar and the flat ritualistic site. She kneeled down on the boot high grass, leaves and bare soil and allowed her breathing to slow and her warm skin to accept the frigid air. The steam from her warm body released a hellish vapor. And then she sensed others. She stood up, inspected the darkness between the oak, birch and pine trees, and a consistent breeze altered the wavy dark silhouettes cast by the trees from the full moon's glow. She kept stepping, unconcerned with her hiking boots crushing tree limbs or cracking pine cones as she then turned around to inspect where she sensed them. Wild animals spewed guttural warnings as they hunted for prey and she heard a Great Horned owl above her snap its beak, "Hoo-hoo-H'hoo-hoo." She glanced up the elderly sycamore tree. Perched on a sturdy branch, the owl flapped its wings as it gazed down at her with fierce yellowish-eyes.

"I want to talk," Artemis said. Scanning the area at her head height, she gripped the weapon handle. In the distance, she could hear a powerful waterfall that sounded like the whoosh from thunderous commercial jet engines as the passenger planes took off after taxing across a bustling airport runway. "Show yourself, right now, if not, if you're living. I'll kill you on first sight. I promise I won't miss."

From the darkness, dense brush, and the fat and skinny tree trunks, grainy spirit women began to appear cascading in an irregular formation. They floated and drifted like pale-gray clouds from all directions captured by moon light as they converged next to a solitary spirit. They gathered as one unit together near her. Artemis reflected that in life she had been beautiful, slender with long flowing hair.

"Leave this place," she said. Her eyes black. She was motionless as the others existed behind her. "This is not a place for the living."

"I don't think so," Artemis said. She stepped toward them and invaded their space. "Who were you? All of you?"

The spirit woman rushed toward Artemis. She screeched at Artemis with her hands claw like. But Artemis stood her ground as the aggressive spirit woman made her threatening pass. The spirit form circled back and maneuvered in front of her sisterhood.

"I'm not scared, I know you cannot touch me," Artemis said. She stepped closer. "I mean no one harm, we cannot hurt each other. Who are you?"

"Leave this place," she said. She hissed and encouraged her sisters to screech, howl and wail at Artemis. They crowded in hissing, yelling at Artemis and they tried to scratch at her.

Artemis took her hand off her gun. She realized there was movement behind the protective acting adult spirits, soft words being exchanged, the innocent voices were just above a whisper.

"Why here?" Artemis said. "Who are you?"

The spirit women began to regroup, gathering close together, words expressed as they floated farther away from Artemis. They started to communicate with the chosen spirit woman. She acknowledged them, her left hand up, she twisted around drift back and to face in front of Artemis.

"This is a place for death," she said. "I told you, I warned you, this is not a place for the living. Leave."

"I've seen a ritual here, under that tree," Artemis said. She pointed back over at the site; she looked up into the massive tulip poplar that defied gravity as it swayed back and forth. "Sacrificed a lamb, they chose it on purpose, my last name is Lamb. Satan's idea I suspect. It sent me here to seek clues. What was your name in life?"

The spirit woman was followed by the other women as they studied over at Artemis, drifting near her, lingering above dead oak limbs and clumps of rotting leaves and dormant ferns. She sensed they had accepted that her statement was the truth as one of them ambled and whispered to the chosen leader. She nodded.

"Lilith, was my given name," she said. She nodded back to her spirit sisters. "My parents named me Lilith. I was a Jew amongst Christians and Muslims. I was an outcast."

And Artemis started to notice the spirit women kept backing away from her in unison, and they meshed closer, and closer together. She caught a tiny golden spirit girl peek out from behind a felled oak stump. The women tried to encourage the spirit girls to remain hidden, but the girls revealed themselves as they were curious, they kept peeking out from behind dense bushes and sturdy limestone boulders.

"My mother was Irish Catholic, my father Presbyterian, but they never practiced any faith. Those little girls, this prophet sacrificed children?" Artemis said. She leaned on her boot toes. She resisted her inner emotions; she focused on her training, on facts. "A child?"

"Yes. Little girls are his favorite," Lilith said, wistfully. "Or one of us was chosen, if they had not kidnapped a girl. We never knew when. If we ate the wrong mushroom, it was all over."

"Is this the Prophet Higgs Boson?" Artemis said. "He's who you refer to? He peddles drugs?"

"Yes," Lilith said. She pointed over at the tulip poplar. "The tree will die, they must feed it, it's what lives beneath that is worshipped."

"What needs to be fed?" Artemis said. She stared over, studied the other women. They all had a common bond. "You were all killed, how can this be?"

Lilith looked forward at Artemis. Her gray spirit particles to swayed and trembled. She frowned and slumped her shoulders.

"I was an addict, all I yearned for was to get high," Lilith said. "I lost my family. I lived on the streets, in the woods, until he found me."

Another of the women drifted next to Lilith.

"Satan sent you?" she said. "Why? We try to hide from The Evil One. We don't bother anyone, anymore, please leave us alone."

"Yes," Artemis said. "I don't know why, who were you?"

"It hates you," she said. She stared at Artemis. "I was Jezebel, I was a prostitute. I gave myself to the master. He betrayed me. My body rots behind you in the soil. I'm being digested and broken down by the monster."

"I'm aware Satan hates me, I'm sorry your bodies were desecrated," Artemis said. She shifted back and looked down at the ground near the tree trunk smothered with mushrooms, dirt and crabgrass. "It tortures me. But I am afraid for a girl."

The women considered Artemis' statement.

"Your truthful," Lilith said. She drifted toward Artemis. She sniffed near Artemis. "I can sense your spirit, you live for truth."

"Satan hates the truth," Jezebel said. "It takes one of us, one by one, it takes one of us at a time. It leaves the children alone; they are innocents. It cannot touch them. Angels take them one by one, the reason is not given."

"You can't go on?" Artemis said. "The reason you are all gray spirits, and not golden."

"To Hell, is our eternal path, we prayed to Satan," Lilith said. "We are all trapped. We did bad things that we will pay for in eternity."

"The children warn us," Jezebel said. She scanned up to search the sky that sparkled with Orions Belt and from light billions of years old. "When it comes, they can sense Satan. They help us."

Artemis stepped back, and she looked back over at the tree. She could detect the uneven surface that was covered with mushrooms.

"What does this have to do with a hospital?" Artemis said to herself. She twisted back over at the spirit women. "How did you get addicted?"

"Don't eat the mushrooms," Lilith said. She gazed back at Artemis. "The mushrooms are death."

"I get you, no worries," Artemis said. And then she heard the muscled twelve-point white stag emerge from the forest; it snapped off a large tree limb as it grunted forward; followed close behind it by the American Indian warrior spirit. "I don't understand what's going on, this is just a bad dream."

"The white stag," Lilith said. "It protects the forest."

Jezebel pointed over at the warrior spirit.

"The warrior caught Prophet Higgs Boson murdering a girl who ran from him," Jezebel said. She held her hand up over at him in a sign of peace. "The prophet is afraid of the warrior, he ran away leaving her on the forest floor. He left her heart next to her. It was eaten by a pit viper as a black king snake constricted her dead body."

"She was not sacrificed to the mycelia, you know what it's called?" Lilith said. She pointed at Artemis. "You talked to her. Before she went on."

"How so?" Artemis said. "I was not aware."

The women looked at each other. They paused.

"We hide in your world, we exist in the light, a light most cannot see," Jezebel said. "But you can see into our world, but a tiny portion. We know of you. We had to test you."

"Our spirits communicate," Lilith said. "We've been watching you, you are well known in our spirit world. We know your true nature. We hope you choose the prophet."

"I'm sorry," Artemis said. She sensed they understood her work, her passion for her duty. "I don't hate, they hurt innocent people. I am bound to protect the innocent. Like Lily-Ann, she was innocent."

"Yes, you don't hate, you are truthful," Jezebel said. She tried to place her hand on Artemis chest, but it waved through Artemis. "You are like the warrior, but you're alive. You have not felt death's sting."

Artemis looked over beside the white stag. The warrior was painted for battle, his spear garlanded with white feathers. He nudged at her as he shoved his spear toward her.

"I don't understand him," Artemis said.

"I do. The warrior prayed at death to always roam the forest to protect it from mankind," Lilith said. "He waits for the prophet, he scares the prophet. He sometimes appeared at our ceremonies and chased us away."

"You could all see him?" Artemis said.

"We were high, but it wanted us to see him," Lilith said. "He tried to help us. We did not listen."

"Lily-Ann," Artemis said. She looked down at the hard ground, the swirled dormant grass and dirt as her voice trailed-off. "She ran for her life..."

"The warrior tried to protect her body, but it's a spirit like us, it's not in your world," Jezebel said. "It sent the stag to find Virgil. Virgil found the body. He chased away the Red Wolf eating her and killed the snakes with his bare hands. He cried and prayed over Lily-Ann. He took off his coat even though it was cold and protected her body, he called, and until they came for her."

"Virgil?" Artemis said. Her mouth gaped open. She searched over at the spirit warrior. "He knew before, he's a cagey fellow."

"Virgil tries to protect the forest," Lilith said. "He's afraid, he's gotten too old. His body fails him. He drinks to kill his pain."

Jezebel floated toward the tree. She pointed down.

"It's the mycelia, it must die," Jezebel said. She pointed back over at the tree. "It's alive, but the mycelia feed off the tree and our bodies. He created it."

"The prophet?" Artemis said.

"No, Dr. Demetrius," Lilith said. She hesitated and gazed up into the swaying tree limbs. The spirit girls started to moan. A fierce wind gust whistled across the valley floor.

"We have to go, sisters, prepare."

"They are twin brothers," Jezebel said. She began to pick up her pace, sailing away from Artemis. "Identical to the other. You will find your answer with them. Protect the child, she's in danger, the prophet knows of her."

And with haste the spirit women all disappeared with the spirit children crying and screaming back into the darkness like a suddenly exposed death ship within the gloom shown by a ship's search light gliding across a night-time ocean. And the forest began to feel colder, it seemed harder to Artemis. The stag huffed and stomped back between the trees and trudged up a hillside. The warrior remained behind, its spear thrust up and at Artemis, before it turned and left. From behind Artemis a familiar voice.

"Oh, look at you, it smells all pine needles and musky out here, those babes could not resist my scent," Satan said. The handsome man strolled with a certainty only from knowing how all things end. "All decked out in your inner badass, don't shoot me, or don't stab me with that thing. It looks wicked. That's a weapon for war, or hunting a human. Boo at you, Artemis."

"This is fun?" Artemis said. She closed her eyes. She opened her eyes. She pinched her cheek.

"Oh, I'm here," Satan said. "This is not a dream. Besides, I can visit you in your dreams, if you like?"

"What do you want? You sent me out here," Artemis said. "Leave those women alone, you could allow them to beg for mercy?"

"Naw, as these humans say, up here's in the Appalachia," Satan said with a twangy accent. "That would ruin my fun. The little girls can go on to those others, when they figure it out. But those women, they made a bargain. I don't let souls out of my contracts."

"Then why show them to me?" Artemis said.

"Remember what I told you?" Satan said. It cackled as it strolled around Artemis. And then it wolf howled. "What did I tell you from the beginning of our play?"

Artemis' mind swirled with thoughts and evidence. But she rolled her memory back in time. She stared up at the faint images of arthritic tree limbs revealed by the full moon's pearly glow and the forests mists.

"Greed," Artemis said. She spat at the ground.

"Greed it is," Satan said. Its clap slow, rhythmic. "Good Artemis, you're learning. I hate you."

"Brothers?" Artemis said. "That's the connection."

"Yes, you earned a magic clue," Satan said. It smiled at Artemis with its dead oblong shaped eyes. "It's right in front of you, but you don't see, yet. Those gray women hiding over there, maybe I should go soul-fishing? I'm out here in the forest, get me a line in the air."

"They're in cult, so what," Artemis said. "I'll tip off Agent Beaky, he'll handle this mess. The malpractice part is becoming obvious and criminal."

"Oh, come on," Satan said. "That's way to simple. Think, think, greed? It's my favorite sin, but then there is an emotion. It leads to all the other sins. I want to teach you that emotion, it's my pin prick into your soul."

"I don't understand," Artemis said.

Satan pointed near her black nylon boots.

"Did I mention?" Satan said. It smirked. "Don't eat those mushrooms."

Before Artemis responded to Satan. It evaporated. And it left Artemis shrouded in the darkness with the four-legged animals seeking a meal, hairy eight-legged spiders guarding their nests, and snakes slithering back to shelter within their earthly holes. She adjusted her night vision glasses, and she began to hike back out from the woods. She needed to go find Agent Beaky.

Chapter 26

"They're brothers," Artemis said. She gripped the warm coffee mug. It steamed over the top and the hazelnut aroma was comforting to her. "He was wearing a demonic mask, now it makes sense. I didn't suspect it was Dr. Demetrius he's not as muscled or thick as his brother."

"Well now," Agent Beaky said. He watched a middle-aged lady in a blue business suit at a nearby table stabbing her fork into her bland breakfast. "How on earth did you find this out?"

Artemis pondered the situation for several minutes. She worried about the fact Satan had revealed itself to her. And a little girl's life was in danger. She needed to get Agent Beaky's help, but she risked him thinking her a paranoid schizophrenic.

"You're right," Artemis said. "I'm clairvoyant, but I have stronger than normal abilities."

Agent Beaky had been in the FBI for many years. He could see Artemis' expression was clear and focused. His instincts told him she was deceptively powerful and skilled.

"I suspected," Agent Beaky said. He pushed his coffee mug across the smooth tabletop and over to his left-side and left it alone. "Military? Kill with either hand? I've watched you, you're ambidextrous."

"Recruited me from college, The Company, that's what I call," Artemis said. "My scores where off the charts, plus, I'm an orphan. Perfect prototype for what they wanted to train me to do for them. They loaned me to the military for specific needs. These days I get files assigned related to a medical malpractice case. But they point me at a societal problem. I hunt it down, and I exterminate it."

"The Company?" Agent Beaky said. He pondered her comment, he gripped his nose and looked down at the fake brown wood tabletop. "My clearance is not up there, not sure what they allow you to tell me."

"I just don't lie well," Artemis said. "It's against my inner code. These people out in the forest are dangerous. I can't manage this alone. They're the worst kind of criminal."

"All right," Agent Beaky said. "Where did you learn about, I guess we'll call them going forward the Demetrius brothers? If it is confidential source, I'll respect your desire for privacy. However, I'll need them if we go for an arrest warrant."

Artemis squirmed and kept her gaze on Agent Beaky.

"I hiked back up into the mountains," Artemis said.

"Alone?" Agent Beaky said. "Are you mad?"

"I'm not scared, if a living animal snuck up on me it was my time to go," Artemis said. She gave Agent Beaky a stare. "I can communicate and look at dead humans, and animals, trapped wandering spirits before they go on into eternity. I've been able to since I was a kid. A black bear or rattle snake, do not frighten me."

Agent Beaky coughed with his fist over his mouth. He leaned in closer to Artemis. He whispered as a hotel guest sat down next to them with a plate of bacon, brown toast and scrambled eggs.

"Who or what did you find in the forest?" Agent Beaky said.

"Spirit women," Artemis said. She sighed. "And there were some spirit girls they protect. The women tried to protect them from me at first, but they knew of my work and calmed down."

"Let me guess," Agent Beaky said. "Murdered? Like what happened to that lamb that subhuman carved up."

"Yes," Artemis said. "And little girls hiding behind them were this hulking Demetrius brother's favorites, and that hospital over there has a less athletic Demetrius brother that is a pure evil roaming inside it. He's not anywhere as big as his twin."

Agent Beaky's jaw line clenched down, and he almost growled.

"From the beginning, before I drove into Selene," Agent Beaky said. "They charged me with protecting Jerome and his family. It was the reason I wear this silly FBI jacket; it's in part as a warning sign, not to mess with Jerome. But now my Welsh DNA's getting triggered, I'll burn in h-e-double-tooth-picks, before I turn my back, I'll state that straight away."

"Yeah," Artemis said. "You seemed to be a walking, talking cliché, what do you have for me?"

"Interesting development," Agent Beaky said. He pointed toward the hotel's active breakfast area in the general direction for the hospital. "Got me a drone, hovered outside of eyesight, took some film and pictures behind the hospital."

"Trucks?" Artemis said.

"There you go," Agent Beaky said. "We watched them load box after box into unmarked shipping containers or smaller box trucks. They appear to move the shrink-wrapped cargo in and out with no worries."

"They sound efficient," Artemis said. "And rather greedy."

"They are, it has to be a profit seeking enterprise," Agent Beaky said. He huffed. "They are all suited up with what looked like hazmat suits, nice, clean and none of the workers stopped to be lazy about, all on point, all with a prearranged purpose."

"What's in the boxes?" Artemis said.

"We can't tell," Agent Beaky said. "We're told by a reliable insider, one of Jerome's assets, its mushrooms and freeze-dried things they called, ah, sorry."

Agent Beaky started to pat down his pockets in search of his smartphone he had set on the breakfast table.

"Mycelia?" Artemis said. She slid the smartphone back over toward Agent Beaky. "In front of you."

"Oh, thanks, can't function without these things," Agent Beaky said. He pointed at Artemis with his right hand forefinger. "Ah, yes, I trust that's what they said."

"I did the internet search," Artemis said. "That's what we looked at that night, out there, when they fed that lamb to it. They have a monster out there, they feed woman and children to it. I'm certain of it. Smart, but sick people, I guess that's how they eliminate the evidence."

"Is that what you were told?" Agent Beaky said. "By those unfortunate souls? They verified, oh, how terrible."

"Yes, but then they are spirits, they got spooked and floated away before I could ask them for more information," Artemis said. She shrugged and yanked over at her backpack strap. "And you can't see them, so they're useless for evidence. Gave up solid intel though, but otherwise we'd need a forensic team to dig up around that tree. And buy ourselves a fire fight with the Demetrius brothers and crew in the process."

"What now, they ran away from a boogie man?" Agent Beaky said. He chortled with a nervous expression. "I don't have your gift."

"You can say that," Artemis said. "Worse than any boogie man I've ever come across."

As Agent Beaky sat back his chair squeaked against the tile surface. His pale blue eyes held their gaze as he contemplated Artemis' statement. He leaned forward and gripped the tabletop.

"Well now, what else?" Agent Beaky said. "Where's this going? It's your eyes, you have this strange look."

Artemis shook her head. She opened her hands and arms wide. She started to say something, but stopped, contemplating the method to explain her supernatural nemesis to Agent Beaky. She rubbed her hands together.

"Satan," Artemis said. She blinked her eyelids. "I hope you don't think me a fool, and need to get me in the psych ward. It knows what I just told you, it monitors me, no reason to hide that fact from you."

Agent Beaky appeared as if something had stung him in the neck. He glanced at a teenager ripping cooked bacon into strips and gobbling them down like snakes. He stared back over at Artemis. He started to speak, but then he stopped.

"I'm not sure, you said?" Agent Beaky said. He stammered as his lips pursed. "You're certain?"

"Positive. I've experienced demons, so forth," Artemis said. "When I first arrived here, I traveled out to a local cemetery. I figured I would meet some wandering spirits, you know, see what I might see. After all in my line of work, the wandering spirits speak the truth. They are the best informants. Cheap, reliable and they'll never be discovered by human bad guys."

"All right," Agent Beaky said. "I… ah, suppose…"

"They have nothing more to hide," Artemis said. She shrugged. "It's one of my investigation techniques. If a file with uncertain death cases, I begin my process at local cemeteries."

"The Company? The people you cannot discuss with me," Agent Beaky said. "If I may ask, as it were. They know about your, shall I express it, abilities?"

"Yes," Artemis said. "Imbedded me years ago, healthcare, they monitor it. I'll leave it at that for our purposes."

"Bloody hell, you're serious, you didn't even blush, and you're half-Irish," Agent Beaky said. His voice squeaked. "Don't mind saying I feel a bit off my shoes, never, never expected. I'll sleep with the lights on."

"Nor did I," Artemis said.

"Why you?" Agent Beaky said.

"I don't know, Satan just appeared, made a big show for me," Artemis said. She pushed the coffee mug in a small semi-circle pattern. "First time it scared me. But then I realized, it wanted something."

"What did it look like?" Agent Beaky said. He waved his hand over his head. "Horns? Tail? I don't know."

"Oh, I stood there crying," Artemis said. "It changed forms, a big cobra snake, black blob, and a handsome dude, and it just toys with me. But it was real. I pinched my cheek to be sure I wasn't seeing things. Did tactile movements. I hope I've not gone all mental. I hope."

They sat across from each other for a few minutes. They heard the busy guest traffic eating breakfast, people discussing important business, or the rat-ta-tat from hotel guests trudging their suitcases toward the checkout counter across the tile floor.

"Demonic rituals," Agent Beaky said. He whispered. "Makes sense, sacrifices, woman and children."

"No, not boys or men," Artemis said. "Little girls, a woman from the group, they said the prophet chose them at random. But always females. They were specific."

"Satan," Agent Beaky said in a whispered tone. He kept his shoulders hunched forward. "You're certain, sorry, my mind's gone hiding."

Artemis considered her next moves. She needed Agent Beaky as an asset to clean up the human tragedy after she managed the Demetrius brothers. And she appreciated his role to protect Jerome's family. But her job required solitude and a focused violence.

"Our friend, Virgil," Artemis said.

"Ah yes, he's a sad man," Agent Beaky said. "The handle guy, likes the hard stuff."

"He's more than a convenient guide," Artemis said. "When I was out there, before we hiked up into the mountain. I noticed an American Indian, he was a spirit, dressed in full on warrior, paint, the whole deal. It follows a living white stag. Huge animal. Beautiful creature."

"You don't say," Agent Beaky said. Held his left hand up. He scooted off the chair. He got up and walked over and refilled his coffee mug. He sat back down. The coffee cup tremored, and brown liquid oozed over the sides. "Sorry, I'm off. You've zapped my mind and I'm terrified with your, ah, informant."

"I'm not sure what to think," Artemis said. "But the women told me he communicates with the warrior. Virgil's sad because he cannot protect the forest. He and the American Indian must have a spirit connection, if that makes sense?"

"I'm learning quite the brain full this morning," Agent Beaky said. He rubbed his forehead. "I'm the lead man in for a drug bust. And I've been launched off into the spirit world. But I can't share this with my direct report. She'll take my weapon and badge away on the spot."

"I need your help," Artemis said. She decided Lily-Ann's murder and Virgil's involvement would complicate her current need. "The little girl, Laina, they have taken her away from me. I think she's in danger; they know her connection to me."

Agent Beaky glanced back over at the hotel's front glass doors as guests walked inside or out of the front lobby into the cold air. A valet helped an older lady step outside.

"Well, you bent one over on me this morning," Agent Beak said. "Not sure what I'll write, or say in my report. I'll help you, children are sacred."

"I've concluded," Artemis said. She blew a long breath through her mouth. "If Satan wants me dead, I'd be dead. It wants something else, not sure what. But I have to protect Laina at all costs."

"Ha, that's a pisser, I'll help best I can figure out," Agent Beaky said. "I'll ponder this, give me a few days. And another thing."

"Yes?" Artemis said.

"Be careful with them," Agent Beaky said. "These boys are dangerous. Might I tag along, next time you go out into the woods?"

"They don't scare me, but Satan scares me," Artemis said. "Sure, I don't think you'll see anything. You'll think I'm talking to air."

"Even so," Agent Beaky said. "What about Jerome's claim and your other work?"

"I care about the girl, she's my prime one going forward," Artemis said. She glossed her hands across the tabletop. "This has gotten way beyond any medical malpractice file. I'll bring in my boss to manage it. I think the evidence will emerge, and we're on the wrong-side. It'll be about money, now."

"I'll say," Agent Beaky said. "What's the next move?"

"I think go back to the source," Artemis said. She considered sharping her work tools. "I need to figure out Dr. Demetrius."

Chapter 27

"I'm brilliant, it's a fact," Dr. Demetrius said. He glanced over at Artemis as he pulled out a rectangular sterile metal tray. He shook the tray covered across the top with wobbly mushroom caps.

"I guess we all need some self-confidence," Artemis said.

"It's how I manage the humidity, temperature, C02, with the right environment," Dr. Demetrius said. "Did I tell you I can create a structure for human organs?"

"Why keep people on life support?" Artemis said without acknowledging Dr. Demetrius'. "Appears from our position a harsh protocol."

"Oh, the staff takes every precaution, we try to keep them alive, after we tried to save them," Dr. Demetrius said. He kept pushing down on the dark soil and kept inspecting his mushrooms. "I'll say it, but never admit it. It's my hospital employer being themselves. Greed. They squeeze out every dollar from Medicaid. It's obvious, they file claims for more money based on the time the patient stays. It is the government's system. I try to ignore them. I'll never say that in the open or in front of a lawyer."

"How does this thing feed?" Artemis said. "I read some papers, it needs a tree, or other waste to feed?"

"You mean like a big compost pile?" Dr. Demetrius said. He slipped on another clean pair of latex gloves. "That's kind of how it works in the forest. Mycelia need the rot; they have enzymes that break it all down. For example, an animal dies in the forest. It's consumed by natural decay, maggots, but the fungi, they are decomposers, they are part of the decomposition system. The animals, like humans, become part of the soil. We go back to the mother earth, our bodies go back inside the fertile soil womb."

"You have a compost pile?" Artemis said. The acid from her stomach licked behind her throat.

"Life emerges, dies, dig a hole, drop a body in the dirt, winter comes, come back in the spring, where did the body go? Just bones to be crushed into nothing," Dr. Demetrius said. He pointed at another tray. "See those, cordyceps, from them, we have potential cancer drugs. They are a strange fungi, an alien like, they have a parasitic existence. I feed them insects; The fungi take over the insect. It's quite startling first time you see it. They eat the insect from the inside out, maybe a way to kill cancer cells inside the body, yet to be discovered."

"You're the hospital's medical director," Artemis said. "How are you going to answer for the death cases, overdoses, and the bodies cremated, how's that the standard?"

Dr. Demetrius pondered Artemis' questions. He cruised about the laboratory and appeared to inspect the metal trays covered with a cheesecloth like material spread over a variety of mushrooms. He was careful, surgical like as he dug beneath into the mycelia networks.

"Not me, DEA, look it up," Dr. Demetrius said. "Passive toxicity, addict dies, the body is a host, it's toxic. Breathe in stray particles, someone gets sick, or worse. The hospital took an absolute position. I might have the nurses wear surgical masks as an added precaution."

"But the families?" Artemis said. "It denied them the right to a proper goodbye."

"We have to treat them, you know the government mandates," Dr. Demetrius said. He plucked off flawed mushrooms and dropped them into a biohazard container. "Bad ones, so, what if one of these deceased patients, their addiction leads to a virus, or worse? We can't see it, you can't see it, its viral. The unsuspecting population gets sick, they trace it back here, and then what?"

"I show up," Artemis said. "After you get named in a suit."

"Shocker," Dr. Demetrius said. He sashayed between the rows of trays for mushrooms and mycelia. "These are all different, unique specimens. It's an endless harvest."

"It sounds harsh, but we have to respond to the claims," Artemis said. She crossed her arms and tried not to touch any laboratory surface.

"It is, I don't like it, but we have an epidemic here," Dr. Demetrius said. "By breathing a body becomes infected. Most of this is not science; its ignorance from the DEA. But we had to take extreme measures. Besides, it is rare any family member shows up after an addict dies, unless there might be some money at the end of a dead person's rainbow. Thus the reason you're pestering me."

Artemis was cautious not to bring up Laina, or the information she had gotten from Dr. Langendorpher. She was uncertain how to approach Dr. Demetrius. He was smart, elusive, and potentially lethal.

"Local lawyer seems up front," Artemis said. She strolled along the laboratory aisle between storage stacks behind Dr. Demetrius, with what she presumed were all mushrooms.

"I've met Jerome many times, he has ethics," Dr. Demetrius said. He snipped off the tops of mushrooms with sharp shears he had retrieved from within sterilized packaging. He stared over at Artemis. "Small town, my dear. He's not fond of me. Besides, we don't have attractive redheads roaming our streets, perhaps you come over to my place for dinner? I have mushrooms recipes galore."

"That's not a good idea," Artemis said. She avoided looking at Dr. Demetrius. "I'm here on business."

"Pity," Dr. Demetrius said. "I'm an amazing chef. As you might imagine, my mushroom recipes are to die for. Besides, I like you Artemis, you're interesting. Your blue eyes are alive."

"I'm a claim handler," Artemis said. "I'm boring."

Dr. Demetrius stopped shearing the mushrooms. He gazed back over at Artemis, again with a smirk.

"You are not like any insurance talking head we've had up here before," Dr. Demetrius said. He dropped the shears into a sealed bin. "You're military, it's in your eyes. You march with purpose, your posture it upright, you've strong hands, athletic build."

"Sorry?" Artemis said.

"You're not a fat, pale, stale male, and like I said, you're military trained, it's obvious," Dr. Demetrius said. He waved for Artemis to follow him. "It's about money, I get it. It's rather a sad journey, money cannot solve the world's problems. But money invested, targeted, ah, we can help vast populations live better, healthier lives."

"World's problems?" Artemis said. She noticed they had strolled away from the lab, and were heading down a long, well-lit corridor toward sturdy chrome double-doors with round porthole windows at about her eye level. "That's an open-ended statement."

Dr. Demetrius pushed back the right side door and on the other side he put on a long overcoat with the hospital emblem on the right breast pocket. He handed a similar one to Artemis.

"Earth is over-populated, plastics, micro-beads are clogging up the oceans, killing innocent wildlife," Dr. Demetrius said. He pointed over toward a storage facility. "But I've developed a temporary solution, it's how I keep this hospital open, let me show you."

"This is your secret," Artemis said. She stepped outside with Dr. Demetrius. The chilly loading dock facility did not emit the typical pungent diesel or fossil fuels smells. She shifted to focus on the busy loading dock, and workers moving with choreographed efficiency the different sized shrink-wrapped wooden containers from storage spaces onto electric powered forklifts, being driven by a hazmat suited driver over toward waiting open shipping containers. "Gene and Loretta didn't want me to see this place, why? It's surprising how quiet this place is. Just the commercial truck noise, but they're outside."

"Stupidity, never mind them, our forklifts are green-powered, batteries for those, I've been experimenting with natural gas," Dr. Demetrius said. He pointed at a yellow painted forklift. "What you're seeing is freeze-dried mycelia inside those boxes. I produce them for a vast array of commercial uses. Our clients can grow them; they just add some water. Once they take root, they provide a reusable, clean resource for study. But I cannot release this to the public, yet. The hospital system blocks me."

"The reason they didn't want the reinsurance company aware?" Artemis said. "What's the deal."

"Greed," Dr. Demetrius said. "Think greed. My creations can replace plastic containers. Imagine the size of that market?"

Artemis tried to focus on every detail she saw, the rangy storage units were upwards of about twenty-feet, all stacked full with pallets of shrink-wrapped boxes. The workers covered in germ-free suits, each face hidden behind safety goggles.

"Billions," Artemis said. "Why the germ suits?"

"Hospital is a not for profit," Dr. Demetrius said. "But they always scheme how to make more money. The suits are to minimize contamination. We don't want to spread candida auris. It gets inside the hospital, a tough fungus to eradicate. But we need to be safe out here, it is a good risk management procedure. I don't want to hurt anybody."

"I take it this gets a lot of attention?" Artemis said. Dr. Demetrius was turning into a sphinx. His personality evolved, softening from her previous sensations. She thought he was trusting her, opening up to her.

"Oh yes, my employer is like the big pharma," Dr. Demetrius said. He winked at her. "Once they vacuum up enough money, and my patents expire, their altruism will kick in, and then share my patents with the world."

"Who are your clients?" Artemis said. "Can't be just anyone given all the secrecy."

"Ah, a good question, we are testing with distribution companies for container manufacturing, we don't disclose them, it might get the plastic lobbies attention," Dr. Demetrius said. He waved over at the foreman. "For now, our pharmaceutical friends, it's an easy platform for drug investigations. Bio companies for experimentation for human organs like ears, livers. The mycelia are clean, as if like stem cells. Some day I'll conquer the meatless market, limitless."

"You're your own company inside the hospital," Artemis said. "You must turn a significant profit."

"That's why they leave me alone," Dr. Demetrius said. He stuffed his hands into the overcoats pockets. "Science, the art of medicine is about discovery, curiosity, and seeking the truth, not money. I don't take vacations, I get bored. Nice car, house, after that it's greed. How much money is enough? You know the age old question. Nonsense."

"That's all you care about?" Artemis said.

"Yes, next time, bring your FBI friend. I'll show him whatever he wants," Dr. Demetrius said. "They need not fly over us with a drone. I'll show Agent Beaky whatever he desires."

Artemis turned toward Dr. Demetrius.

"He's easy to notice," Artemis said. She looked over at a spotless, maintained forklift. "Neither am I in a small town like this, guess it's a good place to hide in plain sight?"

"You're holding out," Dr. Demetrius said. He winked as he held his arms and hands open. "I'm standing right here, it's you and me. Ask me whatever you like."

Artemis was certain he wanted her to take his bait. She reserved her thoughts about Laina, and her mother's whereabouts for another time. It would be the obvious first questions.

"You've a twin?" Artemis said.

Dr. Demetrius half-grinned without showing his teeth. But his dark eyes told Artemis he welcomed the question. His eyes seethed with anticipation.

"I see you've been out in the forest. He's lost his mind, drug addict," Dr. Demetrius said. He slipped his hands and arms behind his overcoat. "Calls himself Prophet Higgs Boson, you know, the God particle. How creative. But he is disturbed, that's who the FBI should investigate."

"You've been out in the forest?" Artemis said.

"No, I don't communicate with drug addicts," Dr. Demetrius said. "He's dangerous, I suspect more so these days. I don't know, but he's a functioning drug user and dealer. Opioids, heroin and the rest, wasting his life, wasting other lives."

"You don't speak anymore?" Artemis said.

"Never, it's been years," Dr. Demetrius said. He stared down at the smooth concrete slab. "Artemis, he's the reason for all the high-security. He is very smart, like me. We scan the hospital campus for his girls. Some of his unfortunates come onto the campus inside in an ambulance. Like that little, Laina, the girl's mother was one of his crew. He prostitutes them. Sick."

"Some might imagine you two are working together?" Artemis said. She gripped her hips over the coat. "He gets them hooked, hospital takes them in for addiction treatment. You both get paid coming and going. A greedy scheme to bilk the government and peddle the drugs to users and other distribution channels."

"Fair question. But I took an oath. I take that oath to heart. I try to heal the sick. And remember, I'm Greek, Hippocrates was Greek," Dr. Demetrius said. He squished his lips together. He pointed over at Artemis. "At first, I wasn't sure about you. I find business people, lawyers, boring. A collection of greedy boxes of hair, but you seem different, you have an edge about you."

"What's your brother doing out in the forest?" Artemis said.

"You're holding out on me again," Dr. Demetrius said. He studied Artemis' face. He nodded. "I'm an arrogant ass, I admit it. But my work is for humanity. My name, my families name will be on those patents well after I'm gone, they are my legacy. I accept the secrecy as a necessary evil to protect my work."

Artemis kept her gaze right back at Dr. Demetrius. She sensed he was being truthful. And for the first time, he was not cautious and evasive.

"He's, into demonic worship," Artemis said. She stopped. She crossed her arms. "Tell you what, I'll take you up on your offer. I'll come back with my FBI friend, Agent Beaky, take a tour, and why don't we all go out into the forest to visit your brother."

"He's dangerous, he's hates me. I refuse to allow him near the hospital, the reason he's paid off the local police, but they're afraid of my employer.

A false move and they all get hammered, but they'll pocket his money," Dr. Demetrius said. He looked downward at the shiny surface. He nodded. "He'll kill me on sight. I have no question about that, or his intentions."

"You'll be safe," Artemis said. "I'm trained for these sorts of, ah, trips. He would need to bring an army."

"Oh, I see. I'm not afraid of death," Dr. Demetrius said, matter-of-factly. "I've been in death's presence, many times. My DNR has simple instructions, after, they'll wrap me in mushrooms, and I'll be buried near newly planted oak trees leading up to the hospitals front doors. A green way, a natural method for burial. I'll fertilize the soil as I decompose."

"I'll protect you," Artemis said. "We'll go during daylight, you'll have the FBI, Agent Beaky."

"I have a bad feeling about my brother, you must realize he hates my mother for leaving us at birth. He has this weird, flawed reasoning," Dr. Demetrius said. "He has no ethics, no higher calling. I'll almost guarantee you he knew you were out there. I'm told he monitors everything. Like I said, he keeps the local police in his pocket."

"I believe you. I think you need to see his ritualistic site. It's about the mushrooms," Artemis said. She backed away.

"That's a suspicious comment," Dr. Demetrius said. "I've heard the rumors. Good sales pitch, Artemis. I'll go. First come visit me with Agent Beaky."

"I'll be in contact," Artemis said. She twisted and walked toward the double doors.

"And you meant to say, mission?" Dr. Demetrius said. He backed away from Artemis and started to stroll farther into the storage facility toward the waiting foreman. "Don't edit your words, makes you appear weak."

Chapter 28

"Artemis?" The voice emanated from Artemis' smartphone speaker.

"Yes," Artemis said. She sat up on her hotel room's bed by stuffing two pillows behind her back. She wiped her eyes. "Jerome?"

"Yes," Jerome said. His voice sounded hesitant. His cadence searching for the precise word. "Been dealing with your request. Your statement, connection to the father has been helpful, and I think well received, ah, by the court."

"You don't sound real confident?" Artemis said. She held the smartphone closer in front of her mouth.

"You're correct," Jerome said. Artemis heard him cough to clear his throat. She thought he was delaying the inevitable news.

"I'm waiting," Artemis said. "Laina?"

"Laina, yes," Jerome said. "I went to visit her, part of my job as your counsel. She's seems healthy, but she's not in good spirits. Ah, another problem has emerged."

"Talk," Artemis said.

"First off, let me handle this," Jerome said. "But I learned the family has a connection to this prophet character. I think they are under his spell."

Artemis sprang off the bed. She searched the room for her suitcase, her tactical clothes and considered if she'd need her tools.

"Take me there," Artemis said. "She needs to see my face. I need to reassure her I've not abandoned her."

"I'm not sure," Jerome said.

"Jerome, that man's out of his mind," Artemis said. She paused. "Come pick me up. I'll tell you something, in confidence, it'll help you with your file."

"It might get hairy," Jerome said. "I'm not sure about this."

"I'm a big girl, you know that," Artemis said. She stopped pacing. "Instead, I'll run down to your office. I need to get out there. Now."

~

"How do people live out here?" Artemis said. "It's remote. I guess some like living off the grid."

"Not well," Jerome said. He drove his modest SUV along a bending blacktopped two lanes road. "The coal jobs, gone, they refuse to move away."

"Why are you here?" Artemis said. She tapped on the SUV's passenger side window with her right hand knuckles. "You're talented enough to practice in a big city. But you came back."

"I guess it was my parents," Jerome said. He gripped the spongy leather covered steering wheel. "They were missionaries, their white chapel is close to where we are heading. I think they instilled in me to focus on faith, family and the truth. I wish I had a greedy bone in my body. It would have made paying for my kids schooling a lot easier. This is home. It's that simple."

"I understand, in part," Artemis said. "These mountains are beautiful, they're magical. I imagine spring is amazing."

"So true, yes, you should see springtime, and the fall colors are glorious," Jerome said. He pointed out toward a mountain peak fronted by a shear rocky limestone face. "I used to hike up there, the view is incredible. But then pot came to town, not the moonshiners, but the growers. They grow it up in the hills. And now, it's worse. They have infested the forest, hide out here, with these evil characters. Drug dealing and the sort."

As Jerome drove Artemis pondered her future, and her coming decisions. Satan created her this labyrinth. It offered her clues and obstacles. Its pinprick into her heart was love. But Satan the hate farmer spread rumor, innuendo and conflict.

"How do you know an all powerful God exists?" Artemis said.

Jerome glanced over at Artemis. He shook his head.

"They write books about that question," Jerome said. He grinned as he drove the SUV farther along the narrow road, he clicked the SUV's blinker as a 1950s rust bucket was squeaking by them from the other direction. He turned the SUV left onto a gravel road with a grassy center hump, canopied by oaks, maples and pine trees toward a pie shaped clearing. "I've sensed pure evil, it's a feeling you get, you know?"

"Oh, I know that feeling," Artemis said. "I ask because of your parents. Mine never took me to church. Ever."

"From my parents, correct, it's true," Jerome said. "They revealed God to me; they encouraged me to confront evil, from that guidance it gives me the power to stand up and protect those that cannot protect themselves."

"How's that show me a God is in the hood?" Artemis said. She sniffled as diffused sunlight splashed inside the SUV. "My allergies are coming back. Spring must be early."

"You answered the question," Jerome said. "Winter to Spring, from death to renewal. God reveals spring because we perceive a renewal is coming, we trust that will happen with our fancy science."

"You lost me," Artemis said. She sneezed. "Excuse me."

"It's about trust, accepting the truth," Jerome said. He stopped the SUV and parked it about a quarter mile from a shotgun style wooden planked house painted dark blue topped with a tin roof. "Let's give ourselves some space. My father taught me about death. He told me in the hospitals he'd watched a person die. Many times their eyes were open, they were in pain, pumped full of morphine, so forth. At the instant they died, they smiled, it was faint, as if their eyes saw something beyond them, a happy vision, he thought. Think about that, what did they see?"

"I appreciate you sharing," Artemis said. She unclipped her seat belt. She scanned out of the windshield toward the home. "Looks like we get to meet this prophet. His twin is over at the hospital."

Jerome stared forward and grunted.

"It was inevitable," Jerome said. He opened the SUV driver-side door. Artemis and Jerome walked across the gravel and dirt, the sturdy man tried to startle Artemis near the home's front wooden door protected by a rickety metal screen door. His face an exact copy of Dr. Demetrius. But his black hair slicked back, and he was muscled and more athletic than his brother. He menaced.

"I speak for the family," he said. He stood on the wooden porch above the concrete stairs.

"And you would be?" Jerome said. He kept stepping toward the front screen door. "Are you a mute?"

The larger man placed his big hand on Jerome's right shoulder.

"I am Prophet Higgs Boson," he said.

"Take your hand off," Jerome said. He glared at Prophet Higgs Boson. "Are you an attorney? Do you have a license to practice?"

"I am a healer," Prophet Higgs Boson said. "I am important for my flocks lives. I cannot be bothered with trivial things."

"Then the answers no," Jerome said. He flicked Prophet Higgs Boson's hand away. "I am. I'm here on behalf of the court, and my client. Go sit on that porch swing, and stay out of my way, or I'll call someone you don't want to meet. And I don't mean the police."

Prophet Higgs Boson stepped back, held his rough hands up, and he gazed down at Artemis.

"I mean no harm," Prophet Higgs Boson said. He pointed over at Artemis. "Your client?"

"Yes," Jerome said. "She need not respond to you."

"Thank you," Artemis said. She stepped out from behind Jerome. She stood motionless in front of Prophet Higgs Boson, investigating, observing, calibrating up into his dark eyes, studying his face, and his body down to his fancy Italian leather slippers.

"Feisty," Prophet Higgs Boson said.

"Nice ride," Artemis said. She nudged her shoulder over toward the shiny black SUV parked next to a meandering stream. "You?"

"My flock provides for me," Prophet Higgs Boson said. "I need reliable transport to meet with my flock."

"Stay out here," Jerome said. He knocked on the door and turned the metal knob. He peeked inside beyond the doorjamb. "Hello, again. Artemis follow me, please."

Jerome and Artemis stood just within the ramshackle home's front door. The ceiling painted smooth, but it had an irregular flow, it set low and created a claustrophobic effect. Toward the back of the house appeared to be a galley-style kitchen, an iron potbelly stove provided heat near the opened back door. Jerome shut the front door to prevent Prophet Higgs Boson from entering behind them.

"We'll still get paid?" A scruffy middle-aged man said. He wore a rumpled red flannel shirt with bib overalls. A box of greasy deep fried food on his lap. "We're havin' to feed her."

"We ain't made a money," a skinny woman in a wrinkled pale green dress. "She ain't our only responsibly."

Artemis looked over at her. The woman stood on the frayed tan linoleum, but her eyes told a different story. Her brown eyes were unfocused, watery. Her once vibrant pinkish skin blotched with discolored acne.

"I'll assure you the state will direct deposit your check," Jerome said. He smiled, nodded and he leaned his shoulders forward. "Can you bring Laina for us? We just want to say hi, and then we'll be on our way."

The man waved backward for them to travel down the center hallway toward the pot belly stove.

"She don't come out," he said. "Help yourself. She's on the left side, last room."

Artemis and Jerome stepped around them, down the short hallway entering a tiny bedroom. A shear curtain covered the south-facing window. The single bed covered with a long forgotten sleeping bag. Artemis spotted Laina stuffed into the corner between the bed and the wall hugging a forlorn pillow.

"Laina?" Jerome said. He leaned down on his left knee. "I brought Artemis. She wants to say hello."

Artemis heard Profit Higgs Boson outside talking to someone. He was into his saving souls act and likely sharing his drug samples; she thought. She leaned down in next to Jerome. The room smelled musty like forgotten cardboard boxes inside a storage unit.

"I wanted you to see my face," Artemis said. She held her hands out. "I'll get you out of here."

Laina held the pillow against her legs back up against her chest. She stared down at mauve shag carpet. She shook head.

"They goin' to hurt me," Laina said, flatly. Her downward gaze certain. "I'm done for."

"Not on my watch," Jerome said. "We're watching. I'll engage the court to get you out of here."

"That woman's like my dead mama," Laina said. She sniffled. She pointed toward the closed bedroom door.

"Has any one hurt you?" Artemis said. She shifted down to draw Laina's gaze into her eyes. "I'm trying to adopt you, do you understand?"

"I ain't leavin' here, am I," Laina said. She looked up at Artemis from above the pillow.

"Not today," Jerome said. "I'm working as fast as I can, I'm sorry. Artemis wants to take you in, keep that in mind. It'll give you some hope."

"I recognize that big man outside," Laina said.

"How so?" Jerome said.

"Give stuff to my mama," Laina said. "He knows my name."

Artemis sat back on her legs, she squeezed her hips with her hands. She fake smiled over at Laina.

"For now," Artemis said. "Stay low, out of the way. I'll deal with that mess. Do you understand me?"

"Better hurry," Laina said. "He's taken my friends, they just up and disappeared. It was him. I just know it."

Jerome glanced over at Artemis. He nodded it was time for them to leave. Artemis slinked closer to Laina.

"Don't you fret little lady," Jerome said. He scowled over at Artemis. "We'll return. I promise you that."

"Come over here," Artemis said. She held her arms open. "Give me a hug. I want you to know I'm not abandoning you. You're part of my tribe. I don't leave tribe members behind."

Jerome got up and turned his back as Laina crawled out and hugged Artemis. She grappled into Artemis. Laina whimpered. She moaned.

"I'm always watching," Artemis said. She whispered. "You're never alone."

"I'm scared," Laina said. Her body shook. "He's goin' to hurt me. He's talkin' 'bout evil stuff."

"The world has scared me many times," Artemis said. She held Laina closer. "My mother always told me it was okay to cry, it makes the fear drain out of you. She told me that's why she always competed without fear, she focused her mind on each fact. The fact is I'm here. I'll protect you."

"My daddy loved you?" Laina said. "That true?"

"Yes, I loved him," Artemis said. And Artemis allowed her brain to unlock her heart. It was what Benjamin would have begged her for. "I love you. I'll protect you with my life."

Laina kept whimpering as she nodded crushing her face into Artemis' neck and shoulder. She wiped her wet eyes across Artemis' right arm.

"Thank you for lookin' out for me," Laina said. She backed away. And scurried back clutching the pillow into her dark hiding spot between the beaten down bed and the protective wall.

After Artemis had released Laina, she closed her eyes, sucked in a deep breath and blew out it out from her lips.

"Just stay down," Artemis said. "Think positive thoughts." She twisted up toward Jerome, and they left the bedroom.

Outside on the wooden porch, the Prophet Higgs Boson was explaining the universe to the wiry little man from inside. They acknowledged Jerome and Artemis.

"Jerome, can you do me a favor?" Artemis said. She gripped Jerome's left forearm with intent. "Walk to your SUV and do me the favor and don't look back."

Jerome's eyes understood the request. He kept striding away across the gravel surface with his brown dress shoes covered its chalky gray dusk. Artemis gave him a few seconds, and she twisted and scampered over toward Prophet Higgs Boson. Before she reached him, she heard Satan's sarcastic voice within her mind.

"Artemis, he's funny," Satan said. "Let him talk."

Artemis stopped. She gazed up into the brown hillside, and then she kept marching across the wooden porch to face square with Prophet Higgs Boson. The middle-aged man slinked behind Prophet Higgs Boson.

"Do not fear," Profit Higgs Boson said. He held his muscled arms wide. "I will provide for my lambs, the girl is safe with my flock."

"I've met your brother," Artemis said. "He's into his mushrooms and other creations. A smart doctor. He's brilliant."

Prophet Higgs Boson grimaced at Artemis.

"He's an arrogant fool," Prophet Higgs Boson said. He crossed his arms. His shoulders back. "He knows nothing, I am beyond him. My ministry will change the world, he is nothing."

"They sent me here to clean up his mess," Artemis said.

"Good, praise Satan," Prophet Higgs Boson said. He reached forward to grasp Artemis' left shoulder. "Do those works, join my flock."

"Not my thing," Artemis said. She allowed his hand to grip into her strong shoulder and feel her muscles. "I am sure you understand."

"You should try our mushrooms," Prophet Higgs Boson said. He huffed. He released his grip and held his hand out toward the forest. "My flock harvests them. These woods provide. Nothing my brother would understand. Try them and you'll journey with me through the universe. We will converge into one spirit."

"Someone has told me not to eat the mushrooms," Artemis said.

"I search into the future," Prophet Higgs Boson said. "I see the mind of gods, Satan gifts me with sight. Join my flock, give your life over to me."

"Stare into my eyes," Artemis said. She stepped closer up to Prophet Higgs Boson. "Look real deep into my eyes. Go on, do it."

Prophet Higgs Boson complied and vacuously stared down at Artemis. She tiptoed upwards with a blank, certain face.

"The little girl inside, is mine," Artemis said.

"Perhaps," Prophet Higgs said.

"Wrong answer. I'm gifted, too. I search into the future, as well," Artemis said. "If she's touched, abused, if she should slip on a rock and skin her knee, guess what the future holds for you?"

"I follow where my lord takes me," Prophet Higgs Boson said. His voice unsteady. His gaze avoided Artemis', and he stared out toward the trees. "They have delivered her for a purpose." He paused, his mouth gaped open. "It's my… Lord's… ah… plan."

Artemis shifted to follow his line of sight. There, at the forest's edge across the flowing cold stream stood the American Indian spirt warrior. He menaced, his eyes fierce, and he held his once sharp spear as if to launch it. He screeched at them in his native tongue.

"You know that spirit warrior?" Artemis said. She pointed over at the spirit warrior. "The one standing over there, other side of the water, looking at you. He likes me. He hates you."

Prophet Higgs Boson ignored her.

"I look at what Satan reveals to me," Prophet Higgs Boson said. But he flinched as Artemis heard the warrior scream over at Prophet Higgs Boson, and she saw the warrior try to throw the spear. It hurdled toward them, but the golden particles dissipated into the air above the stream. Artemis poked Prophet Higgs Boson in the chest with her lefthand forefinger.

"I'll tell you Satan's plan for you, and that idiot worm hiding behind you. If she's harmed," Artemis said. She pushed in closer to Prophet Higgs Boson. She punched his chest again with the back of her left hand fist. "That spirit that just tried to kill you will pale compared to me. I'm alive. And I realize Satan's plan for you, it's clear to me, want to know what it is?"

"I do not fear Satan," Prophet Higgs Boson said. He laughed dismissively. "Satan is my god. I am a valued servant. My lord will not leave me to female humans like you. You are weak."

"Thank you," Artemis said.

"For what? You are a strange woman," Prophet Higgs Boson said. "Women are useful when they obey me."

"I have identified the mess I need to clean up," Artemis said. She backed up and started to stroll away. She was methodical in her steps. She stared back at Prophet Higgs Boson. "It is now clear in my heart, in my mind."

Prophet Higgs Boson shifted close behind her toward the concrete porch steps. He gazed down at Artemis as she ambled away and across the dirt and gravel surface toward Jerome's SUV.

"Tell me of this mess?" Prophet Higgs Boson said. "What has my Lord

Satan told you, a mortal woman?"

"You," Artemis said. She glared back over at him as she smacked hard his SUV on the hood, triggering the loud car alarm. It blared out a theft warning. "You're the mess I've been seeking. Remember my words about the girl."

"Artemis," Satan said. It screamed. It howled from beyond the nearby mountains and across the tranquil stream smothered with smoothed over rocks and pebbles. "So delightful, so sinister, and cryptic, you're learning. I felt your authentic performance. I believed you. I think the wormy man almost dropped a deuce in his pants. Scary, scary Artemis. Oh, the assassin is getting warmed up for action. I cannot wait to feel your hate."

"Leave me alone, I don't hate," Artemis said under her breath. She got back inside the SUV and stared through the windshield at Prophet Higgs Boson. As he was pressing his SUV fob spastically trying to shutoff the theft alarm and the red blinking tail lights. He flipped Artemis off.

"Sorry," Jerome said. "He's a problem."

"Let's get out of here," Artemis said. "I need to travel back home. I've identified my task."

"Very well," Jerome said. He started the SUV's engine. "I'll keep tabs on her. I promise."

"Thank you," Artemis said. "I'll be recommending the claim management come from my boss. I'll encourage him to get up here. He prefers to talk about these matters face to face."

Jerome glanced over at Artemis. He nodded as he shifted the SUV into reverse, and spun it around.

"I'll welcome him," Jerome said. "I just want to get these matters resolved, let these families heal."

"Yeah," Artemis said. She turned soured and kept her gaze on the agitated Prophet Higgs Boson. "Please get Laina out of there. Either way, that man has to go. And by the way, I don't think your claim is about medical malpractice. I think Dr. Demetrius ethically cared and treated the patients."

"Thank you, I guess we'll fight this out," Jerome said. "We understand each other. But listen to me. Don't get your self arrested fooling with that moron. You'll not do Laina or me any good getting tangled up with the police. They'll sit you in a jail cell."

"I know you're right, I think your claims hiding in the hospital garden," Artemis said. She turned back around. "It's one trap door after the other. And if I fall, she'll die."

Chapter 29

"I've never seen you let a file get this complicated," Wylie said. Bemused as he pointed over at Alan the Moon's bartender whistling a tune, dancing and engaging his bar guests. "He's a happy soul."

"What are we having?" Alan said. He piano tapped his fingers on the amber marble bar top. "Hello, Artemis the lamb."

"Alan this is Wylie," Artemis said. She half-grinned.

"Hello, Wylie," Alan said. "What will it be?"

"I'll have a Guinness," Wylie said. He chuckled. He sat back on a solid wooden stool next to Artemis. "This your joint? Kinda place when I was young you'd get a beer and smoke cigarettes."

"It's a good, quiet spot," Artemis said. The ceiling fans wafted cold air down on her. "I never get hit on, mostly a local crowd. Quiet spot, however, must be a soccer match tonight."

Alan whistled as he turned, he grabbed a branded Guinness pint glass and skipped across the heavy duty, anti-fatigue rubber mats to start the two-part pore method at the tap.

"I must pour your Guinness with great care," Alan said. He looked and pointed back over at Wylie. "Patience my new friend."

"He's serious about that," Wylie said. He chuckled as he leaned forward and looked down the bar alley over at Alan. "Understands the process, a good bartender, he's a Brit?"

"Welsh. He'd correct you. Reason I come in here, remember my mother was Irish," Artemis said. She shifted the half-full glass back and forth over the bar top between her open palms. "It's my home base, a place I can look forward to after a long trip into the unknown."

"I bet," Wylie said. He admired the British West Indies themed restaurant. The dark wood, the ornamental mirrors. "Cool joint."

After one-hundred-nineteen seconds, Alan brought over a full Guinness pint. Alan set it in front of Wylie and they all enjoyed watching the turbulent contents as if they were waiting for a scuba diver to emerge from being cascaded and surged up through a turbulent brownish-red sea and up into a calm light brown foam surface.

"Perfection," Alan said. He wiped off any residue and pointed the harp symbol at Wylie. "Enjoy."

Artemis leaned over and clinked Wylie's glass.

"To good health," Artemis said. She sat back after taking a gulp. "I have a tough mission before me. A child's life is at risk. I don't like it."

"You're serious about taking her in?" Wylie said. He crinkled his face as looked over at Artemis. He sipped the Guinness. "She does not understand what you're about. I don't want to know. But she'll be livin' with you."

"I'll figure it out," Artemis said. She flopped her hands on her lap as a bar guest yelled at a television screen watching a rugby match. "Like I said, it's complicated. The attorney suing the hospital offered to help me out. He's a good man."

Wylie acknowledged the comment.

"Small town America," Wylie said. He shrugged. "But you've kept everything straight? I don't have any surprises coming?"

"Good question," Artemis said. She shifted closer to Wylie. "Felt I had this one figured out. I'd get it on a slow track, burn out his credit limit. Keep him burning cash down the road and beg to settle while I searched for the mess I was sent to clean up."

"That makes good sense," Wylie said. He stared up at the silent television screen displaying the hard fought rugby match. "Strange game, they'd hurt me. So, what changed?"

"A word," Artemis said. "After I heard it, I went roaming about the hospital campus. Acted like I felt ill and needed a walk. I found what I was looking for, it was right there."

"You don't want this in a file?" Wylie said. "Reason you had me cross Gandy Bridge for a Guinness."

"Remember, I've got an FBI agent poking into our hospital, he's chasing a drug dealer that turns out is Dr. Demetrius' twin brother," Artemis said. She gripped the single ogee edge of the wooden bar. "I don't get the feeling Dr. Demetrius has been selling drugs out the back of the hospital. They have some interesting business ventures. But it's something else. I found his secret, he's got a serious Achilles heal to hide. I suspect he got away with it for years, and now it has gotten out of control with the opioid epidemic."

Wylie and Artemis sat next to each other for several minutes. They had studied the active medical malpractice claim file down to every grammatical mistake, every misplaced comma. It was also a file seen by higher-ups or worse, it could be exposed inside a court room.

"How's the little girl doing?" Wylie said. He gripped the cold glass. "I've been advised The Company supports your decision."

"I have a tracking device on her," Artemis said. "Best, I can tell she's still alive, she doesn't move around much. It's a depressing situation."

"You're crafty," Wylie said. He sighed. "Let me see if I can help, make a few back channel calls."

Artemis turned her head over at Wylie. She looked beyond him over at another bar guest eating a colorful curried dish. And then she focused on Wylie.

"Never considered it. But maybe speed up the process?" Artemis said. She smiled. She nodded. "Without Jerome finding out, get her under my care and away from that mess she's living in."

"You know something girl," Wylie said. He hesitated. He stopped talking as he looked forward as a restaurant chef approached them. They stenciled his name on his maroon chef jacket. His face was cherub like, he was a fit middle-aged man with mischievous brown eyes. A white kitchen towel draped over his right shoulder as he sauntered along the bartenders alley. He beamed over at Artemis revealing crows-feet near his eyes.

"Graced us with your presence?"

Artemis reached across the bar to shake the man's moist hand. He had sweat along his receding light brown hair.

"You look like you came out of a hot sauna?" Artemis said. "Chef Mikey, this is my direct report Wylie."

"Pleased to meet you," Wylie said.

"As well," Chef Mikey said.

"You sound from across the pond, London?" Wylie said. "Like the happy bartender over there."

"I am, but that one's Welsh, but you sound like," Chef Mikey said. His cheeks puffed with his eyebrows raised. "Not quite redneck? No disrespect."

"North Carolina," Wylie said. He winked at Artemis. "I've heard your accent from my trips over to Lloyd's. Pleasure is all mine."

"Ah, as well," Chef Mikey said. "What can I get for ya, Artemis always gets my fish and chips, kinda boring if you ask me. I can make you Vindaloo, spicy, if you can man-up?"

"Careful Wylie," Artemis said. She laughed and lifted her Guinness. "They mean hot and spicy."

"How about giving us a few minutes," Wylie said. He acknowledged Chef Mikey, he leaned back on the wooden stool. He crossed his arms.

"All righty then," Chef Mikey said. He tapped the bar top, as he proceeded on down the bar checking in on other bar guests.

Artemis waited until he was out of earshot. She made sure that the bartender was distracted. The active bar gave them enough loud sounds to drown out their conversation. She whispered over at Wylie.

"We need to settle this file, keep it quiet," Artemis said. "It could take down the hospital."

"All right," Wylie said. He sipped the Guinness. "That's good to know. We'll keep the file notes bare. After you share it in the file, you write it down, it lives forever. That's your thinking."

"Yes, the lawyer knows the entire town, grew up there," Artemis said. "He'll find out, that's what I'm thinking. I'm trying to maneuver him into a global settlement. He'll not want to be the reason the hospital closes."

"You don't think he has any tangible evidence?" Wylie said. He gripped his left earlobe. "Yet."

"Not something I or he can get at without getting a lot of curious eyeballs," Artemis said. "It's buried. As in composting in the front lawn, a manicured garden with human fertilizer."

Wylie stared up at the television. He uncrossed his arms.

"If I heard you," Wylie said. His face grimaced. He paused as he gazed back over at Artemis with a capricious expression. "A word, and it was there in plain sight, this some kind of riddle."

"It'll make your skin crawl," Artemis said.

"Ha, I've a strong stomach," Wylie said. "I've been at this a long time. Surprise me."

"You ever done much gardening?" Artemis said. She stared back over at the side of Wylie's face as there were new guests walking near the bar area. They tapped on the bar next to Wylie. "Hospital has a strong green initiative. Dr. Demetrius has an abnormal interest in composting. He explained it all to me without realizing it. If not for the fact it's illegal, buried in a mushroom suit seems better than being pumped full of chemicals and stuffed in a metal box. Unless it's your next of kin, and without your knowledge."

Wylie's expression opened up, as if he'd seen a vision.

"What are you thinking?" Wylie said. He whispered over near Artemis. "We might be wise to engage the attorney, get in front of this claim file before someone goes digging in the garden?"

"That's my thinking," Artemis said. "I think I know where they've hidden the dead bodies. In the literal sense."

"Tell you what," Wylie said. He leaned back up. "Oh dear, I knew something strange was going on up there. It's that sixth sense. And I don't' know how you do it, but these death case files you get figured out in short order." He sighed. "I'll talk inside the house about my authority level, because if I follow, it might be a big number."

"If it gets out into the public, a huge number," Artemis said. She pushed the pint forward. "And I found the mess I need to manage. You'll help me with Laina?"

"Without a question," Wylie said. He gripped Artemis' left forearm. "I'll get her on a fast track with a call or two. But you be careful. These folks won't be thrilled with your discovery."

Chapter 30

"Agent Beaky, did you know in the next century the world's population will grow to approximately eleven billion," Dr. Demetrius said. He steepled his fingers. "Consider, how do we feed them? How do we manage infection?"

"It's a problem," Agent Beaky said. He buttoned up his jacket beneath his square chin. "But that's out of my role and responsibility, what happens here, inside this place?"

"I'm answering your question," Dr. Demetrius said. He wore a respirator as was Artemis and Agent Beaky. Dr. Demetrius stood next to a solid storage pole staring upward. "Look around my mushroom farm, take your time, notice the busy drones up on top, so forth, and then I'll show you my lab and our processing facility."

"Gene wasn't real happy with you," Artemis said. The respirator caused her to have an awkward vision of the mushroom farm.

"That's why I'm in charge," Dr. Demetrius said. "He can stay out of the way, the glutton's got bourbon in his desk drawer. Addiction will ruin his career. I need to protect my work."

"Very well," Agent Beaky said. "Mind if I walk a bit?"

"Please inspect, take your time," Dr. Demetrius said. He waved his hands toward the storage bins and the down dark alleyways. "I have nothing to hide. It's science, experimentations."

With a hand-held flashlight, Agent Beaky scanned up and down at the towering storage system. He glanced over at Artemis. He shook his head and strolled down the aisleway, peeking inside the large bins. Careful not to touch anything, he disappeared into the darkness except for the yellow flashlight spotlight and returned after several minutes. And he was being followed by the curious tiny wandering spirit girl. She waved over at Artemis as she smiled.

"Are these consumable?" Agent Beaky said. He clicked off his flashlight. "These are genetically modified?"

"Hi, Artemis," she said. She giggled. And then she slouched down and dangled her arms near her feet. "I don't have anyone to play with. Do you want to play?"

Artemis looked over at her and blew her a kiss. The little spirit girl with scraggly hair and a bland dress understood and she waved back as she disappeared into the darkness.

"These are intended for eventual consumption," Dr. Demetrius said. He tapped on a storage container smothered with mushroom caps. "They are free samples; We share them with interested parties. They have amazing texture, the flavors are pleasing. Almost like a steak."

"To be clear," Agent Beaky said. "Genetically modified?"

"It's what I do," Dr. Demetrius said. He shrugged and waved for them to follow him toward his genetic testing lab doors. "It's more than just food, like these specimens. It's also new drugs to fight infectious disease, protecting the environment from solid wastes."

Dr. Demetrius unlocked the sturdy lab door and they entered the laboratory space. He took off his respirator and encouraged the group to follow his example.

"What I'm showing you is private," Dr. Demetrius said. "These are proprietary. I'm opening up our doors to minimize any potential for the FBI to show up unannounced. I know Gene's been secretive, and to an extent our procedures are justified to protect the public, and as you are both aware, my brother's activities."

"It's private with me," Agent Beaky said. He shifted farther into the lab space. "We'll keep our options open as to the legal and potential criminality."

"I'm in," Artemis said. "Let's keep moving, we'll need some time to get out into the forest. I don't want to get caught at night out there with your brother lurking."

"Ah, good point," Dr. Demetrius said. "I'll be efficient. Agent Beaky what is the largest organism in the world?"

Agent Beaky considered the question as he looked around at the large square shaped laboratory. He glanced at Artemis.

"Not sure," Agent Beaky said. "Where are your technicians? Employees, I see a lot of workstations. Those chrome covered machines look expensive."

"They work at night," Dr. Demetrius said. He stared curiously over at Agent Beaky and then over at Artemis. "It minimized the questions, and, as I've mentioned, I have a mental twin brother. He's the problem. He tries to sneak in here, steal my work. So we modified our work hours, so forth, to minimize an intrusion."

"He is a problem, now that I've met the creep," Artemis said. "I dislike the man."

"Let's deal with him later," Agent Beaky said. He waved his hands forward and encouraged Dr. Demetrius to continue.

"Very good," Dr. Demetrius said. He pointed at the covered containers. "This is where we begin our research. I've studied the fungi genome; In fact, we can get whole fungi genome sequences, publicly available. It's available, do an internet search."

"So you're not reinventing," Agent Beaky said. "An open source approach, if I follow?"

"I'm starting my work at that point, yes," Dr. Demetrius said. "I give credit in my patent applications. I try to be as transparent as possible and not get into trouble. I abide by our industry ethics. It is vital for the long-term emergent science."

"What are you doing, then?" Artemis said. "What's the real point if it's not for money?"

"A question I'm wondering about," Agent Beaky said. He tapped Artemis on the forearm.

"Mushrooms are the outgrowth from the fungi," Dr. Demetrius said. "Why do humans reproduce, right, simple, to advance the species. That's all the mushrooms do, they feed on rot, they grow, the spores they release. The spores can travel over great distances to find a spot to grow, to survive."

Dr. Demetrius walked in front of a storage unit. He opened it and removed a rectangular-shaped specimen tray. He peeled back the white spiderweb like cloth to reveal the mushrooms. He opened a drawer as he retrieved a sterile packaged digging tool.

"These are edible?" Agent Beaky said. He pointed down at the metal tray. "I've seen these in the grocery."

"Wonder what got me researching fungi?" Dr. Demetrius said.

Agent Beaky considered the question. He nodded.

"Family member? Loved one?" Agent Beaky said. He twisted and scanned the laboratory. "It is a typical human emotional reaction. Money is not a strong motivator."

"Yes, well put," Dr. Demetrius said. He placed the metal tray onto a black granite lab table. "Many years ago, my loving mother delivered healthy, beautiful twin boys."

Dr. Demetrius rubbed his eyes with his latex covered thumb and forefinger. He paused as he examined his gloved hands, removed the gloves, put them into a biohazard receptacle and replaced the gloves with a new pair on his hands.

"What happened?" Artemis said.

"My mother died for me to live," Dr. Demetrius said. He sighed. He sucked in a deep breath. "She was allergic to penicillin, or the candida auris got inside her, sad to say, but she was a smoker. Might have breathed in a deadly yeast, a fungus. I've read her medical history to the point I've memorized her case. They never figured out why, or more important, how. It bothers me. I don't want a child to feel like I did growing up."

Artemis turned toward Agent Beaky.

"Dirty secret in medical malpractice, hospital cases that I've had," Artemis said. "Candid auris can be difficult to eradicate inside hospitals. You can't see it, and it spreads without warning. If not managed, you'd almost have to tent the place like a home to kill off termites."

Dr. Demetrius pointed the digging tool over at Artemis.

"Yes, what she said," Dr. Demetrius said. "They didn't have the anti-fungals to treat her. She died a horrible death. The reason I started to research fungi. I think the fungi are the answer to many world-wide problems. I'll tell you one of my closely held secrets, to prove my point."

Dr. Demetrius stared over at them with a perplexed expression.

"I'll keep quiet," Agent Beaky said. "I got it."

"I'm in," Artemis said.

Dr. Demetrius nodded and sighed.

"Gut biome, I think that's where we attack," Dr. Demetrius said. "How do we as a species improve quality of life and survive?"

"Better drugs?" Agent Beaky said.

"No, just the opposite," Dr. Demetrius said. "Better natural resistance. Make our body's immune systems work. It's in the food."

"Genetically change food systems," Artemis said. "You hinted at it, it makes sense now. Mycelia, yeast, the fungi, its limitless food supply. If I follow your thinking."

"Treat a human like a plant," Dr. Demetrius said. "Modify the human genome over a generation or two. Have either of you two at least taken the time to read my patents?"

"Now wait," Agent Beaky said. "That's bordering on illegality. You can't alter food, FDA will shut you down."

Dr. Demetrius started to dig into the dark plant soil between rows of white capped mushrooms.

"More of an ethical issue, I think. But I'll accept the criticism. I welcome peer review. It will advance the science. But that's also why we are only researching; experimenting, we have strict rules dealing with genome DNA sequencing, so forth," Dr. Demetrius said. "We do not share these with the general-public. I'm not a criminal or lacking in ethics. But I have to push my work to that point of no return. I want you to understand my reasoning."

"What are you showing me?" Agent Beaky said. He leaned farther forward. "What's in there?"

"See below the surface," Dr. Demetrius said. He hummed. "The white spider web like strata?"

"Yes," Agent Beaky said.

"That, Agent Beaky, is mycelia," Dr. Demetrius said. "It's what creates all the magic. Mushrooms are just their fruit. It's what you don't see that makes the difference. It's like the air we breathe, without it, we'd all die. But we can't see it."

Dr. Demetrius patched over the disturbed soil. He patted in down with a gentle tap with his gloved fingers.

"New drugs, food," Artemis said. "Eliminate plastics, micro beads, if my memory is good."

"Yes, I'm harnessing nature, my mycelia might make the soil better for dry environments, drought resistant," Dr. Demetrius said. He started to walk holding the metal container. "Let's keep this moving along. I don't have all day. Besides, I want to see what my brother's been doing out there in the forest. He's a concern I've had for sometime. I trust you two can protect me."

"I think it's bad," Agent Beaky said. He pursed his lips and glanced over at Artemis. "I'll follow your lead."

"Very good, wait a moment," Dr. Demetrius said. "Let's put her back inside the holding unit, keep her safe, and warm. I almost messed this up."

"You really love those things," Artemis said.

Dr. Demetrius slid the metal tray back inside the refrigeration unit. He checked the internal temperature, the humidity control dials.

"It's just my life's work, no big deal," Dr. Demetrius said. He turned his head ever so slight back over at Artemis. "If you love something or someone, you'll protect them, maybe with your life?"

"Yes," Artemis said. She turned to step toward the metal doors.

"Ah, for your mother, it's the love for your mother," Agent Beaky said. "I get it. What's next?"

Chapter 31

"I'm at the hospital," Artemis said. She encouraged Dr. Demetrius and Agent Beaky to continue along with the hospital tour. She covered the smartphone with her hand. "I'll catch up."

"I'll be re-filing our claim," Jerome said. Artemis had been expecting this tone. It was flat, certain. "I have had some evidence, we discovered, rather troubling. You hinted at it. Thank you."

"If that's what you need to do," Artemis said. Young orderlies in white uniforms scampered by her and sprinted back toward the main hospital. "We'll deny it, and the process begins. Or should we meet and discuss, should I have Wylie fly up?"

"I'm not sure we'll want my findings in public," Jerome said. Artemis heard him breathing hard against the telephone microphone. "It's the community I live in, remember. I am troubled by what I've discovered."

"I take it you found actual evidence," Artemis said. She pondered Jerome's tone, confident what he had found. "Give me a hint? But I think I know the answer."

"Are you within earshot of Dr. Demetrius?" Jerome said. "I'll share, but it's between us?"

Artemis turned and realized she was alone in the well-maintained hallway. She thought someone was a good risk manager to have kept any potential tripping hazards out of the area or along the marble floors. The walls painted, fresh and clean. Clear, concise signage bolted to the walls with black arrows pointing toward departments.

"I'm alone," Artemis said. "Just me and the hallway."

"You're correct, I too don't consider this is a clear medical negligence case," Jerome said. "I think the medical records spell out that Dr. Demetrius and the staff tried to save lives. I don't question that at all. I don't question that motive. It's what happened after."

"He was adamant with me," Artemis said. "But I get lied too regularly. Let's say, the truth gets shaded based on the shoes they're wearing."

"I can imagine, but I found a source," Jerome said. "A superb source, works over there at the hospital. I'll say that he's suffering, he's troubled by what he saw. But he can't afford to lose his job, his families at risk."

Artemis leaned back on her black hiking boot heels.

"But we're still talking medical negligence?" Artemis said. She pushed forward with her free hand against the smooth, warm wall surface. She breathed in the sanitized air. The building temperature abnormally warm.

"Seems the doctor hopes composting will be a strong green initiative that he's pushing at the hospital and within the community," Jerome said. "I'll leave it at that. You expected this?"

Artemis realized her instincts were correct.

"I'm not shocked," Artemis said. "I've been walking the grounds, let's say we understand each other."

"Perhaps I should talk to someone with a large authority level?" Jerome said. "It should be a good-sized number. It would be the right thing to do. And, trust me, I don't want to be the man that caused the hospital to shut its doors, we need it here."

"Are you sure?" Artemis said. Jerome sounded as if he were shifting papers across his desk. "I'll need something. I'm not questioning your motives, I need hard evidence."

"I suspect in the doctor's mind he's being green and ethical. I assume you'll disagree," Jerome said. "I'll use my smartphone, send you a picture, will that do the trick for everybody?"

"Yes," Artemis said. She looked down at her smartphone screen. "I have secure app you can upload the file, it'll available for internal use. Restricted to those with a higher clearance, we have a robust encryption protocol. Fair?"

"Fair enough, I can keep my end quiet," Jerome said. "Email me the link, you'll have it before sundown."

"Do I need to share this with Agent Beaky?" Artemis said. She stood up and started to walk toward the processing facility. "I think I know what you're telling me, it was what, let's say, maybe, I heard someone down the hallway tell me. It was not malicious; it was a fact. But it caused me a sick taste in my mouth."

"It's not defensible, we both know it's illegal," Jerome said. "I'd take it into the courtroom. I'd need the morning to show my evidence. It would be an expensive day for you all. And yes, Agent Beaky would then need to consider criminal charges."

"I've had cases like this," Artemis said. She nodded. "My direct report's name, Wylie. He'll want to come pay us a visit, his procedure. We'll settle these files. Let's try to keep it quiet."

"I welcome his visit. I'd prefer to keep this as quiet as possible, too," Jerome said. "Artemis, this is a painful issue for me. You understand the situation where I sit. I have the sword of Damocles above me."

"I get you," Artemis said. She closed her eyes. She blew out a long breath. She opened her eyes. "I'll be back in contact soon. And about, Laina, we're making progress with her?"

Artemis listened as she assumed Jerome was shifting his office chair around behind his desk.

"Funny thing about you, you must know someone important," Jerome said. "Seems the court fast tracked her case based on your background study. I got the paperwork in today, like magic. They overnighted it to me. I had not asked for anything of the sort."

"Imagine that," Artemis said. "I'll be in touch, thank you."

Chapter 32

"This is my brother's habitat?" Dr. Demetrius said. The forest was blustery, the ground hard with recent white snowfall skiffs pushing down grass communities. He stood upright as he thrust his arms above his head to manage his breathing after the brisk hike up the hillsides. And then descending with Artemis and Agent Beaky onto the flat valley. He walked toward a clearing through boot high sedge grass that slapped his pant legs and over toward the enormous tulip polar. "He's lost his mind. Upside down crosses? My beloved mother. My father, well, I don't know what to say. This is a stain."

"We didn't see his face, but yes. We both think it was him, and his followers," Artemis said. She stepped over a decaying, pockmarked tree trunk and smashed limbs, pointing upward without looking. "We kept down, up there. Along the hillside rim. We had a guide bring us here. It was a troubling night."

Dr. Demetrius observed the ritualistic site. His hands shoved into his coat's pockets. As dusk approached, he piercing yellow sun peeked above the devious tree line casting long shadows that crept toward them across the forest floor. Artemis' pale cheeks ruby red from the frigid breeze spanking her face.

"You've never been out here?" Agent Beaky said. He strolled up toward the tree. "It's quite the tree. I've never seen a place like this, ever."

"This is an evil place," Dr. Demetrius said. "He knows I'm here. We are surrounded by the Amanita; they are amazing, but dangerous if not respected. And they have all been disrespected."

"How so?" Agent Beaky said. He scanned the tree limbs for cameras. He glanced over at Artemis. "Easy to hide up there, I suppose. Cameras?"

"I have a twin, Agent Beaky," Dr. Demetrius said. He kicked at a husky red cap mushroom with his hiking boot. It wobbled. "I'm sure you've studied behavioral genetics, twin studies? We sense each other."

"Why are we surrounded?" Artemis said.

Dr. Demetrius crouched, his hands dangled over his knees. He pointed over at Artemis' legs.

"Around your black boots, to be clear they should not be there," Dr. Demetrius said. He yanked off a leather glove and touched the ground with his bare right hand palm. "It's late winter, this should be impossible. All these examples, they are from the Amanita genus."

Dr. Demetrius remained kneeled down, he studied the dirt and grass surface, he swept away dead black leaves and brown pine straw. He flicked away small tree limbs, flung away cast off bark, and he turned his head and dropped the side of his head onto the soil. He then sat back up, wiped away the grime stuck to his cheek and ear. He dug his fingers into the dirt, he sifted the dark-brown soil through his fingertips. His dark eyes, his fingertips, intense, observant.

"Warmth," Dr. Demetrius said. "Way too much warmth, perfect moisture, not wet, not dry. I'm afraid of what I'd see below the surface. This should not exist, but it exists. I feel it."

"What did you hear?" Artemis said. She moved closer to Dr. Demetrius. "What are you sensing? It's in your eyes."

Dr. Demetrius sighed. He acknowledged Artemis.

"As if a giant blind hydra sleeps under are feet," Dr. Demetrius said. "It shifts. Blind, in total darkness, it seeks a strong root system, like the tree behind me. This should not have happened."

Agent Beaky walked over closer to Dr. Demetrius. Artemis turned and looked up toward their former hiding spot certain the cult knew that night they were being watched; The location was obvious. She wondered if Satan had put thoughts into the women's minds to allow themselves to be humiliated. She sensed evil near the rough tree trunk. As if evil steamed up from the ground to enrapture the tree, the bristling thicket and wash across the red, maroon and pale green mushroom caps.

"Drugs alter the mind," Artemis said. She had not turned to look over at Dr. Demetrius and Agent Beaky. "Sad."

"True, it's brain chemistry," Dr. Demetrius said. He stood up, he stepped by Agent Beaky and gazed up the tulip poplar at the sturdy limbs covered with partial leaves. With his right hand he followed the coarse tree bark down and strolled around the massive tree trunk. "This tree should be bare, those leaves up there are not natural for this time of year. It has some yellow blooming, almost impossible."

"What's this, Amanita?" Agent Beaky said. He pulled out his notepad. "How is that spelled?"

"Amanita," Dr. Demetrius said. He pointed down at a large red capped mushroom, the top covered with white wart-like growths. "Amanita muscaria, that one. It's a classic mushroom, fly agaric, used for centuries as an entheogen. These are all full of anatoxins."

Artemis looked over at a confused appearing Agent Beaky.

"I'll ask," Artemis said. "What's entheogen, mean, we're lost."

Dr. Demetrius pursed his lips and clasped his hands together. He searched and scooted through the knee high grass and the decaying tree limbs covered with a vast alien shaped mushroom varieties, ferns, and greenish moss.

"Ah, see here," Dr. Demetrius said. He marched forward. He swooped his right hand downward. "This is a beautiful example, the common name is fly amanita. A classic gilled fungi, basidiospore, but I would not eat this, it has a powerful hallucinogenic."

"I don't follow," Artemis said. She stepped closer to Dr. Demetrius and Agent Beaky.

"It's psychoactive, used in spiritual, for sacred purposes, if you believe in that nonsense," Dr. Demetrius said. He smirked over at them. "In Greek, entheos, in English it means, *full of the God*, get it? Ever used the word, enthusiasm? It's the root. It comes from the hallucinogenics properties. In the 1960s, Hippies used to love them for their *trips*."

"They eat these," Agent Beaky said. He pointed downward. "The cult your brother leads, they eat these to get high, so to speak."

"I would assume they take them, like I said, on a trip," Dr. Demetrius said. He turned to examine the mushrooms that littered along the grounds, they were meandering across lower tree trunk wounds and decay, fallen logs, or hidden by black rotting leaves. He pointed. "Over there, those, Amanita Caesarea known as Caesar's mushroom, and over there, a nice example of an Amanita citrina, better known as a false death cap, these two are edible. But where are you, where are you my love?"

"What do you mean?" Artemis said.

"I would second that," Agent Beaky said. "Your tone concerns me. And rather strange."

Dr. Demetrius ignored their questions. He tiptoed amongst the mushrooms, the wilted leaves, brittle limbs, and he stepped over a large limestone rock outcropping. And he smiled. He kneeled down and he was gentle, loving, as he cupped a mushroom within his palms.

"I knew she was near, let me introduce you to them," Dr. Demetrius said down at the mushroom. He smiled back over at Artemis and Agent Beaky. "Amanita phalloides, we know this beauty worldwide as a death cap. Eat her, you'll die a horrible death."

Agent Beaky kneeled down across from Dr. Demetrius.

"Looks like something from the supermarket," Agent Beaky said. He squinted his eyes. "May be too pale greenish, but otherwise, it appears harmless, like a white mushroom."

Dr. Demetrius pulled away his palms and he swept away the leaves, dirt and twigs near the thick mushroom stem.

"That's her gift, she has a honey, sweet scent. I'll not find out today," Dr. Demetrius said. "She lures you in, she appears like an edible mushroom. So innocent looking like her edible sisters over there. But I would not touch her out here deep in the mountains without exam gloves; she's toxic. And, she's thermostable, you cannot cook the toxins out of her. Take her home and eat her, she'll wait and attack the liver, kidneys. She's an assassin."

Dr. Demetrius leaned back on his heels, his arms and hands dangled over his knees. He inspected the trees, the forest floor, and beneath his boots.

"What are you thinking?" Artemis said. She leaned down with her hands on her thighs looking over at Dr. Demetrius.

"I'm scared, the death cap, she's the great deceiver, but she should not be here, not during this time of the year," Dr. Demetrius said. He stood up. He walked over and touched the tree, he glossed his hand along the rough gray-brown bark.

"Are we being watched?" Agent Beaky said. He scanned around the darkening forest. He gripped his weapon. "Should we move along?"

"We're always being watched," Artemis said. "It's too early for them, they know we'll be gone soon enough."

"They don't fear the authorities?" Agent Beaky said.

"Bought and paid for," Artemis said. "Jerome assured me they go about their sick business, local well-known secret in a small town."

"They don't scare me, they are fools, and my brother is a bigger fool," Dr. Demetrius said. He followed his right hand down the craggy tree trunk all the way to the ground where its muscular root system lived. "What's beneath this tree, now that scares me. I'm not sure I'd even want to dig."

"Digging for what?" Agent Beaky said. He strode near the tree and Dr. Demetrius. He looked back and winked over at Artemis.

"Look around you," Dr. Demetrius said. He pushed his hand against the rough tree trunk. "Tell me what you see, Agent Beaky."

Agent Beaky glanced over at Artemis. He inspected the area, the tree families, the dense forest thicket, the rock outcroppings. He looked down at the red and white, greenish mushrooms.

"I see life," Agent Beaky said. "This tree has leaves, the trees across the valley are naked, bare. The nearby grounds covered with mushrooms, but it's cold, and it's late winter."

Artemis treaded through the grass and over toward Agent Beaky and Dr. Demetrius.

"We didn't tell you what happened out here," Artemis said. "The night we watched your brother's ritual."

"Show me the spot," Dr. Demetrius said. He pointed at the ground. "From where you watched him. I guess he was here? This soil troubles me."

"Yes," Artemis said. "They bring in their stuff, it's sick. They did terrible things to the women. And an innocent animal."

The strong breeze whistled through Dr. Demetrius thick, dark hair. He flipped up his jacket collar.

"My brother is a sick man," Dr. Demetrius said. "As I told you, he's got issues from childhood."

Artemis, Agent Beaky and Dr. Demetrius hiked up the steep hillside and found the exact spot that Virgil had guided them. Dr. Demetrius examined down at the forest floor, the tall tree, and the ritualistic site.

"Your turn," Agent Beaky said. "Tell me what you see?"

Dr. Demetrius glanced at Agent Beaky and over at Artemis. He touched a nearby tree and slid his hand down its trunk. He crouched down and pealed back some brush.

"See, mushrooms, death caps," Dr. Demetrius said. He peered back up at Artemis. "The forest is dying, it appears alive, but one of my darlings is feeding off it. Tell me more Artemis. What happened that night? What sleeps beneath the tulip poplar down there?"

Artemis acknowledged Dr. Demetrius' question. His gaze was penetrating. But she saw behind him near a fragile oak sapling, the spirit of the American Indian appeared. He stood quiet, a warrior, and he pointed his spear garnished with white feathers over toward her. And she realized the warrior spirt was not trapped; His proud eyes. And then she heard that all to a familiar voice from beyond.

"Oh, Artemis," Satan said. "Tell the poor bastard. He's the creator, not his brother."

"Your brother has quite a group," Agent Beaky said. He squinted. "Right, Artemis? Are you all right? Are you well?"

"I'm fine. Agent Beaky and I were here," Artemis said. She shook her head. She waved back at him. "Virgil, the grocery store guy, down the hill behind us, he guided us up here. We thought it was drugs, drugs being made at the hospital, so forth."

Dr. Demetrius stared down the darkening lavender and blue hillsides and farther downward inspecting the site from right to left.

"I see the pentagram they scratched into the ground," Dr. Demetrius said. He pointed down at the site. "This is evil. And dangerous."

"I'll say this," Agent Beaky said before Artemis could collect her thoughts. "I'll not write what I saw in a report. I'd get tossed out of the FBI, trash my career."

"Artemis?" Dr. Demetrius said. "Did something emerge from underneath that tree? It makes sense why the soil down there is so arable. As if someone is roto tiling the spot like a gardener. I suspect the ground breaks apart with minimal effort. And reveals a monster."

"Oh, come on Artemis," Satan said. "Tell him, he's going to find out from your over-active friend. It'll be fun. I'm so excited to see his face."

"Down there they had a ceremony," Artemis said. She pointed toward the tree. "Your brother wore a goat mask. I thought it was you. We're confident it was him. He's a big, muscular body."

"I can understand the confusion," Dr. Demetrius said. "But my twin likes to weight lift. Always has, I suspect he's rather large these days, and aggressive."

"He is. He shouted a chant, something like that?" Artemis said.

"You're stalling, Artemis," Satan said. "I'm getting into this, it's so gratifying, please, please go on."

"Yes," Agent Beaky said. "Ah, a satanic ritual, how I'd express it, yes, I think that's correct."

"I'm clairvoyant," Artemis said. "I think you should know that."

Dr. Demetrius stood up, still and quiet as he observed Artemis. He looked down at his boots. He shrugged.

"I suspected you had unique skills," Dr. Demetrius said. He nodded gazing down the hillside. "How interesting."

"Your brother, or someone I thought was you," Artemis said. "They put on a show for us, in part for me. I think he can sense me."

"Oh, I'm almost there," Satan said. "Please, go on, and you, my dear, are way more than clairvoyant. So humble, I hate it. You need to get a big ego. Show off your skills, girl."

"They brought out a lamb, it ate some mushrooms his followers had hand-picked," Artemis said. She strolled closer to Dr. Demetrius. "The lamb ate the mushrooms, and it died within minutes. And then it happened."

"It flopped dead as Dante," Agent Beaky said. He huffed. "I'll never forget that night."

"And?" Dr. Demetrius said. "What happened?"

Artemis sensed that Dr. Demetrius had already concluded what had happened. It was in his eyes and from his PhD in mycology. It was his creation hiding down below the tulip poplar.

"He's got a clue," Satan said. "Now finish him. Finish him."

"They cut the lamb into pieces," Artemis said. She bit her lower lip. She stared pensively at Dr. Demetrius. "Fed it to the thing under the tree. It's got to be a mycelia thing, or something like it. It acted like an octopus. Like you said, a giant blind hydra."

"I'll say," Agent Beaky said. "I'd say more like a blind kraken, it was huge and aggressive."

Dr. Demetrius acknowledged Artemis. He pondered her story.

"It's true, he, or one of them stole a box of my mycelia," Dr. Demetrius said. He looked at Artemis as wrinkles emerged across his forehead. "The mycelia can absorb toxins, in this case, unless I miss my guess, opioids. Addictive, dangerous, and for my brother, I suppose profitable."

"Greed," Agent Beaky said. "At the cost of innocent lives, no worse example for a human, but we'll get him."

"For now," Dr. Demetrius said. His voice monotone. He nudged his head toward the tree. "I recommend not digging that thing up. My brother has done the work for you. Take samples, this Amanita collection stuck to this tree scar, they will produce the results you'll need. Test the mushrooms for heroin, fentanyl. It hides in the meaty tissue. It might be in trace amounts this far from the tree, but your medical examiners will find them. It's all the evidence you'll need I suspect."

Artemis sensed her opening to send Agent Berkey off Dr. Demetrius' trail. But she needed to make Dr. Demetrius an asset to help her extract Laina.

"I guess it was his way of composting?" Artemis said. She stepped closer to Dr. Demetrius. She whispered in his ear. "You have a nice garden at the hospital. A green project. I've learned you have a unique method to develop fertilizer for your experiments."

Dr. Demetrius stared down. He looked at Agent Beaky, and then slowly back over at Artemis. His eyes as if lost contemplating a deep thought.

"They didn't send just anybody, did they?" Dr. Demetrius said, wistfully. He glanced at Artemis.

"No, they charge me to go clean up these messes," Artemis said. "Your brother created this mess down there stealing your work from you and the hospital. I'm here to clean him up."

"Am I under arrest?" Dr. Demetrius said. He looked back over at Agent Beaky. "Artemis?"

Artemis gazed over at Agent Beaky. She winked at him to play along, even though he appeared confused and uncertain.

"Oh, Artemis, you're so crafty," Satan said. "The American Indian warrior likes where you are going, always better to lure them to their death, easier than dragging a dead body. Smart."

"We're listening," Agent Beaky said. He gripped his weapon. "It's up to you and with Artemis' guidance. I guess."

Dr. Demetrius pressed his lips together. He squinted at Artemis.

"He used my work to create that monster, I know it's down there. It's huge, and I suspect hungry," Dr. Demetrius said. He pointed his thumb backwards toward the tulip poplar. "But we have a much bigger problem than this site, or my brother."

"What on earth do you mean?" Agent Beaky said. "We'll dig that thing up and set it on fire, burn the forest to the ground. If need be to eradicate this cult and that thing."

"Amanita phalloides, the death caps," Dr. Demetrius said. He pointed down at the greenish mushroom attached at the intersection of an oak tree trunk and decaying bark. "They are spreading, it's a worldwide phenomenon. If not stopped, it could be a human disaster beyond my imagination. And I now know... I know where the death caps mother sleeps, and eats. She's like the queen inside an ant farm."

"Oh, he's so smart," Satan said. "But I hate his brother more, yes, I hate his brother. I think ole Dr. Demetrius is about to go soft. Pity. I think it's a stress response."

"How do you know this?" Agent Beaky said. He looked over at Dr. Demetrius and then over at Artemis.

"I'm an expert, I'm a genius," Dr. Demetrius said. "Read the online news sites. But, I am afraid, we're too late. My brother has made me a fool. Are family name will be trashed for eternity. I've helped murder human beings."

"I need your help," Artemis said. She gripped Dr. Demetrius' arm, she shook him back into her presence. "Help me, you help yourself, you understand me?"

"Not sure how," Dr. Demetrius said. "What other option do I have, my brother has betrayed me. I'll end up being accused of mass murder. I've gone numb. I cannot grasp the magnitude. Innocent people out picking wild mushrooms, curious children playing in a field."

"I'm adopting a little girl," Artemis said. "That's my point."

Agent Beaky stepped closer to her and Dr. Demetrius. He scanned up into the darkening sky.

"Congratulations," Agent Beaky said. "Good on you."

"Unless your brother kills her first," Artemis said. "Remember the girl you thanked me for taking in? Remember her?"

Dr. Demetrius glanced over at Agent Beaky, down the darkening hillside, and back over at Artemis.

"So cunning, Artemis," Satan said. "It clicked inside his brain that you've not told Agent Beaky about his composting activities at the hospital. Oh, I hate you so. You told him the truth, but left out a lot of other truths rotting under the hospital's garden. Brilliant. I'm about to explode."

"It's true. I've been studying your little friend," Dr. Demetrius said. "How d'you figure that out?"

"She has a wearable device, placed between her thumb and forefinger," Artemis said. She pressed at the exact spot on her right hand. "My expert witness, she's rather thorough in her physical examinations."

Dr. Demetrius stood still and quiet. His mouth gaped open. He stuffed his hands into his coat pockets. His eyes unable to focus on any forest object. A Great Horned owl clawed into a tree limb above them. It hooted down at them. It snapped its beak.

"I guess that makes sense," Dr. Demetrius said. "Given your business. I assume your capabilities. Damn, I never thought. It was so simple, so green."

"I assume you sort of got her mother's consent, first," Artemis said. She raised an eyebrow. "Right? She's gone but I think I remember you took care of that issue, in the medical records for clinical trials."

Dr. Demetrius sucked in the air, and he held it. He appeared sheepish, he looked over at Agent Beaky, and then back over at Artemis. He nodded like a good boy.

"Why yes, yes I did. I've been using her data with our artificial intelligence platform," Dr. Demetrius said. He stuttered. "She's fascinating to observe. I'm trying to study how her genetic code changes, you know, to make her genetically stronger, as a human. Help her out. She needs a break."

"Interesting," Agent Beaky said. "It's not illegal?"

"We have human studies, clinical trials all the time," Dr. Demetrius said. His grin shifted up and down. His gaze darting back and forth. "We get them lined up, Gene handles that part of the paper work. It's all part of science. With her, well the clinical trials at phase one."

"I've been tracking her," Artemis said. She gave Agent Beaky a thumbs up. "But you know where she is all the time, too?"

"It's true," Dr. Demetrius said. "She's in good health. I checked on her yesterday; her vital signs are good."

"I doubt I'll get her out of the court system in time, and I don't want to get arrested," Artemis said. "Your brother knows I know, he'll make his move. It was in his dark eyes, he's obsessed with her."

"He's sick," Dr. Demetrius said. He wiped his eyes. "I'm sorry. I hope you get her back. But I'm getting a bad feeling."

"We'll know when they come back here, with her, a couple days, best case," Artemis said. She pointed downward. "We'll both know, won't we?"

"Ah, I just caught up," Agent Beaky said. "Smart move, a risky strategy, not sure I'd get that approved. But it's the best option for now. I'll tote in a high-powered rifle. I've taken the shot before, I'm prepared if we need to protect her."

Dr. Demetrius frowned and the jagged wrinkles crisscrossed his forehead. He covered his face with his hands.

"I would never never hurt a child," Dr. Demetrius said. "I study her, yes, and the others for their better health. To protect future generations. They give me harmless baseline data, the data helps me save other lives, I improve lives. I don't want to hurt anyone."

"I know that, now, it depends on where my investigation takes me," Artemis said. She whispered in a low tone. "The community needs the hospital. If we keep this quiet. We have the funds to settle the claims."

"My brother is a pure evil," Dr. Demetrius said. He wiped his eyes. He shook his head in disbelief. "I thought it was a coincidence, a child moves away, the data stopped. The devices need fuel, magnets, and a laser field. Now, I'm feeling sick to my stomach. I think I understand what he's done to these innocent children. Dear God above. Their bodies are down there, beneath the surface decomposing, more like being digested. All you will find under that soil are bones and a mycelia monster."

Dr. Demetrius kneeled down and covered his mouth.

"He's sacrificed women, and girls, never any men or boys, best we can tell," Artemis said. "He feeds them to your mycelia."

Dr. Demetrius began to weep. He dropped to his all-fours, and he vomited until he started to dry-heave and convulse. Agent Beaky and Artemis gave him space, and waited for him to compose himself.

"Ah, such a kind heart," Satan said. "Just sad, guess this human needs a stomach for it. Mass killing takes a certain human mind set. I've had my champions, but they are rare. Artemis, you just mind-thumped down on poor Dr. Demetrius. Beat him into a corner. I am impressed."

"This must end," Dr. Demetrius said. His breaths hard, and his lungs begged for oxygen. "He knows my secrets."

"He's in a network we're following," Agent Beaky said. He stepped forward, leaned down and patted Dr. Demetrius on the back. "Artemis, soon, we must dig around that tree, burn it to the ground."

"That's my thinking," Artemis said. "I had to figure out if both brothers were my mess-makers, and now, I know for sure."

"The mycelia absorb the toxins, they feed," Dr. Demetrius said. He wiped mucus from his mouth. "It feeds off, sorry, breaks down the dead with enzymes. But that thing down there has to be a huge monster by now. My brother manipulated it into a mindless killing machine. Its fruit, the mushrooms, they are deadly."

"What are you saying?" Agent Beaky said. He kneeled in closer to Dr. Demetrius.

"Drugs, fentanyl," Artemis said. "Heroin. Like he said, it hides in the mushrooms."

"Drugs, the mycelia are making drugs using the mushrooms as cover, no question, heroin mixed with fentanyl," Dr. Demetrius said. "A genetic trick to influence the mycelia to produce his product. I engineered my mycelia to respond like artificial intelligence, a genetic learning machine. It has no ethics, it is not a sentient being."

"Yeah," Agent Beaky said. "But we'll end this sooner, than later. Thanks to Artemis and with your cooperation."

Dr. Demetrius shifted back and forth, he shook his head as if prepared to leap from a high up balcony from a towering skyscraper.

"You can dig all you want, you don't understand," Dr. Demetrius said. He closed his eyes. He covered his face with his hands. "All you'll find is death, those poor unfortunate souls being broken down one cell at a time going back to the soil. But that's not the bigger problem. They're at least dead."

"Artemis, wait for it, wait for it," Satan said. "This is the big reveal, remember what I told you when we first met? Oh, I'm dizzy, I'm almost there."

Artemis felt a strong cold breeze snap against her face. She ached at her knees.

"We're too late," Artemis said. "Devil is in the details, the genetics, the AI learning."

"Correct, and it's all my fault," Dr. Demetrius said. "The death cap, the Amanita phalloides. They are spreading. They're like a virus now, burrowing like a giant blind mole-rat, learning as it grows. She'll birth colonies, her fruit pop up in fields where children are playing, in forests, and it's unfortunate to say, every street in every city and town. It's all happening underneath us. I suspect its tentacles are underneath us right now."

Agent Beaky got up and strolled closer to Artemis.

"Like playing a child's wack'm-o game?" Agent Beaky said. "They pop up here, pop up over there, so forth."

"Yes, but a deadly game," Dr. Demetrius said. "Kill this monster for sure, cut the head off. But it'll mutate, and keep growing under our feet. It's like a cancer just under the skin, sometimes the surgeon keeps finding new roots, and they have to go fishing to excise out all the growth. Leaves an ugly scar behind."

"I don't mind saying," Agent Beaky said. "You make me a nervous lad, this is a mean business."

Artemis heard Satan's satisfied moan.

"Oh, Artemis, that was just terrible news," Satan said. "I warned you, mass killing is my work. The demons just can't keep up with me. And from what I just watched, the other Demetrius brother's got the stomach for it.

Sad."

"I'm such a fool," Dr. Demetrius said.

"Oh yes, yes you are," Satan said. Its cackle vibrated across the valley and whistled through the tree limbs.

Chapter 33

"They assume I've lost it," Agent Beaky said. He buttoned up his dark blue jacket. He hunched forward. "I need to go back to Lexington, right away, to get grilled, I expect. I'll be back soon, I hope."

"Why now?" Artemis said. She gripped the table edge as she leaned forward. "We might need to move in quick, like tonight. She's not got long."

"I feel you," Agent Beaky said. "Seems my sentences about amanita, mushrooms, so forth, got their attention."

"It's all true, those are facts," Artemis said. She reached across the hotel's breakfast room table to grab his left forearm. "Guess they don't want to send anybody else out here with us?"

"Manpower shortage, budgets," Agent Beaky said. He gripped Artemis' hand with right hand. He patted down on it. "I'll get it worked out, I promise. We need help, that mob is too large for the two of us."

"Yeah, I'm good, but not against an army," Artemis said. "Scumbag knows we're in the area, he's waiting for us. He'll kill her for the sport of it. He thinks he'll get away with it. I avoid the police, I scared they'll arrest me, lock me in a jail cell."

Agent Beaky and Artemis sat silent, and still as they pondered the situation. Artemis sat slouched back on the unforgiving chair. She was confident she had eliminated Dr. Demetrius from her kill list. He was arrogant, overconfident, but not a threat to society. His brother was a different story; he was an intelligent drug dealer, a sociopath. A serial woman and child abuser. She had looked into his eyes; his eyes gave his soul away to her. He was the reason they sent her. The Company always sent her into uncertain situations to determine the ultimate sanction, and in Artemis' mind, Prophet Higgs Boson was about to get sanctioned.

"Tracking her?" Agent Beaky said. He pointed over at Artemis' smartphone. "Just trying to understand."

"I am, my direct report, Wylie, he's coming up to manage the claims, he'll get it all settled, it's just money," Artemis said. She sipped warm coffee from a common hotel mug. "I've got her setup on my phone with an alarm for nighttime, but I sleep very little now."

"Not much of an appetite, as well, my heart's pounding," Agent Beaky said. He gulped and he blew air through his open mouth. "Children are different. I don't like to have children in harm's way. Sorry, but you look like a ghost bit you? I don't want to say the name. What's been biting at you."

"Yeah," Artemis said. "Satan's torturing me. It keep dropping clues in front of me."

Artemis glanced over at Agent Beaky. She was confident he was a kind man and devoted to his career. If given the opportunity, he'd be a good father and loving husband. He kept himself fit, careful with his diet. But she realized he feared the one certainty that all humans fear from birth; it was his death. Artemis had seen death up close from her childhood. She was not afraid; It was a simple calculation based on a reality. She'd catch a bullet, get knifed from behind, die in a random car accident, or perhaps a genetic flaw that killed her body. But she would die someday, and then forevermore view the planet from a different visual perception.

"Sorry, lass," Agent Beaky said.

"I'm being toyed with," Artemis said. She pulled her hands back; she crossed her arms. "I have little control over this case. I have little control over my life. But I'll keep going forward. For her."

Agent Beaky stared over at Artemis. He gripped his hand over his mouth. He nodded as an old man limped behind him toward the hotel's two-gallon stainless steel coffee maker.

"I, I," Agent Beaky said. He fidgeted with his lips. "I don't want to think. Even say it, the name. I'm sorry."

"I get it. Satan's a scary problem, it plays with my mind. It places obstacles in front of me. I have no idea how to manage a child. Satan knows my weak spot," Artemis said. She sighed. "But I'll not turn my back on her, she might die, but she'll die knowing I tried to save her. If I die, I'll go out for the right reason."

"I admit it. I'm terrified," Agent Beaky said. "They will kill us if given the chance. I'm certain. But I'm duty bound. They would not listen to my plea. I have to head back."

"You should understand, from my childhood. I've had this gift, or it's a curse," Artemis said. "I've never viewed my tasks with hate; it's just a factual step-by-step process. I'm responsible to protect a lot of innocent people; it's my job. It's not a personal vendetta, does that make sense?"

"It does, but aren't you afraid?" Agent Beaky said. He followed with his active eyes the old, wobbly man with a full head of thin gray hair step away from the stainless steel coffee dispenser clutching a steaming white mug spilling the brown contents along the tile floor. "How do you do it? In the mind..."

"Oh, I'm scared. I'm scared for her; she doesn't understand. I allow my emotions to accept the reality, if need be, I cry to release that obstacle so I can clear my mind," Artemis said. She opened her arms. She examined Agent Beaky's crinkled face. "Do you love someone? You've never loved someone like you love them, now?"

Agent Beaky's eyes locked in on Artemis. He blinked, blew C02 through his lips, and rubbed his forehead.

"Am I that obvious?" Agent Beaky said. He sniffled. He kept rubbing his forehead. "I've never been out on a case with a clairvoyant, and one that can sense Satan. I don't want to even say my girl's name. I don't want, it, to read my mind. I must protect her. I think I've gone mad."

Artemis breathed in a deep drag, she held the breath and released it between her thin lips. Her eyes clear. Minimal guest traffic roamed the front lobby. It was a common late winter day.

"You can't hide from Satan. I accept that I don't have any control," Artemis said. She rubbed behind her neck. "You're focused on missing out, not being a father. The chance to provide a happy home that's full of children, where you have a big Christmas tree littered underneath with presents."

"I, I, why yes, you think I should take in a deep breath? Like you did," Agent Beaky said. He breathed in through his nostrils that flared and back out his mouth. "I've met someone. I'm devoted to her. Yes, we're making plans, children for sure."

"Love her?" Artemis said. "With no second thoughts?"

"Yes, without reservation," Agent Beaky said. He pushed his chest forward.

He smacked the tabletop with his hands. "I love her. I've never been devoted in this way. Dwi'n caru hi, as my mother would have said. I do, I love her."

Artemis smelled pungent cleaning detergent as the nearby Hispanic maid dipped a string mop into a bucket and splashed out the excess water through a wringer. The hotel coffee maker percolated a bland coffee brew. And she remembered her father making his bespoke coffee blend on Sunday mornings. His coffee was rich and vibrant like his personality. Her mother would be sit on an antique stool behind a marble counter. Content to sip her green tea amused from watching her loving husband make Artemis pancakes dotted with fresh fruit. Her mother allowed Artemis to have buttermilk pancakes on Sunday mornings as a celebration for the new week. During the week Artemis' father made her healthy fare focused on her mother's demand that she have a nutritious diet lacking in sugar.

"After my parents' accident," Artemis said. She sighed. "I was alone. I had no next of kin, no family. My parents were orphans. But my parents had provided for me; they had planned for me."

"If you don't mind me asking," Agent Beaky said. "What sort of accident? Car wreck?"

"Gas leak," Artemis said. She shrugged. "Just bad luck, my father loved to cook, he preferred natural gas. The fireman found them snuggled together. I guess they wanted to reassure me, but it was just a fact. I knew they loved each other, devoted to each other, as you said. I know they loved me. I keep that sensation close. It guides me."

"Ah, but they died together," Agent Beaky said. He pointed over at Artemis. "They were not alone."

"And that's what makes me different," Artemis said. She stared over at Agent Beaky.

"Sorry?" Agent Beaky said. "You lost me. Am I that nervous?"

"I'm comfortable being alone," Artemis said. She leaned forward. "I prefer to work alone, but let me ask you, Special Agent Nero Beaky, would you kill for her?"

Agent Beaky sat back and contemplated the question. He stared up at the ceiling tiles. He observed other hotel guests mill about the stale lobby area.

"Absolutely, I take your question to heart," Agent Beaky said. "Without reservation. If it were the right thing to do. I'd go to jail if need be. I'd take a bullet to protect her life."

"Obvious answer," Artemis said. "Why?"

"That's easy, now," Agent Beaky. He glanced over at Artemis. He waved his right hand at her. "I love her. I'll protect her at all costs."

"And she'd always know you loved her?" Artemis said. "Right?"

"I would guess so," Agent Beaky said. "Yes, I could live, or I guess die with that, yes, I could."

"But what if you'd be dead? You understood the mission will get you killed," Artemis said. "That's the hard part, not having control. People want control over something they cannot control. I figured out that's what clouds the mind. You're dead either way. Why get wound up on useless emotions that burn energy."

"I don't fully understand," Agent Beaky said.

"I've never felt alone, ever, it is as if my parents are always nearby, with me, following me," Artemis said. She smiled. She wiped away tears in the corner of her eyes. "I'm never afraid to go into a hot job. I'm scared. And then it's like I feel, my parents have my back. Sending me positive energy to seek courage. I release all the tension in my mind and body. And go do the job. To do the right thing."

"You have a curious mind, you're emotional, but not," Agent Beaky said. "I don't want to see what you see."

Artemis acknowledged Agent Beaky's comment.

"I temporarily lose the wandering spirits, and I get terrified," Artemis said. She blinked her eyes. She wiped them. "I'm not sure if there is an all powerful God, a Heaven. But those spirits I see, they all search for something. Or they flee from something. I realized years ago there is another dimension that separates us. I'm not a believer there is one all powerful wizard pulling the up or down levers. But there's something beyond me, us, it's what gives me hope. It's what drives me to protect the weak. To stand up to defend a child. I'll go knowing I lived with integrity. My parents had integrity. I hope they are proud of me."

"It's Heaven," Agent Beaky said. "I'm sure of it. If there's ah, you know the name, there's a God, with a capital G."

Artemis looked at Agent Beaky certain he had never seen a wandering spirit fade into a bright crease in space and time. He would never understand that life's meant to live without a net. And what it felt like to step off a high ledge uncertain if the guide wire would be there, or even after if the guide wire would hold his weight firm and strong.

"I exist within the maybe. I work for people I've never met," Artemis said. She pointed over at the hotel's check-in counter. "They could stand right over there, I'd not recognize them. But I realize they, as in The Company, they hired me for a reason."

"If you don't mind," Agent Beaky said. "You sound rather cold-blooded, in a way."

"I don't hate, I'm not cold-hearted," Artemis said. "I understand that in the human condition there are human cancers, genetic flaws. So Agent Beaky, what do doctors do about cancers?"

Agent Beaky paused, he touched the table top as if it were covered with acid. He looked back over at Artemis. She gave him what he wanted to see, an assassin's dead certain gaze.

"They heal the patient," Agent Beaky said. He paused. "No, but they kill the cancer."

"Go back to Lexington, figure out how to keep your job," Artemis said. Her voice a low monotone. "When you return to Selene, the cancer will be dead."

Chapter 34

"So, this is our problem hospital, nice looking facility, clean," Wylie said. It was a cloudy, crisp day as he had walked away from his four-door rental car as he pressed the car fob and the car's taillights blinked white and red. He marched up toward Artemis as healthcare workers strolled behind her. Patients and families limped, walked and helped others step toward the front doors. "Well girl, we're ready to go?"

"Yes," Artemis said. She hugged Wylie and smacked him on his back. "This girl has them inside, I have them separated."

"I brought a large authority level with me, rather cold up here, geez," Wylie said. He pointed over toward the hospital's large rectangular shaped garden. "Over there is shall I say, the spot?"

"It is, I'm not sure how many, it's not something I want to dig up," Artemis said. She turned her back to the garden space setting dormant toward the end from a harsh winter. "You want to walk it?"

"No, I'll take your word for it, besides I hate cold weather. I can see my breath like I'm smoking, again," Wylie said. He bundled up his thin gray overcoat and turned toward the hospital's busy front doors. "Creeps me out, but we have to save this place. If that mess over there gets out, this place is gone. And we might need to update our resumes. Or, worse."

Artemis led Wylie into the hospital lobby. He signed in at the guard desk, snapped on a guest badge, and they walked into an elevator off the main lobby and they traveled up into the administrative floor.

Inside the large, ornate conference room, Jerome sat with his stenographer and legal files. Wylie and Jerome shook hands and everyone exchanged greetings. Wylie sat down across from Jerome.

"Nice to meet you Wylie," Jerome said. "Sorry under these circumstances."

"As well," Wylie said. "Let's get this over with, agreed?"

"Agreed," Jerome said.

Everyone understood going forward they were on the record and being recorded. The stenographer turned to focus on Wylie. Her fingers along the machines keys.

"I'll go first. I don't want to wear this tie all day," Wylie said. He scooted the high-back chair forward. His dark-gray suit jacket open with his arms on the conference table. "We both know the proximate cause for your claim? That garden outside has the evidence, buried underneath. We both appreciate there are unfortunate human beings that died inside this hospital. I assume we all prefer not to disturb them out of respect for the dead, and their families?"

"We agree," Jerome said. "Thank you. I should point out I live here. I don't want to hurt anyone. I don't want to reopen wounds that have begun to heal."

"It's clear, Dr. Demetrius, the hospital staff all had a duty to care and treat for your clients loved ones at the time they were patients inside this hospital," Wylie said. He paused. He kept his arms and hands open. Kept eye contact with Jerome. "As best we can read, they tried their best to save those patients. Our experts think the records ring true. I consider that to be true. I don't consider the evidence points toward a criminal intent while treating them. We don't think they breached their duty, while the patient was alive. But, the result after is illegal. It was a scheme, as irrational as I've seen, to further Dr. Demetrius' research. But after the fact, he buried the problem out front under the garden space. We do not deny these facts. We do not intend or desire to disturb them."

"We agree," Jerome said.

"Dr. Demetrius breached his duty, as a physician and as the medical director in what happened after the death, the incorrect ah, disrespectful, disposal of the deceased. I trust I've made my point?" Wylie said. He leaned back off the table. "Can we all agree to stipulate that?"

"We agree," Jerome said. "It's a fact and we don't want to go make a big spectacle about it here in a small town. At a hospital we all need. Mostly, a place that they provide good care for our folks."

"Very well," Wylie said. "So, this exercise is to determine damages. And now, I'll shut up."

"For the record, I'll express for the plaintiff side," Jerome said. He glanced toward the stenographer. "We are in agreement as to the physician and hospital staff duty, the breach of that duty, and causation. We seek to come to a remedy for damages." Jerome acknowledged Wylie's seasoned, efficient approach. "To be clear," Jerome said. He cleared his throat. "I am here on behalf of the noted claimants, the families for the deceased, as recorded in my filing. I should remark it that every human life has value. Those unfortunate people had value, but we will stipulate they contributed to their own demise. Addiction is a terrible disease. We hope and pray we can come to a respectful resolution for this dispute."

Wylie nodded and pulled at his white dress shirt color to loosen its tight grip.

"I accept your statement on behalf of Caduceus Re, the hospital, the system we reinsure within the captive model," Wylie said. "We do not dispute it. We will not argue the facts to your claims. We admit to the proximate cause. And to speed up this resolution, I have worked with our captive manager to arrange for a global settlement that we will work to come to a final agreement after this meeting."

"I guess we can bring in Dr. Demetrius and Gene," Artemis said. She sprang up, and left the conference room.

Wylie swiveled back the conference room chair, he stood up, he moved and sat at the far end of the conference table in front of gold leafed framed portraits of the hospital's deceased former CEOs. As Gene and Dr. Demetrius entered the room, he got up and introduced himself to them. They sat in front of Jerome. Artemis walked down the conference room and sat next to Wylie.

"All right," Wylie said. He sat back with his hands on his suit pants. "Dr. Demetrius, Gene, it's Jerome's time to ask questions. We will not interrupt him. To keep this meeting quiet, Dr. Demetrius. Gene will act as your counsel and as general counsel for the hospital. Do we all understand each other?"

Gene sat up on the high-back chair. He squirmed over at Dr. Demetrius.

"In other words," Gene said. He nodded over at Wylie. And then he slouched back over at Dr. Demetrius. "If everyone cooperates, meaning you and me, we'll keep this out of the newspaper."

"I do," Dr. Demetrius said. He stared down at the table. He was sullen and quiet.

"Dr. Demetrius," Jerome said. "I too, am sorry we are at this intersection, but I assume you understand why we're here?"

"I do," Dr. Demetrius said. He interlocked his fingers on the conference room table. "I'm sorry."

Wylie tapped on the tabletop. He held his hand up for Jerome to wait. He pointed at Dr. Demetrius.

"Thank you," Wylie said. He gazed over at Dr. Demetrius until Dr. Demetrius acknowledged him. "No kiddin'."

"I don't understand," Dr. Demetrius said.

"I do," Jerome said. He half-grinned back over at Wylie.

"The number one thing we look for in medical malpractice claims, number one," Wylie said. He nudged over at Artemis. "What did I teach you?"

Artemis pushed forward. She half-grunted.

"If a physician says, or writes, that they are sorry without being prompted," Artemis said. She smirked back over at Wylie. "It creates the fertile ground to settle the file. With special emphasis on the word, fer-tile."

"Good. Now just tell the truth, we'll get this behind us," Wylie said. He sat back in the high-back chair. "Sorry, go on, Jerome."

"It's true," Jerome said. "Seems so simple, but juries want to believe you. They're human. They have families, and they get sick."

"I understand," Dr. Demetrius said. He waved his right hand back and forth. "Soft skill technique, I suppose. But to be clear, I am sorry. I don't understand what got into my head."

"As the saying, none of us have clean hands," Jerome said. He clicked his ink pen, he scanned down at his notepad and he checked off a note from his list. "If you will, tell me about your practice, your background."

For the next twenty minutes, the group listened to Dr. Demetrius recount his childhood, his formal education, his training, and how he ended up in Selene, Kentucky.

"Dr. Demetrius," Jerome said. He slid over a piece of paper, eight by ten from his firm's letterhead with the firm's brand and contact information printed across the top and bottom. "This is a list of names, do you recognize these names, and if so, why?"

Dr. Demetrius' eyes moved across the piece of paper. He mumbled the names as he read left to right and on down to the bottom.

"I treated them all," Dr. Demetrius said. "They are all

deceased. If I may, we, I, tried to save them. I swore the Hippocratic oath. I am Greek. It is my sacred duty to heal the sick.

I would never, never." Dr. Demetrius pointed his right hand forefinger up toward the ceiling. "Before God as my witness, never allow a human being to die without trying to help them, never."

"Thank you, I respect your passion. I respect your words," Jerome said. He held up the paper. He held it up toward Wylie and Artemis. "I enter this into our record."

"If I may," Wylie said. "We'll accept your evidence, perhaps ask the question. Then we can then start our conversation, negotiation I guess, perhaps back over at your office?"

Jerome stared over at Gene and Dr. Demetrius, and he took off his reading glasses. He pointed over toward Wylie down the conference room table.

"Good, you are to the point. I see where Artemis gets her no nonsense approach," Jerome said. He shifted his notebook to square. "Thank you, Wylie. Dr. Demetrius, just tell us, in simple terms, what happened with these patients, after they died?"

Gene shoved his lumpy body into Dr. Demetrius, and he thrust his left hand up.

"If I may?" Gene said. He gazed back and forth at Wylie and Jerome. His forehead glistened with moisture. His lazy eye attempted to keep up with his vapid head movements. "If I may?"

"Please," Jerome said. "I'll not interrupt you."

"Go for it," Artemis said. Wylie shrugged and readjusted his eyeglasses. "Start digging."

"It was hospital policy," Gene said. He stuttered before his brain dump. "The… the staff, sorry, Dr. Demetrius tried to save these poor souls. These children of God, I… I pray for them."

"Get to it, brother," Wylie said. His eyes squinted as his face hardened.

"They empowered us to keep them alive," Gene said. He hesitated. He wiped his face with his puffy hands. "CMS, you know, Center for Medicare, Medicaid Services, well, they'd pay us. I… I mean the hospital, more, more money, based on keeping the patient longer. If they stayed longer, we got more money; it was the rules. It was hospital system policy."

"They were dead," Dr. Demetrius said. He closed his eyes as he huffed. "We put them on life support, it was temporary, to get them beyond what is it, twenty days?"

"Twenty-one," Gene said. "Nobody seemed to care; you know,

company policy. A few days wouldn't matter; these poor souls were dead, but we could squeeze out more revenue. The revenue our not for profit could put to work to make more profit."

"Simmer down," Wylie said. "I need not come back up here?"

"I don't want to go down that rabbit hole, pure greed," Jerome said. "Let's focus on the patients, the human lives. Dr. Demetrius?"

"Oh, okay," Gene said. He slumped back. "Just trying to help."

"Yes, I understand," Dr. Demetrius said. He supported his left elbow with his right hand. His left-hand fingers glossed over his mouth. "No one came, I noticed. I said to the nurses several times. No one ever came to check on them. As if we had left them adrift at sea, like the wooden fishing boats from my childhood in Greece. Nobody cared anymore."

"But some had children," Artemis said.

"Yes, I accept your point," Dr. Demetrius said. He gazed forward as if counting the tables wood grains. "I remember the first time. I made it down to the morgue. We left the body there for several days. So, late one night, I signed it out. I made a name up, they never checked. I wrapped the body in a mycelia mesh, burial wrap with button mushrooms I'd sewn into it with the mycelia. And I buried the body deep in the hospital garden. No one saw me; it was a dark area I knew we didn't monitor."

The stenographer stopped typing and she stared over at Dr. Demetrius. It was as if she'd lost her ability to breathe. Her mouth gaped open, and she stopped blinking as her skinny fingers rested above the machine.

"Remember, you're under an NDA," Gene said. His moist fingers crawled across the table like land slugs.

"Yes," Jerome said. He sighed. "We all understand. Can you manage this? I need your assurance."

"I guess so," she said. She began to type. "Yes. I can do it."

The group paused and waited for Dr. Demetrius.

"Well, after that," Dr. Demetrius said. "My research started to have better results. It was an accident. I hate accidental science, it's not efficient."

"What does that mean?" Jerome said.

"The mycelia, fertilized from the soil from the garden, after a few months," Dr. Demetrius said. "They started to come alive, they started to propagate huge mushroom crops. So, I started to target the victims. After, I mean, after we tried to save them. When the hospital put them on life support, I'd plan where to bury them. We created a back story; it was with the DEA's help about toxicity."

"I'm lost," Jerome said. "DEA?"

"Like a contact high," Gene said. "If you touch fentanyl powder you'll get addicted, or worse. Too much can kill you, accidental overdose. The bodies were toxic and dangerous."

"It was a perfect ruse," Dr. Demetrius said. He nodded his head over toward Gene without looking at him. "Like he said, scare the uniformed. We got the patients in; they had never signed consent as they were comatose, or any DNR's - do not resuscitate. After they died. The bodies were left for my discretion, and so, I realized the remains were useful. And it was a green burial; eco-friendly, they gave back to the living, in a twisted way."

"I managed the families," Gene said. "They just assumed what I said was truthful. And then you come along poking about."

"Yes, I started to pay attention," Jerome said. He patted his long fingers on his client list. "You all have too many eyes and ears here to have kept this a secret."

Dr. Demetrius turned his eyes from looking down at the conference table and twisted his head to look over at Artemis.

"The children," Dr. Demetrius said. He gazed at her glass-eyed like his pupils were lost in a clear water puddle. "Laina?"

"Yes, that's her name," Artemis said.

"I was trying to help her," Dr. Demetrius said. "At her genetic level. I tried to make her addiction resistant, you recognize that addiction can be handed down from a mother to a child?"

"I do," Artemis said.

"The mushroom spores," Dr. Demetrius said. "I engineered them to attack the human genetic structure, to discover a method to stop addiction. The micro bots fed me the brain activity. I was getting close to a break-through. CRISPR technology opened the door for me, it became an obsession. I was obsessed."

"You tracked them?" Artemis said. "Like tracking an animal."

"I did. I'm sorry," Dr. Demetrius said. "I monitored them, where they traveled, and their vital signs. Solid base line data points. It was easy. I imagined studying them from afar over their lifetimes, discovering how the genetic structure responded to their environment. It was exciting."

"Do you realize what happened to them?" Artemis said. She stared back over at Jerome who winked at her. He sat back watching, observing Dr. Demetrius.

"At first, I assumed they moved away," Dr. Demetrius said. He frowned.

"I had one die inside the farm; it was a coincidence. I discovered she was an untreated diabetic. Poor thing had a stroke. I found her in a bin; she was tiny; fragile little girl. It was terrible. Her mother had died a week or so before. I buried her next to her mother. But the others, I think my brother. Well…"

"All right," Artemis said. She covered her face with her hands. "I guess. Let's get this over with."

"I'm still monitoring her," Dr. Demetrius said. His countenance perked up. "She's strong, good vital signs. But the others, I don't understand, him."

"I'll deal with him," Artemis said. Dr. Demetrius avoided her eye contact. He hunched forward. "I was not out to hurt anyone. I got lost in my research. My pride got ahead me. Like I've said, I'm sorry. I'm sorry for all of this mess."

"I figure you have what you need?" Wylie said. He wiped his right hand across his bald head.

Jerome acknowledged Wylie. He shifted his notepad side-to-side.

"I have one demand," Jerome said. He pointed at Gene. "Non-negotiable, and I could lose my law license from not sharing this tragedy. I could get cross with the law, as well. I'm too old for jail. I'd like to keep practicing."

"I'm listening," Wylie said. "We aren't sitting clean and easy over here either."

"The garden," Jerome said. He pointed toward the conference room's tall rectangular windows that faced above the hospital garden. "Bulldoze the garden, make it a grass park where children play and patients can walk outside for fresh air."

"Oh, lands," Wylie said. He looked over at Gene who unloosened his red tie. "That is your call."

"We'll do our best," Gene said. "Not sure I'm in a bargaining position, Jerome. But I'll make it happen."

"Gene, just bulldoze the garden," Jerome said. His voice an octave lower. He dagger pointed over at Gene. "It's a simple solution, make the space a permanent grass park. And place a big marble headstone at the front area, share the names and dates for those souls buried there. And another thing…"

Gene nodded. He was obedient like a well fed golden retriever after it got caught playing in the garbage.

"We'll do that for sure," Gene said. "And?"

"The park will be a memorial park. I know these families," Jerome said.

He managed his emotions, his face blank, certain. "On the marble head-stone, write something like, in memory of those who lost their lives to addiction, to the opioid crisis."

"I consider that beautiful," Wylie said. He looked back over at Artemis. He tapped her on the arm. "Clever, Jerome. How 'bout we throw into the tab, and perhaps a little scholarship for the kids?"

"I like that," Jerome said. "Thank you. I think you, and I, will get along well."

"Jerome," Wylie said. "I think you have what you need?"

"I do," Jerome said. "I'm tired. This has been a horrible experience that I'll never be able to comprehend."

"I've brought a gentleman with me, he's back at the hotel," Wylie said. He stood up. "Finances structured settlements for us. I expect a good method for these people, help them manage the money?"

"Yes, we should go to my office. I'm sure you've done the math," Jerome said. "I can work through each file, get them over a lot quicker, and quieter. And we can all get on with living."

"That's a good plan," Wylie said. He loosened his red club tie. "Besides, hospitals give me the creeps."

They all started to leave the conference room. Wylie stopped Artemis. He waved over at Jerome.

"We are all off the record," Jerome said. He closed his leather note-book. "Wylie?"

"I've got this," Wylie said. He squeezed Artemis' left arm. "You finish up, get that mess cleaned up. I'll see you back in St. Pete. We need to get a Guinness, and you tell me about your plans for Laina's upbringing."

"I'll clean up the mess," Artemis said. "It's what I do."

"Yeah, I know what they tell me," Wylie said. He hugged her. He breathed out his mouth. He stammered. "Just be careful. I don't want to train a newbie, again."

Chapter 35

"What'll you have?" The petite waitress said to Artemis. She blew a pink bubble and popped it with her big front teeth. "We have a chef's special."

"Oh, two egg omelet," Artemis said. She investigated down at her smartphone screen. The warm diner air spiked with a bacon, butter, and sausage aroma. "No milk, I get a bit lactose intolerant, messes with my stomach."

"Oh, I'll ask the chef," the waitress said. She wrote the order with a stubby pencil. "I'll double check with him."

"Thanks," Artemis said. She glanced up at the waitress that wore a white long sleeve blouse. Pancake batter blotted her orange rubber shoes. "Water works, it's how I make my eggs at home. Simple."

"We have a vegetarian medley, today," the waitress said. "It's a real healthy special, can't get enough veggies? I think the chef bought to many and now he's trying to get them out before they spoil. If you ask me."

"Sure… that's great," Artemis said. She glanced back down at her smartphone screens blipping a red icon as she monitored Laina's every movement. "Sounds good, thank you."

"Anything else?" the waitress said.

"Ah… no, but thank you," Artemis said. She set the smartphone on the table. "Just coffee, black coffee. My dad always told me to drink it black. I still do. Creature of habit, I guess."

"Never know what's in it, non-diary," the waitress said. She giggled.

"My Daddy told me the same thing. I'll come back and check on you, sweetie."

Artemis sipped the black coffee. As she stared out the diner's windows at the modest local town traffic, she was confident Wylie was well on his way to close the medical malpractice file. It was about money and the dead would not be resurrected from the hospital garden. The file sealed deep inside a courthouse vault. She suspected Wylie was sitting on a narrow plane seat, reviewing his structured settlement agreements, and the related claim files as the commercial plane cruised the lower stratosphere toward Tampa International Airport.

It heartened Artemis that Jerome was doing the legal work to help her extract Laina from depravity. But in the meantime, she had to keep a close monitor on her. Artemis was certain that Prophet Higgs Boson had a demented plan to feed her to the mycelia underneath the tulip poplar. A charismatic sociopath, obsessed with pleasing Satan. And it was clear to Artemis that he had learned of his brother's research methods. The secrets inside the mushrooms genetic code. The giant mycelia nourished from sacrificed human and animal decay birthing fungi infused with a powerful opioid payload. A lethal criminal enterprise masked as harmless mushrooms. Prophet Higgs Boson the ultimate mess The Company sent her to clean up. Her next steps, she pondered, inspect her tools. They were razored sharp. Her semi-automatic 9mm was holstered underneath her dark blue zip-up cardigan was her backup weapon. She preferred to look her targets in the eyes to verify their demise.

"Here you go," the waitress said. She slid a milk glass diner plate in front of Artemis. "Two egg omelet, no dairy, chef used half cup water, and the veggie special, enjoy."

"Thanks," Artemis said. She inspected the common white diner plate and realized the vegetable medley within a brown gravy included chopped up mushroom caps. She searched over at the sit-down counter; an older man wearing a green flannel shirt ate a similar order. The mushrooms and the vegetables were cleared from his plate. He sat on a padded red Naugahyde stool with a chrome base sipping orange juice from a jelly jar glass. She twisted around and noticed other guests at square tables having consumed or about to eat the vegetable special.

"You okay?" The waitress said. She kept chewing and squishing the bubble gum. "Everyone loves the veggies. I'm trying to be a vegan, help me lose some weight. I got to make my belly disappear before summer. I go inner tube rafting, don't want the boys calling me a pig and makin' me oink."

"Oh, I'm good," Artemis said. She shrugged off her initial concern about the mushrooms as mild paranoia. "Sorry, I didn't sleep much, thanks."

"You're fine," the waitress said. "I'll come back, here's the check, sweetie."

Artemis ate her breakfast, paid her bill with cash. She strolled back toward her hotel pepped up by the frigid morning air and sunny blue sky. She kept monitoring Laina's movements, nothing special was happening. Laina had not left the home. A good sign. Agent Beaky was out of her path. But she was certain Prophet Higgs Boson was lurking, waiting. She opened her hotel room door and was about to inspect her tools, but she burped. She blushed. Inside her stomach it rumbled like she had disturbed a sleeping dragon. She bounded into the bathroom. Sweat started to bubble out of the back of her hands. She swept moisture from her face and forehead. Her body quivered and tingled from an instant heat rash, panting through her open mouth. And she vomited her breakfast. After her stomach emptied, she curled onto the frigid bathroom floor, clutching the porcelain toilet, shivering, sensing the cold surfaces.

"Artemis..., Artemis... I... told you," Satan said. It cackled inside Artemis' brain. "Don't eat the mushrooms. And you silly human, you ate the mushrooms."

Artemis awakened within a dreamlike state. No longer inside the bathroom or her hotel room; she traveled without walking within a strange latticed, oval shaped whitish tunnel. At the bend for another tunnel, she saw Satan. Attired in a black velvet tuxedo, a black silk bow tie and black shoes shined to a high polish. Inside the tunnel it rained a sparkling golden dust.

"Where am I?" Artemis said. She stared down the curved tunnel; It appeared to be never ending with offshoots after offshoots on either side or above her.

Satan stood up tall. It wiggled its bow tie with its pointy fingers and it pulled down on the velvet jacket at the labels.

"I hate to visit this hood, we are within the mycelia golden meridian," Satan said. It smirked. "This is not permanent; I can lurk here for a short time. This is a philosophical holding tank. It gives me time to consider my options for a permanent location back in Hell for my new souls. Or, if they have been chosen by the humble angels. Do you like my pointy tail? I think it gives me a chill look. Hip but serious?"

"Am I dead?" Artemis said. Her mind blurred by a whirlwind temporal paradox. "I ate mushrooms. I'm stupid. I failed."

"Don't stress, you're such a ball of stress. I lurk here for the unsuspecting," Satan said. Its sharp tail waggled behind it. "I'll do all the work. I just want to take you for a trip."

"I'm in purgatory?" Artemis said. Satan pulled her along as if she was floating above a pearly, rubbery endless airport moving sidewalk. "It's not possible. I failed."

"Come on, loosen up, this is big fun. You heard me, so don't stress," Satan said. It strolled as it hummed a minstrel tune next to Artemis. "Do you like my horns? I picked them special for you. What did I tell you when we first met?"

Artemis stared over at Satan, her vision covered its image within a frothing haze. But its eyes glowed deep blues and blood reds and the center was black, ominous.

"I… don't," Artemis said, "know."

"Silly girl, remember, I'm an idea," Satan said. It clapped its thorny hands. "I'm in your mind; I'm not a fairy. You're now inside the mycelia highway; the place for rot. Mind you, it's not Hades; this is not permanent. You're seeing the back side of purgatory. I created this inverted wormhole to have fun with you. We are upside down, but in my existence, it's all the same right-side up or not. A cool gyroscope trick I play on humans. You don't get motion sickness?"

"I'm lost," Artemis said. "I failed Benjamin, she'll die. I failed her."

Satan stopped strolling. It pushed its fingers back over at Artemis's waist holding her levitating in space like a child's circus balloon.

"You are such a ball of stress. I think these horns make my human face look longer, what do you think?" Satan said. It huffed. It wave for her to follow it. "Relax girl, this is a tour within the golden middle way. Think Aristotle, life in balance. And believe me, he was a wacky dude. My dear, you are quite safe with me. I can't take you. Pity. But I'm making progress with you. I'll get inside your soul, it's my long-term game plan."

Satan sashayed toward long windows that sparkled from reflected convex, flat or concave light as it yanked Artemis along behind it with an invisible tether without her operating her legs.

"I want to live," Artemis said. "I have to save her."

"By the way, I have to thank you. You've sent me several instant hall of fame souls, as in pure evil, give me a capital E, for Evil," Satan said. It put a thumbs up in front of Artemis. "I didn't even have to waste time with making plans for them in here. It was obvious, the big entity no one can see, did not want them. After all, I am a public servant. Career politicians have nothing on me."

"I did my job," Artemis said. "I was doing my job."

"Yes, you did," Satan said, in a rhythmical, slithering cadence. "You're so talented, athletic, even ambidextrous, nice genetic touch. Also cunning, tactical, a gifted assassin. But you lack one emotion. I'd hate you to learn it. You'd be a perfect addition for my underworld. And for Benny's sake you need some good luck. Oh well, I share bad luck. It's what I do."

As they cascaded down the mycelia highway, Artemis eyes started to clear. She floated near Satan as if being showered through a car wash under a constant golden mist. But it was a dry mist, it was warm. The tunnel meandered in all directions with new openings, after new openings within an endless spiderweb labyrinth.

"What do you want?" Artemis said. She glanced at the back of Satan's human head. His black hair styled to perfection as she avoided its tail's sharp tip end snap at her and snap at her.

"I'll explain later," Satan said. It stopped in front of a long, concave window. "Look inside, I present to you my first deadly sin, wrath. I prefer this concave shape, rather crowds them in together. A tiny claustrophobic hint to liven the party."

Artemis understood what she saw were the newly dead, now lost human spirits searching for eternal next-steps. She looked up at the white bone like mycelia; it appeared like a thick whitish rubber tubing covered in a stringy mesh. And it had random lumps pass above her along the ceiling like a male's Adam's Apple during a pizza party and beneath her.

"Why wrath? You ask," Satan said. "The next six you have to guess, and the why. It'll be fun to voyeur. Artemis, these are my tools to slither across the earth. Part of my big fun. They work better than your razor sharp tools. Alter the mind, deaden feelings and then let hate do its magic."

The new spirits lashed at each other. They screamed. But they were just out of reach from the other. Their spirits bounced off the invading curved glass, ping and ponging off it and scrambling back like rapid animals. Twisting their shoulders, sniffing the air and planning their next assault.

"They're like rapid dogs held by a short leash," Artemis said. "They are angry creatures. They accept violence as the answer."

"Very good, even from a killer, like you," Satan said. "They can't quite get to their prey, an ex-wife, a former boss, maybe a random English foot-ball fan. You call it soccer, in the states, Artemis. That one's a postal worker, retail postal work can make a woman go out of her mind. They're tribal. The best part they can't get at their target. It's maddening for them. Oh well, let's shift to the other side, Artemis. It waved its pointy right hand. Over here, on the other side, tell me, Artemis, what do you see?"

Satan encouraged Artemis to turn her shoulders, and she faced another long window. The spirits behind the convex glass were hiding, avoiding any contact with any other spirits like abused, abandoned dogs.

"They're all afraid," Artemis said. "They are frozen by inaction. It scared them to live. Fear. They lack contentment."

"And now they're dead," Satan said. It tapped and tapped on the glass with its horns. "Pity, at least the murderers, those crazy ones over there, did something. I gave these spirits extra space, but they're so timid. They don't roam the space well."

Artemis' mind was clearing; her eyesight focusing. She sensed Satan's putrid fragrance. The golden particles less invasive.

"Neither had discipline," Artemis said. "They could not calm their minds, to live in balance."

"Ah, good girl, the reason you're a gifted assassin, you are disciplined, focused, calm as you slit throats," Satan said. It wiggled its tail. It smiled to reveal sharp fangs dripping with mucous. "You get me, you get me, so. But let's keep coasting along. Time will not let me waste you away. Stinks. I mean sniff. No kidding take a good sniff? It stinks over on that side in the worst way. This sides sweeter, a fart with a dash of honey?"

Satan yanked Artemis along behind it and on over in front of another long window. Behind this window, it piled the human spirits over each other into a chubby mass across a comfy, overstuffed couch. They sat watching and playing video games and mindless reality television shows. Along the coffee table a pile of golden tickets set waiting. The tickets blazed in a golden radiance.

"A golden ticket to Heaven," Satan said. "All they have to do is get up, and grab the ticket. The crease opens, poof, they are off to eternity."

"Sloth," Artemis said. She pushed her hands against the shiny mycelia next to the flat glass. It felt real to her, spongy, warm, and alive with diges-tive activity. "They were too lazy in life; they never took a chance. Now, they'll wait. Forever."

"You can't hear it," Satan said. It grinned like it expected total darkness to drape across the window. "Added a constant grandfather clock tick and tock, it reminds them not to waste time. But they lack the ability to pay attention. I left the glass simple, flat. Uninteresting if you were to ask for my opinion."

"I think I know what's behind me," Artemis said.

"Oh, good, let's go voyeur in," Satan said. They turned and moved toward the opposite side of the tubular environment. The mycelia wobbled, and it sounded like it digested a meal. "And what have we here, wow, they are at it?"

"Over exercise, obsession with fitness," Artemis said. "The reason some are chained to elliptical machines, or those treadmills. They can't stop lifting weights. They obsess with strength, but it does not earn them courage."

"Pointless when you're dead," Satan said. "They don't even sweat now, I don't get them. Although that girl over there in the skin tight shorts, way hot, to bad. I can make her hotter. Get it, Artemis? Oh, I kill myself. Let's keep touring; it will only get worse, so, much worse."

Satan snapped its fingers, and Artemis floated in front of another window. Behind the concave window, the spirits were obese; they were lethargic.

"Gluttony," Artemis said. "They can have prepared foods. Their wine glasses are large, topped off."

"The smells from behind the window," Satan said. "Oh, to die for. Get it? I pushed the glass in, fatties needed to flop into each other."

"But the food and drink disappear when they reach over for any of it," Artemis said. "It's torture."

"Ah, I hate them so," Satan said. It snapped its fingers and Artemis faced the flat window behind her. "Now what do you think?"

"More torture," Artemis said. "Poor nutrition, obsessed with being thin, but they aren't healthy. Nothing in moderation."

"Yes, yes," Satan said. "All the food and drink, like the other side, but?"

Artemis watched the thin spirits. They had the same food, the drink, all piled on tables, and stuffed into the corner nooks. They likely had the same smells. But they refused to acknowledge the food's presence. As if it were poison.

"Torturing themselves, body issues," Artemis said. She leaned her forehead against the warm glass. "Both sides are extremes, the glutton can't stop eating, drinking, but they all hate themselves, that's the connection."

"Oh hate," Satan said. "Oh, how I hate them all. But can it get worse?"

Artemis sensed her body drift away from the glass. She flew backwards across the mycelia highway within the golden meridian shower. Satan presented her in front of another long window as the mycelia above her gulped and burped again.

"Now, only four to go," Satan said. It smacked its thorny hands together. "These are my favorites for human torture. My favorite tools. Killing is so easy, boring. But torture before and after death, perfection."

Artemis saw through the flat, wide window glass. Each spirit held a golden ticket to heaven.

"I'm confused," Artemis said. "They can go to Heaven."

"Yes, but they don't want their ticket," Satan said. "Why?"

"Envy," Artemis said. She breathed a deep breath into her lungs. "They want the other spirits ticket; they think it's a better ticket. Ignorant that in theory God will treat them all as equals."

"Artemis, in theory? You sound like you're becoming a believer?" Satan said. "Now that's not a good thing for a trained killer, might make you go all gooey and weak. Keep in conflict, grill-fiend."

"The spirits behind us," Artemis said. "The extreme opposite. They lack any joy from life."

"Ah, right," Satan said. It snapped its fingers. "Let's see."

Artemis stared into the area behind the glass. Each spirit giving up their golden ticket to another spirit. And none of them trusting the obvious bright crease for eternal peace.

"Blinded by good works," Artemis said. "Nothing accomplished. They dither with each other within circular logic."

"Yes, oh, yes," Satan said. "But they'll be out of there soon, the humble boobs will just snatch them out of there. They're harmless. Boring."

"They were supposed to inherit the earth," Artemis said. "At least eternity will be kind to them."

"Oh, you are such a softy, as you tell Wylie," Satan said. "Let's keep moving along, those spirits are boring to me."

Artemis cascaded, helpless in front of another window. Within the space behind the convex glass, the spirits roamed again like ping-pong balls inside as if within a wind-blown jar.

"Pride," Artemis said. "Has to be pride."

"How so?" Satan said. It stuck its forked tongue out from its pale lips. Its jackal eyes glowed blue and red. The black center menaced her. "I beg for more."

"Their expressions are of self-importance," Artemis said. "They shift around the room begging for notice, but no one can understand them.

Until they walk through each other, disturbing their spirits. They are then insulted, feeling disrespected."

"Ah, yes, getting disrespected and making emotional decisions, dumb, dumb, way too easy," Satan said. It frowned. "The window behind us, boring. I mean those spirits needed to get a life. Oops, and now they're dead."

"Do I need to look at them," Artemis said. She stared forward. "They are meek, shy, they won't be here long. They took being humble to an extreme."

"Yes, very good, yes, they'll get snatched soon. You are getting the hang of this, here, here, for Artemis," Satan said. It pulled Artemis over toward the next window. It was convex. The space pillowed on pure white couches, leather beds, or lace covered the beds. "These hellions, now, this is what I'm hating about. I gave them room to roam. It's soft with lots of bouncy for action."

Artemis winced, she turned her eyes away.

"No," Artemis said. "That's disgusting."

Satan purred as it watched the active scene.

"Come on, Artemis," Satan said. It poked out its forked tongue wiggling it. "I'll not release you without you seeing them, turn your eyes back over, come on. Take it all in. Or, Benny stays with me, for eternity. Laina meets her tragic end."

Artemis stared into the wide and deep room where nothing was hidden. Dark, animalistic demons joined with the new spirits. The hulking demons were hairy beasts and with sharp inward horns and flapping tails. The spirits unable to escape from them as if in solid human flesh but the demons were spirits as well thrusting and jabbing the human spirits.

"This is my masterpiece," Satan said. It stepped closer with its forked tongue against the convex shaped glass and left a moisture streak with foamy drops starting to drip downward. "The demons get to go all out, notice, that one over there. It is raping her from behind. She looks startled. In life she was not into that experience. Torture her spirit in her exit only hole. Fun to hate. The male spirit facing her, he wants her. But he's trapped with two demons. See, the demon spirits trapped them in an orgy they can't enjoy. The demons take them instead and perform terrible acts the spirits would never get down with while alive. Torture. Like that macho appearing dude, he lusted for any babe that moved. See, he's the one over there on that bed, ouch. He'll never be able to gargle that taste out of his mouth. But wait, he's dead. I hate the expressions. It's shock mixed with helplessness. I am such a creative. But if you hate what you do, you never work a nanosecond throughout eternity."

"Lust," Artemis said. "The demons are between them all, the demons let them realize what they desire, sexual obsession, but they can't have it."

"Oh yes, lust it is, but with a twist, they lack control," Satan said. It clapped its hands. And then it frowned. Its tail pointed up behind it. "Window behind us, boring. I mean boring as Heaven."

"Chastity," Artemis said. "Something like that?"

"You sunk my battleship, well-done, Artemis, I hate video games," Satan said. It leaned in closer to Artemis. Its putrid aroma off putting even in a dreamlike state. "They never get laid, ever, never had any carnal fun. I'll spare you, boring scene, let's fly along."

Artemis zapped in front of the last wide, flat window.

"This one," Satan said. It cackled and then it howled. "What did I tell when we first met?"

"Greed," Artemis said. She floated just above the mycelia surface as her eyes started to become drowsy. Her vision deteriorating. But she breathed in deep breaths. Her heart beats steady and certain. "The golden tickets, they refuse to share with the others."

"And?" Satan said. "Come on girl, give it up."

"They all have half-tickets, but multiple tickets, they hoard their stash," Artemis said. She stared at the tickets. "But the serial numbers are mismatched. They can't go on without a full ticket with matching serial numbers."

"It's so delicious to watch, they can have all they want," Satan said. It howled. "If they just shared what they had, worked together, they could get what they need. They would realize the others have a match they need, and vice versa. But they refuse to share. They have a lot of time to contemplate this I'll promise you that, Artemis Lamb. Maybe we should sit back, perhaps we should order some popcorn?"

Artemis' breathing was heavy, her irregular breaths fogged the window. She sensed she was swimming upward within black ocean water toward a singular white dot. The dot expanding, becoming larger and rounder as she surfaced.

"It's almost time," Satan said. "Pity, the window behind it, boring, so boring, it's painful to glance inside."

Artemis opened her eyes wide, she gripped her fingers together. She flapped her legs.

"The widow, she's alone," Artemis said. She glanced over at the poor woman. "She'll give her last two dimes to her children, costing her her life. She starved to death."

Satan snapped its fingers together. Artemis proofed from the mycelia highway. They stood near a white granite monument in the dark cemetery.

"Come find me when you're prepared to bargain, you'll know when," Satan said. It growled. The sound reverberated as if trapped inside an empty cathedral. "Let's do this cemetery. I felt welcomed here. I need a comfortable place for my best work. Game on girl, I'll come visit you in the hospital."

Chapter 36

"You're lucky," Dr. Demetrius said. He felt under Artemis' chin, he pressed his fingers inward against her larynx. "You're starting to have a better pulse. Your temperature spiked, it's come down."

Artemis blinked her eyes. She stared down at the hospital bed, her body covered with pale blue sheets and a white cotton blanket. She heard the medical machine blips. The light fixture behind her buzzed from electrical voltage.

"How did I get here?" Artemis said. She pulled at her right arm, she saw the luminous IV line taped to her right hand. "That stings."

"Maid walked by your hotel room," Dr. Demetrius said. He tapped his mobile device as his dark eyes found her electronic health record. "She peeked inside because you left your door wide open. I think you tried to crawl out of your hotel room."

"Your brother tried to kill me," Artemis said. She started to move and shift under the bedsheets. "Where's my smartphone? I need to find her."

"Police think they broke into your hotel room, police likely helped them. They'll have taken your smartphone. Trust me, it's not in here," Dr. Demetrius said. He gripped Artemis' right hand wrist. "Your pulse keeps improving. I think you'll live."

"I have to get out of here," Artemis said. She shook her head. She wiped her eyes. "I have to find her, now."

"Pumped you full of some high-end milk thistle, activated charcoal,"

Dr. Demetrius said. He set the mobile medical device on a countertop, stuffed his hands in his white lab coat pockets. "It helps to regenerate your liver, we've gotten you hydrated. I think he slipped you Amanita Muscaria, took you on a short trip. He's got people all over town, he's been following you."

"Yeah, I knew better," Artemis said. She groaned. "Don't eat the mushrooms."

"If he wanted you dead," Dr. Demetrius said. "He'd slipped you Amanita phalloides, remember the death caps? I'm curious, did you take a magic trip?"

Artemis glanced up at Dr. Demetrius. She grimaced.

"You've taken them?" Artemis said. She opened and closed her eyelids. "Feel like I got hit in the head."

"I did once," Dr. Demetrius said. "I'm a scientist. I wanted to understand them. But I'll never do it again, scary. I wanted to understand addiction, but not get addicted."

"I can't find Laina, now," Artemis said. "If she's on the move. I have to get out of here, get out there."

"I can help you, you need me," Dr. Demetrius said. He patted her on the leg. "I've been following monitoring her. She's maintained the same location. I'm the one that put a micro device in her palm. She's not moved in days."

"And those micro bots?" Artemis said. "Going through her brain."

"Yes, I did." Dr. Demetrius said. He nodded. "I can help you, and you can help me. This madness has to end, he's killed innocent people; it's in part, my fault. That monster comes from my experiments, my work."

"I can manage him," Artemis said. She leaned up and shifted forward. "She's my prime one at all costs."

"Her vitals show me she's doing fine," Dr. Demetrius said. He sucked in a slow breath. "A lot of inflammation, it's her temperature, heart rate, they are up."

"Stressed?" Artemis said.

"I would think so," Dr. Demetrius said. "My brother must be near her, being well, himself."

"Are you sure you can manage?" Dr. Demetrius said. He adjusted the metal bed rail downward. "And, thank you."

Artemis slung her naked legs over the side of the bed. She gripped the edge of the bed. She re-gripped the cold metal rail beneath the thin mattress.

"For what?" Artemis said. She looked back and forth along the gray speckled tile floor, and over at the side table topped with glass containers for tongue depressors, and packaged otoscope specula tips. "Clothes? What time is it?"

"Wylie, Jerome and you," Dr. Demetrius said. He pointed over at a black padded chair with a plastic storage container. "Over there, you all saved my medical license, allowed me to continue my research. I'll never be able to repay the hospital, or you all."

"Oh, we don't hurt the wrong people, what time is it?" Artemis said. She slipped bare footed downward onto the cold tile floor. She gained her balance, as Dr. Demetrius gripped her right forearm.

"Wait, let's not make a mess," Dr. Demetrius said. He removed the IV line with practiced precision. "Get your balance first. Can you manage? It's two-thirty in the afternoon. You were out all morning."

Artemis faltered as she grasped Dr. Demetrius' hand, her knees sank downward, but she sucked in a deep breath and then she righted herself.

"Your brother's responsible for killing people," Artemis said. The natural adrenaline from conviction, coursed through her veins as she stood up. "This place is at the core for an epidemic. I agree, it has to stop. Let me get dressed."

"I'll be outside," Dr. Demetrius said. He guided Artemis over toward her clothes and her personal effects. Before he closed the door behind him for the patient room. "Your weapon is in my office. I've got it locked in my desk. I'll not alert security."

Artemis lifted the blue plastic container onto the bed. She examined her clothes. She pulled open the hospital gowns tie strings and took off the powder-blue gown.

"Artemis, oh, Artemis," Satan said. It enraptured the room with a soft, pale blue mist. "I told you not to eat the mushrooms."

"You warned me," Artemis said. She tried to ignore Satan's presence as she got dressed. "Where is she?"

"Are you prepared to bargain?" Satan said.

Artemis paused, after she had dressed; She leaned back on her boots. Her arms dangled at her sides. She closed her eyes.

"If you let her go," Artemis said. She stared over at the ruffled hospital bed sheets. The blue mist spun like a cyclone over the padded chair. "Kill me. Allow her to live, let her seek happiness."

Satan's melodic laugh vibrated from wall-to-wall and against the windows. And then it appeared behind Artemis, sitting on the cushioned chair. Artemis scooted back toward the closed door. She crouched down, her hands dangled over her knees as she faced Satan.

"She means nothing to me," Satan said. Clothed in a bespoke dark gray Saville Row suit, red pocket square, and pale blue bow tie. "I came here because of you. It's always been about you. I don't care if she lives or dies."

"Let her go," Artemis said. "Make that monster go away."

Satan winked, its wide-tooth smile sparkled. It crossed its long legs. It tapped its sharp finger nails along the armrests.

"Like my loafers?" Satan said. It wiggled the expensive Italian leather shoe with a silver buckle. "Humans lust for these. I don't get it. I like to keep them priced out of reach, just beyond the average humans finger tip. Envy is useful to deploy."

"I'll kill him, either way, you know that," Artemis said. She pushed her back up against the door, thrusting up and gripped the doorknob with her left hand. "If you take her, she'll go on. Her spirit will go on without a question in my mind. She's an innocent."

"True, I welcome that moment," Satan said. It growled. "But, as her spirit visits my world amongst the mycelia. I will torture her. I'll keep her lost wondering in a dark funhouse for a thousand years. For my own funzies like the tiny spirit girl in Dr. Demetrius' mushroom farm. Remember her? She's so sweet, boohoo."

Artemis pressed her forehead over against the smooth, cold wall at her right side. She stared downward at the tile floor.

"What then?" Artemis said. "Will you let the spirit girl go on, the one inside the mushroom farm. She's harmless. If I cooperate?"

"Now we begin the negotiation, I hate you," Satan said. Its forked tongue rattled forward like a venomous snake searching its territory for prey. It snapped its fingers. It stared forward. "I just released her. I'm watching a bright crease appear in front of her. She's giggling, she's smiling. And now she's gone on into that strange existence."

"What then?" Artemis said.

"Get your weapon from your former foe, now friend, I suppose," Satan said. Its voice gurgling, growling and hissing. "It's disgusting how pathetic Dr. Demetrius has fallen. Go get your throwing knives, a dagger, oh, I hate that curved one made from titanium, bring it for sure. You prefer your tools to be razor sharp, and they are, I protected them. Those are the tools for a serious assassin. You'll find them safe and all snuggled together."

"If you kill her," Artemis said. "I can't stop you."

"True, ponder on that," Satan said. It pointed at her. "If you accept my offer. You'll feel me your truth. I want to feel an emotion from you. I demand an honest performance. If you accept the role, I expect your artistry. Come on Artemis, be an artist, live a little."

"But what?" Artemis said.

"Torture," Satan said. "In human terms, it's a good appetizer. It tickles my appetite, but I want a fancy entree."

"How do I do this?" Artemis said. She leaned her back on the door, she stared above Satan at the open window blinds. "You know she's my prime one. I'll kill anyone in my path."

"I do," Satan said. "Such the focus, oh, prepared for battle. I am excited for all your blood and guts, delicious."

"Where?" Artemis said.

"You know that answer," Satan said. "Look over at me, nothing to be afraid of, I'm Satan."

Outside the door Artemis heard the typical hospital sounds, the squeak from gurney wheels being pushed near the door. She looked down and cracked open her eyes. Satan stood up and transformed from the handsome man and into a pale blue angel with muscled feathered wings. His face was beautiful beyond the written word in any language from any human century.

"The cemetery," Artemis said. She squeezed back into the corner between the metal door and the patient room's interior wall. She gasped. She clenched her teeth. "I'll be there."

Satan flapped its wings. It pointed down at her.

"Let the doctor tag along with you. I want to praise him," Satan said. It floated higher toward the ceiling inside the hospital room dominating the space. "Be prepared to act swift, have all your pointy tools strapped to you."

"He'll not see you," Artemis said.

"I am revealed when I want to be revealed, silly human," Satan said. It flicked a middle finger at her. "I cannot promise you her life. Unless?"

Artemis reached forward as Satan puffed into a blue dust. The dust disappeared as it tunneled through the HVAC ceiling duct.

"Unless, unless," Artemis said. She reached forward. All she grabbed at was air. "What?"

Satan chuckled through its whisper.

"You give me what I want. It's a simple exercise in free-will," Satan said. "See you soon, my human plaything."

Artemis stood up inside the brightly lit hospital room. She checked her clothes and belongings. She understood her next steps. Satan kept luring her, revealing clues that kept blooming along a hidden path triggered from within her desire to care for another human being's soul and his innocent child.

Chapter 37

"I'm sorry," Dr. Demetrius said. He slumped against the hallway wall outside of Artemis' hotel room door. "It was my brother. I don't understand him."

"They trashed it," Artemis said. She flicked up the light switch as she moved farther inside the dimly lit room. She stepped over the manufactured wood desk shoved into the first double bed. The drawers yanked out and crushed into kindling. The lamp between the beds smashed; It lay helpless beneath the far windows. She searched down to find her opened suitcase. They had scattered her clothes like it had been a college toga party. She kneeled down to inspect the sturdy suitcase. "They were all high; it's all haphazard, unprofessional."

"I keep failing," Dr. Demetrius said. "I don't understand why my microbots, the sensor quit. You saw them in my office, the blip died. I don't know how we'll find her. My life has become a nightmare."

"I realize why," Artemis said. She crouched down inspecting the suitcase interior. "We'll go meet the answer."

"How?" Dr. Demetrius said. "That's an odd response."

Dr. Demetrius stepped farther inside, he looked into the dark bathroom. He clicked on the light. He was cautious not to touch any of the mirror shards scattered across the tile floor and beneath his boots.

"I have a plan, I will make it in plain language later," Artemis said. She kept her eyes down on the task at hand. "Sometimes you have to dance with the real Devil, to get what you want."

"I must stop him," Dr. Demetrius said. He stepped back from the bathroom doorway; he crossed his arms. "I'm responsible for this. I'll do whatever you ask."

Artemis tapped on the inside wall of her large, black fabric suitcase. She glanced up and back over at Dr. Demetrius.

"We're in luck," Artemis said. With her right hand she made a fist, she punched into the side panel, it cracked it open. She pulled out a long tan leather chef's roll. "Took my computer, my smartphone, both are encrypted. They are worthless and useless. But they left behind my tools. Sloppy."

"What's in that chef's roll?" Dr. Demetrius said. He stood behind the desk, gazing down at the top of the tousled bed. "Are you some fancy part-time chef, too? Remember, I'm an excellent cook. My cutlery are amazing, a bespoke Japanese set."

"No, I use this roll for easy transport," Artemis said. She flattened the comforter and bed sheets and shifted the storage bag onto the first bed. She unrolled it to reveal her throwing blades, daggers and knives. "These are my work tools."

Dr. Demetrius shifted his gaze downward at the sharp knives. He kept quiet. He covered his mouth this his right hand fingers tapping them over his lips.

"Those aren't surgical or culinary," Dr. Demetrius said. He pointed down at them from a safe spot. "What do you do? It's not malpractice insurance, not with those. Those look military."

"I'll explain, soon, I promise," Artemis said. She selected a four and a half inch dark-gray serrated knife with a sturdy black nylon handle. And then she clutched a twelve inch stainless steel blade with a cord handle, and then a compact, folding dagger made from titanium. "I'll hide these inside my coat, for now. In the meantime, something, how do I say this. IT wants to meet you. And then we'll go find your brother, and Laina."

Dr. Demetrius pondered Artemis' words. He twisted his head, and he peered over at his reflection cast back at him from the room's smoked glass windows and the late afternoon sky's.

"You said, it," Dr. Demetrius said. "A something, not someone, correct?"

"Wait," Artemis said. She studied her remaining tools. She nodded and pulled out a long two sided blade, with a round black handle. "This might be useful, unless I miss my instincts they'll be a group waiting for me out there."

"What is that thing," Dr. Demetrius said. "Why did you say, it? Again, I don't understand."

"Russian beauty, doubled-sided blade," Artemis said. She gripped it and twisted it. "Ballistic knife, pull this trigger, it's spring-loaded, knife detaches, so forth. They are illegal to possess without a ticket. I have a ticket."

Artemis wrapped her remaining tools and stuck the storage roll back inside the suitcase's hidden compartment. She stood up, and looked back over at Dr. Demetrius.

"I did say, it, you heard me," Artemis said. She shoved the suitcase behind the second bed and between the back wall. "I need to go make a deal with it."

"It?" Dr. Demetrius said. He mumbled as he turned his head to the side. "It."

Artemis covered her tools with her blue sweater and zipped up her parka. She stepped over the desk and back out into the hotel hallway. Dr. Demetrius followed her as he shut the hotel door behind them.

"Walk with me," Artemis said. She marched toward the elevators. She checked her tactical watch. "We're going to Most High Cemetery, that's where the deal goes down."

"My brother is a drug dealer," Dr. Demetrius said. He pressed the round metal elevator button. "I guess that's a good place to meet, I'm not educated on these matters."

"No," Artemis said. "You'll see. You'll be scared. But…"

"Ah, but?" Dr. Demetrius said. The mauve skinned elevator door opened. They got inside, and Artemis pressed the button for the ground floor. "What?"

"When it comes, pinch yourself," Artemis said. She stared forward. "You'll know you're not dreaming. Besides, you'd already be dead if it wanted to take you; it's a fact."

"I can't understand you," Dr. Demetrius said.

"It wants something," Artemis said. "You'll see."

"I'm scared. I don't understand why," Dr. Demetrius said. "My stomach is churning, should I be? And you keep using it, and not he or she? It is a strange pronoun to use. I'm confused."

"You should be. It is not human," Artemis said. As the elevator door closed. "Don't feel lonely. I'm scared, too."

Chapter 38

"Wait for it, it'll be here," Artemis said. Her breath's foggy vapors covered back across her face. "Try to slow your heart rate. Take in deep breaths, control the breaths."

"I'm trying," Dr. Demetrius said. His chest heaved. "I'm about to throw up, stomach acid at the back of my mouth. I get a mild esophagitis. How are you so calm?"

Artemis scoured the cemetery for movement, the golden ensconced wandering spirits had evacuated to safer perceptions and she looked up into the tentacled oak tree. The ominous raven's black eyes stared back down at her. She and Dr. Demetrius stood next to each other at the center of the frigid Most High Cemetery. They heard the black-winged bird's sharp claws dig into the leprous tree bark as it peppered them with a low croak, after a murmured croak. It was joined by black crows across a distant thorny limb. They cawed at them. The haunting white granite monument that centered the cemetery was shrouded with a gray expectant late afternoon murkiness.

"What's our goal," Artemis said. Her teeth chattered. "What do we agree is our goal?"

"Find Laina, we'll find my brother," Dr. Demetrius said. He followed Artemis' upward glance to see the raven twist its beak and snap at him. "I guess cemeteries are a quiet spots for these matters?"

Artemis inspected the cemeteries nine sections and the seven iron gates.

Certain Satan would enter soon. From behind her she heard Dr. Demetrius scamper behind the gnarled oak tree trunk.

"What's that?" Dr. Demetrius said. He whispered. His shaking left hand fingers pointed out beyond Artemis. His eyes glistened with uncertainty. "Looks like a tall man, odd, he's coming our way from across that field. He's near that downed tree."

A human form wearing a horned goat mask gallivanted through the cemeteries iron gate bars that whistled through the body like it was made from air. The black suit it wore, tailored to perfection. The pants with a sharp crease with an inch and a half cuff at the bottom. And Artemis understood that Satan had announced its presence.

"Focus on the goal," Artemis said. She gulped. "If you keep your mind on the goal, you'll get through this. Remember, it wants something. Otherwise, we'd be dead."

Satan kept the goat head mask on and it marched forward. Its hands and arms swaying with an ease and savoir-faire.

"Oh, I want something, Artemis," Satan said. It stopped walking and stood next to the gaudy center monument, sauntering back and forth with its hands in its pants pockets. "Thank you Artemis for bringing Dr. Demetrius. You listened. I cannot express to you both how often humans lack the ability to listen."

Artemis shifted closer to Dr. Demetrius. She waved for him to remain back and next to the old tree.

"What do you want?" Artemis said. She tried to keep her mind blank and not calculate her next moves or ideas.

"Good, Artemis, keep your thoughts vapid," Satan said. It tapped on its wrist. "Always efficient with time, get to the point. I'll do that since you need time. Hello, Dr. Demetrius. I've been begging to meet you for some time now, and here you are with my new friend."

"We're not friends," Artemis said. "To be clear."

"Ah, truthful to the end," Satan said. "I hate that."

Dr. Demetrius stepped from behind the bulky tree. He pointed over at the iron gate. His shoulders back.

"Cute trick, skinny man," Dr. Demetrius said. He scanned up and down Satan's human body. He grunted. "Otherwise, take off that silly mask, who are you?"

Satan hummed a funeral dirge and it pulled out its long fingers with sharp nails and it steepled them.

"Don't take the bait," Artemis said. She crowded in closer toward Dr. Demetrius. Her left shoulder in front of him. "Keep your cool. Breathe."

"I wore this mask for you Artemis, I perceived you'd appreciate my artistic nature," Satan said. It lifted off the mask to reveal the handsome face. It stared over at Dr. Demetrius with a wide-toothed smile licking its lips with a forked-tongue. "Your idiot brother that I inhabit wears this. I gave it to him. It was a gift. I'll give him another one, later. I suppose. It depends on Artemis' skills."

Satan flung the goat mask aside; it bounced off a headstone and it cracked down the center splitting the nose apart.

"This is absurd, what's, your… tongue," Dr. Demetrius said. He whispered. "Who are you, we have a child's life at risk? If you can help fine, otherwise…"

"Oh, simmer down doctor, in due time," Satan said. It meandered over toward a grave stone. It leaned forward and pointed downward with its knife-like left hand forefinger at the name, carved across was a former human life with beginning and ending dates. It stared back over at Dr. Demetrius. It smirked. "Thank you for this one, he was not a bad man, at first. Until, well, he's not doing well now. He was part of your brother's crew. He prayed for me. He worshipped me like a good boy. I responded with his wish. As Artemis knows, I don't break my contracts. Ever."

Artemis stepped over and kneeled down to read the name. She could barely read the name from the reflected light.

"Charles R. Hall, I think. I don't have my smartphone. He died last year," Artemis said. She glanced back over at Dr. Demetrius. "Did you know him? Treat him?"

Dr. Demetrius shifted, stepping by Satan, he scowled back over at it. He stood behind Artemis. He bent his knees, used his smartphone flashlight as his shaking right hand gripped Artemis' right shoulder as he mumbled the name from behind her.

"Yes," Dr. Demetrius said. He released his grip. He stood back up contemplating the name. Mumbling the name as he stared up at the emerging Moon and Orions Belt. "He was a patient. Coal mining accident, he had constant back pain, soft tissue injury. Sorry, sorry that he ended up with my brother, did my brother kill him?"

Satan hissed. It sashayed away from them and over toward the ornate white granite monument. It clapped in a methodical cadence. It crushed the brown grass under its shiny shoes.

"No, your brother was not his proximate cause, oh no," Satan said. It cackled. It dagger-pointed back at Dr. Demetrius. And it turned back around toward the white granite monument to admire the craftsmanship with its back to Dr. Demetrius. "You did. You killed him." It shrugged. "I hate this monument. It is so full of ego. Well done to this dead family. Come to think of it. I think I might have most of them."

Before Artemis could block him, Dr. Demetrius sprang from the headstone, he screamed at Satan. Satan turned around just in time for Dr. Demetrius to slam it into the monument. Satan's arms dangled and it smiled and panted at Dr. Demetrius. Dr. Demetrius balled up his right hand into a fist. He gripped its neck and crumbled Satan's body down onto the ground, stuffing it back against the white granite.

"How dare you," Dr. Demetrius said. He pointed down at Satan. "I've never murdered a person. I've devoted my life to saving lives."

"Careful," Artemis said. She sprinted in behind Dr. Demetrius and grabbed and clutched his waist. She tugged him back hard and maneuvered Dr. Demetrius back and away from Satan. "Let go, not a good idea. Keep your focus, it is toying with us. Be careful."

Satan hopped back up, it adjusted the jacket lapels, and swept its hands over its pants leg. It inspected the suit for scratches or imperfections.

"Such passion, my, my," Satan said. It sniffed the cold air. It licked its moist lips with a forked-tongue. "But, to be accurate. You prescribed him powerful pain medications. Correct?"

Dr. Demetrius paused as he stared at Satan. He blinked his eyes and pawed his right hand fingers at Satan as if answering a strange image with a question that blinked inside his visual consciousness.

"To ease his pain, yes," Dr. Demetrius said. He searched the sparkled, icy grass tips for answers. He glanced at Artemis for assurance. "I, I... treated him with the best options available. There are government approved protocols. The man was in severe back pain. I tried to help him."

"Got him addicted," Satan said. Its pointy fingers and hands help upward, its arms open like an innocent televangelist begging for a senior citizen for an automatic month-to-month offering. It stuck its forked-tongue out like a snake sensing the environment. "You didn't follow up, staff looked the other way. But... you all... got paid?"

"I, I... accept that point," Dr. Demetrius said. He snorted with his hands on his hips. He shook his head as he scratched his forehead. "But I cannot be at two places at the same... time. I am sorry he got addicted. I am. We have hospital services to help. It's a constant... problem, prescribe too little, they are back in the office. Prescribe too much supply, we have an addict to manage."

Satan cackled. It howled over at Dr. Demetrius.

"I can," Satan said. It wiggled its body. It poked its pointy forefinger into its left cheek. Its voice in a sarcastic, child like tone. "It's a gift. As Artemis knows, I am a public servant."

"I don't understand," Artemis said. She stepped in front of Dr. Demetrius and encouraged him to step away from Satan. "What do you want? You made your point. I have to protect her."

"I can be at many places," Satan said. It waved its left hand fingers at Artemis. "All over this planet at the same time. A cool trick. That's all, Artemis. Chill out. I've got a plan for you. But I am playing with Dr. Demetrius now."

"Whoever you are," Dr. Demetrius said. He stood next to Artemis. His chest heaved. He scanned back and forth at Satan and over at Artemis. "I did not kill anyone. Do you always talk in riddles? I do not understand, what do you want? We need to find a child, help us good-man, or we're leaving this madness."

"Be careful," Artemis said. Her voice low and reluctant.

"Yes, be careful with me. I gave you a pass from your violent stunt. And I am not a good-man," Satan said. It pointed at her. Its voice deep, commanding, and guttural. "You should listen to Artemis. She understands death. I just wanted to thank you and all your colleagues. You have made my work so, so, much easier. You, an indirect path, I suppose in your mind. But, I believe you. You meant, first, do him no harm. I'm paraphrasing. Nice fellow that Hippocrates. But Dr. Demetrius you just got busy with your genetically modified mycelia and that fabulous mushroom farm. You are an amazing farmer. You are. Your magic mycelia has grown into epic proportions out there in the forest. Thanks to your brother, and a composting technique he learned from? Wait for it... right Artemis? His brilliant brother."

Dr. Demetrius contemplated Satan, and he gazed over at Artemis.

"How does he know this?" Dr. Demetrius said. His voice sullen, his eyes searching the headstones, the monuments. "Artemis?"

"Epigenetic's is part of my trade craft, remember, this Devil's in the tiny genetic detail, life trauma works for the soul," Satan said. It howled. It pulled forward its French cuffed sleeves to reveal the innocent white cotton and black pearl cufflinks. "Untidy, but effective for a mass killing."

"I see now, I think," Dr. Demetrius said. He sighed. His voice sparse, low. "Opioids, over prescribing fentanyl, that's your point? Did you lose a loved one, if so, I am sorry."

"Focus," Artemis said. "It has gotten into your mind."

"But, I assure you the vast majority of physicians, hospitals, we all seek to cure patients, help them manage their pain," Dr. Demetrius said. He nodded. "However, we have colleagues, facilities they focus on money. It's an unfortunate part of our times. Greed."

"Tens of thousands of humans, wiped out, heroin laced with synthetic fentanyl, ah I hate it so, a perfect killer," Satan said. It shimmered, it wiggled its arms and happy danced. "You should know Dr. Demetrius. I don't have any loved ones. I'm not capable."

"Try to focus on the goal," Artemis said. "We'll get past this, focus on the goal."

"I had you, you were full of pride. A boring sin, but in your case, it was useful. Pity I wasted my time," Satan said. It screwed the tip end of its shiny shoe into the concrete walkway. Grinding a concave depression into the cement and sand mixture. It pointed over at Artemis. It stuck out its forked tongue. It snapped at her with its sharp fangs. "Until that one messed up my plan. And your heart and mortal soul slithered away from me. Oh, you were within my clutches. I felt your black heart."

"Who are you?" Dr. Demetrius said. He stepped back. "You're sick. Or, something else… I'm in a nightmare. Simple, I'll awaken from it. Splash water on my face."

"Want to see? The something else…" Satan said. It stood up straight. It stared over at Artemis for an uncomfortable half-minute. It grinned and blinked its jackal eyes. "Artemis, she's my special project. Oh, how I need her in my army." It clapped, and it clapped. It bent at its knees. "Ready, yay."

"Never," Artemis said. "What do you want?"

"We'll see about that," Satan said. It leaped ten foot forward to face Dr. Demetrius. "Thank you for your research, your creations are spectacular. They are effective for mass killing. Perfect. You are a genius for the black arts."

Dr. Demetrius froze, he bent back as he stared into Satan's dead eyes that glowed blues and reds and then turned into black orbs.

"I meant for the mycelia to protect life," Dr. Demetrius said. His voice just above a whisper. He began to understand what he was interacting with and the consequences. "Create life for generations, new foods, green products. Oh god… God please protect me."

Satan tapped Dr. Demetrius on the top of his head. Dr. Demetrius crinkled his face. Satan flashed its five fingered hands close to Dr. Demetrius' face.

"Well then, don't be… sad, I know how to insult a Greek boy," Satan said in a childish voice. "But your brother stole a box of your super-duper mycelia, and a package of mushrooms all meant for a university research facility. Oh… darn."

"I've seen it," Dr. Demetrius said. "I did not prevent it, a monster."

"Sometimes bad luck counts," Satan said. It poked into Dr. Demetrius' chest. "Remember your comments about penicillin? Oh, you were so proud of your research, not going to stumble into your solutions? Not the big bad Dr. Demetrius, he was above accidents. Brilliant. He's a genius."

"How do you know that?" Dr. Demetrius said. His face wrinkled, his eyebrows narrowed. "This cannot be real."

Artemis elbowed him. She stared forward.

"Pinch your cheek," Artemis said. "It is real, be careful. It is not to be played with. Back up."

"Do that, pinch your cheek. I'm real," Satan said. It fidgeted its fingers at Dr. Demetrius' cheeks. It howled. "Do it. Do it."

Dr. Demetrius pinched his cheek. He winced. Satan patted him on the head.

"I don't believe this," Dr. Demetrius said. "I'm going to die, wait, I'm already dead."

Satan gazed at Dr. Demetrius and glanced over at Artemis.

"Any who, in your brother's case, I mean, dumb luck counted," Satan said. It turned its head side-to-side staring, inspecting at Dr. Demetrius, poking out its forked-tongue. "He buried the mycelia under a huge life giving tree. He started to mix in the ground-up heroin with synthetic fentanyl, and he kept the soil nice and moist, and warm, like any good farmer. A good farmer like you. He's a quick study. But he's gone mental. Has mumsy issues. I think of him in this crease in time as a shepherd giving back to his flock. Mind you an addict flock flapping inside a constant stormy black cloud."

"I'm humiliated," Dr. Demetrius said.

"Mushrooms started popping up," Satan said. It backed up and began to stroll in a circle around Dr. Demetrius and Artemis. "And those were some loaded fungi, let me tell you. Wow. And then, he figured out what you were doing with those dead addict bodies over at the hospital. He stole your work, genius, if you want to get ahead in life just steal from the artist. It's easier than having the creative brain and doing the work. He started sacrificing girls, drugged up women to worship me from his hate for his mother campaign lunacy. A twisted fellow, but hate, oh, he feels the hate. He gets me."

"Focus on the goal," Artemis said. "Focus."

"Chill girl, I hate you," Satan said. It waved and flicked its hands for Artemis to step away. "We'll get to you in a few, so, doctor, your mycelia started feeding on human flesh, sometimes animals. It enjoyed a delicate lamb the other day. A rare delicacy. Yummy."

"A killing machine, I admit it," Dr. Demetrius said. He covered his face with his hairy hands. "They have manipulated it for evil. I had no idea it would morph into a killing machine."

"Oh how delicious, you get me now Dr. Demetrius," Satan said. It patted its chest with its hands. It hugged its self. "And it hides in plain site, growing inch by inch under your shoes. Death caps, the toxic mushrooms, they have spread all over the world, like, wait for it, a fungus." Satan stepped back and it howled, it cackled. "Get it? Spreading like a fungus. Oh, you should do an internet search on this one. It is such a luscious killer, it pops out of the ground. A bulbous, greenish, innocent looking assassin, a bit like Artemis, begging to be taken home and consumed at their own peril. Perfection."

"I must stop him," Dr. Demetrius said. He held his breath as he peeked through his fingers over at Satan. He pinched his cheek. "What are you, you don't have human eyes? Now I understand, I think. Artemis is this, well, a sort of Lucifer?"

Satan stopped strolling, it backed up and put its hands on its waist. It paused, smirked, wiggled its forefinger back over at Dr. Demetrius.

"I chose Satan, not Lucifer, not Beelzebub, not Prince of Darkness, or from the Greek, Diabolus. This time, I'm Satan, but, you're a smart one," Satan said. It wiggled its forefinger in the air and caused the all the black crows to flop dead on the hard ground behind them. "Now pinch your cheek, again. See, I'm right here. This is not a dream. Watch this, I'll put on a real show for you. Killing those scrawny birds was easy. My raven felt disrespected up there."

"Back up," Artemis said. She grasped Dr. Demetrius' right forearm. "Keep still, focus on the goal, can you stay still?"

"I think so," Dr. Demetrius said. "Are we going to die?"

"I don't know," Artemis said.

And Satan morphed into a muscled Black Cobra springing up off its tight coil. It poked out its mucus forked tongue; It slithered on the grass passing Dr. Demetrius, it hissed, and it slinked in between Artemis in a horizontal figure eight-making infinity shape. And then it morphed into black particle orb and glided above the monument, kissed the decaying cherub statue, glided around it and then it disappeared behind the white granite mausoleum. After a moment, the slender, handsome man returned from the other side. It had changed into a black velvet jacket, pressed pants, its shoes understated Italian leather with shiny silver buckles.

"I hate humans, I chose a better jacket. You attacked me Dr. Demetrius. I discarded my other jacket because of you, you silly human," Satan said. It clapped. It bowed to Artemis and over to Dr. Demetrius. "My show is over. I trust you both felt my performance. Dr. Demetrius always, always remember, I hate those that worship me, like your brother. No kidding, I hate him. I hate all."

"You made your point," Artemis said. She stepped in front of the sobbing, whimpering Dr. Demetrius. He had collapsed to his knees. He had defecated in his pants. Basting in an ammonia fragrance as he shivered and moaned.

Satan spat forward with its lizard like forked-tongue. It snarled at Artemis.

"You're a special cause for me," Satan said. It growled at Artemis. Its razor sharp tail revealed. It snapped over at her. "A challenge from God, and your crafty father and disciplined mother."

"My father?" Artemis said. She looked down and then back up. "You have my father? No way you have my mother. You're lying."

"Oh, no, missed out on him, and her, it sucked," Satan said. It hissed. "But when you were born, your father took you and your mother to what's left of the Temple of Artemis. A place Diodorus Siculus called, a wonder of the world. It was in the ancient Greek city of Ephesus. Woo-hoo... he was being cool for your mother."

"I've never been there, you're lying," Artemis said. "My parents never told me anything like that, you cannot deceive me. I have followed your instructions. Tell me where Laina is, now."

"Yes you have. And you have been to Ephesus. They named you after the temple, the goddess, you didn't know that, did you?" Satan said. It shrugged. "I was there. Observing. The reason you fascinate me. It's all about your faithful parents. They were orphans. An Irish Catholic Olympian, competed in the pentathlon, married an older American Presbyterian obsessed with antiquity and biblical relics. What an interesting human couple. Your old man had one last active sperm, a lucky shot and poof. Artemis Lamb was conceived from the lovers union of a pure bred Irish female with a male American mutt."

"You're a bastard," Artemis said. She leaned down. Her shoulders forward, her hands and fingers primed. "I'll not let you disrespect my parents."

"Thank you," Satan said. It stepped closer to Artemis. "Kill me, you redheaded assassin. Give it your best shot."

"I'm better than you," Artemis said. She screamed as she cried. Artemis knew she could not take Satan. She focused her mind on her goal. "What do you want?"

And then Satan transformed into a beautiful angel with baby blue skin and long curly hair. Its countenance draped in a soft baby blue, its wings in baby blue, as it fluttered as if a kind butterfly over colorful flowers and green grass during a bright spring afternoon.

"See me now, Artemis. I am Satan, as I appeared when God cast us from Heaven," Satan said. It fluttered and danced in the air. "Am I not perfection?"

"What?" Artemis said. "What do you want from me?"

"I'm the Devil. I live in your mind," Satan said. It floated toward Artemis. "I live in your dreams. I am the great deceiver."

"Why are your torturing me?" Artemis said. She swung at Satan. She spat at Satan. "Just kill me you disgusting creature, get out of my mind. If there is a God in Heaven, I will take you down. Face me, you're pathetic and weak. I am not afraid of you."

"Oh how delicious, sob for me," Satan said. It guffawed. "Boohoo, oh, that's right, it's all for you. I'm so scared of you."

"Why?" Artemis said. She whispered. She wept. "My parents loved me. They loved me without condition. You cannot steal that from me. You do not have that power over me. Tell me where Laina is? You can torture me, kill me. I will never fail Benjamin."

And Satan floated still and quiet. It had opened Artemis' soul, the pinprick it slithered into as she had allowed it to journey deeper within her mind.

"Well then, you did ask me. I'll give you Laina's information, I will, I promised you. But first, it was your crafty father, he obtained a special object," Satan said. It waved its right hand, and it caused Dr. Demetrius to fall into a deep trance. His moaning now silent, his body still and reflective. "The meteorite that had been housed in the original temple. A special object that the Greeks once worshipped. I don't understand why. A fancy rock. Or, was there more about this rock? Your father understood what his human hand possessed. It was his moment in time. He didn't waste his moment."

"I don't understand," Artemis said. "Tell me what do you want? She's running out of time. I can feel it."

"Silly human, he understood what he was holding. The meteorite was the matter as God created matter. Part of a singular particle as the universe expanded from the Big Bang. I was close to God then," Satan said. It flapped its wings and stirred up a dust devil. It caused the tree limbs to wave and interlock as if caught in a harsh winter storm. The black-winged raven flew away toward the approaching darkness. "As old as time itself. Your puny father discovered the shiny meteorite strolling along with your mother eating figs in a Greek market. But he realized what it was, so, like I told wonder boy over there, luck counts. But your dad, and your mumsy they were a strange breed. True believers, I mean down to their genetic core."

"That's got nothing to do with me," Artemis said. "I need to find Laina, help me. Please. His brother will kill her."

"Oh, yes it does," Satan said. It landed on the cemetery grass. "Your father took you and your mother to the temple grounds at Ephesus that very night. It was a clear starry night. A lot warmer and nicer than this hard scrabble town. He did not hesitate. It was his moment. He knew it. With your mother next to him, he prayed over your bassinet as you slept. He placed the meteorite on your heart and then on your head. He whispered a prayer for God's divine grace, and that you would always live your life with integrity and with honesty in your heart." Satan gazed up into the sky that cast starlight and shone distant planets beyond reason and understanding. "Oh, how disgusting the scene. I almost vomited, but I'm not human. I just shook my head and flapped my wings at the absurdity."

"Just leave us I'll find her my way," Artemis said. She looked away from Satan. She fell to her knees. "You're lying. You always lie. If I die, I'll go on. I'm not afraid."

Satan swayed its wings in place, and then it flew over toward Artemis. It breathed hot air all over Artemis. It smelled pungent, dank and like a rotting dead animal. It snorted at her like an evil dragon testing its prey.

"Well, your father didn't keep it," Satan said. It growled. "He wasn't greedy, which I didn't understand that night. It was worth a lot of money for the right buyer, or one of your father's antiquity clients. So the fool took the meteorite, and he dug a deep hole. He buried it on the temple grounds in front of the last remaining column. He thought it belonged to eternity, he was adamant telling your mother. It was to be buried at its rightful spot in the universe. Oh Artemis, your parents were true believers. I watched them dig that hole together."

"My father loved me," Artemis said. "I feel him every day. You cannot steal love from my heart. You do not have that power over me."

"Oh, I suppose. But what got God's attention? Your father spoke the Ephesia Grammata," Satan said. Its wings barely flapped and stirred. It stood reflective and contemplated its existence. "The six magic words from Ephesus. Your father went deep, deep, impressive for a mortal. He knew his stuff. The dude was gifted with a brain and your parents had a faith in God beyond reason. They had a faith that would have made Job blush."

Artemis cried for the memory of her parents. Her mind a sandstorm from Satan attacking her brain matter. It offered her no mercy as it pelted her mind with sweet memories and soft kisses.

"He prayed that the meteorite was a gift made by God, as God made the universe," Satan said. It fluttered its wings. "He praised God. He thanked God for baby Artemis. He was thankful for God's breath that caused the four winds, from God's sweating brow came the blue seas, and God made the land for his creatures to live. And guess what? God was pleased with your father and your mother. I'm not kidding. I'm not lying. And I prefer to lie, or at least shade the truth. But that night, Artemis, no kidding, your parents impressed God. Cool gig impressing God, if you can get it right."

"Are you happy?" Artemis said. "Do you have any dignity inside that black soul?"

"Never. And none is my answer. So, your father just kept at it, he prayed a prayer for mercy, a prayer for Jesus' mother, Mary. You might not know, but Mary died in Ephesus," Satan said. It flapped its wings. It blinked its eyes. It sprang back and onto the white granite monument. "Your mother lit a candle, she said a prayer written by the Apostle Paul. And then your parents held hands, they sang an out of tune song about love. Disgusting. It sounded awful. And then… They offered to sacrifice you to God. Why humans do these things, I do not understand. But you were on the chopping block. No kidding. They were prepared to push in baby Artemis, they were all in, they were not bluffing. Oh no. They fascinated me, you fascinate me. You live for truth. I do not fathom your DNA."

"I'm alive," Artemis said. She scooted back away from Satan. "You're a liar."

"You can't elude me, don't even try," Satan said. It flew down toward Artemis. "Calm down. I want you to understand why I will offer you a deal. This is a bargain. I must be going easy to offer you this bargain. I'll give you a chance. The stakes are even and I never play fair. But for you, Artemis Lamb, let's play the game straight up. I'll accept whatever happens."

"You're lying," Artemis said.

"I lie for my purposes. I tell the truth when it suits. Your parents pleased God," Satan said. "Guess what happened as your parents cried like little children clutching their precious baby?"

"I have no clue," Artemis said. Her arms dropped to her sides. "Where's Laina?"

Satan kept swaying its wings, but it stared aimless into the heavens at thoughts beyond time, understanding and consciousness.

"In a moment, then you'll understand my offer. So, God sent my former brother, Archangel Gabriel," Satan said. Its pale blue eyes gazed upward. Its expression full of disappointment. It whispered like a lost soul. "Gabriel appeared in front of your parents. Angels emerge through the visible light from the time to a time when God gives them a task. And my former brothers and sisters appeared with him. They all came. They all hung out with him, curious what was up with this mortal couple. They are the curious types, an introverted crowd. Well, the whole congregation showed up and you and your parents were surrounded by a host of angels. God does this on special occasions, seems they program most humans for weakness these days, which makes my job easier. But, not Mr. and Mrs. Lamb, no, not those two humans. They were true believers. They gave their lives to God. It was not about them. I felt it. It was about their devotion to God. I was stunned, they lacked any ego. Nothing. They fascinated me."

"That's not true," Artemis said. She shook her head. "We never, ever went to church. I don't go to church."

"Be quiet. Be still. So, go figure, an Irish Catholic married an American Presbyterian. Both were orphans. And not one church welcomed their union. Not a single holy man, priest or minister would accept them into their flocks, not one. They never said a word to you, but they always knew what you could see. They never thought it was about them, it was about God," Satan said. It allowed the winds to blow, the sky to fade to gray. It whispered. "That's kind of the point. Your parents never, ever turned away from God. Pity. So, I'm everywhere across this planet. All the time, and your parents understood that. I inhabit inside church's, too, it is true. I do my best work inside those places, church, synagogues, prayer houses, you pick. It is about proper use of my mental tools, the deadly sins I deploy. Words and deeds used with purpose, creates my magic."

Artemis sensed Satan was building up energy. It was stabbing and thrusting darkness.

"What do you want?"

"Sanctimonious greed, oh, that sin is my best work, best ever. Artemis you understand proper tool selection. I have enjoyed your previous performances," Satan said. It laughed with a certain gargled rhythm. "But you have lacked a certain, how do I say it, a darkness behind your eyes. I need you to feel that darkness."

"That's not the reason you're here," Artemis said. "What do you want? I came here in good faith. Take my life and let her go free."

Satan growled with satisfaction. It howled.

"Ah, smart girl, but I have no faith, good or not," Satan said. It waved its sharp fingers. "Gabriel took you from your parents, yes, Archangel Gabriel held you in his electrified, luminous hands. The power of God coursed through his entire being, a radiant soul faithful to God during the wars.... The war... that I lost."

"You're lying," Artemis said. "Just kill me, leave Laina alone. I'll give you my life for hers."

"There you go, you did it again, and you mean it. I felt your truth," Satan said. It snapped its thumb and forefinger. "You did it without hesitation, you accepted fate without reservation. I hate that about you. I don't understand you, you're so stinking honest, yuck, it is a disgusting flaw. And you are an assassin. How?"

"I'll never be a fraud," Artemis said. She clenched her teeth as tears billowed from her eyes. "Kill me, I'm not afraid."

"Oh, Artemis you passionate diva. But then, you're not a diva," Satan said. "Gabriel held you and he shared you with all our brothers and sisters. They were all so humble and kind gazing down at you. I was left as an outcast, left watching, alone."

"I'm lost," Artemis said. She hunched downward.

Satan sighed. It gazed across the universe at the intersection where God lives beyond the light and total darkness.

"My brother took out his golden sword, and touched your baby forehead," Satan said. It shrugged and fluttered its wings. "Ever wonder why you can see the dead held in limbo? See all those golden particles, those wandering spirits hiding from visible light?"

"I loved my parents," Artemis said. She closed her eyes, and she breathed in the cold air. "You will never block my love for them. My choice. The one thing I have is free will."

"Silly girl, Gabriel gave you a divine gift for vision, you see the truth. You're marked, Artemis. I cannot touch you without repercussions," Satan said. It sighed as it vacuously flapped its wings. "Which makes you interesting for me, for as long as you live. I will torture you. I can do that for my own purposes. But I cannot kill you. I'm blocked by them… they… won the war… they deployed… love."

Artemis sat back. She scanned the cemetery. She sensed a presence all around her, a power beyond her comprehension. They were there, but she could not see them.

"You caused Agent Beaky to leave," Artemis said. She gazed over at Satan. Her expression certain. "It was you."

"Yes, it was easy to twist the minds of foolish men," Satan said. Satan remained still, it focused on Artemis' eyes. "Now, if you want to find Laina, accept my offer."

"I'll die for her, you know that," Artemis said. She remained kneeled down and bowed her head. "If she goes free, take me."

"Too easy. You now know I cannot do that. But, I'll tip the scales for just this one tiny ask. Give me a feeling, a simple human emotion. Remember, you cannot fake it with me," Satan said. It waved its wings back and forth and it hovered over Artemis. "All I want you to feel inside you is, hate. If you promise to give me pure hate, I will give you the when and where, do we have a deal?"

"What about Benjamin?" Artemis said.

"Yes," Satan said. "I'll not forget Benjamin's spirit. I'll accept his spirit being released as part of our contract. But, what do I get?"

"Hate," Artemis said. She closed her eyes. "I'll give you hate in its rawest form."

Artemis understood the boots her freezing toes and feet set inside. Satan held all the cards for Laina's life. And Satan just grinned down at her. It waited. It waited for her answer with lust and greed inside its dark void. It waved it right forefinger toward her. Satan had trapped her because love was pulsing inside her heart.

"Ah, we have come to an understanding," Satan said. "I need your answer. You're truthful words."

"Or else?" Artemis said. "If I fail."

Satan snapped its thumb and forefingers and then Benjamin's spirit appeared in front of Artemis. She gazed back up as he floated in mid-air, helpless to move on, ensnared in Satan's web.

"I'll keep your boyfriend, Benny," Satan said. "His child dies, and you're left all alone, again. Now, do we have a deal?"

"Deal, how do you want it?" Artemis said. She squinted her eyes and allowed Satan's penetrating sting to slice through her heart. She touched her left breast from feeling the puncture wound.

"Be creative. Give me your best performance. As long as it comes from your mortal soul. So, when that Shepard Able out there kills this Farmer Cain," Satan said. It stared down with black eyes and over at Dr. Demetrius. It screeched and earthquaked the ground. It screamed at blank faced Artemis. She stared forward at the white granite monument. "I want pure hate to course through your veins like a Black Death! You will show me you have no mercy, you will kill them all! You will show me you understand what pure hate feels like. I demand the heart of an assassin!"

Satan breathed out a dragon's hot breath, it flapped its wings and then snapped its right forefinger and thumb. Dr. Demetrius awoke from the trance. Artemis acknowledged Satan that she understood her task. Dr. Demetrius crawled up off his knees and he stood up, he wavered, he shook his head.

"We'll find another way," Dr. Demetrius said. He huffed. "Please don't kill me, I mean us."

Satan floated over toward Dr. Demetrius.

"You two should go find Virgil," Satan said. Its voice a low growl. "And his American Indiana warrior friend. They will guide you into a hell on earth. There you'll find the child and your idiot brother."

"When?" Artemis said. She opened and closed her eyes. Her shoulders ached as she stood up, she avoided eye contact with Satan or Dr. Demetrius. "I need to know that?"

"I would not waste anymore time, midnight tonight, when the clock ticks a second beyond the hour, the sword goes down, the heart carved out," Satan said. "Ah, as my ole pal Shakespeare wrote, the game is afoot. Now, tally-ho. You will have but a pin-prick in time to satisfy my contract."

Chapter 39

"You all goin' huntin'?" Virgil said. He looked over at Dr. Demetrius. His large hands pressed down on the quarter inch plywood grocery store counter top blotched with condensation rings and coffee stains. "Hm, I guess ya brought that with ya."

"How's your spirit friend?" Artemis said. She marched up in front of the checkout counter. She ignored Virgil's suspicious stare over at Dr. Demetrius. "Your American Indian spirit warrior friend?"

Virgil stood back, and he searched Artemis' blue eyes. He inspected over at the smartphone that Dr. Demetrius held.

"Please," Dr. Demetrius said, low. His right hand shaking the modern communication device. "We need your help, it's for a little girl. I now understand, it's my fault."

"You packin' under that coat," Virgil said. He pointed over at Artemis. "You two askin' for something?"

Artemis unzipped her parka. She revealed the sharp knives strapped to her upper thighs. She stepped closer to Virgil, placing her favorite dagger with a curved blade on the counter. Her loaded Glock remained holstered at left rib height.

"I'm here to extract Laina," Artemis said. She clutched the dagger. She snapped open the blade. "I need you to guide us, but in a new direction. Prophet Higgs Boson has her; he knows our prior path our location. He found where we watched them the first time. I am certain. He's waiting for me."

Virgil reached forward to touch the ominous titanium blade. He glided his calloused left hand forefinger tip down the custom-made shaft.

"Serrated at the bottom, good craftsmanship, or, should I say craftwomanship?" Virgil said. He sighed as if he gargled noble sediment and shale. "This ain't no huntin' knife."

Artemis snapped the blade shut, she replaced the dagger inside a black pouch clipped to her heavy duty nylon belt with a quick release buckle.

"I'm not hunting for animals," Artemis said. With a blank expression she held her gaze at Virgil. "And I never hunt for sport, never, will you help us? You know the forest, you and the spirit warrior can guide us to the sight without them detecting us, or tipoff the direction we are coming from. But, to be clear, they know I'm coming. This will be a dangerous job."

Virgil pushed his tongue up into the gap between his upper front teeth and lips. He glanced back over at Dr. Demetrius, and down at the aged counter top. He hunched his shoulders. But then he nodded as he pushed back, his shoulders wide and upright.

"First time I laid eyes on you," Virgil said. He patted the countertop with his right hand. "I felt you brought trouble, it was in your eyes, they noticed everythin'."

"If you don't want to come," Artemis said. "I understand. I'll go in either way."

"Please, help," Dr. Demetrius said. He stumbled and pushed a potato chip display over onto the grocery store's linoleum sliding bags over next to the soda pop machine. The bags of chips scattered. The floor puffed dirt from Dr. Demetrius stomping at them. "Sorry, sorry, I'll fix this. I'm scatter brained."

"We'll have a river to cross out there in the sticks," Virgil said. His snort deep and ominous. "It's shallow, the warrior knows the best spot. I guess you should know he saved my life, you'll get it. He's my friend."

"Take me there," Artemis said. She stepped back as Virgil leaned down behind the counter to reveal the metal cash register and the colorful scratch-off lottery ticket display. "How do you communicate with the warrior?"

Virgil pulled up the countertop and limped forward. He had put on his heavy winter coat; He held a double-barrel shotgun balanced in his left hand, a revolver shoved between his denim blue jeans and his red and black flannel shirt. "I guess my coat pockets full enough with shells and bullets for this mess."

"Do I need a weapon?" Dr. Demetrius said. He had repaired the display and retrieved the potato chip bags. His right hand fingers fidgeted with his coat's dual zipper.

"No," Artemis and Virgil said in unison. They glanced at each other. They walked together across the wooden planks and down the concrete steps and on outside into the wintry air. Dr. Demetrius followed them close behind. Virgil turned back to pad lock the metal door. He latched the screen door. He patted the wood siding like it was an old friend he was seeing for the last time.

"What's next?" Dr. Demetrius said.

"We hike up, no other way, it's goin' to get dark, quick-like," Virgil said. He breathed in a deep reflective breath as he gazed up at the lumpy hillsides covered with black oaks, sassafras, and shadbark hickory. The sky fading from powder-blue toward dark-gray with random skinny white clouds drifting toward the horizon. He pointed over at a exposed specimen across the two-lanes road within a low spot centered by a pre-painted aluminum double-wide trailer set on a cinder block foundation. "See that red maple, she gives me syrup. If we go through a dry spell, I'll water her, always in the early mornings. She needs just enough for her roots."

"I bet she's amazing during springtime," Artemis said. She sensed Virgil understood the task, and that he might not return. Aware that no person knows their scheduled last day amongst the living. "I'd like to try the syrup. I'll bring Laina back, no matter what."

Virgil stared over at the big tree. He half-grinned.

"I'd like that," Virgil mumbled. He sucked in another deep breath and let it out. "Children are like saplings, you know, they need time to tryin' to grow. Once they grow, might give ya back syrup. It's how things are. Just one man's thinkin'"

"If you get me close," Artemis said. She stood next to Virgil with clear eyes and clarity of spirit. "I'll manage this. All I'm asking you is to get me in the area."

Virgil kept his gaze forward. He shrugged as he started to walk.

"Warrior, he's waiting for us," Virgil said. He pointed over at a narrow meandering dirt path crowded-in by rye grass being invaded by dead spidery crab grass leading into the Appalachian hillsides, and on toward the mountains. "He knows the way. He sent me a place to meet up, I know the spot. It's a nice fishin' hole, you'll see."

Virgil waved for Artemis and Dr. Demetrius to follow him. He kept the antique shotgun barrel pointed downward.

"How do you know this is the way?" Dr. Demetrius said.

"At night out here, like it's goin' to be tonight," Virgil said. He kept trudging forward; They started to move between soaring trees and dense thicket. His boots crushing the gravel surface. "You can see stars that guided ancient peoples; it's the same stars we'll be following."

"Crazy to think about," Artemis said. She pushed back a tree branch, ducked underneath it and it wobbled behind her. "Light from billions of years ago."

"I don't understand this thinking?" Dr. Demetrius said.

"Hush," Artemis said. She looked back at Dr. Demetrius. "He's answering your question, just listen."

"Oh, yes, a riddle," Dr. Demetrius said. He pointed forward. "I see, yes, yes, his method. His protocol."

The hillside grade started to incline and it became a steeper trail. It zigzagged before blue-gray limestone boulders with captured prehistoric shellfish fossils across the rough surface or husky black walnut trees with its pungent lemon-spice scented fruit, scattered around its trunk, its husks decaying into black from their former pale green. The passage disappeared behind white ash tree limbs or grayish-blue boulders painted by green moss, dormant ferns, and evergreens that pricked at their coat sleeves. A broad-winged hawk flew over them as they navigated steady and strong along the bumpy rock and dirt route that was encroached by merged tree roots enraptured into an embrace that at their bases looked like dark-brown and black petrified anaconda skins.

"My parents let me hike out here alone," Virgil said. He stopped to watch a squirrel scratch up a gnarled oak tree. "Quick critters, but back in those days we didn't have much to fear. I was too big for most animals, except for adult black bears, but wouldn't ya think they was just as scared of me, as I was of them."

"I would think so," Artemis said. She saw farther along that the tree mishmash and brush jumbles were disappearing, and a clear opening beckoned. Beyond the opening across the gorge was an abrupt drop off were jagged limestone rock walls were topped by struggling trees that bent with the winds and scrag bushes. The shear rock formations carved out from weathers ruthless assault from millions of timeworn years.

"I got lost this one time," Virgil said. He grunted. He wiped beads of sweat from his receding gray hair line with his thick forefinger. He flicked them away. "It got dark, quick like. I got religion fast that night. I'll tell ya that for sure."

"Survival training," Artemis said. She stooped downward under a thick tree limb that leaned toward the dirt path. "Clear night, follow the stars, listen for running water. About right?"

"Quite a logical plan," Dr. Demetrius said. "Interesting, it's nice out here. It's cold, but it smells musky like a forest should. It clears my lungs, might like to hike this again."

"Kinda of a trick to stay alive with your brother out here," Virgil said. "Just sayin'."

"The warrior?" Artemis said. She heard running water. She kneeled down on the decaying dark-brown, black leaves and pine straw and looked beneath them down a shear limestone rock wall. The drop off to the bottom to the forest floor over thirty foot. "He guided you home?"

"First time I met him," Virgil said as the blue sky had faded to a darker gray. "Lost, crying, like any boy. I thought I was dead, you know. I figured a bobcat would get me. I heard 'em growling."

"Sorry," Dr. Demetrius said. "That sounds terrifying."

"It was. Well, he appeared in front of me," Virgil said. He pointed toward his left side as he turned his shoulders. "Down over there, doctor, those rock steps, a fat man's misery."

Dr. Demetrius stepped over toward a roughhewn rock wall with a natural earthen opening guarded by an adult cockspur hawthorn with spiky bare limbs.

"Oh, how convenient, check this out," Dr. Demetrius said. He stepped onto the rock step smoothed over from time, consistent hiking use and extreme winter ice storms and blistering summer heat.

"Take your time," Artemis said. "Easy to slip. Keep you balance, use the sides to steady yourself. What did he say, Virgil?"

"At the time, I didn't understand him," Virgil said. He pushed his hands against the coarse rock wall and stepped down with careful steps along the natural spiral staircase. "No clue, he just pointed his spear at me, but he was smiling. Happy like I guess. He encouraged me to follow him. I think to calm me down he kept smiling and hooting encouragement. I just followed him, not long. I was back home, happy to be alive."

At the bottom of the rock stairs Virgil pointed through a tunnel made from a naked tree limb canopy. At the end of the crosscut Artemis noticed the white stag foraging for grass, twigs, and scratching the soil with its hooves. And she heard running water and farther down the stream the burble cascade from a powerful waterfall.

"He never fails. A strange thing, as I've aged, he hasn't. Sniff that fresh air, but you get me, don't ya, Artemis?" Virgil said. His boots crunched the wet soil. "Follow me. It's a good fly-fishing spot on down, see that canvass back. Nice lookin' duck family. The waters full a water-dogs and such. I bet on down there is a family of black beavers building a damn. Ran across them the other day. They all part of nature, can't help themselves. Buildin' a damn is what they do."

As they hiked from underneath the tree canopy along a boot high grass menagerie, they stood at the edge of an active, clear stream. An easy depth to cross over the flowing waters, maybe twenty foot wide, and over onto the muddy dark-brown bank. The white stag turned and loped across the cold stream. Its hooves splashed water and crunched into the brown and gray river bed crowded with smoothed stones and pebbles. A tiger salamander dove and burrowed into its nest. They followed the white stag across. On the other side, the spirit warrior stood waiting, holding his wooden spear, gripping the shaft beneath the Sonoran flint arrowhead. But he looked concerned and uncertain.

"Hey there partner," Virgil said. He held his right hand up in a sign for peace. "What's the matter?"

"What in the world," Dr. Demetrius said. "I'm done for…"

"We have an unwelcome visitor doctor, just chill out," Artemis said. She gazed behind the warrior. Along their uncertain dirt path stood a handsome man in a fancy suit. "Just stay here, with the warrior. I'll manage this."

"I take it that's a problem, but how'd he get out here wearing that get up?" Virgil said. He pointed over at the tall man. His expression curious and surprised. "I'll stay here, for now, unless you need me, just make a sign."

"I'll make it go away," Artemis said.

"She does mean, it," Dr. Demetrius said. "I'd recommend trying to act invisible."

Artemis acknowledged them. She walked along the stony trail alongside the working stream. The smooth rocks becoming larger farther along the pure waters as she saw in the distance between the hillsides, bigger shouldered boulders being frothed and bathed by the powerful current.

"Oh, how nice," Satan said. "Such a quiet spot for us to meet, one last time."

"We have a bargain," Artemis said. "I know what I'm doing."

"Oh, I know, we have a contract," Satan said. It stepped closer to Artemis. Its jackal eyes blazed blood red with molten dark-blue at the center black dead orbs. "Once you step by me, I will not intercede. I will inhabit none of the humans. Your destiny awaits the fates. We will be watching."

"We?" Artemis said. She looked at Satan with suspicion. She scanned the leafy bushes and bare tree limbs.

"I am forbidden this time," Satan said. "My dark-matter slithers across the universe. But those behind the invisible light controls the clocks. I submitted my plan. I don't know what happens next."

"We have a deal?" Artemis said.

"Ah, I look forward to feeling your hate," Satan said. Its stare a dull black void. It pointed its sharp fingernails up. "I will be so pleased to send this on."

"And then you let Benjamin go on," Artemis said.

"Yes," Satan said. It clapped. "Perhaps a little taste?"

And behind Satan high in front of a massive willow tree growing at a right angle near the bend in the river, hung Benjamin's spirit. He gazed downward at Artemis. He tried to smile, but he failed. His spirit near a red cardinal and his grayish-brown life partner. Artemis sensed Satan dissolve into particles as Benjamin spirit evaporated. And Artemis saw darkness descend over her future path. She turned and went back toward Virgil, Dr. Demetrius, and the spirit warrior as the white stag kept foraging for trigs, grass clumps and scratched at the pebbles.

"It's time," Artemis said.

"Yep, daylights 'bout burnt off," Virgil said. He nodded over at the warrior, he looked back at Dr. Demetrius.

"This will be dangerous?" Dr. Demetrius said.

"Yes," Artemis said. "You can stay here. I'll manage this."

"You're here to kill my brother?" Dr. Demetrius said. He looked at Artemis with a blank, certain stare. "Have I earned death, too?"

"Easy brother," Virgil said. "I wouldn't tangle with her."

Artemis acknowledged Dr. Demetrius. Her eyes clear. She gripped the dagger handle with her right hand.

"The child is my prime one," Artemis said. "If you stay out of the way, we'll all get back out alive."

"He's prepared for you, you know that?" Virgil said. He wiped his lips with his flannel shirtsleeve. "I'd expect a terrible fight."

"I ask this," Dr. Demetrius said. He interlocked his fingers below his waist. He looked downward at the waters flowing by his waterproof boots. "Let me try to reason with him, if I die. It's just my time. Artemis, will you protect my research?"

"You mean that monster out there?" Virgil said.

"No, it has to be eradicated, I don't know how, yet," Dr. Demetrius said. "But my brother is a mass murderer. I'll not let our family name continue to be stained. It's all I have to honor my mother's spirit."

"Yes," Artemis said. She stepped forward. "Your name will remain on those patents. I'll speak to them if we have a worst case. If not, you keep practicing, keep researching. We go."

And they began their journey now guided by the spirit warrior's body acting as a bright searchlight with the hefty white stag. They stepped along the moist dirt passage and up into a steep hillside covered with a murky fog over the dense forest that smelled musty, dank, and tinged with sulfur smoke. And Artemis noticed there we no birds in the gray sky anymore or wild animals hunting amongst the trees and rocks. It was as if the smell from death had chased them all away.

Chapter 40

"I hear something, look. I see light, light," Dr. Demetrius said. He pointed forward standing near a soaring tulip poplar in a loud, spastic voice. The solitary trees emerged from parallel evolution; either deciduous or evergreen, they stood together with their brethren scattered by nature as silent witnesses into the darkening night as Artemis and her group hiked up the trail. The next day, the trees would compete for sunlight beyond their crowns, while the fungi hyphae would seek nutrients for survival interconnecting their anchor root systems beneath the soil. But they would all hold within their rings and spirit a deep genetic scar from the violence that had happened the night before over in the valley. "It's coming from over there, I think. Yes, yes, over that hill."

The spirit warrior turned and shoved its spear back over at Dr. Demetrius. It put its translucent hand in front of its mouth. His intense eyes ablaze.

"Simmer," Virgil said. He crouched down with the shotgun pointed downward. "Keep down. Keep still. Think like an animal."

"Dr. Demetrius," Artemis said. She kneeled down and stared into his eyes. "We are being watched. Cameras are everywhere. Or worse, they might be close, hiding, waiting for us, understand? Any odd movements get attention. Sounds. Follow the warrior, careful with your steps, control your breathing."

Dr. Demetrius looked down at the black rotting leaves, pine cones, and dark-brown fertile soil. He gripped onto an oak tree limb's rough bark that sprinkled shards on the ground and across his boots. He nodded back at Artemis with intension.

"Sorry," Dr. Demetrius said. "It's just my nature."

"Let's go," Artemis said. "Keep a lookout."

The spirit warrior encouraged the white stag forward. They followed the brawny animal that traversed the trail up the dense hillside and on toward an emerging yellow light being cast downward from above them as they hiked by thorny limbs and scrub brush. Irregular shadows blanketed the wavy surface across as the broad leafed kudzu smoothing the underbrush and onerous fescues. They crested the hillside, and the stag sauntered away from them. It snorted. The spirit warrior bent onto one knee behind a white ash tree aware that Prophet Higgs Boson could see his presence. He waved for them to follow and scatter side-to-side.

"They are sick people," Virgil said to Artemis. He grunted as he squatted behind a slate boulder covered with spongy moss living with an ancient chestnut tree. "Over there, they have Laina. A cotton ropes around her neck. She's tied to the big tree."

"I have her in my sight," Artemis said. She crept closer to Virgil. "Scumbag has tied her hands behind her."

"I am ashamed, my family name," Dr. Demetrius said just above a whisper. He kneeled down to touch a frail tree about waist high that had emerged from the soil. "A child. This sapling shivers during winter, protected by a deep sleep waiting for the spring. Sunlight shafts from the above canopy will share warmth to encourage photosynthesis. A life. A fragile life. I must protect it."

"Stay low, stay quiet," Artemis said. She understood what Dr. Demetrius contemplated. She started to make her count. Prophet Higgs Boson took the goat mask off the table and he placed it over his face. He gripped the Kris sword and set it on the lacquered yellow oak table. The sturdy table was about six feet long and four feet wide. A wooden bowl set next to the sword. It overflowed with greenish death cap mushrooms.

Prophet Higgs Boson opened his muscular arms wide, gazing up into the fading light, and he appeared to begin his satanic ritual as if presenting his show toward the spot Artemis and Agent Beaky had surveilled them before with Virgil. He spoke words to praise Satan. He became louder after he spotted the white stag loping along the ridge-line. "Virgil, how many?"

"I'd say, five grown men, there, and over there," Virgil said. He pointed toward the massive tulip poplar. "Seven women, and Laina. That's all I see. No animals, not another child."

"They have guns," Dr. Demetrius said. He wiped his face with his right hand palm. "He has to be stopped."

"Yes they do," Virgil said. He glanced over at Dr. Demetrius and then at Artemis. "And they'll use them on us, but good news."

"They are all using shotguns," Artemis said. "No one has a rifle, AR-15, or a lethal gun. Basic weapons for home defense."

"I don't understand?" Dr. Demetrius said. "They'll kill us, they will kill the little girl. He must be stopped."

"Shotgun has a wide spray pattern," Virgil said. "Knock you back, a defensive weapon most times."

"Doubt that," Artemis said. She sniffed the kerosene smoke billowing up from the torches. "Likely loaded with slugs. For now, we are outside their range. But, the two closer to us, they have handguns. The one I can make out looks German-made."

"They are looking toward us," Dr. Demetrius said. He ducked downward behind sleeping hemlock, winter ferns, and honeysuckles. "Can they see me?"

"Keep cool," Virgil said. He waved with his right palm facing downward for Dr. Demetrius to keep low. "They expectin' us to pay them a visit, the men are all lookin' into the forest. But notice, they turn watchin' their master, guns dropped, all random like."

"They can't see us up here, we are in the Goldilocks zone. The torches they've lit across the half-circle perimeter act like a stage light. They can see just beyond blackness the first four or five feet," Artemis said. "Dumb. If we were higher up, they'd notice us. But they can sense us. It is a basic human nature. Hope they're high, hallucinating. Either way, I'll manage them."

Artemis counted five men and seven women. Laina whimpered, the rope around her neck tight. Her hands tied behind her. The rope pegged her to the life-giving tree. The satanic group wore white robes with pointy hoods and held them together with black cord belts. Prophet Higgs Boson the lone one wearing a golden sash. His robe ornate with a golden symbol embossed at chest level.

"I'd freeze to death," Virgil said. "They are half-naked, again. They must be on somethin' serious. Ain't no bourbon handle involved."

"Sad human outcomes," Dr. Demetrius. He huffed. "They feel nothing, Virgil. They're addicts. Their brain chemistry has them feeling euphoric. But they are experiencing breathing depression given this cold night. They are seeing life in a foggy perception. It will slow them."

Artemis realized Laina's life clock was ticking away. Prophet Higgs

Boson becoming more and more agitated in his ritualistic speech with his vapid sermonizing movements toward his flock. He grabbed the rope and pulled Laina over closer toward his leather sandals. Clear in Artemis' mind the straight forward sequence to kill the five men. But Prophet Higgs Boson would kill Laina during the fire fight. But she noticed the men were all rigid, nervous, the first two would be killed without being able to scream from the ballistic knife being plunged into their lungs, and her dagger's simultaneous slicing their carotid arteries, jugular veins and collapsing their larynx. They would die in less than a minute. She recalculated. She would kill the first two, a commotion will get the other three searching the dark forest. Have Virgil fire a shot into the air. And then she'd run toward Prophet Higgs Boson before they reacted or fire a shot at her. The women would scatter from being frightened and disoriented. But if she miscalculated, and if she's late to the party, Laina's murdered in front of her eyes.

"Virgil," Artemis said. She gazed over at him and at Dr. Demetrius. "Take Dr. Demetrius around to the other side. I'll wait. Unless that idiot touches that sword with ideas to harm Laina. If he does, I'll shoot him. I can pick him off from here. But I need to crawl in closer for a better shot."

"I get ya," Virgil said. "Make a commotion over there?"

"Yes. Once I'm down lower. Or, like I said, if he touches the sword, go in, shoot on sight," Artemis said. "But let me manage these two on my side. Then fire your shot. Run away from the spot because they'll fire into the forest. I'll take care of the prophet, he's my responsibility."

"I got your back, sister," Virgil said. He patted Dr. Demetrius on his left thigh. "Let's go, brother. Times a waste'n."

Artemis watched the sullen Dr. Demetrius. He nodded at the ground as he scowled. He picked leaves of grass and looked up into the clear night sky at white stars, stoic planets, and the emerging pockmarked full moon. Part of Artemis' mind hated the fact she predicted typical human nature. The stare from his dark eyes told her the future. His decision had been made certain from her guaranteed death statement for his brother. His mind grappling with reality and time closing in on his moment of no return. But her love for Benjamin bound her to protect Laina's life, and then to earn his spirit's freedom from Satan's grip. She recalculated her kill sequence. The mission now straight-forward, ending with Laina's extraction from Prophet Higgs Boson's death grip.

"Life is short; The art is long," Dr. Demetrius said. He smiled without showing his teeth. He made the sign of the Christian cross with his right hand, whispering a prayer for his mother's soul. And he leaped over the brush and thicket evading Virgil's attempted grasp. He charged through the hardy musk thistle crammed together with kudzu, ferns and fescue. He marched into the kill zone with his shoulders back and his hands held high. He shouted. "Do not shoot, do not shoot. I come in peace."

"They'll kill him," Virgil said. He stared down. He wheezed. As he glanced back over at Artemis. "I'll get goin' - I'll watch for ya, after ya deal with those two, I'll fire off a shot, and I'll come in and try shootin' them bad guys."

"Take your time, Dr. Demetrius has given us our opening," Artemis said. She winked at Virgil as she motioned for the spirit warrior to drift in the opposite direction. The warrior thrust his spear at her as he moved away. "This is my job. I'll manage this, just hang back after you shoot, and just be there for Laina."

Artemis stared at Virgil to convey her truth to him locked within her blue eyes. The truth that life was uncertain, the best intentions never matter, and evil wins battles during long-winded wars fought with heart felt desire.

"I get ya," Virgil said. He pinched his right earlobe. He nodded. "I didn't consider it that way."

"If I don't come out," Artemis said. "You be there for her. But Prophet Higgs Boson's mine."

"I'll do my best," Virgil said. He fist-pumped Artemis before he limped away.

Artemis took off her winter parka shedding it on the ground, exposing her skintight tactical sweater and her shiny razor-sharp tools. She focused her vision down the shadowy hillside. Her endless training about to be tested. She relaxed her shoulders, her mind clear. All her five senses focusing into a singular centripetal force toward extracting Laina. In the moments before her violent tasks she had sensations as if her parents were on either side of her encouraging her, whispering for her to seek courage. To honor their memory by doing the right thing for humanity.

Chapter 41

"Silence, you women back away, begone," Prophet Higgs Boson said. He jerked at the cotton rope and pegged Laina back to the tree as she whimpered and squeezed her legs toward her chest. He twisted back and stood behind the table to face his twin brother. "Stay still child, do not shoot, he is my brother. He is weak, not like us my flock. But, let him speak. I command this."

Dr. Demetrius strode from the darkness, he stepped across the dormant calf-high grass and indifferent dirt blotches, and downed tree limbs after he sprang beyond the torch lights. The armed men allowed him to scurry farther into their ritual site. The robed women near the circle backed away from instinct and experience. He faced his brother from across the yellow oak table.

"I demand you stop this madness," Dr. Demetrius said. He shouted at his brother. He pointed over at Laina. "Do not touch that child!"

Dr. Demetrius gifted the opening that allowed Artemis to begin her work. She calculated Virgil being slowed by age and affliction. He would not appear until well after she finished the job's planned sequence of events. She knew Dr. Demetrius' pride, his ego, his sense of righteous indignation encouraged him to risk his life in memory of his deceased mother. She monitored the brothers' quarrel. And having bargained with Satan, she was not about to be merciful.

"You cannot understand my power," Prophet Higgs Boson said.

"I can help you," Dr. Demetrius said. He tapped on the table with his left hand. "I can get you help. I can get everyone here to help. Stop this. You are addicts; There is no shame; it's a disease. We can treat the disease."

"You know nothing," Prophet Higgs Boson said. "These are my flock, they will not abandon me. You have given us the mycelia, its fruit we share with mankind."

"You're peddling drugs, heroin laced with fentanyl, it's a death sentence," Dr. Demetrius said. "What you created is a monster, a toxic monster. I came to destroy it."

"Never," Prophet Higgs Boson said. He brandished the sword swaying it back and forth over the table. "It sleeps, but we must worship it. We must feed it with the blood of an innocent."

"I will not allow you to touch her," Dr. Demetrius said. He stood tall, watching the sword's movements without flinching. "You will have to kill me first. I will not betray our family name."

Artemis heard the brother-to-brother argument that was escalating into higher octaves. She focused on efficiency. Each step meant time off Laina's life clock after Satan had predicted it was ticking toward one second after midnight. The first man with his back to her was portly, diminutive and perspiring through his pointy headed cloak. He death gripped his shotgun. The knife needed to puncture his left lung and slice with an angular blow toward the heart muscle threw fat, muscle and dense human tissue. She sprang over an oak tree stump smothered with moss and ferns with a powerful forward somersault. Gripping the ballistic knife's round handle with her left hand. With the top of her hand above the blade tip, she thrust with her left shoulders big muscles penetrating into the man's back an inch left of his spinal cord and deep into his left lung shifting the blade down and to the right to capture his heart's aorta or left pulmonary artery, clipping either would work to flood his body with his own blood. With her right hand grasping the sharp titanium dagger she slit his throat with a deep carving action beneath his unshaven chin from ear-to-ear cutting the left external carotid artery, left internal jugular vein, across his vagus nerves and larynx and the right internal carotid artery and external jugular veins. It took her less than three seconds and a minimal gasp from him as he collapsed back into Artemis' arms and chest. His mouth and throat spewing his twelve pints of red blood draining and puddling onto the forest floor. She smelled burning kerosene mixed with his personal body odor as she dragged him back using her big muscles and thighs into the brush by hoisting him under his armpits. In the darkness she made certain he was dead. If anyone looked over for him they'd assume he stepped into the forest to take a piss. She kicked the shotgun away, and she sped along the perimeter ten foot from the torch lights visual reach and on toward her next target. She paused kneeling down to manage her breathing, her heart rate, and she looked and listened as the Demetrius brothers argued. Her vision saw Laina cowering behind them near the tulip poplar's trunk.

"You are a menace brother," Dr. Demetrius said.

"Join me," Prophet Higgs Boson said. "Become a leader in our army, Satan's army."

"I cannot accept evil," Dr. Demetrius said. "I am a sinner. I let my pride get in between me and God. I accept my sin. Stop with this madness. Repent, save your soul, brother. Honor our mother."

"Satan will accept you, come with us, brother, our mother was a whore," Prophet Higgs Boson said. He scooted the wooden bowl across the table. "Eat, mushrooms nourish the mind. They will open a new world for you. You can travel with me across time without leaving the forest."

Artemis watched the two men argue from within the gloom as she crept up on the next target. She placed her boot steps on predetermined spots on grass clumps, decaying solid wood, or dirt patches to minimize any sudden movements or noises. The next target was taller and thinner than the last target that lay dead awaiting rigor mortis to arrive.

"Those are toxic," Dr. Demetrius said. He pointed down at the bowl. "You know that."

Artemis' next male target appeared to her to be a true Satan believer. He lightly held his shotgun with his left hand fingers that he thrust into the air after Prophet Higgs Boson's statement. He screamed his allegiance to Satan. His body steaming from the intersection from cold mountain air and giving off human heat.

"Good bye," Artemis whispered in a calm tone. She bent her knees down as she leaped from within the stringy fescue jumbled with hemlocks and honeysuckle. The man turned, curious, but his eyes were stunned to see her cocksure predatory gaze emerging from beneath him. With her right hand she slit his throat with the two-sided ballistic knife while plunging her titanium dagger up into his chest. The neck wound punctured his carotid artery and jugular veins as deep as she could manage, using her right hand and shoulders to maneuver the blade from left to right in a swift practiced move. He spewed his blood, mucus over Artemis. His eyes bulged as he dropped his gun and reached for his searing neck. With her left hand, she plunged the dagger just below his xiphoid process, and she twisted it upward with her left wrist, corkscrewing it to create internal havoc to sushi his heart muscle. He spat his blood, mucus and internal air as he died a silent death. As she balanced his hemorrhaging body with her hands, shoulder muscles, and thighs, dragging him back into darkness as she searched for the next targets. Two of the five lay dead having bled to death in less than two minutes. But Laina's life clock kept ticking towards one second beyond midnight. The next two stood close to each other, Artemis was in good luck, she'd save time with a twin-killing. They were half-baked watching the Demetrius brothers lethal argument. She jerked the dead body back through the boot high fescue and in behind a tree stump. In the pitch blackness she verified her second kill. She leaped backward wiping blood from around her face and eyes, but she kept her stare on the next targets. She monitored the brothers' argument as they were giving her the extra time needed to extract Laina. Gazing underneath the table Artemis verified that Laina remained immobile, curled in next to the unforgiving tree trunk. The fifth target ignored her work, as he loitered over closer toward the ritualistic table. His back to the next two targets, the shotgun pointed up, his right hand fingers near the trigger. She sniffed the air, he was smoking a thin joint. Her five senses conjoined with supernatural phenomenon.

Artemis searched behind her into the woods and thicket, she had not detected Virgil's whereabouts. He had not fired his weapon. She suspected he was terrified by her skills, questioning her violent methods as he was dragging his good leg along the path. His wide chest likely heaving deep breaths while he hid within the forest's protection. The best result possible she thought and helped to keep him out of her way. She blocked her mind about Virgil. It was the different mindset between the predator and its prey. And she was the predator. She focused on the next targets as she veered in behind the two men. She kneeled down as she studied their body movements, their hands, feet, and overall size, calculating her approach. One smoked an off-label cigarette. From the torchlight, his eyes appeared glossed with a milky haze, glassy-eyed. He spoke to the other man in a low, monotone with a twang. Underneath the table Artemis re-verified her visual on her prime one, Laina.

"Prophet predicted this," he said. The other man nodded in agreement. Their last living conversation on planet earth.

Artemis pulled out her third knife. A custom-made twelve inch blade forged from stainless steel with a nylon-wrapped handle as she gripped the ballistic knife in her right hand, and the blade with her left as she balanced her weight on her boot's toes, shifting back onto her heals, her right leg lifted upward toward her chest as if to practice the high-jump like her mother taught her and to build up momentum before she bounded forward with a somersault passing a hulking pawpaw tree, leaping upward with her knees snuggling under her chest and then unfolding her body, descending and jabbing the men beneath their shoulder blades by thrusting down hard with a deep penetration, in an instant engorging their lungs with blood and internal fluids. She powered her lethal maneuver downward toward their heart muscles by harnessing gravity, lowering her hips and thrusting down with her thighs and butt muscles. The weapons piercing, slicing through to the other sides of their upper chests. The targets spat blood, air and mucus. But they started to cough and wail before she could slit their throats. Their bodies collapsing hard onto the scrub brush; But, they shattered her silent battle. Artemis sensed she was exposed, visible from the sparse torch light. Laina's life clock ticked faster and time was closing in on her expiration at one second beyond midnight. Artemis slit the men's throats with a practiced precision. Her next target was now Prophet Higgs Boson, while she had to out-maneuver the fifth guard's shotgun slugs by running in a zigzagged or halting pattern.

"I predicated you," Prophet Higgs Boson said. He screamed at Artemis. He pointed at his brother. He growled back over at Artemis flexing his thick neck and shoulder muscles. The goat horns pointing at her like a doomed Spanish Bull. "I knew she would come. You betrayed me brother, you betrayed me."

"Get help," Dr. Demetrius said. He threw the wooden bowl filled with death cap mushrooms at his brother. It bounced off Prophet Higgs Boson's goat mask. "You betrayed human kind, you're a monster, a mass murderer."

Artemis started to scamper toward Prophet Higgs Boson. As the fifth guard turned toward her holding his shotgun level with her, she stopped running and restarted again as the barrel was shifting back and forth gauging her speed. And then she saw Virgil appear behind the man; he had his shotgun down, the hammer cocked and his right hand forefinger on the trigger.

"Set it down partner," Virgil said.

The robed man with the pointy hood concealing his face whipped around toward Virgil. But he was younger, relaxed from the cannabis, and his reflexes quicker than Virgil's. They both fired their weapons. Virgil was flung backward into an oak tree trunk, he crumbled after being gut shot, his shotgun slid away from his fingers. His head flopped down as he clutched his belly. He moaned as his fingers tremored. The robed man stumbled, he seesawed, but then fell to his knees. The weapon dangling in his hands and fingers. Artemis retraced her steps, retrieved the ballistic knife from the dead man's back, she turned her shoulders, dropped onto her left knee. She pulled the trigger, and it flew like a launched arrow from a marksman and caught the man in the side of his neck, snapping his hyoid bone. The razor-sharp blade tunneled deep and it lodged beneath the man's dead eyes.

The cult's women were no longer under Prophet Higgs Boson's spell; they were screaming and running away from the ritualistic site into the forest. Artemis pulled the twelve-inch blade out from the fourth target's dead body. Sheathing it. She gripped for her Glock preparing to take her kill shot. But as she was about to run forward she felt a searing, penetrating pain in her right calf. She understood it was a small knife wound. She yelled as she grabbed the knife from its scabbard and held the blade at ninety degrees, spinning back to eliminate the one target she had not accounted for. But she stopped the blade's progress as the terrified face of a young girl gazed up at her. She was small, wearing a dark coat with blue jeans, maybe ten, perhaps older. Prophet Higgs Boson's next sacrificial lamb. But Artemis' training caused her to halt the knife's momentum from slicing the girl's delicate neck. She screamed as she stopped the death blow, sheathing the blade back to her quick release scabbard.

"Hide," Artemis said. She snarled. She limped back. "Now."

The girl skedaddled behind a fallen oak tree. She peeked above it. Artemis searched with her free right hand behind her and glanced at her right calf. The pocket knife wound tottered. It bleed. It stung. But she could manage it later. The Demetrius brothers were struggling, wrestling. But Prophet Higgs Boson's was a larger, muscled body as he over-matched Dr. Demetrius. Artemis got a visual on Laina. But Prophet Higgs Boson glanced over at Artemis as she was charging toward him, gripping at her weapon, her eyes guaranteed his death. He shoved Dr. Demetrius away, snatched the rope, yanked Laina over and slammed her onto the table. He retrieved the Kris sword. Dr. Demetrius sprung back up. He roared. "Never, brother, stop." As he dove at Prophet Higgs Boson, as he tried to twist in and shield Laina from the sword. Shoving his body between them. But Prophet Higgs Boson with his left hand shifted the wavy blade tip toward his brother while holding Laina's neck with his right hand. Dr. Demetrius's fierce energy helped the sword to plunge into his chest at the exact spot his heart muscle thumped. Dr. Demetrius clutched the sharp blade, it sliced a jagged, bloody schism across his palms and fingers. He spat his blood as the long blade thrust deep and it emerged out his back through his winter coat. Dr. Demetrius puffed air, he spat out mucus and blood, he stared at his brother. His final living snapshot. Prophet Higgs Boson yanked the sword back out, as Dr. Demetrius collapsed to his knees. Prophet Higgs Boson shoved his brother down with his right foot.

"Brother," Dr. Demetrius said. He gasped. His blood flooding his lungs, and across the forest floor. "I…"

"Go to your God," Prophet Higgs Boson said. As Laina wiggled, she screamed and flapped her legs to break free from his powerful grip. "Now innocent one, I must please my lord and savior, Satan."

"No," Artemis said. She jumped closer toward the table, dragging her right leg. She gripped for her Glock as he was within an easy kill shot. But she tripped on a sturdy tree limb leaning against a small lime-stone boulder hidden by crabgrass and ferns. As she fell forward onto her right knee, the gun flung and it skidded across leaves and pine straw and bounced against an innocuous pine cone and just beyond her reach. Artemis screeched. She crawled at the gun, digging her fingers into the dark-brown soil.

"I sacrifice this child," Prophet Higgs Boson said. He sneered down at Artemis as he jerked the Kris sword high, the wavy blade sparkled from reflected torch light, glistening along the sharp edge with Dr. Demetrius' mortal blood. His goat mask staring up toward the heavens and stars.

And as if time ceased for Artemis, the American Indian warrior's spirit appeared in an instant in front of Prophet Higgs Boson. The warrior screamed words from his native language as he tried to throw his long spear that no longer killed into a living body. Laina kept struggling pushing upward, scratching at the Prophet Higgs Boson's thick forearm as she fought for her life. But she was no match for him; he was many times larger. From a place the visible spectrum cannot see, Artemis heard her mother's voice. A soft voice with a velvety Irish accent.

"Artemis, my darling," her mother said. "How did I teach you? How does an Olympian throw a javelin?"

Artemis glanced up into the clear night sky and she saw Orion's Belt glowing down at her from deep space. The timeless stars twinkling encouragement.

"With joy," Artemis said. Her left hand smacked down at her thigh for the blade. She whispered. "With her heart. With a happy spirit."

The American Indian had graced Artemis the split second before midnight that she needed. As if her deceased father helped her get off the hard ground, his spirit shoved her upward and she heard his voice in her mind. "I believe in you punkin', listen to your mother." Artemis held the twelve-inch blade by the nylon grip. An eight ounce blade made for longer than normal throws. She sensed the balanced weight. She remembered watching her mother practice throwing a javelin during bright summer days. Her mother advising her time and time again to relax her shoulders, turning her back to the target line, allowing her body to buildup energy from natural flexibility and to release the potential energy by the soft flick of her wrist. And Artemis had been taught well, from her knees she twisted her shoulders perpendicular to Prophet Higgs Boson. With a soft face, clear eyes, she calculated the wind, the humidity, the weather, the correct height, and she snapped her shoulders back to square and flicked her left wrist releasing the blade at the exact last nanosecond. She launched it through space and time, defying gravity, reason and pure logic collapsing across the bluegrass and crabgrass after emptying all she had remaining in her mind, body and spirit, remembering to crawl toward for her Glock. But she was left powerless, scratching her hands, her fingertips at the weeds and dirt to hurdle, to push, to fight, then peeking upward to see Prophet Higgs Boson about to thrust the Kris sword down, to kill Laina, and to carve out her heart. But her razor-sharp blade found its mark; It clipped Prophet Higgs Boson's neck, severing open his external carotid artery, specking his white silken robe with red blood drops and then it lodged behind him into the tulip poplar.

"Got you," Artemis said. The spirit warrior twisted toward Artemis as he held up its spear. She sprang up, she hobbled forward, she fell again. But she got back up rushing toward Laina.

Prophet Higgs Boson stumbled; he dropped the Kris sword. It clattered off the table. Surrendering his grip from Laina. His carotid artery slashed open as his neck spewed red blood like molten lava coursing out from a crack in the earth's core. He stumbled backward attempting to keep his blood from escaping that no longer was destined to cycle through his heart and lungs. Artemis' penetrating cardiac injury hacked open his circulatory system causing him to hemorrhage and release his systemic loops internal pressure. Artemis balanced herself, she rose onto her good leg. She limped, and stepped, she hopped, aware she had a contract to settle with Satan.

"Laina," Artemis said. Her chest heaving, her lungs begging for oxygen. "You're safe. I've got you."

Laina said nothing, sobbing, crawling off the table. Artemis unclipped her hands. Laina hugged Artemis at her waist, whimpering. She gripped

Artemis. Her fingers invading behind Artemis' belt loop. "I thought I was all alone."

"You're in my tribe, I don't leave my tribe behind," Artemis said. She kneeled down, she grimaced as she hugged Laina. "Listen to me, I need to do something. You cannot watch me. I want you walk away. Turn your back on me. I need to take care of that scary man."

Laina glanced over at the moaning Prophet Higgs Boson. He was scooting, hustling back and away from Artemis, his sandals pushing back against dirt clods. Helpless, his body draining energy, he propped against the tulip poplar. Blood spilling from his mouth. Laina nodded. Artemis searched around the ground beneath the table for the Kris sword.

"Go," Artemis said. She looked over at Virgil, he was soaked in his own blood. "Maybe check on Virgil. He needs your help. And there's another girl, here, she's hiding. Find her."

"I'll find her," Laina said. She ran toward Virgil.

Artemis stood back up and limped over in front of Prophet Higgs Boson. She stepped beyond him; she found her knife; she yanked it out from the tulip poplar. She used his fancy silk robe to wipe his blood off the blade. She smacked the goat mask off his face with her left hand. She searched down at him. Still alive; his blood dripped from his lips and down his chest. Artemis sheathed the twelve inch blade. She understood the action she had to perform; she had a price to pay. A mortgage to close. A payment that would alter her soul forevermore. But the payment was for Benjamin's spirit, for his immortal soul to drift into tranquility.

Artemis turned and found the Kris sword. She limped over to pick it up. She studied Dr. Demetrius' body laying in his blood, his dead eyes staring up at her. The soft breeze cooling her skin. Artemis gazed up into the stars, she gripped the swords handle and she allowed the uncoiling Black Cobra within her soul to emerge from her inner-self. She shrieked like an Irish banshee as she twisted around and plunged the wavy Kris sword deep into Prophet Higgs Boson's chest just centimeters right from the midsagitall plane and his breastbone. She shoved it hard with her shoulders and hips. He coughed, he spat blood, his eyes widened. His body convulsed. His heart muscle tissue contracting and spasming. He spat out a bucket of mucus as his thick neck bulged with a trapped air-pocket.

"This is for Lily-Ann," Artemis said. She snarled. As Prophet Higgs Boson's blood splattered her face. "The innocent girl you raped and murdered."

Artemis' eyes began to turn molten blue. They transformed into a cooling dark red. And then the Black Cobra slithered up from her soul, and she allowed hate to enter her heart. Her eyes metamorphosed an arctic black, devoid of feeling. A colorless black found in deep space within dark matter's void. She sneered and she shifted the sword south and then she carved north inside Profit Higgs Boson's no longer beating heart. The human tissue and the muscles squishing, the blood expelling a putrid carbon dioxide.

"That's for the women you raped," Artemis said. She growled as her face was but a whisper close to Dr. Demetrius' twin. She sniffed him like a predator before devouring its prey. She hissed like a snake before its strike. "I'll twist this blade, and slice you from the east and then west for the addicts you harmed. I'm taking your life. I'm taking you. You can hear me. Wake up Prophet Higgs Boson, I'm slicing your heart out like you did to innocent girls and woman you victimized."

And the microsecond before Prophet Higgs Boson eyes went blank and they would open for his evil spirit's first meeting with Satan. Artemis snatched the long Kris sword back out from his chest. As his blood was dripping off the blade. A crafted sword made for a ceremony, a sword made for rituals, and a sword meant for violence to be the last resort. A sword she preferred using over her own tools, lest she would always remember the hate-filled act. She shifted back; With both hands gripping the handle. As her Japanese master had taught her basic exsanguination methods and to respect animals at slaughter time by a swift decapitation of white-mustached pigs or Wagyu cattle, she turned her relaxed shoulders away from her target. With a practiced, swift movement right-to-left, keeping her wrists flat and cocked at ninety degrees. She focused down at one inch below Prophet Higgs Boson's square jawline, and she allowed the razor-sharp blade to slice a deep channel, freely, precisely, and letting the shaft shatter his larynx and the tip end slice through his muscled neck and out the other side, cutting in half his carotid artery and jugular veins. Prophet Higgs Boson's eyes bulged, his neck splattering Artemis with his mortal blood a nanosecond before his death. He gushed air and mucous. His lifeless head leaned right from it almost being decapitated. His dark eyes gazed at nothing living, but were now eternally in Satan's presence.

Artemis' chest heaved. She inspected her work like a seasoned contract killer. She spat at the carcass. She wiped blood and sweat from her eyebrows and forehead with the back of her left hand.

"I ended your mess," Artemis said. She tossed the Kris sword into the forest. With her hands into a fist, her body tremored as she wailed from the depths of her soul. "You're no longer a societal problem. Your predatory days are over. Go to Hell. Go meet Satan!"

Artemis slipped, she stumbled backward as her words reverberated across the valley and the forest and tussled the tree limbs. She smacked her head back against the table. And then she heard Satan's cackle. It howled as she closed her eyes. She cried as she was splayed against a table leg, she lay crumbled across from Profit Higgs Boson's body aware that her soul forever scarred and damaged.

Chapter 42

"I found her," Laina said. She stood next to a scrawny girl with long brown hair and a dark coat. They fidgeted next to each on the other side of the lacquered table. "Virgil's still breathing, he's just whispering for now. Best I can tell."

"You're safe, get away from here," Artemis said. She glanced over at Dr. Demetrius' body. She gripped the table with both hands to help her stand up, and pointed the girls away from the death scene. "Let's check on Virgil."

Artemis limped around the table. The torch lights beginning to fade. She stopped, she glanced back, and yanked the pocket knife blade out from her calf. She flicked it away, clenched her hands into fists, as her blood bubbled a modest circle away from the wound. She would soon tie a tourniquet, confident the wound would heal even though the knife was caked with rust. She dragged her foot over the dirt, rocks and grass to retrieve her gun and holstered it. And she yanked her ballistic knife out of the dead man's neck, cleaned it off with his robe. She had retrieved all of her tools, accounting for everything she brought into the forest. And Artemis stared over at Virgil's slumped body, she understood Virgil had been gut shot at close range. There was nothing she could do for him out here; They were deep within the forest, high-up an Appalachian mountain.

"You won't kill her," Laina said. She stepped next to Artemis. She huffed after every third word. "I know Hazel, she's not mean. She is nice, please don't kill, her."

"Calm down," Artemis said. She blinked her eyes and wiped her face. She steadied herself. "Let me get a clear thought. You're safe. You're both safe. Let me breathe, calm my pulse."

"My daddy told me too," Hazel said. She scampered by Laina. She stepped and stumbled backwards in front of Artemis. "Please don't kill me, I'm sorry. My daddy told me to stab anything that moved."

"Please don't kill her," Laina said. She pressed her hands together like she was praying to Artemis.

"Girls, stop, you got me good, Hazel," Artemis said. She pointed down at a spot next to Virgil. "Stand over there, be quiet. Be still. I'll not harm you, ever. Just let me talk to Virgil."

Artemis wiped the blood and sweat from her face with her black sweater sleeves. Her knee joints popped as she kneeled down. She saw Virgil's hairy hands covering over his flannel shirt. Soaked with his thick red blood. The ground beneath her tremored. She touched his scruffy, unshaven face under his chin.

"Virgil?" Artemis said. She moved her head down closer, gripping his sturdy neck to lean his head back to help him breathe. "You did good. You saved Laina."

Virgil coughed. He gasped for air. He alligator stared over at Artemis. His body was warm and effusing steam against the cold mountain air.

"Good?" Virgil wheezed. His blue eyes were getting lost within a foamy tidal surge. Artemis sensed his time left with the living about to catch his last frothy wave, and then his soul would drift out toward the sands and float out into calm eternal seas.

"You did good," Artemis said. She sniffled as a single tear dripped down her face. "Without you, I would have failed."

Virgil half-grinned as he expelled his last breath. And behind his eyes, Artemis watched bright shooting stars beckoning his soul to follow them. And she felt his body release all the tension from his life. Behind her, Artemis heard the spirit warrior chant in his native tongue as he danced with a purpose she suspected was for Virgil's soul.

"Oh, how sweet," Satan said. It clapped and it clapped. It wore a red velvet jacket. "Very touching scene. Virgil's off, his spirit will have a brief stay to sober up. Otherwise, I missed out on him."

Laina and Hazel screamed and hid behind an oak tree and scrub bushes near where Virgil's body leaned. Artemis held her hand up and she stared back over at them. She shifted, turned, and pushed her back against

Virgil's body. The earth beneath her tremored, again. And cracks started to appear across the ritualistic site.

"I made it happen," Artemis said. She pointed at Satan. "Let Benjamin go."

"In due time," Satan said. "I came in formal wear, seemed appropriate after watching such a hate filled show. I considered a top hot with tales, a basic black. But, I went with velvet, so soft, I felt it appropriate from your performance. The color is perfect, it works given the river of blood you created. It favors my skin tone, yes, I amaze myself, I'm such the creative."

"Why?" Artemis said.

"You killed for a reason, sure, the life for that child," Satan said. It pointed at Laina. "But you killed with hate, you were unmerciful. Hate filled your heart. I felt your performance. I do not remember a performance like that from a sane human. And I feel you are sane, well, most of the time."

"We have a deal," Artemis said. "Let Benjamin go."

"To be clear, Prophet Higgs Boson is now learning," Satan said. It hyena laughed, it cackled as it smacked its pointy fingernails and hands tougher. "He didn't get the lust section. I don't accept requests. Ever."

"Yeah?" Artemis said. "Do tell."

"Oh," Satan said. "There is a special place in my Hell for child abusers. I even avoid that section. Yuck. Makes my blue wings shiver, which is not a good look for me. I have a responsibility to my public."

"And his brother?" Artemis said. She looked over at the spot where Dr. Demetrius' dead body lay. "He tried. He admitted he was a sinner. I think that helps him."

"He's no longer on the list. I almost got him," Satan said. It shrugged. It snapped both its thumbs and forefingers. "Yet, he'll be wandering the hospital halls until they decide what to do with him. He's got a lot explain' to do, as Virgil might have said."

"I did my job," Artemis said. She spat blood from her bruised lips. "We had a deal."

Satan paced back and forth.

"The cru de gras," Satan said. It faux shivered. "I was still not sure you could get there. But you did. Your eyes turned black. Such an epic ability. So, we had a contract; you met all my terms and conditions. I'm pure evil, but I have standards. I have a reputation. I'm not like a career politician, ah, please."

"Let Benjamin free," Artemis said. She slumped, she leaned back against Virgil's body.

"Not yet, I have one last truthful nugget for you," Satan said. The ground under Satan's shiny shoes began to shift and rumble. "Meet me, and I'll have your Benjamin, back in Old St. Pete, you know the park, you know the statuary?"

"Yes," Artemis said. She glanced up into the trees that started to shake and flap. It sounded like a commercial plane engine was about to land on them. "Near the banyan trees, she stands alone, she looks out toward lower Tampa Bay."

"We'll be waiting at the next full moon," Satan said. And the spirit women appeared at the forest's edge. Satan waved its left hand, and it harvested the souls from Prophet Higgs Boson's flock.

"Let them roam?" Artemis said. She looked at them as they disappeared. Aware the innocent spirit girls were still hiding behind them within the forest's darkness.

"Those girls, little ones out there you're thinking about, they are not mine," Satan said. It waved them away. "You must be joking?"

"The women know they made mistakes in life," Artemis said.

The spirit women dissolved in the air as the earth shook beneath Artemis. This time the tremor harder, the ground cracking, splitting open.

"They were crafty," Satan said. It sighed. "Mercy, oh yuck, is never my gig. Ah, they, will be by soon to collect those girls hiding over there. It's what they do. It's all happy, humble and stuff. Disgusting."

Artemis looked up at Satan. It stared down at her with a smirk. It opened its arms, held its hands wider open, and the handsome face winked.

"They?" Artemis said.

"Yes, they are coming," Satan said. It tapped the ground with its shiny shoe. Over near the tulip poplar the ritual table shook, it leaned into a opened shaft that spewed air. "Something's hungry, you woke it up with all this blood and guts you served it. Well done my dear, well done, but not, I think sashimi, no, not sushi. I think raw. But these bodies will be delicacies for this critter. Oh, those mushrooms near Virgil's boots, don't eat those."

The red-topped toadstools beneath Satan started to wobble like an invisible, lost pinball was bouncing off them.

"Girls," Artemis said. She pushed her back up the tree trunk as she scooted off Virgil. She never took her stare off Satan. "We have to move, now."

"In the meantime, I might recommend you follow the spirit warrior," Satan said. It turned and it pointed over at the spirit warrior. It snapped its fingers and it disappeared. Artemis heard its voice and its laughter resonate across the forest and into the hillsides. "It's about to get wicked, think Old Testament."

Chapter 43

"Girls," Artemis said. She pointed toward the heavily treed hillsides. The limbs began to spasm, waving at them and raging back and forth. She heard a crack as the top of an old tree snapped, shifting off, it fell to the ground with a hard thud and rolled over the brush, crushing the plant life. "Go, now." She pointed over at the spirit warrior. He leaped up and down as he gazed up into the darkness. He pointed his spear up, he yelled a word from his native language.

"Laina, Hazel," Artemis said. She searched for them. She screamed. "Now." They bolted from behind the trees and scampered toward the spirit warrior. Artemis followed them limping and hopping behind them the best her body allowed. She refused to look back over at Virgil's body as the mycelia beneath her boots pushed its white bony tentacles upward, grappling, searching for food to ingest and to decay. Artemis glanced left and saw Prophet Higgs Boson's body being devoured and being jerked underneath the soil. His lifeless body being enraptured and torn into fleshy pieces by the strong white mycelia emerging from beneath the massive tulip poplar.

The spirit warrior brandished his spear for them to follow him. He guided them toward a traversing upward path hidden within the forest. Artemis could see him lead them up the hillside toward a shear rock outcropping. She sensed electricity along her arms and neck as she heard the whip snap from lightning bolts that showered the forest with a flashing pure white light. As Artemis caught up with the girls, she encouraged them to advance toward the spirit warrior who waited for them. He smiled, nodded and waved for the girls to come toward him.

"I'm scared," Laina said.

"I'm scared, too," Artemis said. She trudged up the hillside along a narrow path. The tree limbs lurching back and forth, the path shook as dirt and rocks trickled off and stumbled over the ridge as a steep drop off emerged beneath them. The ground kept shaking as hard boulders kept cascading down the slope, killing anything along their uncertain paths. "Just keep looking at the warrior, focus on the warrior."

Near the hilltop, the spirit warrior pointed them into a natural cave concealed by bulky trees and thorny limbs. It was dark within the dampness, except for the lightning show that from time to time revealed the spirit warrior's face as he stood sentinel guarding the cave opening. After each lighting strike he would smile, he would nod and hold up his spear over at them as he observed the ritualistic site below. The white stag stood deeper inside the cave.

"What's he doing?" Laina said. She shivered and hunched down close to Artemis and Hazel. Artemis hugged them close.

"He's protecting us, and the stag," Artemis said as the stag snorted. It heaved out hot breaths. Artemis realized the muscled stag's body shared warmth inside the modest cave. It was not inside the cave by accident. "It's his way, his spirits way. He uses whatever is given from the forest to help us survive."

A thunderous rumble came, a bright flash from lightning as the mountain quaked down to its core. Artemis thought it sounded like a daisy cutter bomb dropped in Afghanistan. A bomb meant to clear out trees and brush for a helicopter to land.

And they watched the spirit warrior raise his spear into the air, as he whooped, he hollered from his native language.

"I ain't ever been in a storm like this," Hazel said. She whimpered. "Are we goin' to die?"

"Are we goin' to die, Artemis?" Laina said. "Tell me."

"Girls," Artemis said. "Be brave and be strong. You cannot live in fear. We cannot control the future. Let's just keep together, hope for the best. I'll show you a secret. Look at me."

Artemis sucked in a deep, deep breath. She held the breath, she paused and then she let it out through her lips.

"I don't like secrets," Laina said.

"See?" Artemis said. "Take deep breaths, my mother taught me, hold them, and then let out. Repeat it, you'll see. You'll calm down, do it like me."

The girls watched her, curious, suspicious, and they followed Artemis' example. They looked at each other as they sucked in deep breaths and exhaled. And after a moment they nodded over at Artemis. The stag scratched at the cave floor, it snorted.

And then a bright flash. A unique flash like none ever sensed by Artemis. A thick flash shown across the silent warrior's face. A shockwave. He whispered a prayer, he whispered a chant as he kneeled down on one knee, he gazed forward, his mouth gaped open, as if in awe from the electromagnetic thrusts popping down and zapping the earth's crust just beyond the cave's shelter. A power kept thrusting into the land and spirit world beyond understanding. A huge rumble shook the cave, rocks kept falling, spraying them with dirt and dust and then a large boulder smashed down from above. It crashed, passing through the warrior, falling beyond the cave and down the steep hillside. An old tree limb fell over the opening, its branches spiking at them. The girls screamed and clutched at Artemis. And Artemis realized, sometimes lightning strikes the same spot twice. They heard the sounds from total devastation. As if an earthquake arrived with a bunker busting bolt that had consumed its target. The sounds from a fierce whirlwind enrapturing anything unprotected. And after the last bolt shook Mother Earth, there was an odd total silence as if as nature reclined contemplating the purposed violence.

"It smells like smoke," Hazel said. "My hairs were all electrified. Did you get all electrified?"

"Me too," Artemis said. "Watch the warrior, wait for him."

And as rapid as the storm had materialized, it was gone. Silence reigned. The fierce winds calmed. The forest regained its poise.

The spirit warrior stared back over at them. Bewildered. He said something that Artemis thought meant it was safe to come out of the cave as the white stag trudged around them; it nudged the large tree limb away from the cave opening and shoved it over the slope.

"Why didn't it rain?" Laina said. She looked up at Artemis. "It ain't wet. Don't it rain when it thunder and lightening?"

"Nothin's wet," Hazel said. "It ain't wet, no where."

Artemis stood with Laina and Hazel listening to the forest for several minutes searching for any movement. The spirit warrior and the white stag stepped back down the narrow path. And then from within the forest emerged an innocent white haired doe, it foraged for grass; it bit at bare tree twigs. From above the doe rested a fierce Great Horned owl, dark camouflaged, its sharp talons gripped the thick tree limb. And she heard birds chirping and communicating.

"We're safe now, girls," Artemis said. She set Laina down onto a felled tree stump. She unhooked her tools, and slipped off her tactical sweater, and exposed her tight black thermal top. "Wear my sweater, I'll go find my coat, later. We can go now. I'm not sure what to say."

"What happened?" Laina said. She wiped her eyes with her tiny fingers. She tried to grin before she cried. She sniffled. "You… saved… me…"

"You're my tribe, let's follow the warrior," Artemis said. She held her hand out for Laina. She hugged Hazel. "Let's just go back down the trail. I don't know what to say, what to do."

Hazel pointed over at the tulip poplar engulfed with a smoky haze enrapturing its limbs.

"It's like the grounds steaming," Hazel said. "It must a been a big fire or whatnot."

"I think so," Artemis said. "But the warrior wants us to follow him. Be careful. Let's go back down into the valley. Be patient with me. I'll limp it out. Keep to the right side nearer the rock wall."

At the bottom of the narrow path, they stepped together toward the ritualistic sight. But the electrical storm had wiped the area clean, there were no bodies, the table gone, and the soil seemed tilled by a farmer in anticipation for a new spring time planting. As they kept walking, they noticed Virgil's body gone. Dr. Demetrius' body gone. There were no signs that the mycelia lived beneath them. And there were no mushrooms littered across the ground. It was now a quaint valley area within the forest's dark, smokey haze. And the tulip poplar soared toward the moon's glow.

The spirit warrior grunted at Artemis. He thrust his spear over toward the far end of the valley. From within the gloom emerged three spirit girls. They drifted forward draped within a golden meridian. The spirit warrior said words to Artemis. Words that Artemis could not understand, but words and an expression she sensed.

"Go in peace," Artemis said. She held up both her hands. The spirit warrior held up his spear, he smiled and nodded at them. He disappeared into the thicket followed by the white stag. And they dissolved within the tall grass and plants. "Girls, I'm not sure what to think, to do. Let's just walk over there and find out. It's all we can do. I think we're safe."

Artemis limped and lead Laina and Hazel across the forest floor.

"Hazel, where's home?" Artemis said as they walked together. "Do you have a family?"

"I do, you killed my daddy," Hazel said. She shrugged. "It's okay, he beat me. He stole me from my mother."

"Where's she?" Artemis said.

"She's in town," Hazel said.

"I'll get you home," Artemis said. The spirit girls were drifting closer and closer. "Don't stress. I'll get you home. It will be a long walk, but you'll fine. I promise."

Laina stopped walking. She covered her mouth as she pointed at one of the spirit girls, she ran back and hid her head behind Artemis' waist. The little girls faces were unveiled, they appeared scared, afraid and their eyes searching. Artemis sensed something beyond them had allowed Laina and Hazel to see the spirit girls. She thought there was a loving reason, a reason about to be revealed. A wisdom beyond her grasp.

"Do you know them?" Artemis said. She crouched down and held Laina. "Don't be afraid."

"I know her. The girl on the right," Hazel said. She waved over at her. "She disappeared from school. Had signs all over town with her photo. They never found her. I reckon we know why now."

And the girl from the left side drifted near Artemis. She tried to touch Laina on her arm. Laina hid her face. Her lips trembled.

"Did you know her?" Artemis said. She brushed back Laina's stringy hair from her face. "It's good to cry. My mother told me it released toxins from the heart."

"I thought you didn't like me no more," Laina said. She mumbled a name as she backed away. "Everybody hates me, they leave me all alone."

"You're my best friend," the girl said. She tried to hug Laina, but she was no longer living. But Laina's face calmed as she opened her eyes after she felt her friend's happy spirit pass through her. She wiped her tears away. And Laina tried to smile as she nodded.

"You'll always be my best friend," Laina said. She whispered. "I miss you."

Artemis' mind swirled with questions. She understood that in life these blameless spirit girls experienced an unspeakable trauma. She lacked the ability to comprehend terrible human flaws and why their lives were stolen. But Artemis was an assassin. Her job clear in her mind. She did not hate; it was not about hate. Until Satan tricked her. The Company she worked for sought to find and eliminate human beings that were societal problems. And they empowered her to remove them. The Company campaigned a silent war about the balance between good and evil. Accepting within their mission that violence is a resource left for human cancers.

"I'm not sure what to do," Artemis said. "I don't want to leave you all out here. I won't leave this place without a solution."

And just as Artemis uttered the last word about an uncertain next step, her red hair was fluttered by the four winds. She sensed a presence. A powerful presence not like any sensation she had ever had before. An energy approached them from beyond the horizon.

"Something is comin'," Hazel said. She pointed over beyond Artemis' left side. "It's a man, or woman, I don't know?"

A tall image of a human being approached them, Artemis realized it did not appear as a man, or a woman. It lacked a true color; almost translucent. It's countenance serene; it smiled with kindness in its sparkling eyes. Its facial beauty ageless; its golden hair shimmered. And then the being transformed from one into three beings. They lacked any wings and wore simple white silk tunics. They were bare-footed and yet they did not touch the ground. And Artemis sensed a pure love, the sensation reminded her how she felt sleeping between her parents on a Sunday morning before her father made her pancakes.

"Hello, my darlings," the center being said. With its golden hands held open. It cast a bright golden light over them. "Do not be afraid. We love you all. We accept you all. You are beautiful."

The spirit girls appeared entranced by the beings. They smiled and giggled with expectations. Laina's friend wandered toward them with no fear in her eyes.

"Will they be safe?" Artemis said. She blinked her eyes as if she did not believe what she was seeing. She pinched her earlobe. "Who are you?"

The center being ambled near Artemis.

"Hello, Artemis, we're what you call angels, God sent us for these children," the angel said. The angel smiled as it turned to gaze over at the other angels. They all blew Artemis a kiss. They showered calmness, and golden tranquility across the valley. The center angel floated closer. "I remember you, Artemis. I doubt you remember me. You were a tiny baby. The night we welcomed your parents into our tribe."

Artemis pinched her cheek, again. It hurt. The moment was not a dream.

"I don't understand," Artemis said.

"It's not about understanding," the angel said. "There are riddles that will never be solved, and questions that will always go unanswered."

"Are you taking them?" Laina said. She stepped closer toward her friend. She gazed up at the angel.

"Yes," the angel said looking down at Laina. "Do not worry; she's safe with us, in a happy place. Where children play and laugh all day under a warm sun. You were brave tonight."

"Why did I hate?" Artemis said. She started to cry. "My parents taught me never to hate, but I did."

The angel skimmed over the grass to hug Artemis, it held her as the other angels encouraged the spirit girls to follow them. And Artemis felt like a baby wrapped in a soft blanket. Safe. Secure. Loved. An unconditional loving spirit enrapturing her down to her mortal soul.

"A happy warrior defends the truth, we fight a constant war with Satan," the angel said. The angel smiled down at the little girls, at Laina, and then over at Hazel. "The spirit warrior gave you a safe place to hide. He gave you all he had to give."

"I'm a killer," Artemis said. "I never killed with hate in my heart. What am I to do? I've never believed."

"Don't cry, Artemis," Laina said. She tugged at Artemis's right hand fingers. "It'll be… all right, I guess."

"Satan is the great deceiver," the angel said. And three white feathered spirit doves flew across the valley and they perched high on an oak tree limb. They defied the darkness and shown pure light. "It will return. Do not fear Satan, fear that your heart turns cold. That your soul allows hate to enter your spirit forever. Do you understand?"

"Not fully," Artemis said. "My mind is always in conflict."

"You're a human being. You've learned a lesson," the angel said. "Satan tricked you. It's what Satan does."

"I kill people, thou shalt not kill," Artemis said. She held her face in her hands. "I'm an assassin. My parents would be ashamed of me. I think. But my mother spoke to me, my father was near me."

The angel looked down at Laina.

"Say goodbye," the angel said. "But you'll meet her again, do not fear the night, my love. You are never alone. You are loved."

And Laina and her spirit friend tried to hug. They tried to understand viewing each other from different prisms from within the light that few humans will ever see.

"It is your chosen path," the angel said. The angel's face clear, humble and translucent. It neither smiled nor frowned. "Hate is a seed that only you can allow to grow. You have free will my love. Can you feel pure love without experiencing pure hate? Would the universal clocks cease without the gravitational balance between good and evil? Artemis, always remember that timeless light always defies dark matter. It's there, it waits, like the twinkle from the stars. You must decide to seek the sparkle waiting in your heart."

And Artemis accepted the riddle. From her childhood, the answer hidden within the golden meridian. A sacred place where balance existed between good and evil. A place where Satan could only lurk, but did not control. It was her choice, her journey to decide to allow love to guide her journey. Her free will mattered, and that she accepted her imperfections and understood that a limitless love waited for her hidden behind the event horizon.

"Thank you," Artemis said. She whispered. "I love you. I don't know why I said that to you."

"Go home my darling, let Satan speak. But you must choose if you want to listen. After, we look forward to Benjamin's spirit becoming part of our humble mass," the angel said. It floated back and over toward the spirit girls and the other angels. "Smile happy warrior. Live to fight for us, fight for truth, fight for pure love. And know we'll always be watching. You are never alone."

And the angels nudged behind the spirit girls. They all giggled from excitement. Laina's friend waved goodbye and they sailed together into a curved diamond shaped crease that opened within the spectral light and closed leaving behind visible light within the darkness.

Artemis stared at the spot that was no longer revealed. She was thankful for her life, thankful she had extracted Laina. But she was sad that Virgil lost his life. She gazed over at Hazel.

"I'll get you home," Artemis said. She scanned the valley. "I'll get you out of this darkness. Let's go find my parka, Laina you need a coat. I don't need you getting sick. I think that's a good direction to hike back out of here."

"What'll I tell my ma?" Hazel said.

"Tell her the truth, let's get out of here, I've a flashlight somewhere in my tool kit," Artemis said. She began to limp forward. "She might not believe you, but tell her the truth. You can't go wrong always telling the truth."

Chapter 44

"Angels are so, how to say it?" Satan said. It gazed up at the darkening skies as a full moon was being revealed. It almost snapped its thorny fingers but stopped. "Nice, so nice, yes, so humble. I mean, just yuck. And forget the pure love crap."

"Where's Benjamin?" Artemis said. "Let him go."

"He'll appear," Satan said. It stared over into the dark-green and brown banyan trees that dominated downtown St. Petersburg, Florida. It studied along busy Beach Drive as the fancy cars rolled and squeaked in both directions. The cars lining up at the valet station with arriving guests flipping keys and sharing cash tips. "I'll not cheat you. Besides, those others you met, they are watching me. I have to give him up, my game with you has ended."

"What do you want?" Artemis said.

"That's the little girl?" Satan said. It pointed over at Laina. Her legs dangled from a park bench. "Do you like my new suit? It's bespoke. I chose a pure black silk, the bow tie had to be dark red. I'm Satan, I have a stereotype to keep up."

"You realize that," Artemis said. "You're stalling. I don't care about your suit."

"I suppose I am," Satan said. It steepled its fingers. It winked at Artemis. It's expression playful, disappointed. "I made a deal with God about you."

"So what," Artemis said. She crossed her arms. "You're the great deceiver, it's what you do."

Satan started to pace around Artemis in a circle.

"It is, I hate it so," Satan said. It clapped and it clapped. "After your parents escapade in Greece, well, I had to play a game with God. After all, I'm stuck with them, for eternity."

"I loved my parents," Artemis said. She closed her eyes. "You'll never take that away. I have free-will."

Two young men wearing short-sleeved dress shirts and black clip-on ties waved over at them. They stood next to a metal rack stuffed with religious pamphlets. The one on the left wore a baseball cap and had a scraggily red beard with mischievous eyes. He grinned and pointed with both hands over at Satan to come hang out and listen to their brand of good news.

"He wants to save my soul," Satan said. It waved its left hand and a puff of wind knocked over the rack and polluted the grass park with religious themed paper. "That takes some stones to offer to save my soul. Sad. If they only understood."

"They weren't bothering you," Artemis said. She opened here eyes; She stared down at the hard concrete path that bisected the rectangular-shaped park. She looked up and pointed over at a group. "You missed the dudes over there trying to save the planet, or the one over there guilting people into protecting children."

"Stop, don't tempt me. Hate, so much hate to share," Satan said. It rubbed its palms together. "I hate them. It's just that simple."

"You won," Artemis said. She looked at Satan. "But you had to cheat. You tricked me."

"I'm Satan," Satan said. "Don't be a fool like Prophet Higgs Boson. After you almost sliced his head off. I enjoyed that, it was terrible, and so satisfying. I think I'll let his head dangle for eternity."

"I guess there is a higher power," Artemis said. She shrugged. "I understand now. I'm not as conflicted with my work."

"Conflict, oh please," Satan said. It appeared exasperated. "Such an interesting word from the English language. From Latin, conflictus. I exist for conflict. Without mindless conflict, my work gets tricky. Hate blinds the truth. It's a key to my war strategy."

"I did my duty," Artemis said.

"Yes, and you did it conflicted with hate in your heart?" Satan said. It pointed at Artemis. "Right?"

"Yes. Where's Benjamin?" Artemis said. She turned to keep Laina in her eyesight. "I have a child waiting to sense her father, one last time."

"Well then, always little miss efficiency," Satan said. It hummed a derogatory minstrel tune. "When you were a teenager, I asked God to play along with me. God always plays along, you might read the news about all the conflict in the world. It's my work. But, you understand now, God plays a longer term game. I admit it."

Artemis understood Satan wanted to turn its metaphorical dagger deeper into her soul. But she had prepared to let it bleed her scars. She accepted her wounds as part of her truth. If she allowed Satan to cause her to feel, she was free from its grip.

"You murdered my parents," Artemis said. She stared down at her brown loafers. "That's your little secret?"

Satan growled. It hissed. It leaned in near Artemis. It smelled putrid and rotting.

"Yes. Good guess. Sent in my best demon," Satan said. It hyena laughed. "Left the gas on, which your father would never have done. He was meticulous. You were away to summer camp. Since their daughter would not disturb them. Oh my, those two, they made sweet, sweet love. It was disgusting; They had love in their hearts. Mom never faked it. So they were all empty, snuggled together as they drifted off to sleep. They died from breathing in the carbon monoxide fumes. Simple and yet a perfect stab wound into your life."

"Feel better?" Artemis said. "I know you don't have them. My mother's spirit spoke to me, so did my father's. They saved me. They helped me save Laina."

Satan's eyes started to molt into a dark reds and then dead black. It smirked and stuck out its forked tongue and wiggled it.

"I told God I'd teach the child touched by Gabrielle's sword to learn about hate," Satan said. It again leaned in toward Artemis. It tapped a finger on Artemis' chest. "I got that emotion to boil inside you. I start with hate. I tried with Job. He didn't take my bait. But you were able to get it. I felt your performance. Authentic."

"I accept that fact," Artemis said. "I allowed hate in my heart. It's the truth."

"Just so you realize, I won. I worked for decades to make you into my own image," Satan said. It sneered at Artemis. "Humans learn to hate each other, a child's heart is pure at birth. Then the child learns racism. The addict gets a taste of alcohol, a nasty drug, or both, addiction lurks in the genetic code. It's one of my best inventions. Tarnish the exhilaration from a first kiss with mass marketing pornography. It's easy these days. Almost borders on the boring. But then you come along. Assassin with a loving soul, you are a strange human."

"I'll never give in," Artemis said. "Are you finished? Give me Benjamin. Allow him to go free and release his spirit."

"Fine, by the way, I am on the clock," Satan said. It frowned. It winked. "One last point, I influenced you to become a killer. The Lamb's little girl, a killer, an assassin. I wonder how they would feel about that?"

"I am," Artemis said. Her skin blushed. The temperature cooled as she sensed the nearby rumble from an approaching subtropical storm. "I accept my truth."

"That's all I wanted," Satan said. It looked up into the fading blue sky and back over at the harbor waters. "You're in conflict. And I am pleased with your hate. Come back after the storm. He'll be waiting near that concrete babe. Until next time, Artemis Lamb."

And Satan vanished. Its cackle vibrated across the banyan trees and along St. Petersburg's city streets and buildings.

Artemis sat down next to Laina. They watched children playing around the banyan tree trunks and kicking up the sand, yelling and giggling.

"Always remember to send a thank you note to Jerome," Artemis said. She hugged Laina. "He'll appreciate it. He's a kind man."

"Why?" Laina said. She scrunched her face, looking up at Artemis. "Will people here make fun of me, cause I talk funny?"

"Yes, but we have lots of people here that talk funny. You'll not be alone. Besides, Jerome did the legal work," Artemis said. She smiled knowing that Wylie, and The Company had influenced the legal system. "I adopted you."

"Adopt?" Laina said. "I don't understand."

"You can stay with me forever," Artemis said. "Or until you get old enough and get sick of me."

"You my mama, now?" Laina said. "My mama and daddy dead. I ain't got no one. Do I need to get a job?"

"You'll decide, ah, no, you're in my tribe of two," Artemis said. She gripped Laina's left hand. "Call me Artemis. I'm your friend. I'll take care of you. We'll go shopping tomorrow. I'll buy you new clothes. Let's find fun clothes, life's too short for boring."

Laina studied Artemis' face, at her thick red hair. She remained quiet and pensive. And after her hazel eyes reflected on what she sensed about Artemis. She wiggled her legs and nodded.

"I believe you," Laina said. She watched the tourists strolling by her. She scanned over at the banyan trees. She whispered at Artemis. "Are you be still killin' people?"

"Yes, I'll have another file," Artemis said. She gripped Laina's hand. "Don't ever, ever tell anyone. Deal?"

"Deal, I'll keep quiet," Laina said. She waved her legs back and forth. "I can't lose you. My daddy found you special for me."

"Let's walk over there," Artemis said. She pointed forward. "Near the statue looking out at the bay waters."

Artemis and Laina ambled over toward a statuary painted white.

"Why are we here?" Laina said. She gazed up at Artemis with her inquisitive hazel eyes. "We're standing on the grass. It's hot."

"We need to say goodbye," Artemis said. She sucked in a deep breath. "I'll cry. It's just what I do. My mother taught me to cry, to let the toxic feelings go. She promised me it released demons."

"Why?" Laina said. "Why we here?"

"Your father, his spirit. He's coming," Artemis said. She sniffled. "He'll not be back, we'll get a few seconds. But he'll know you're with me, as the full moon's revealed."

"I don't see anybody," Laina said. She scanned the area. She touched the concrete statuary. "This is weird."

"It'll be him in spirit," Artemis said. "You'll feel his presence, he'll whisper to you. I promise."

And as if on Satan's cue, the sub-tropical storm crossed over and cleansed the grass park and the downtown buildings and streets. The tourists, the children, the locals ran for cover. But Artemis calmly opened her umbrella and provided Laina shelter from the rain. She inhaled the petrichor from the dry soil accepting the warm drops.

"You know what they call that smell?" Artemis said to Laina.

"No," Laina said. She sniffed. "It's funny smellin'."

"It's the petrichor," Artemis said. "They knew it as the blood inside the Greek gods, a story from mythology."

"Oh," Laina said. "I never heard about that."

"I'll teach you," Artemis said. She stared to cry. "I'll teach everything my father taught me. Everything my mother taught me. And I'll tell you everything I remember about your father."

From within the mists after the late evening thunderstorm migrated along and shifted out into the Gulf of Mexico, the full moon appeared to travel higher into the evening sky. And Benjamin's spirit appeared next to the statue. He smiled looking down at Laina. He blew her a kiss from beyond all reason and time, from a heart that no longer pulsed in the living world.

"Thank you, my love," Benjamin said. He smiled at Artemis. He glossed his hand over Laina's head. "I can go now. I will always love you."

Artemis cried a cloudburst of tears as Benjamin evaporated before her and his spirit folded into another existence. Gone from her life and he would never return.

"Did you love my father?" Laina said. She looked up at Artemis. "He was here. I felt him touch my head. Was it him?"

"Yes, it was him," Artemis said. As she let the tears fall. "I loved him with all my heart."

Laina stared around at the palm trees, the live oaks, and over at the large marina littered with boats resting in slips or moored farther out in the dark-blue harbor.

"You're my mother now," Laina said. "I decided."

"Just call me Artemis," Artemis said. "I don't know how to be a mother. You can teach me. Do you like fish and chips?"

"I guess," Laina said. She held Artemis' right hand. "I'll show you how to be a mother. I'm a good worker."

"Let's go hang with Alan, and Chef Mikey," Artemis said. She wiped her face. She re-grasped Laina's hand. "They'll show you, let's go hang out, let's be, and we'll figure out life."

"Did my father like fish and crackers?" Laina said. She started to walk along the wet grass with Artemis. They stepped on the concrete path and on across busy Beach Drive.

"This is home now," Artemis said. "I'll tell you everything I remember."

"You're strong, aren't you?" Laina said. She grinned up at Artemis. "You can do a lot a pushups. You got strong hands."

"Yes I am," Artemis said. She winked down at Laina. They wandered into the Moon Under Water. They found the empty table next to the front windows within the Snug section. After a moment, Chef Mikey sauntered over to the table. He hugged Artemis.

"Hey girlie," Chef Mikey said. He beamed at Laina. His hands on his hips. "Little one, good to see you. You want to try my fish and chips?"

"You sound funny," Laina said. Her eyes were hopeful. "I'm just kiddin'. I sound funny, too."

Before Chef Mikey answered, Alan sprang up to the table.

"I will do the service," Alan said. He had skittered out from behind the dark wood bar. He smacked his hands together. "Where are you from? I know this. Wait, I know this."

"Kentucky," Laina said. "You're funny."

"Yes, yes," Alan said. He pointed forward at the windows toward outside as tourists and locals ambled by the restaurant. "Kentucky. Laina from Kentucky. I'll discover a nickname for you, but I must think it over. I must contemplate this. My creative spirit will answer this vital question."

"I like you, girlie," Chef Mikey said. He flipped the white towel over his other shoulder. His chefs smock dirty from cooking and cleaning a commercial-sized kitchen.

"Hot back there?" Artemis said.

"Hot as hell, a place I hope never to visit," Chef Mikey said. He wiped his cherub shaped face. "I came out to cool off. I didn't know this girlie had returned to grace us with her presence."

"Oh, now, I'm Welsh," Alan said. "Mikey, he's English. And now we have, Laina, Laina from Kentucky. Glad to have you back."

"Ever been across the pond?" Chef Mikey said to Laina.

"Pond?" Laina said. She stared over at Artemis.

"You know," Alan said. "The Atlantic Ocean. Chef Mikey and our families came across the Atlantic Ocean to live here."

"No," Laina said. She turned her head back and forth at Alan, Chef Mikey and Artemis. "Should I?"

Alan tapped his forefinger on his wristwatch.

"Wait. You must come now, Laina from Kentucky. I think there's just enough light left outside," Alan said. He waved for Laina to follow him and Chef Mikey out of the Moon Under Water's front doors. Alan held Laina's hand as they descended beyond the front doors, the host station and down the tiled steps.

"Why?" Laina said. Artemis hustled behind them.

"Little girly, I predict," Chef Mikey said. "Ya going to lose your mind. I know what's coming."

Alan stood on the concrete sidewalk, as they were immersed within the tourists and locals. He stared up into space as if searching for a celestial being. Finally, he pointed up with his right forefinger.

"Look, Laina, look," Alan said. He hunched down on his knees, and he pointed up from behind Laina. "It's flying in a low earth orbit. See that tiny dark speck?"

Laina gazed up. Her eyes following Alan's forefinger upwards. And then she saw the fast moving spaceship. She pointed.

"Is that God?" Laina said. She hopped. She pointed.

"No, funny one," Chef Mikey said. He stared down at Laina. He turned and grinned back over at Artemis.

"It's Skylab, it's flying across the night sky," Alan said. He chuckled. "It's where astronauts live up in space, looking down at earth. They can see you, Laina from Kentucky."

"I see it, I see it," Laina said. She screamed as she pointed up. She hopped upwards thrusting her hand up. "Can they see God?"

"God can see them," Chef Mikey said. He patted Laina on her head. "God sees everything. I'll go fix you up my special fish and chips."

"Can God see me?" Laina said. She stopped hopping. She turned to stare at Alan. "Is God up there?"

"Oh, lass," Alan said. "God protects those astronauts; they're up there learning about the magic in the universe. They'll help us all as they share what they discover. I promise you that."

"I hope God helps my daddy," Laina said. She nodded back over at Artemis. "I hope he's safe, and not near mean people."

Artemis wiped her eyes as she sat back on a nearby burnt orange cushioned bench seat. A kaleidoscope of humanity strolling by her as they were living their normal lives. She gazed up at the full moon and she whispered a prayer for eternal love. And Artemis wondered about what they hid within the bright light she could not see. She hoped that those that loved her and that she loved were always near her just shaded from her view by the visible spectrum. She smiled over at Laina. And she realized, it was what Benjamin would have wanted. She had given Laina a place to call home.

The End.

ABOUT THE AUTHOR

Nathaniel Sewell lives in St. Petersburg, Florida. Amanita was Nathaniel's 5th novel. He can be found from time to time on his bicycle enjoying God's beauty, or enjoying a Guinness inside The Moon. Feel invited to come sit next to him at The Moon, order an adult beverage, or not, and chat about life.

ALSO BY NATHANIEL

BOBBY'S SOCKS

FISHING FOR LIGHT

5TH&HOPE

A YEAR INSIDE THE MOON

If you enjoy his novels write a review on Amazon.com, or like his page on Facebook or Instagram.

www.nathanielsewell.com